Love and Forensics

LOVE AND FORENSICS

An Imprint on Life

Charles Curtis

Copyright © 2013 by Charles Curtis.

Library of Congress Control Number:		2013912405
ISBN:	Hardcover	978-1-4836-6718-8
	Softcover	978-1-4836-6717-1
	Ebook	978-1-4836-6719-5

All rights reserved. No part of this book may be reproduced or transmitted in any form or by any means, electronic or mechanical, including photocopying, recording, or by any information storage and retrieval system, without permission in writing from the copyright owner.

This is a work of fiction. Names, characters, places and incidents either are the product of the author's imagination or are used fictitiously, and any resemblance to any actual persons, living or dead, events, or locales is entirely coincidental.

This book was printed in the United States of America.

Rev. date: 08/20/2013

To order additional copies of this book, contact:
Xlibris LLC
1-888-795-4274
www.Xlibris.com
Orders@Xlibris.com
131397

Prologue

Terri Sutton, a beautiful five-feet-eight-inches-tall brunette with green eyes and an anxious smile waited impatiently for her husband Chris. She waited with their fifteen-year-old son Gavin and their attorney. While they waited, they heard the banging and clanging of cell doors as they opened and closed. They heard the din of prisoners as they went about their duties they were assigned. They listened to the barking orders of prison guards as they issued their commands.

They smelled the odor of coffee as it drifted in from the cafeteria, the smell of dinner being prepared. The smell of disinfectants and waxes used to keep the prison clean. The odor of vomit from where someone had evidently gotten sick and the disgusting odor of urine that was drifting in from the latrine.

Terri was there to pick up her husband Chris, her precious, blue-eyed, blonde haired six-feet-two-inches-tall husband. The father of their son Gavin, her darling husband of almost eighteen years was finally getting out of the Monroe Correctional Complex in the State of Washington.

The eighteen years they had been married of which only two wonderful years had been spent together. They were the two happiest years of her life, which had flown by so swiftly. The fifteen years Chris had been locked up seemed like five hundred years since he had been in a prison cell.

Chris and Terri loved each other so much that even being apart for a few hours was like a crushing blow to their hearts. Fifteen and a half years of their life when they could only see each other for a few hours at a time except for a forty-eight-hour visitation every two months. Those were the times when they were able to hold each other and laugh and cry together.

It was over fifteen years since their baby boy Gavin had been born. Chris had not been there when Gavin was born; he was not there when Gavin was baptized. He hadn't been there when Gavin his son started kindergarten. He hadn't seen him lose his first tooth, Chris didn't get to help when he rode his first bike, and he was not able to take his son fishing.

Gavin was at the Monroe Correctional Complex with his mother waiting for the father he had always seen behind prison walls. The father he had only seen dressed in a prison uniform. But also the father who always showed his great love for Gavin and his mother, a father who was always there to give Gavin great love and encouragement.

A prison guard stopped by to tell them it would be at least two to four hours before Chris would be processed and released. He asked, "Do you want some coffee or a soda?" Terri replied, "Yes, decaf coffee for me and our attorney, black with no cream or sugar please. Could you also get a diet soda for my son."

Gavin said, "Mom, I know Dad was sent to prison for a murder he did not commit. I know part of the story, but I do not know all of it. Could you tell me how dad showed up in prison in the first place?" "Well, Gavin," Terri replied, "it is a very long story. It's a tale of a very strong love between your father and mother. I guess we had better start from the very beginning."

Terri sat for a moment, pondering how to tell the strange saga to her son. A son she had raised by herself. She could hardly believe this stalwart young man was a product of her loins. He looked so much like her husband Chris, the same chiseled, handsome face. The same mannerisms; however, he had her dark hair and green eyes.

Finally, she decided she would tell Gavin the whole story. At the same time, the special intimate details she would remember in her own mind. The story was fresh in her mind, even though it had taken place over a period of fifteen years.

"Gavin, the story begins with both sets of your grandparents the Olsons and the Suttons," Terri began.

Chapter 1

Both families had farms close to each other. They were located in the small farming community of Towner, North Dakota. They farmed part of their land with wheat and oats. They raised beef and dairy cattle, pigs and chickens. The two families' farms were within walking distance of each other. The Olsons and the Suttons were the best of friends. All four had grown up together; they all enjoyed the same things. The families went to the same church. They went to movies and card parties together. In fact, at this time both families were expecting a baby.

One day near the end of February when the thermometer hit twenty-five degrees below zero and the wind was at a brisk twenty miles per hour, it was at that time Clovis Sutton turned to her husband George. Clovis said, "Honey, you better warm up the four-wheel-drive pickup. It's time to take me to the hospital in Rugby. I'm about to have the baby."

George lunged up and went outside and got the pickup running, then silently thanked God he had studded snow tires. George packed blankets, food, and water for the trip just in case they got stranded. He drove the pickup to the fuel pump, making sure the vehicle had a full tank.

He went back to the house, then helped Clovis out to the pickup. George said, "Clovis, I hope that you can hang on until we make it to the hospital. It's over twenty-two miles from here. The icy roads had snow drifting over the top of them. He brought along some snow shovels just in case."

The roadway was fairly clear in spots, Then George would hit a drift five to thirty feet long, and sometimes the four-wheel-drive pickup would not make it all way through a drift. Then George would get out with the snow shovel. He would clear the snow away and start again.

They finally made it to Highway 2 where George saw a snowplow. George stopped by the snowplow and got out to talk to the driver. George told the driver, "My wife is about to have a baby. How is the road from here to Rugby?" The snowplow driver replied, "It's bad, just follow me. I will take you his far as the Pierce County line. I will call the Pierce County snowplow driver and have him meet us there."

Thankfully, that's the way it worked. George waved thanks to the McHenry County driver, then followed the other snowplow driver. He plowed the road right up to the emergency entrance at the hospital. The snowplow driver had called ahead, and the emergency staff was waiting for them. They placed Clovis in a wheelchair and rushed her into the hospital. George yelled, "I'm parking the truck, then I will be right in." Clovis feebly answered, "Okay."

George quickly parked the truck and rushed inside. The hospital staff told him where to find Clovis. He rushed up the stairs ignoring the elevator. There was no way he was going to slow down. Just as he entered, the room nurse took his coat and handed him a hospital gown. Putting the gown on, George went to Clovis's side taking her hand in his.

All of a sudden, the baby let out a huge squall. He didn't seem to like the idea of being brought into this world in this inclement weather. He kept it up all the time the doctor was cleaning him up. Then the doctor handed him to Clovis, telling her, "You have a beautiful eight-pound-ten-ounce baby boy."

This is when Clovis gently took the baby boy in her arm. Taking her time, Clovis talked softly and soothingly to him. The baby immediately stopped crying and looked up at his mother. It was as if he knew exactly who this woman was, and he probably did as she had talked to him and sang to him in her womb.

George looked on in wonderment as he beheld his wife and his son. The doctor asked if they had a name for the birth certificate. George and Clovis both answered at once, "Christopher Alan Sutton."

Both the Suttons and Olsons raised Black Angus beef cattle. In addition, each had a small herd of Holstein dairy cows. So they had their own milk and churned their own butter. They also raised pigs and chickens mostly for their own use. Clovis Sutton and Gloria Olson both had large gardens. So in the summer, they always had fresh vegetables.

In the fall, the women canned what vegetables they could. They purchased plums, peaches, pears, and apricots, which were also canned. In the spring of the year, Sam Olson and George Sutton would plant wheat and oats, which in the fall they would harvest. During the summer, they would put up hay for their livestock.

In April of that same year, Gloria Olson was rushed to the same hospital at Rugby. Once there, Gloria gave birth to Terri. Terri was a beautiful baby girl with long dark hair, green eyes, and the longest eyelashes you ever saw.

As soon as the toddlers were old enough, they became inseparable. The kids would share their toys. If one of them got scolded or yelled at, they would both cry and hug each other. One day when the children were in their terrible twos, Gloria and Clovis were having coffee together.

Suddenly, the mother's heard a lot of giggling, tittering, and laughing. Gloria went "uh-oh." She got up and walked into the other room. She came back putting her fingers to her lips, motioning for Clovis to come and see. She whispered, "You have got to see this to believe it."

Little Chris had gone to the refrigerator; he had opened the door. Then he took out the chocolate syrup for the ice cream. He took the syrup into the other room, proceeding to pour the chocolate all over himself and Terri. There was chocolate syrup all over their bodies, in their hair, on their faces, in the carpet, all over the walls, and on the furniture. They were now in the process of finger painting themselves and each other.

The two young mothers could barely keep from laughing out loud. Clovis and Gloria cleaned up their children and scolded them. Then made Chris and Terri help clean up the mess they had made. When the children were done, the mothers had to clean it properly.

The children almost never squabbled; however, if Chris did something which annoyed Terri, she would blink her long dark eyelashes at him, saying, "Chris, I am going to cry." At this point, Chris would give Terri a hug, saying, "I'm sorry, Terri, please don't cry. I won't do it anymore."

One day when Terri was almost four years old, she asked her mother, "Mom, how old do you have to be to get married?" Surprised, her mother told her, "You should be at least eighteen years old. But, honey, I hope you go to college before you get married." "How old would I be when I finish college?" asked Terri. Her mom replied, "You would probably be twenty-two years old."

Putting her hands on her hips, Terri said, "Well, when I am twenty-two years old, I am going to marry Chris. Then we are going to have sex, sex, sex." Shocked, Gloria asked Terry, "What do you know about sex?" "From television, Mom, that's where they kiss and hug a lot." You can rest assured afterward Terri's mother was very careful about what television program Terri got to see.

As the years went on, Chris's kindness and tenderness to all living things became apparent. He would see a baby bird fluttering on the ground not quite able to fly. Chris would locate the nest, then climb up the tree. He would very carefully put the baby bird back in its nest.

Animals seemed to sense Chris meant them no harm. One day, Chris was sitting on a log with Terri beside him. He told Terri, "Be absolutely quiet."

Then he made a chittering sound. Still very cautiously, a mother raccoon came out of the bushes. Chris put some bread and sugar cubes on the ground in front of him.

The mother raccoon came slowly, and stealthily toward them every so often she would stop. Then she would look around as if watching for enemies. Finally, she grabbed a sugar lump, then she ran back toward the bushes. She stopped just at its edge, then turned around and stared solemnly at Chris and Terri. Ever so slowly, Chris laid some more bread and sugar cubes on the ground. The mother raccoon set up blinking at them. Only then did she eat the first sugar cube.

Then turning around, she scampered into the woods. Terry started to laugh; however, Chris quickly put his hand over her mouth, saying, "Shhh." Just as fast as she had left, the mother raccoon was back. This time, she had her three little babies with her. The racoons all ran up, grabbing the bread and sugar cubes. They retreated fifteen feet where they sat and ate the bread and sugar cubes.

When the raccoons were finished with their food, they sat and eyed the children quizzically. Chris knew, and Terri put out four more slices of bread after the raccoons devoured them. Chris started talking in very low tones to them. Chris told Terri to speak to them but in a real soft tone so they would not get scared. Terri cooed, "You look so cute with the masks around your eyes. I think we will call you the bandit queen and her posse." The raccoons sat and listened, turning their heads this way and that. Realizing there was no more food to be had, the raccoons wandered off.

Chapter 2

Early one January morning, the snow started falling. First came soft, fluffy snowflakes. Then it turned into the ultimate raging blizzard. Both the Olsons and the Suttons put their dairy cattle into their nice, warm barns. They herded the beef cattle into huge pole barns. They put out large bales of hay for the cattle just in case.

Also, in case of a white out, they ran ropes from the house to the barns. Thus, if the storm got bad enough, they could check on their animals without getting lost.

The heavy snow kept coming down for three days, then the temperature started to drop. George Sutton told his wife, "At least the wind isn't blowing. I have never seen the wind blow when the temperature drops below thirty degrees below zero." No sooner had George finished talking when the wind started to blow.

For the first four hours, it was just a light breeze. After which, it turned into gale force winds. You could hear the wind howling and whistling as it beat around the house. If you have ever encountered anything like that, you will know it is one of the most frightening, melancholic sounds you will ever hear.

After ten hours of this, George said, "I better check on the animals." He dressed in heavy arctic coveralls and a parka. He put on his heavy gloves and two pair of heavy duty socks and insulated boots. Clovis handed him a walkie-talkie, saying, "In case you get in trouble, you can call us. On second thought, you better call us every ten minutes just to be on the safe side."

"I'll be all right," George grumbled, "but if it will make you feel better, I will call every ten minutes." George immediately headed out into the storm. He kept his hand on the rope at all times. Ten minutes later, he called, saying, "I fed the chickens and pigs. They are warm and cozy. I'm heading for the dairy barn now."

Ten minutes later, George called again, saying, "The dairy cows are all taken care of. I will now make a quick check on the beef cattle in the pole barns." When he called next, George said he was done watering and feeding the beef cattle and was heading back to the house. He called once again when he was by the dairy barn, saying he'd be in the house in five minutes. Eleven minutes later, having still had not heard from him, Clovis and Chris put on their warm winter clothes to go in search of George.

Just as they had started out, Chris went back getting a walkie-talkie. Chris said, "Mom, we should stay about three feet apart. That way, if I talk on this walkie-talkie, you may be able to hear the other walkie-talkie." Clovis and Chris grabbed hold of the rope and began following it. Every ten feet, Chris pressed the walkie-talkie and spoke into the microphone. The wind seem to be abating somewhat. They were now able to see for ten to fifteen feet.

As they followed the rope, they kept calling on the walkie-talkie. Clovis told Chris, "We need to find your father, and we need to find him fast. Even with arctic clothing on, if he isn't moving, he could freeze to death." When they were almost to the dairy barn, Chris once again keyed the mike, calling "Dad." Clovis stopped, saying, "I heard something, Chris." Surging forward, they found George on his hands and knees.

George was awake struggling to get up, a large icicle lay beside him. Clovis and Chris helped him to his feet. George put an arm around each of their shoulders. With Clovis keeping one hand on the rope, they slowly made it back to the house.

Once inside, they had George take off his clothing. They sat him on the couch, then removed their own outerwear. When they returned to talk to George, he had recovered completely. George asked Clovis to get him some coffee to help him warm up. Clovis asked, "What happened?" George answered, "Did you see that large icicle lying beside me? It fell off the barn and caught me on the head. Thank goodness, I had my cap on with my parka hood over that. But it just took all of the remaining energy out of me.

"When the icicle hit me, I dropped my walkie-talkie into the snow as I fell. I heard it, but searching I just couldn't find it in the snow." Chris said, "I found it, Dad. I put it in my pocket." George motioned for Clovis and Chris to come closer so he could give them both a big hug. The storm lasted for another three hours, then just gave up.

The next day dawned calm and clear, a mild ten degrees below zero. The air was so clear that you could hear the snow crunch under your boots. Every breath you took left a small vapor cloud in front of you. Icicles hung from the house and the edges of all the outbuildings. Everywhere you looked, the trees and everything else was clothed in white.

It looked as if Jack Frost had painted a beautiful picture. The trees all had a soft mantle of fresh snow on their branches. There was not a footprint or tire track anywhere in sight. The wind had actually blown all the snow off the driveway. However, in other places, there were snowdrifts twenty to thirty feet high.

Chris went with his father while they fed the chickens and gathered the eggs. To show he was dominant, the rooster flapped his wings and crowed. The pigs came grunting to the trough. Being pigs, they ate like pigs. Chris loved feeding the cattle because they were so gentle and their sweet breath was soothing to him.

After they had finished feeding the animals, it was time to milk the cows. Chris enjoyed milking time. First, they would clean the cow's udders. Then placing a strap on the cows' backs, they would hang a bucket underneath it. There would be a hose attached to the bucket and another to the milkers. They would then place the milkers on the cows' teats. The Suttons had four buckets of this type, so they were able to milk four cows at once.

While they were being milked, the cows would chew their cud contentedly. When they had finished milking, they placed the milk in a refrigerated container. Later, a milk truck would come to pick it up. After they were finished with all of their chores, George and Chris went back into the house. Clovis had just finished fixing breakfast, and the table was all set. She had made pancakes with homemade butter and maple syrup to put on them. There were also fried eggs and homemade German sausage. As they sat down to eat, Clovis said, "The Olsons called saying they are coming over later." They ate heartily for farmers work hard and need the extra calories.

When they had finished eating, George and Chris helped Clovis clean up the kitchen and helped with the dishes. A bit later, a car horn honked Sam, Gloria, and Terri Olson came to the door. Gloria Olson stated, "Now that the storm is over, it has deposited large snow banks all over the place. What do you say we have some fun and help the kids play in the fresh snow."

First, they decided to make not one but two snow forts twenty feet apart. The wind had packed this so firm that the men were able to take a couple of old saws to use on it. They cut the snow into two-by-three-foot blocks. Then Clovis, Gloria, Terri, and Chris took the blocks, making sure both of the forts were four feet high.

Sam Olson turned to George at the same time, saying, "I suppose you know what we need to do now." With that, as quick as a flash, all of the adults rushed into one snow fort. Chris and Terri stood there bewildered until all of a sudden, they started getting hit with a hail of snowballs.

It didn't take long for Chris and Terri to get the idea. They ran for the other snow fort, then Chris and Terri started making snowballs. They started lobbing these back at their parents. It was great fun until both sides finally got tired. After that, George got out the toboggans, and they slid down the snowbanks until they got cold. Then everyone went inside to warm up with hot chocolate.

Chapter 3

Chris and Terri excelled at school. They were very good students. Both of them always received straight A's in all of their classes. They studied together whenever they had the chance. They not only studied their own lessons but studied books on every subject. Much of what they studied was way beyond their grade level.

One day while still in eighth grade, Chris looked at Terri and asked, "We will be starting high school in the fall. Do you have any idea what courses you think we should take?" Terri pondered this for quite some time before she replied, "We need to start thinking of high school as a stepping stone to college. College will be a path for our occupations in life."

Terri said, "I think we should take biology, chemistry, and all of the algebra courses, trigonometry, geometry. We also need to take every computer course available because computers are definitely the wave of the future." "But," Chris protested, "those courses sound awfully hard. I don't even know if I'm smart enough to pass them."

"Christopher Alan Sutton, you never in your life ever got anything except straight As in school. These courses just seem hard to you now because you don't know anything about them. You will find they are actually easy if you just take them one day at a time.

"Now if you're through scaring yourself, Chris, how about I beat you at arm wrestling?" Chris laughed knowing full well he could whip Terri at arm wrestling any day of the week. However, he made her work hard letting her win every other arm wrestling match.

"See," Terri said, "you're not as tough as you think you are." Chris just laughed and reached over and tweaked her nose. Next, Terri asked Chris if he would teach her how to shoot his .22 rifle. Chris answered, "Yes, but the only thing I will ever shoot at are targets. I can't bear the thought of hurting any living thing. That is why you'll never see me go hunting."

Chris took Terri to the side of a hill where they set up some pop cans on a log. Chris began by showing Terri the safety features of the .22-caliber rifle. He showed her where the safety was, where the sights were. "Always use caution, and, Terri, always keep the rifle pointed downrange. Never point a gun at anyone even in jest. Always check to make sure whether your gun is loaded or unloaded."

Having told her all these things, Chris then proceeded to show Terri how to hold and aim the rifle. When she was ready, Chris had her start shooting at pop cans. After firing almost a box of ammunition, Terri started to become fairly good at it. She was able to hit twenty-five pop cans in a row.

After they had finished, Chris had Terri check to make sure the rifle was empty. Chris showed Terri how to clean the rifle. Terri said, "I enjoyed that, Chris. We will have to do it again. I think I'd enjoy shooting a pistol sometime. Do you think that could be arranged?" "I think so," said Chris, "but it's going to be a while I'm saving up to get .38 special Smith & Wesson. But Dad said I cannot have one until I'm sixteen, but when I get it, we will do some serious target practice."

In June, after Chris and Terri had graduated from the eighth grade, their families planned a celebration at George Lake. George Lake was twelve miles south of Towner on Highway 14. They were going to enjoy a day of swimming and enjoying a good picnic. The day was absolutely gorgeous, and the water at George Lake was gently lapping at the shore. The sun had a golden glow, and fluffy large white cumulus clouds slowly floated overhead. A flock of mallard ducks were swimming around in the lake. The ducks chose to ignore all the people swimming. As far as the ducks were concerned, this was their lake, and it was the people who were the intruders.

Chris and Terri laid in their swimsuits on beach towels on the soft, warm sand. For quite some time, they were content to just lie watching the clouds float by. Suddenly, Terri pointed to a cloud and said, "Look, Chris, that looks just like a large elephant." Chris said, "I thought it looked a lot more like our seventh-grade teacher." Terri laughed, saying, "You're not very nice, Chris."

Chris stood up, saying, "Let's go swimming, Terri." So they ran across the sand jumping into the water. The water felt very cold at first, but after a couple of minutes, it felt tantalizingly refreshing. Chris was a lot faster swimmer and teased Terri saying she was a slowpoke. To get even, Terri snuck up behind him and pushed his head under the water.

After that, they would dunk or splash each other every chance they got. Then they had a contest to see who could swim the fastest underwater. Once again, Chris won, then they decided to take time to get some rest. So they went back and laid on the beach towels to soak up the sun.

Their parents called, telling them it was time for the picnic lunch. They had hamburgers on buns with tomatoes lettuce and onions. There were also hot dogs fresh off the barbecue. Their mothers had made homemade potato salad and for dessert, fresh juicy watermelon. Terri said, "Why does everything taste so good when you are on a picnic?"

When Chris and Terri had finished eating, George Sutton told them, "Don't go swimming for at least an hour, or you might get the cramps. Also don't swim out very far. George Lake is shallow for a long way out. But then within five feet, the water is thirty feet deep."

Chris and Terri lay on the beach towels for a long time just enjoying the sunshine. When they got tired of doing that, they got up and started skipping stones across the lake. Chris got in a real good one. It made fifteen skips and a pitter-patter. Terri could never get more than seven skips across the water. Chris smugly told her that it was a guy thing, so Terri stuck out her tongue at him.

About an hour and a half after eating, Terri took off running into the lake. When she was quite a way ahead, she yelled back, "Come on, Chris, you old slowpoke, I know I can beat you." Chris jumped up and ran as fast and far as he could, then he started swimming furiously. He was very scared. He yelled, "Terri, come back here, you are going out too far."

Chris was able to see Terri was now in trouble for she had turned around and was trying to come back. Chris saw that Terri was having trouble moving her arms. Then Terri started to go under. She spluttered, "Chris, help me I'm drowning." Then she started to go down again.

Chris had never swum so fast in his whole life. He got to where Terri had just gone down within two seconds. He took a deep breath and dived down Terri was only three feet under the surface and struggling to come back up. Chris grabbed her from behind beneath her arms, giving a large kick. He brought them both back to the surface.

Terri was conscious but coughing and gasping for breath. Chris swam back toward shore with her until he was in four feet of water. Then putting one arm under her arms and the other under her knees, he started carrying her back to shore. Terry in turn put her arm around Chris's neck, whispering in his ear, "You are my hero." Chris blushed and replied, "I had to save you, Terri, you are my best friend."

Terri's and Chris's parents came rushing over. "What happened?" they asked? Terri replied, "I was drowning, but my best friend and my hero saved me. I owe my life to him, and I will never ever forget it." Terri's parents thanked Chris over and over again for saving their daughter's life.

Chapter 4

After helping their parents on their respective farms all summer long, Chris and Terri entered Towner High School that fall. The classes were not near as hard as Chris had feared. As a matter-of-fact, he rather enjoyed the harder courses he had chosen. Terri told him, "See, Chris, these are the type of courses that stimulate your mind. They will start to make you realize what you are really capable of doing."

Every night after they had finished their chores, Chris and Terri would study together. They were not satisfied with what they were learning in school. They asked their teachers for any advanced courses they could study. In addition, they talked their parents into subscribing to several computer magazines. They studied all these books and magazines with a real yearning for more information.

Before long, Chris became a whiz at math and computers. When anyone would comment on this, he would answer, "You may think I know a lot, but compared to Terri, I don't know anything. She is absolutely phenomenal. She's got me beat hands down. I think it might be a girl thing."

After a long cold hard winter in late March, the weather started warming up. There were only a few patches of snow left on the ground. Terri said, "Chris, I have spring fever. I think I would enjoy just taking a walk." As they sauntered along, Terri said, "Oh, look, Chris, there is the first crocus. I just adore them they are the very first sign of spring." Chris replied, "Yes, along with these pussy willows over here."

In May, Chris hurriedly grabbed Terri, saying, "Come on, Terri, you have to see this." Chris was carrying a large pair of binoculars. Terri asked, "Chris, what do you want me to see?" He replied, "Just wait you will see." They walked past a large grove of poplar trees surrounded with brush and tall grass. Terri said, "Oh, how beautiful. It is no wonder you wanted me to see this."

Lying in the grass not twenty feet away was a whitetail fawn. It was trying its best not to be seen. It had white spots on its delicate brown body, and Chris and Terri stood looking at it. Terri said, "Oh, what a pretty baby she is. So cute. Can we go pet it, Chris?" "No," he replied, "if we touched it, we would leave our scent on it, and the fawn's mother would abandon it."

They went a distance away from the fawn and kept watch. Soon its mother stepped out of the trees and nuzzled the fawn. They watched in awe as the baby got up to the doe and started nursing. After it was done nursing, the doe and the fawn slowly walked into the woods.

Terri exclaimed, "Chris, that was fantastic. Thank you for showing it to me." "Yes, it was," said Chris. "That was very special, but you actually saw the fawn first. That is not what I was going to show you." They walked until they got to the base of a hill, then Chris whispered, "You have to be really quiet, Terri. Follow me and try not to make any noise."

Chris moved very silently. When they got almost to the top of the hill, he got down and started crawling. Terri did the same following Chris until he stopped in a hollow. The hollow was shielded by some very tall grass at the top of the hill. Chris carefully crawled to the very top, motioning for Terri to do the same. When she was in position, Chris handed her the binoculars, pointing to a hole on the hill on the opposite side of them.

Terri carefully put the binoculars to her eyes, then she focused them. To keep from gasping, she clutched Chris's shoulder. Sitting in front of the hole was a mother fox playing with her five little kits. They silently watched for an hour passing the binoculars back and forth. Finally, they quietly left. After they had gotten far enough away, Terri gave Chris a hug, telling him, "Today was one of the best times that I ever had. Thank you very much."

Chapter 5

In the summer, after they had finished their sophomore year in high school, Chris and Terri both took their driver's licenses and passed. They had both been driving vehicles on their parents' farm for years, as have most teenagers who lived on farms in North Dakota. It was a problem of sheer necessity, as their parents needed the extra help.

After passing his driver's test and getting his driver's license, Chris immediately went car shopping. He located a 1982 half-ton Ford pickup V8 with a straight stick transmission. It was in excellent condition and had low mileage and was also a very good ride. Chris told Terri, "I can use it to help my dad around the farm, plus it is good transportation."

It wasn't long after purchasing the pickup that Chris went and talked to Terri. After hemming and hawing for a while, he finally asked Terri if she wanted to go to a movie in Minot with him. Terri laughingly teased Chris, "Is this going to be a real date, or is it going to be like best buddies?"

"Terri, I would like this to be a real date. I just hope it's not going to ruin our friendship. I also hope we haven't developed a brother-sister relationship after all these years." Terri walked up to Chris, put her arms around his neck, and kissed him passionately. Chris couldn't help himself for he replied in kind.

Terri asked, "Now, Chris, did that happen to feel like a sisterly kiss to you? If it did, I would be very surprised. I don't think anything could ruin the beautiful friendship we have after all this time. Besides, sweetie, I have waited for years for you to ask me out on a real date.

"But it seemed to me like all you ever wanted to do was play basketball or baseball or football. Or maybe you wanted to go fishing or swimming, all of which I admit you are very good at." Chris grinned and winked at her and said, "Well, Terri, I have noticed you have changed quite a bit too. For one thing, I notice you never take your shirt off like you did when we were kids."

Terri laughed and swatted him. "I just don't happen to have the kind of muscles you guys have. Girls just happen to grow in different places than guys do." "And quite nicely, if I may say so myself," Chris said, then added, "You look perfect."

So Chris and Terri started dating. They went to movies in both Minot to the west and Rugby to the east. Chris really enjoyed taking Terri to horror movies. He loved the way Terri would grab on to him during the scary parts. Terri just loved it when they went to chick flicks because she enjoyed the mushy scenes.

Terri wanted to teach Chris dance lessons, but she didn't know how to start. So she decided to talk to her mother and Clovis Sutton, Chris's mom. The ladies in turn asked their husbands to help them. The Olsons just happened to have a very large basement, and in it they had a good sound system. So they just reorganized it to make it into a dance floor.

One Saturday afternoon, both families gathered in the basement with poor, unsuspecting Chris. Gloria Olson put on some waltz music, then Terri walked up and curtsied to Chris, saying, "If I may have the honor of this dance." Bewildered, Chris replied, "But I don't even know how to dance." "That is what we are planning to teach you," Terri replied. "The one thing you find plenty of around Towner are dances. I think you will make a very good dance partner if we teach you."

All afternoon and several others were spent teaching Chris the rudiments of dancing. Before long, Chris became expert at the waltz and polka, two-step and line dancing, even ballroom dancing. Terri smiled, gave Chris a big kiss, saying, "Thank you, honey, for being such a good sport." Chris just blushed, saying, "It was my pleasure; in fact, doing anything with you is a great pleasure."

Terri told Chris, "Even though it is summer, we have to keep our up our goals for college. We will be taking our SAT and ACT tests this coming fall, so we have to keep studying for them." They found several practice tests of both sets, which they studied over and over again. When they were satisfied with the studies on those tests, they went to Minot State College to find some new material.

When Chris and Terri were satisfied, they knew everything that were on the tests. They stopped to relax and take their minds off it for two weeks. Then they went back and went through everything again.

Towner was a very small community, but it did have a dance hall and almost everyone in the surrounding area came to the dances. There was a time for fun for young and old. They were mainly wedding dances and would have a live band. Almost everyone for miles around knew each other. Chris and Terri would go to these dances and twirl around the floor. Chris found he really enjoyed dancing and was thankful to Terri for teaching him.

Both Chris and Terri loved attending these functions. They enjoyed the fast dances of the young crowd. They could perform the polka with the best of them, but their true love was the waltzes and the two-step. When they did these dances, they could hold each other tightly, whispering into each other's ears.

The kids started back to school the day after Labor Day, but this year everything was different. Sometimes they would ride to school on the bus; however, more often Chris would drive them in his Ford pickup. One day, Terri said, "Chris, you had this pickup for almost three months now. I believe it is time you gave it a name." Chris said, "And I suppose you have a name for it." Terri said, "Indeed, I do. I think you should name it Henry." "Okay," laughed Chris. "Henry it is."

Chris and Terri were both caught up in the flurry and activity of school life, talking to friends they had not seen all summer. They helped to prepare for the homecoming game and the dance afterward. It would start with a bonfire the night before the game with all of the students standing around sharing stories and laughing. They would be roasting weenies and marshmallows by the fire.

Chris and Terri helped decorate a float for their class, and they also decorated Henry, Chris's pickup. They had a homecoming parade which wound around Towner led by the high school marching band. Horns were blasting, and people were yelling. They ended up back right where they started by the football field.

Terri was a cheerleader. Chris was a football player. Both wore the red and white of the Towner Cardinals. The Towner High School band played, the cheerleaders yelled, and the football players tried their damnedest. But alas, the Towner High School football team was defeated this time. However, one thing Towner has always been known for, and that is good sportsmanship. Everyone congratulated the winning team and prepared to celebrate with a homecoming dance.

One thing Chris and Terri realized even at their young age. You will never be able to win every time. Sometimes the victory is not in the winning but in the trying. If you have tried and gave it your best shot, then you're definitely not a loser.

Fall came, and with it the scattering of red brown and golden leaves, which fell to the ground, then crackled underneath your feet when you went to walk on them. The air got a definitive chill, letting you know Jack Frost was here and winter was not far behind.

And with the fall came the hunting season. There was always a very large variety of game to choose from. There were deer, duck, grouse, pheasant, wild turkey, and wild geese. It almost seemed like all the men from around the

Towner area were going hunting. One day, Terri inquisitively asked Chris, "Why don't you ever go hunting? Both of our fathers and everyone else we know go hunting."

Chris pondered the question for a moment before answering, "Well, Terri, sweetheart, I really do love guns. I myself have a .22 bolt-action rifle, a 12-gauge pump shotgun, and a .30-30 lever action rifle. I have also just purchased a .38 special Smith & Wesson revolver. I enjoy using all of them for target practice.

"I know it probably sounds strange coming from a person who loves guns and coming from a guy who was born in North Dakota and raised on a farm. However, I just can't bear the thought of hurting any living thing whether it is a human or an animal." Terri grabbed Chris, hugging and kissing him. She said, "Oh, Chris, my darling, that doesn't sound strange to me. It just shows me you have a really big heart."

Chapter 6

Then one Saturday, it was time to take Their Act test. Everyone who wanted to take it had to sign up before hand. At exactly eight o'clock, everyone piled into a classroom. When their names were called, they all had to show proper identification. They were told if there was any cheating, they would be immediately kicked out.

When they were then handed their ACT tests, they were told not to open them until the timer went off. The instructor said to work as fast as possible. If they couldn't solve a problem, they were to skip that one and come back to it when they were finished."

When the instructor told them to start, the classroom went silent except for the clicking of pencils. Everyone could feel the tension in the room. At ten o'clock, the instructor told everyone to stop and put their pencils down. "You will now have a fifteen-minute break."

When they had all filed back into the classroom, they were told at one o'clock, the tests would be over. At that time, anyone not finished would have to turn in their paperwork anyway. If you had completed your tests before that, you were to hand in your tests and silently leave the room.

Once again, the instructor told them to start again; and soon, the pencils started clicking. Who could believe thirty students could remain so silent. At 12:15, Terri got up and handed the instructor her test paper and test booklet. Ten minutes later, Chris followed her.

Terri was waiting for him in the lobby and asked Chris, "How do you think you did on the test?" "Absolutely crappy," Chris replied. "Well, actually, I think I didn't really do that bad. How about you, Terri?" Terri said, "I know I did all right, but that's not what I'm worried about. We both need to have done much better than all right. At least if we want to get into one of the better colleges."

Chris thought about what Terri had said for about four or five minutes before saying, "Terri, it seems like we have studied for the ACT tests for years. With your help, I felt like we were invincible. In my heart, I'm going to believe we did great. At least until after we see our test scores."

"Chris, you are absolutely correct, and you have lifted a great weight off of my mind. At the very least, I know that we will we be able to get into a college even though it may not be the first college of our choice." The following Saturday, Chris and Terri went back to the same room. Following the same procedures, this time it was to take their SAT tests.

Chris and Terri were elated when the SAT test was completed; however, the day was not over yet. They had been invited to a masquerade hayride that evening. After several rejected costumes, they had decided to go as George and Martha Washington.

Chris painstakingly put on his powdered white wig, which amused Terri to no end. She laughed out loud as she helped him put on his bluecoat. Terri said, "Now all you have to do is buckle on your saber, George. Do you realize I had to search all over to find this tricorne hat?" Chris said, "Terri, you did a splendid job, and you look great as Martha Washington."

Chris opened the door to help Terri into his pickup, being the gentleman he was. He did this every time. This time was just a little harder though, getting Terri's large dress to fit into the front seat. Then they were off going to a Halloween masquerade party hayride.

The wagon loaded with hay was the genuine thing, and they were helped onboard along with thirty or so of their friends. However, the part that wasn't quite so genuine was that there not was a four-horse team pulling the wagon. Instead, it was pulled by a 454-horsepower, four-wheel-drive Chevy pickup truck. In chairs on the back of the truck were some people playing guitars, violins, even an accordion.

As the hayride headed slowly north, the band started playing. Everyone in the hay wagon started whooping singing and clapping their hands. A string of cars followed them, flashing there lights and honking their horns.

The caravan turned left into the forest reserve north of Towner. Then they all pulled up around the large bonfire. Once there, everyone piled out, and several more musicians joined the little band. It became a loud, boisterous shindig. They had corn roasting by the fire. Also, someone were barbequing a couple of pigs.

Everyone laughed when they saw Chris and Terri were dressed as George and Martha Washington. They started teasing them, telling them they had to sing a song from the time period. Terri whispered to Chris, "We can do this." He nodded yes. They started singing "Yankee Doddle." Everyone started laughing, then joined in along with the band.

After everyone else got absorbed in the singing, Chris and Terri snuck off to walk around. They went to where the Forestry Park had a walking bridge over the Mouse River. There was a clear full moon that seemed to hover just over the treetops. Terri held her hand out, taking Chris's in hers. Chris whispered, "No matter where we go in life, I will always treasure this time and place."

"Life has been very good to us, Chris. I feel as if we have been overly blessed. I keep worrying that the axe will fall someday. That something really bad is looming in our future." Chris said, "Terri, don't think like that, sweetheart. It is more than likely just your imagination. Even if it isn't, we will get through it somehow. Some rain is always bound to fall in everyone's life."

"Okay, Chris, I know I was probably just being melancholy for a moment. From now on, I will just enjoy being in the present. Besides, my mother always told me to thank God for bad times. For without them, you would not be able to enjoy the good times."

Chapter 7

On the way home from school one brisk December afternoon, Chris pulled over to the mailbox. Along with the other mail was a letter from his ACT test. Terri urged him to open it. They tore it open looking for the test results. Chris was dumbfounded. He received a 32 out of a possible 36. He handed it to Terri who gasped, saying, "This is incredible, Chris, I will never be able to beat you."

Chris said, "We will see when we check your mail." Sure enough, Terri's test scores were there. Terri asked, "Chris, would you open it for me please? I'm afraid to look at it. Ever since I took the test, I knew I had failed miserably." Chris slowly opened the envelope, taking the results in his hands. He frowned as he slowly studied it.

Terri was almost crying as she asked, "What is it, Chris? I know it's bad. I was so looking forward to going to college with you. Please just tell me." Chris grabbed Terri, hugging and kissing her. He said, "Honey, I'm sorry, I can tell you were looking forward to failing.

"But alas you will be going to college with me after all. I hate to be the one to tell you this, but you aced your ACT test." Relief just came all over Terri as she started crying. "Chris, you are a big butthole, but I love you anyway."

One week later, their SAT scores came back. This time, they took them into the house and put them on the table. They had decided beforehand they would open each other's envelopes. They drew straws to see who would go first. Terri got the long straw, so she opened Chris's envelope. "This is really fantastic, Chris, you got 1400 on your SAT score. That's very good, sweetie."

Next, it was Chris's turn, and he opened Terri's envelope. Slowly, after looking it over, he stated, "This is terrible, Terri, you maxed your ACT test but you only received 1500 on your SAT. How are you ever going to live with yourself that you didn't quite max your SAT test?" This started both of them to giggling and laughing. Chris grabbed Terri as they started dancing around the room.

Terri gave Chris a solemn look and said, "Chris, it is not too early to start doing research on colleges." They started by looking at brochures from different colleges. The ones they weren't interested in, they eliminated right away. Both Terri and Chris decided they wanted to go for a business degree. From there were several different occupations they could choose from. Anyway, this is where their hearts told them to go.

Terri and Chris started filling out college scholarship application forms. Terri and Chris were surprised at the number of scholarship applications which applied to them. But they painstakingly filled out the application forms they were most interested in. Their parents were very curious, asking Chris and Terri what college they were planning to attend. They replied they had not decided on a certain college yet. But whatever college they chose would have to accept both of them.

Chapter 8

On a very frigid day during the Christmas holidays, Chris asked Terri if she wanted to go ice-skating. When she replied yes, Chris said, "Some of our friends are planning to have an ice-skating party at the Denbigh Lake. We need to go early to help get the ice cleared off the lake."

Chris drove his pickup to the shed where they put in the snow shovels and firewood. Then they went into the house where they got an ice chest filled with hot dogs, hot dog buns, and marshmallows. They put all of this into the back of Chris's pickup. When they arrived at the lake, they found twenty or so of their friends already there. They all got out their snow shovels, and in no time at all, they had cleared a very large patch of snow off of the ice.

They placed the firewood on the bank of the lake along with firewood which others had brought. It looked like there was enough firewood to last for the evening and then some. Chris took some firewood setting it up to make a campfire. Kneeling down, he put some kindling in the center of the firewood. After lighting the kindling, it took another twenty minutes to get a nice roaring fire going.

During this time, several more cars and trucks had pulled up to the lake. It was only 6:30, and already it was very dark. A myriad of stars glowed in the evening sky, and the air was crisp and clear. It was so still you could hear the cracking of the fire and smell the pungent aroma of the wood as it burned.

Chris and Terri sat on the tailgate of the pickup putting on their ice skates. They could hear the plinking of a guitar along with the voices of a young couple. Their voices were clear and harmonious as they sang Christmas carols. It wasn't long before everyone standing around the campfire joined in.

Chris and Terri started ice-skating hand in hand as other couples twirled on the ice around them. Chris started getting pretty cocky, telling Terri, "We will show them how to ice-skate. We will perform an ice dance." They were doing pretty well until Chris got little bit wild. All of a sudden, he fell down and slid thirty feet backward on his back. Of course, this accompanied by the hoots and laughter from Terri and everyone else.

Chris got up dusted the snow of his body and nonchalantly made like this was all part of the act. Terri came up to Chris linking her arm into his, saying, "Nice try, honey. But there is no one who believes you did that on purpose. In fact, a guy standing over there caught it all on the movie camera." At that, Chris started laughing. He said, "By golly, I'm going to ask him if I can watch it with you later. I'll bet I did look hilarious."

Chris and Terri decided to roast a couple of hot dogs and marshmallows by the fire. After they had finished eating, they sat on a log singing Christmas carols with everyone else. Someone had put a pot of coffee on the fire to boil. The aroma was so entrancing that Terri asked, "Why does coffee smell so good in the open air?" "I don't know," replied Chris. "It just does. In fact, it smells so good that I'm going to go and grab us both a couple cups of coffee."

When he came back, he handed one cup to Terri, saying, "Let it cool a bit first. I remember the first time I took a sip of boiled coffee. I burned my mouth and have been very careful about it ever since." As they sat sipping their coffee, a gentle snowfall began. At the same time, a shooting star flashed across the sky. Chris asked Terri, "Did you make a wish?" She replied, "Yes, I did, but I can't tell you what it was because then it won't come true."

There were many other things a person could do in North Dakota in the wintertime. One of Chris and Terri's favorites was snowmobiling. They would put on warm coveralls, and Chris would fire up the snowmobile. Chris would drive with Terri behind him. She would have her arms around his waist. Then he would gun the engine, and they would be off through the soft, powdery snow.

The new generation of snowmobiles are very fast and very powerful. You could easily get a speed of seventy to ninety miles per hour. But you have to be very careful for many people have died because they just weren't paying attention. You could wind up hitting a culvert, a barbwire fence, a log, a fence post, or something else.

But if you are careful, snowmobiles could be a lot of fun. On this particular day, the snowmobile ride was great. There was nice soft snow blanketing the ground, and it was balmy eight degrees above zero. Chris made a sudden quick turn. Terri being unprepared flew head first into a snowbank. Chris stopped as Terri pulled her head out of the snowbank. Spluttering, she looked at him, saying, "Chris Sutton, you did that on purpose."

Chris laughed and said, "I did not, but you do look like a snowman. But not at all like an abominable one, you look more like a desirable snowman." That did the trick, and Terri started laughing and ran into Chris's open arms.

One nice weekend in February, both the Olson and Sutton families decided they would like to do some ice fishing. No, this is not where you go fishing and try to catch him some ice. In the northern states, the lakes get very thick with over 2 feet ice over them. The ice is thick enough that you can drive your car right out onto the lake.

The Olsons and the Suttons were going to Buffalo Lodge Lake near Granville, North Dakota. When they were almost to the lake, Sam Olson stopped the car. He said, "Look at that. Do you think he's trying to hide from us?" Twenty-five feet from the car stood a large snowshoe rabbit. He was standing up everything about him was the purest white except for the tiny black spots at the tips of his ears.

They drove out upon the lake where Sam Olson, and George and Chris Sutton took out the ice auger. There they drilled several holes through the ice. Then everyone including the ladies baited their hooks with smelt. All the fishing lines had bobbers attached to them if the bobber went down, it meant you had a fish on the line. Within five minutes, all three of the ladies had caught a fish. George Sutton said, "He thought this looked like sex discrimination to him."

During the next hour, Gloria, Clovis, and Terri got several more fish while none of the men had even gotten a bite. George went to get a thermos of coffee and some sandwiches. He then handed out sandwiches and poured coffee for everyone. Immediately, all three men's bobbers went down. No sooner would they pull a fish out of water and get the line back in than another fish would strike.

Meanwhile, the ladies sat in folding chairs, eating their sandwiches and sipping their coffee. Finally, the men were not getting any more bites, so they sat down to enjoy their coffee. Of course, the coffee was ice cold by this time. George swore, "Those are the most prejudiced, blankety-blank fish I've ever seen. In fact, now when I think about it, every time I've ever went ice fishing, I've never got a bite until I got a hot cup of coffee; in fact, I don't think I've ever had a hot cup of coffee while I have been ice fishing."

Chapter 9

By the time they had entered their senior year in high school, Chris and Terri had finally narrowed down the number of colleges to four. The colleges they had chosen were Harvard, UCLA, the University of North Dakota, and the University of Washington.

They filled out their applications to everyone of them, then it became a waiting game. While they were waiting, they filled out more scholarship applications and kept up their studies. Of course, they were anxious, but there was so much to do the time passed swiftly.

In January, Terri was notified she had received a scholarship worth $25,000 a year. Then two weeks later, Chris was awarded two different scholarships for combined total of $12,000 per year. But it still wasn't over yet in February, after what had seemed like an eternity. Within two weeks, both of them had received replies from all four colleges. Not only had they both been accepted by all of them, but every college was offering both of them a full ride.

Chris and Terri were elated, but now they would have to decide to which college they would be going. They deliberated long and hard. They weighed both the pros and the cons. Any of these colleges would give them a good education. Harvard was definitely the most prestigious.

After much thought, they finally narrowed it down to the University of Washington. The part which had finally won them over was the fact it was close to both the ocean and the mountains. Chris and Terri had neither been out of the state of North Dakota and had not seen either one. They were both really excited about this; plus, it would give them a great educational opportunity.

Looking back, in a way, it seemed like they had just started high school. Now they were nearing the end of their senior year. The senior prom was drawing near, and there was no doubt about who they would be going to it with. All week long, Chris and Terri had help decorate the Towner High School gymnasium.

This year's theme for the prom was Dreams That Will Last a Lifetime. There were streamers and banners to put up. They were on the committee to find a band and not just any band. What you had to do was pick just the perfect one. They found a photographer who wanted them to pick out and then put up the proper background.

Terri and her mother went shopping for a dress for the prom. Terri finally decided on a beautiful long black low-cut gown. Her mother told her to try it on. When she came out of the dressing room, her mother told her, "Go look in the mirror. You look absolutely stunning."

On the Saturday night of the prom, his dad told Chris, "Take the family car. You don't want to take Terri to the prom in a truck. You would be an embarrassment to all of us. I already cleaned the car inside and out and waxed it so go to the prom and enjoy yourselves."

The moment Chris stepped into the Olsons home, his jaw dropped. This was a Terri he had never seen before. Terri wore this sleek black gown adorned by a string of pearls around her slender neck. Terry's already beautiful shoulder-length dark hair looked absolutely gorgeous tonight. When Chris saw the high heel shoes, long eyelashes, the lipstick, Chris stopped like he was thunderstruck. He said, "Terri, I've never seen you wear lipstick."

Terri laughed, saying, "Chris, I'm the same girl you've always known." Terri then had Chris turn around surveying him. Terry said, "Chris, you looked very handsome in your tuxedo too, but at the same time, you look very nervous." "I am nervous," Chris replied. "I can't help it, but you just look so beautiful."

Chris took the corsage he had brought, trying his best to pin it on to Terry's gown. However, his hand shook so badly he was having a hard time doing it. Both of Terry's parents couldn't help laughing. Terry's mother finally said, "Chris, let me help you with the corsage. The way your hand is shaking you will stick Terri with the pin."

As soon as they entered the prom, they had their pictures taken. Chris and Terri danced almost every dance. Gazing into each other's eyes, they just couldn't seem to get enough of each other. Holding each other tightly as they danced, Chris and Terri softly sang the tunes the band was playing.

Several times, one or another of Chris's friends would come to them and want to dance with Terri. Chris would gently say, "Sorry, buddy, this is my night with my girl." "I wish this night could last forever," whispered Terri. "It will," Chris replied, "but mainly in our memories; besides, we will have lots of other wonderful times."

After the band played the last dance, the evening came to an end. Chris bowed to Terry, saying, "Madam, if you will allow me to escort you to my carriage." Putting her arm through his, Terri said, "Where to, my prince?" Chris replied, "I happen to know where there is a lone oak tree close to Kopperdahl Hill. There we will be able to watch the fluffy white clouds float beneath the silvery moon."

After they got there, they were sitting in the car with their arms wrapped around each other. They were gently yet intensely kissing. Suddenly, Chris pulled back with a look of wonder on his face. He gazed deeply into Terry's beautiful green eyes. He exclaimed, "Oh God, Terri Olsen, I love you so much that it hurts."

Terri laughingly replied, "Have you just now figured that out, buster? Haven't you realized we have loved each other all of our lives?" Chris answered, "Yes, I know, but I never realized that a person could be this deeply in love."

"Chris, I suppose this is the time you will say you want my body?" Terri asked. "If you really want it that much, I will willingly give it to you." Chris replied, "Terri, I do want your body, and a lovely body it is. However, I do not want you getting pregnant. We both have to finish college, so we are just going to have to wait until after we get married." Terri burst out laughing. "So now we are getting married, my love. Was that supposed to be some kind of a marriage proposal?"

Chris said, "Terri, will you step outside of the car with me for a moment." After they had both got of the car, Chris fell to his knees. Chris took Terry's hand in his, saying, "Terri Olsen, heart of my heart, love of my life. After we have finished college in four years, will you marry me?"

With tears in her eyes, Terri replied, "Chris, all of my life I have been planning to marry you. Of course, I will marry you. As you know, Chris, I enjoy watching love stories on the movies or on television. In not a one of them I have ever watched have I ever seen as corny a proposal as you just made. But it doesn't matter, Chris, you did it in your own way, and I love you with all my heart mind and soul.

"But on the serious side, Chris, we both have a full ride to the University of Washington. I don't want to have to wait the full four years to get married to you. I can wait, but if we can get married sooner, I would like it." Chris said, "Terri, maybe we should have a talk with our parents. We both trust them. They are smart and reliable. Maybe they can help us come up with a decision."

Chapter 10

The very next day, Chris and Terri asked both sets of parents to meet with them at the Suttons home. Terri told their parents it was to help us discuss their future plans. They all said they would be more than glad to help. Chris and Terri and their parents sat down at the dining room table.

Chris started the conversation. "First, I would like to tell all of you Terri and I have decided to attend the University of Washington. That we both had received a full ride to college. In addition, I got scholarships worth $12,000 a year. But Terri received a scholarship for $25,000 a year."

Suddenly, Terri blurted out, "Chris is taking too long and going into too many details. Last night, Chris asked me to marry him, and I said yes." Their parents were all startled at first, then they hugged Chris and Terri and offered congratulations.

Gloria Olson spoke up, saying, "While we were all expecting you two to get married eventually, however you are both so young, I hope t you aren't pregnant, sweetie." "Mom," Terri replied, "that's a big part of the problem. We have never made love because we decided to wait until we get married. Chris wants us to wait to get married until after we finish college. Personally, I don't think I can stand to wait so long."

Clovis Sutton broke into the conversation, "Maybe you could just wait until after you finish your sophomore year of college. That way, you will be halfway through college, and you will know more about life. Also, by this time, both you and Chris will be older and more mature."

"That would be splendid idea," Sam Olson remarked. "We could plan a big church wedding for you right here in Towner. What do you kids think of this idea?" Chris and Terri both agreed that it was a brilliant idea. Suddenly, Chris looked around, then he asked, "Where did Dad go?" No one had seen him leave, but Clovis Sutton had a strange smile on her face.

Then the door open slightly, and George beckoned for Chris to come outside. You could hear that George was talking to Chris. After a couple of minutes, they walked back inside. Chris had a huge smile on his face.

Chris walked up to Terri and said, "Dad gave me something to give to you. He told me if you don't like it, I can get you a different one." Opening his hand, he showed her a two-carat diamond ring. "This used to belong to my grandmother; it was her engagement ring." Terri said, "Oh, Chris, it is beautiful." Then she slipped the ring on her finger where it fit perfectly. She hugged Chris, saying, "Now everybody will know we are engaged."

After that, Terri hugged Chris and his father, thanking him for the ring. George told Terri before his mother passed away, his mother had told him, "I will bet you anything, those kids will get married when they grow up. If they do, I would love to have you give them this ring. It has been so precious to me."

The next morning, Chris called Terri, saying, "Hi, get up sleepyhead. I'm coming over in a few minutes. I would like very much for you to come with me." "Where are you going?" Terri asked. Chris said, "I'm heading to Minot to trade my pickup off for a car. I have heard there are a lot of steep hills in Seattle. I don't think my straight-stick pickup would be the ideal vehicle for out there."

Terri was ready and jumped into the pickup as soon as Chris got there. "Will you tell me why you need me for this?" she asked. Chris answered, "Terri, sweetheart, this new vehicle will be for both of us. My father told me a long time ago that you don't ever make a major decision without the approval of both partners. You are my partner now and always."

Chris and Terri looked at what must have been over thirty different cars. They went to over fifteen different dealerships. Then they went to a restaurant to sit down and decide on what car they were going to buy. When Chris ordered a hamburger, Terri told the waitress, "Do not put any onions on the hamburger, I may have to kiss him later." Chris reached over and gently tweaked her nose.

Curious, Terri asked Chris, "Have you decided which car you would like to buy?" He replied, "Yes, I have picked out one I really like, but I want to know which one you like first." They decided the only fair way to do it was to write the name of the car which each of them liked on a sheet of paper. Then they would both turn the papers over at the same time. After they did that, Chris and Terri both burst out laughing for they had both picked out the same car.

The car which they had picked out was a shiny black 1986 Monte Carlo. It had a sunroof, styled wheels, leather interior, air-conditioning, tilt wheel, power windows, and a cruise control. And the best thing was, it had very low miles. There were only eighteen thousand miles on the odometer.

Chris and Terri went back to the dealership. After some dickering, they traded the pickup and some hard-earned cash. After signing the paperwork, the salesman handed Chris two sets of keys. Chris gave Terri the second set of keys, saying, "These are yours. Now we will see how this Monte Carlo handles you get to drive."

Terri laughed, saying, "You asked for it," and she hit the accelerator. The Monte Carlo was out of there like a shot out of a cannon. Terri burned out of the dealership tires squealing, smoke coming off the tires, the smell of burning rubber. At first, Chris sat there with his mouth wide-open, then he broke out laughing.

When he finally could control himself, Chris said, "I love you. I always knew you had a little bit of the wild side in you." "Yes, Chris, I know, but this car handles like a dream, and it was just begging for me to try it out." Chris said, "Regardless, Terri, you are my sweetheart and one of a kind."

Chapter 11

It was a very small graduating class. Towner was a small town that was slowly getting smaller. It is the capital of McHenry County located just off of Highway 2. But Towner like a lot of the towns in the Midwest had a population problem. The time of the small farm with lots of children had just about disappeared. Over a period of years, farmers slowly sold their small farms to their larger neighbors. It took a lot more acreage nowadays to make a living. Consequently, not as many farms, not as many people, not as many children.

Chris and Terri were very excited about their upcoming graduation. As co-valedictorians, they were expected to give a speech. And decided to work on one together. It seemed everyone at school knew about Chris and Terri's engagement. They were both congratulated repeatedly. All the girls had to see and admire Terry's ring. Everyone promised they would be there for the wedding in two years.

Graduation week just seemed to fly by. There were dinners, awards, and finally the big night. The graduates filed into the high school gymnasium. It seemed like all of Towner and the surrounding area had come. With so many people in the gym, and it got unbearably hot.

The ceremony began, Chris nudged Terri, whispering, "Is it just me, or is everyone really long-winded tonight?" Terry elbowed him, telling him to be quiet. Then there was an announcement for the valedictorians Terri Olson and Chris Sutton to come up. As Chris approached the podium, he said, "As co-valedictorians, we did not want to bore you with two speeches. So we have written the speech together. We tossed a coin, and Terri lost. Therefore, she gets to give the speech." Terri solemnly walked up to the podium.

"Members of the school board, Superintendent Hartley, Principal Buxley, parents, fellow classmates, and friends. Tonight as we complete our scholastic journey of the Towner school system. It is with mixed emotions I greet you. We are all happy that we have finished this portion of our lives.

"Now we will be moving on to our future vocations. Some of us will be fulfilling our dreams by furthering our education. Others will be pursuing the great patriotic dream, by joining the military forces of our great nation. Still others will join the labor force. May they become the new captains of industry. Some will find happiness by working on and eventually taking over their parents; farms. This is all well and good. The central part of the United States is known as the breadbasket of the world. We must have men and women to fill this need.

"However, our happiness is tinged with a bit of sadness. We will be leaving our homes, our families, and our loved ones. We will embark on life's journey. Some of us may never see each other again. Towner and the surrounding area has been our rock, our life support, our salvation. Here with the support of our parents, our teachers, our friends, we grew to maturity and adulthood.

"Thank God, for our memories, they will be the only things which will always remain the same. We can return from time to time, but nothing will ever be exactly as we remember it. Which is a good thing, because anything that remains the same becomes stagnant. In closing, remember life only passes this way once. Good luck and God bless."

After what seemed an eternity, the diplomas were handed out. The graduates all threw their hats in the air. The applause grew as the graduating class stood up and filed outside to the high school lawn. What a relief! The school lawn was much cooler with a nice, refreshing breeze. The sweet aroma of freshly mowed grass took the place of hundreds of hot, sweaty bodies.

Friends and relatives crowded around the graduates congratulating them. There were a lot of tearful good-byes and "don't forget to write me" among the classmates of the last twelve years. After thirty minutes of this, Terri whispered to Chris, "We need to get out of here. I don't want to go to any graduation parties. I just want to be with you."

Chris took Terry's arm as they made their way through the crowd. It took like what seemed like forever. Every couple of feet they kept getting stopped and congratulated over and over again. Eventually, they made it to the Monte Carlo where Chris opened the door for Terri, then he got in on the driver side this time. They drove around town for a while, then decided to drive down to the river. The official name of the river is the Souris River but in North Dakota is known as the Mouse River.

Chris took the old river road parking by the railroad train trestle. They got out and walked to the middle of the trestle. There they sat down on the ties dangling their legs over the edge. Chris and Terri quietly sat holding hands listening to all the night sounds. Fish splashing, crickets chirping, frogs croaking, the soft hoot of an owl. On the bank, the wind gently moved the branches of the trees, which cast their shadows on the river, with a quarter moon hovering in the clouds overhead.

Chris looked at Terri, and they both blurted out at once, "I will miss this." Then Chris wrapped his arms around Terri and kissed her tenderly. Chris stated, "At least, I won't have to miss you, honey, because you will be going with me. Because you are the one person I want to be with always."

Chapter 12

Chris and Terri decided to help their parents on the farm until it was time to leave for Seattle. Chris helped mow the alfalfa on both farms. After a couple of days of leaving it lay in the sun, they would bail it into huge round bales weighing one thousand five hundred pounds.

Many farmers would say these big round hay bales sure beat the small rectangular bales they used to have. The small bales weighed anywhere from 80 to 150 pounds a piece. They were loaded by hand, and it was backbreaking work. There was one great thing about these big round bales. There was no way they were going to be moved without a tractor equipped with a farmhand with a grapple fork on it.

While the men were working in the field, Terri was helping her mother and Clovis Sutton with canning. They canned pickles both sweet pickles and dill pickles. Terri loved the smell of the fresh dill weed. They also canned beets, peaches, pears, plums, and apricots.

Around the week of the Fourth of July, Towner would start to fill up. There were many people who had grown up in Towner but then had moved on to other places. Around the fourth, they would slowly start to filter back from other towns, from other states, from other countries. They came because they knew at that time they could meet old friends. They also came back for the annual street dance and the Fourth of July rodeo.

The street dance was usually held the night of third of July. A large portion of the street would be blocked off. A semitrailer would be parked alongside the street, and the band and its instruments would be on it. By the time the band began to play, many people would be well lubricated with alcohol.

With wild yelling and foot stomping, the street would fill up with people dancing. There would be three times as many standing on the sidewalk watching and visiting. Chris and Terri were in the midst of it. They were dancing and laughing meeting old friends that had left Towner years before.

Terri jokingly told Chris she had seen a couple of people who were not too sober. Chris added, "I couldn't be positive, but I thought I might have seen one or two who were." The next day, they packed an ice chest full of pop and watermelon. They packed another chest with sandwiches, cold fried chicken, potato chips, and loaded all of this in the Monte Carlo. Chris and Terri were headed for Towner's annual Fourth of July rodeo.

The rodeo is held north of Towner and was started in the early 1950s. Chris and Terri were lucky they were there by ten o'clock because within an hour, the place was packed. They had parked right in front where all of the action could be seen. Terri remarked to Chris, "It seemed pretty dusty here at the rodeo." He replied, "The crew from the rodeo have a water truck and try to keep the ground watered down. But with all of the traffic, the horses, and other animals, it seems to get dusty within a half hour."

Terri asked, "Chris, have you ever thought of entering to become a rodeo contestant?" Chris answered, "Well, I can't say I never thought about it. But then I had a little talk with my bones and my body." "And what did they tell you?" Terri asked. "Well, they said they didn't like being bruised, broken, spindled, or mutilated.

"However, you will notice a lot of our friends are riding in the rodeo. Many of them started rodeoing, doing so even before they began school. The only thing they could enter at that time is what is called mutton punching." Terri said, "Okay, Chris, all right, I will bite. Just what in the hell is mutton punching?" "You will just have to wait and see," Chris smugly answered.

The first event was saddle bronc riding. Those horses would come out of the chute like dynamite unleashed. The cowboy would be spurring the horse one hand on the reins and the other hand held high in the air. The rider had to stay on the bucking horse for at least eight seconds to qualify. To place high, you had to have a horse, which really put on a show. Of course, the harder the horse bucked, the harder it was to stay on for eight seconds.

Next came, bareback horse riding, followed by barrel bending. Afterward, the event which really scared Terri was bull riding. Those Brahma bulls would just glare at you as if they were meat eaters. They acted like the thing they would like most in life was to get you on the ground. Once there, they would like to stomp or gore you to death. Terri was very glad Chris had decided not to rodeo.

The announcer stated, "The next rider will be Jack Wilson coming out of chute number two. He will be riding a bull called Hell's Fire. This is not your ordinary bull. When he comes out of the gate, boys and girls, watch out. He is very dangerous, having already put several cowboys in the hospital."

Terri's heart was in her throat, and she was gripping Chris's arm so hard she could see him wince. When they opened gate number two, Terri learned the bull lived up to his name. He came bellowing, bucking, snorting, and charging out of that chute. He would swap ends, throwing his rear end high in the air, twisting and turning. One could see Jack Wilson's body snap with every jolt. Hell's Fire's only objective was to get that creature off his back.

After what seemed like an eternity, the whistle finally blew. Jack Wilson had made an awesome ride. Now his only problem was to get off of the bull's back. Seeing his chance, he flung himself to the ground. He hit that dirt running with Hell's Fire hot on his heels.

This is when the rodeo clown's stepped in. The clowns are not there just to make you laugh. Although they do that too, one clown yelled and waved a red cloth at the bull to get Hell's Fire's attention. Meanwhile, another clown rolled a barrel close to the bull and jumped in. Then he stood up in the barrel, waving his arms and making noises. The bull glared at the barrel, then pawed the ground lowered his head and charged. The clown ducked back inside the barrel.

The bull charged the barrel, knocking it over thirty feet. When the clown popped his head back out, Hell's Fire pawed the ground, getting ready to charge again. But by that time horseback riders were able to haze the bull back into his pen. The crowd broke out into thunderous applause. Chris handed Terri an ice-cold pop, saying, "Terri, you are shaking and sweating like you had rode that bull yourself." "I felt like I had too," Terri told Chris. "I hope the next event will be a little tamer."

The next event did turn out to be a whole lot tamer and very enjoyable. It was mutton punching, the event Chris wouldn't tell Terri about. This event was limited to children six years old and younger. They would be riding sheep. Terri squealed with delight when the fifteen contestants walked out into the arena. They were all wearing jeans, Western hats, and cowboy boots. They all took a little bow and walked off.

The gate opened for the first contestant. He had his hands clutched deep into the sheep's wool. That sheep took off running around the arena, then it stopped and baahed bewildered. One after another, they came out of the chute, then it was time for the last little cowboy's turn.

This little guy had style his sheep calmly walked around the arena as he clutched the wool with one hand while waving his other hand to the applause of the crowd. The sheep came to a dead halt, and the little cowboy jumped off. Then he took off his hat and did a little curtsy. It was not until the hat came off, and long golden hair fell to the shoulders. That was when the crowd realized it was not a little cowboy; it was a little cowgirl. Not since Jack Wilson's ride on Hell's Fire had you heard such applause. The little cowgirl received the coveted belt buckle prize.

Chapter 13

Chris and Terri spent the rest of the summer helping their parents on the farms. As the time drew near for their departure to Seattle, they decided to call Terri's aunt and uncle in Butte Montana. Chris and Terri were hoping for a place to spend the night so they wouldn't have to get a hotel room. Because this could be very dangerous for them to be in the same motel. Chris also thought he had better call his uncle in Federal Way, Washington, for the same reason.

Luck was on their side. Both families would be glad to have them visit. They also had separate bedrooms for both of them. They decided to drive out early so they could take their time and enjoy the scenery. They took off on the tenth of September. It was very exciting to be leaving. But there was a bit of sadness to be leaving a place they loved and grew up in. Chris and Terri had so many happy memories in North Dakota.

The trip was enjoyable. Terri had so much fun teasing Chris. He is so kind and tenderhearted. He was also very gullible believing everything Terri told him. So he was easy to tease. The Monte Carlo was very comfortable. Chris said, "It sure beats driving my old pickup." Chris and Terri really enjoyed the trip, looking at scenery they had never seen before. Chris and Terri had great conversations. They were able to talk about any subject under the sun. Nothing was taboo, except sex, that is. Although they did talk about eventually having a family, they decided they wanted to have at least two children.

They arrived in Butte Montana around nine in the evening. Terri's aunt and uncle were waiting for them. Butte is an old copper mining town. In its heyday, Butte Montana was one of the wildest cities in the west. Copper mines at one time dotted the city. The Mountain Con mine, the largest of them, went down into the earth for almost a mile.

They stayed in Butte for two days, then took off for Seattle. Chris and Terri were awestruck by the mountains. They loved North Dakota. It is a very friendly place, and to them it is beautiful. But it is flat, flat, flat. When they finally arrived in Federal Way, Washington, they told Chris's uncle Mike they could not believe the traffic. Mike laughed, saying, "You came in the evening when there's hardly any traffic. Wait till you see it at rush hour." The next day, they drove to the University of Washington. They wanted to look around and sign up for our classes.

The University of Washington is located on the north side of Portage and Union bays. Chris and Terri were amazed at the vastness of the campus. Of course, it has to be large with over thirty thousand students enrolled. They found the admission and registration offices. There they signed up for classes and were assigned to dorm rooms. They were given a map of the campus, so they wandered around checking where all of their classes were located. They were told that they could move into our dorm in two days.

While they were there, they purchased all the books for their classes, then drove back to Federal Way. When they got there, Chris stated, "Maybe we should go find a store where we can buy each of us a computer." Chris and Terri got back in the car and found the way to the South Center Mall. To them, it looked like everyone in Seattle had decided to go there at the same time they did. But they did find and purchase the computers they wanted.

When Chris's uncle Mike came home that night, he asked Chris, "Did you have any problems getting lost today?" Chris answered, "Only once, that was when we left till we got back." For the next two days, they drove around trying their best to get acquainted with Seattle. Even with the maps, they managed to get lost several times. But at least they were slowly getting to know how to find their way around.

After the two days were up, they went back to the University of Washington to check into their rooms. Terri's dorm room did seem to be very large, but it did have two beds and two desks. So she realized she would be getting a roommate. Terri was just hoping she would be nice. It would be terrific to have a friend.

After Terri was settled in, she went to meet Chris. They went to the cafeteria. Chris and Terri were both striving for a business degree, and both signed up for all the same classes. Chris had lucked out at his dorm. He had a single room all to himself. After they had finished at the cafeteria, they checked out the Suzallo library. They were totally amazed at its size. They were told it is one of the largest libraries in the world. It looked like it was a great place for them to study. Every reference book that you could ever want, plus nice long tables and wonderful overhead lighting.

Holding hands, Chris and Terri walked back to her dorm room where they quickly kissed good-bye and said, "See you in the morning." When Terri walked into her room, she hesitated because someone else was already there. An African-American girl turned around with a warm friendly smile on her face. She stuck out her hand, saying, "Hi there, I'm Tatiana Brown. I guess I will be your new roommate." So Terri introduced herself to her as Terri Olson.

Tatiana had a bubbly personality was very tall with a finely sculpted body. She had a beautiful face, short hair, and almost a regal bearing. She also had a soft, resonating voice. Terri didn't know it at the time, but Tatiana would come to be her closest and dearest friend next to Chris.

The girls sat down on the chairs in their room and started sharing their stories. She was surprised to learn that they had a lot in common. Terri asked Tatiana, "Where did you grow up because you have a slight Southern accent?" She replied, "I was born and grew up in Georgia, the second of five children. I have one older brother Bill. I also have three younger brothers Kendrick, Kyle, and Kevin. My mother is very well-educated, having been the first in her family to earn a college degree.

"In Georgia, I spend a lot of time on my grandparent's farm. I have always loved animals this comes from having been around them since I was very young. My grandfather always let me help him with the chores and drive the tractor. It was an ideal life. But then three years ago, my father suffered a heart attack and passed away. My mother sent job applications to companies in several different cities. She had loved my father very much, but she couldn't stand living in a area where she was constantly reminded of him.

"My mother was accepted at a software firm and moved our family to Bellevue, Washington. That is where I finished my education. I graduated from Bellevue High School. From the time I first started school, my mother told my brothers and I to study hard every night. I want to see all of my children getting a higher education. I don't want to see them with low-paying jobs."

Tatiana told me, "I set my goal on college from a very early age. I am planning on a business degree. Now how about you?" Terri told her about her life in North Dakota, saying, "You will have to meet my fiancé Chris. I have loved him ever since we were toddlers on our parents' farms. Chris is the kindest, most tenderhearted person you will ever want to meet. Chris is a big guy, but he wouldn't hurt a fly."

They stayed up talking until it was time to go to bed. In the morning, they went to the cafeteria where they met Chris, and Terri introduced him to Tatiana. Afterward, they all headed off to class. For Chris and Terri, a couple of small town kids, it was quite overwhelming at first. Some of the halls were absolutely enormous, and the professors would be down on the stage. There were TVs everywhere, so anywhere, you sat you could see the professors up close.

What bothered them the most at first was that they were not able to ask questions one on one. However, there was one thing they had learned long ago, and that was to follow along in their book and take tons of notes. They also knew the secret to college as anywhere else is study, study, study. One day, Tatiana remarked to Chris and Terri, "You guys seem to make studying seem so easy."

Chris answered, "It should because we have been doing this together ever since we were in the first grade. We developed a technique very early that you need to be able to pinpoint the real important parts. Some things in every course are just plain fill." Terri piped up, "What Chris is trying to say, remember the important parts. The rest is all just logical or common sense."

Chapter 14

All three of them were sitting in the cafeteria one evening. They had finished eating and were just visiting. Tatiana said, "In all my life, I have never seen two people as well suited to each other as you guys. That includes all of my married friends. Would it be okay if I ask you a personal question?" Chris and Terri nodded okay. Tatiana said, "I have never been in a serious personal relationship with a man. What I mean to say is, I have never been in bed with a man. But I know of other single couples who do that all the time. But I have never yet seen you two sneaking off somewhere together. Is there a problem?"

Chris and Terri both started to laugh and said, "No, Tatiana, we are not laughing at you. Chris and I love each other very much, and yes, we do want each other very much. But we have made a decision for both of us remain virgins until we get married." Tatiana looked at them in awe, saying, "This will be my inspiration. I have read in books about couples who used to do that in the past, but I have never heard of it in this day and age."

One day, as the three of them were walking across campus, Tatiana observed there was almost always some type of protest or demonstration going on at the campus. Terri immediately replied, "I have noticed it too. I also noticed as soon as a protest or demonstration starts, it does not take long before others begin to join in."

Chris jumped right into the conversation, saying, "Let's run a test to see just how gullible people are. I have an idea. Let's start our own protest. Berwick, North Dakota, has become so small they are only a couple houses left in it. Let's start a protest saying the University of Washington won't put a subsidiary in Berwick."

All week long, Chris, Tatiana, and Terri made signs which read, "Berwick students not getting the education they need." They printed up pamphlets to hand out to people. The pamphlets told about how the underprivileged students of Berwick were starving not for food but for a higher education.

They let thirty other students who had a very large sense of humor into their plan. Then they held a meeting and decided to go full bore. Those who were in on it would carry signs and pamphlets. They would shout and yell and carry signs and wave them in other students' faces.

When the group started, the following weekend plan worked like a charm. They stacked piles of excess signs and pamphlets to the side. One would have thought they were street corner preachers trying to save the world. It didn't take very long before other students joined in, and by noon, there were over two hundred students protesting. The only fly in the ointment was when one student came up to Chris. He got into Chris's face and told Chris, "You are full of crap, I am from North Dakota, and I'm familiar with Berwick."

Terri saw Chris take the student aside and talk to him. Pretty soon, the guy started laughing, patted Chris on the back, and then left. But pretty soon the student returned with a sign that read, "Give me Berwick or give me death."

All day long, the original group was recruiting suckers to take their place on the following day. Individually, they had to each convince one or two other students how important this was. Everyone in the original group told the new recruits; unfortunately, they had a huge commitment the next day. They would be unable to be there the next day, but it was very important they take their place.

Terri was afraid it worked all most too well, for the next day, they wanted to sleep in. But how could they sleep when there is a large crowd outside all chanting, "Save Berwick, save Berwick, save Berwick." Tatiana and Terri showered, dressed, then they went to meet Chris. They all decided to spend the day roaming the Seattle waterfront. It was almost a picture-perfect day except for Chris muttering, "Save Berwick every once in a while."

Chapter 15

Chris and Terri found out one thing about Seattle. It rains here once in a while. From old-time Seattleites, they learned that they could forecast the weather. It was very simple one; just had to look at Mount Rainier. If you are not able to see Mount Rainier, it was raining. If you were able to see Mount Rainier, it was going to rain. In fact, Mount Rainier is a very beautiful, majestic mountain just to the southeast of Seattle. It is still an active volcano, although the last time it erupted was sometime between 1820 and 1854. However, there are witnesses who say they observed volcanic activity as late as 1899.

I sometimes laugh when in the summer, I hear a comment like, "I can't believe Mount Rainier still has snow on it." Mount Rainier always has snow on it; in fact, it has some of the largest glaciers in the continental limits of the United States. And the glaciers will continue to get larger until sometime in the future. That will be when Mount Rainier erupts with cataclysmic fury and sheds its snowy white coat.

One morning, Chris met the girls at the cafeteria, laughing. He said, "The guys in my dorm don't think I ever study. They don't realize I spend every night studying with you at the Suzallo library. In particular, one of the guys in my dorm Chou Lin thinks I never open a book outside of class.

"Yesterday morning, Chou Lin came up to me. He asked, 'Mr. Chris, you know we have very important mathematics test today?' I jokingly told him, "No, I did not know t there was a test today. What chapter is the test on?' He said, 'Oh, Mr. Chris, is on chapters 28, 29, 30, 31, and 32. I hope you be okay.'

"I told him, 'I hope I could somehow manage to struggle through it.' After the test was over and the scores were handed back, Chou Lin proudly showed me he had gotten a B on it. 'What you got on it, Mr. Chris?' I really did not want to show him my score, but I finally showed him my A+. He exclaimed, 'You very smart fellow, Mr. Chris. No need study.'"

As we were nearing the middle of our sophomore year in college, Chris and Terri were both very thankful for Tatiana. They were very determined to stay virgins until their wedding, but that doesn't mean there were not very close calls. Sometimes they would be locked in the middle of a very passionate embrace.

Tatiana seemed to have a sixth sense because every time it seemed like Chris and Terri were just about to give in to temptation, the cell phone would ring. They would hear Tatiana's voice on the cell phone, saying, "Just giving you guys a little reminder like you asked me to." This seemed to be enough to always cool them off. They both always thanked her for she was their guardian angel here on earth.

It got to the point if the two of them were going to watch a movie that had a romantic love story. They would invite Tatiana to watch it with them. She would say, "Look, guys, I feel like I'm intruding on you." Terri would tell her, "No, Tatiana, you are not intruding. As of now, you are the official chaperone."

One of their greatest delights was when Tatiana invited them to meet her family. Mrs. Brown was a wonderful cook and an inspirational person. Chris and Terri were able to see where Tatiana's ambition and drive came from. Mrs. Brown, or Mama Brown, as they came to call her, could motivate anyone. The young couple loved to hear her tell of growing up in the Deep South. It was still very segregated when she was young. However, she had not let it bother her much.

She told stories about going to her grandparents' farm and about the creek which meandered through it. Mrs. Brown told them of catching crawdads, turtles, and catfish. She told of her struggle to reach her highest goal a college education. How from there she went on to work at the state capitol building. After a period of time, she wound up working as an aide to the governor of the great state of Georgia. Mama Brown had a way with stories, and while she talked, it seemed as if you had been transported back in time.

Maybe it was about catching a monstrous catfish which must have weighed at least one hundred pounds. Or maybe it was swiping a watermelon from the neighbor's watermelon patch. Taking the watermelon you had swiped, putting it in the creek to get it just so nice and icy cold. Later on a hot and humid August afternoon, slicing it up and sharing it with your little brothers and cousins. One could just imagine savoring every little bite of the watermelon as the juice rolled off your chin.

Mama Brown was a born philosopher. She would stop after telling a story of the good old days. Then she would tell everyone, "The good old days are whatever days you are living right now. You can pick and choose at life and feel sorry for yourself. Or you can decide to live every day to its very fullest.

"Say someone has a job they just hate or a boss. They just can't stand to be around. Are you sure it's really the job or the boss? Are you doing the very best you possibly can? It may just be all in your attitude. If one decides in their mind something in life is not up to one's standards, of course they are going to hate it.

"Let's take the same boss or the same job and find one little good thing about it. The next thing you know, you will find another little thing and then another and another. Before you know, maybe the boss and that job don't look as bad as you thought at first. But suppose it is true, both the boss and the job are that bad. Then whatever can be holding you back? Don't let the door hit you on the backend on the way out the door. Carefully look for another job because there is always a job there for someone who really wants to work."

Chapter 16

Chris and Terri had set June 16 as their wedding date. As the time for the wedding drew near, there were many things to get ready for. Their parents informed the couple everything was ready to go in North Dakota. Both sets of parents had already planned the rehearsal, the rehearsal dinner, the wedding itself, and of course, reception afterward.

Terri had already asked Tatiana to be the maid of honor, and she had accepted. Now Tatiana and Terri had to shop for a wedding gown. If one happens to be shopping for wedding gowns, then Seattle's a great place to be. Or maybe not because there are so many stores to choose from, and the choices are so many and varied.

Terri had thought this task of purchasing a wedding gown would be so simple. All she had to do was go to the store, pick out a gown, voila, you are finished. Maybe for some ladies that's the way it works. However, it definitely did not work that way for her. After two weeks of shopping and dozens of gowns, she was totally exhausted. Terri told Chris, "I might just get married in my blue jeans." Chris laughed and said, "You would look good in anything, Terri. Whatever you do is great with me."

Then one day, out of the blue, Tatiana called saying, "Terri, you have to come to Bellevue and check this out. I think I have found the one perfect wedding dress made with just you in mind." Chris and Terri went there immediately, but she made him go to the arcade across the street. Terri told Chris it was bad luck for the groom to see the bride in her wedding gown until the wedding.

The moment she walked into the store and saw the wedding gown, Terri was tickled pink. Tatiana was right. This dress was just absolutely perfect. It was a beautiful, full-length gown. It was a little low in the front but not too low. The veil went down to become a five-foot train. She was very excited as the attendants took her measurements, then told her the gown would be ready in a week.

With that finally out of the way, Chris and Terri went shopping for a tuxedo for Chris. He asked Terri, "How come you get to see what I am wearing to the wedding? But I don't get to see what you are going to wear?" She kissed Chris, then told him, "It's just the rules of the game, buster."

They picked out a wonderful-looking gray tuxedo for Chris. When he tried it on, he looked absolutely stunning. Chris then told Terri his theory. "When ladies are just little girls, they have dolls. The little girls enjoy dressing those dolls with various articles of clothing. But eventually, these little girls grow up and become beautiful young ladies. They can no longer play with their dolls and dress them as they want to. So instead they get a boyfriend or a husband. That way, they can use their expertise practicing on them." Terri broke out laughing, but she still had to give Chris a good swat.

Chris thought they better start searching for an apartment so it would be ready for them when they got back. Terri thought it was a great idea, but it still took them three weeks before they located a nice three-bedroom apartment in Bellevue. This would give them an extra bedroom in case their parents or friends came to visit. And Chris and Terri would be able to use the third bedroom for an office.

Finding the apartment was just part of the problem. Now they still had to furnish it. The couple had to find furniture by searching through the want ads and got some great buys. Tatiana and her brothers helped move the furniture in. Then Tatiana sat back laughing while Terri had Chris and her brothers reposition the furniture several times.

Terri finally got everything positioned just like she wanted it, then they all sat down to relax. Chris mentioned, "We still need bedding, towels, and cooking utensils. Also, at the very least, we need the basic spices for the kitchen." Terri told him, "We still have a week left before we need to leave. Tomorrow looks good for me. I'm just too tired to do it right now." Chris responded, "You would not be so tired if you had not made us move every piece of furniture twenty times."

Terri winked at him, saying, "You got that part right, sweetheart. You guys were good sports to put up with it." Everyone sat around relaxing, watching TV; and then the next day, they finished their shopping. Chris and Terri put the sheets, pillows, pillowcases, and blankets on the bed. Terri thought it looked great. She caught Chris looking at her by the bed smiling wistfully. She grabbed his arm, taking him back into the living room. She told Chris, "Let's sit down and watch TV, honey. We have waited this long. We are not going to spoil it at this late date."

Chris gave her a quick kiss, saying, "You are quite right, Terri, and I love you for it. You know, it is funny how one or the other of us has always had the strength or perseverance at the right time and the right place." The time has finally arrived at long last. They are so excited. The young couple are flying back to North Dakota for their wedding. Tatiana is with them; however, she will be flying back alone while they go on their honeymoon. Chris and Terri haven't decided where they are going on their honeymoon yet.

Chapter 17

Back in Towner, everything seemed to move so quickly, yet at the same time seemed to stand still. First of all was the wedding rehearsal at St. Cecilia Church. There they were instructed on what to say and what to do at the actual wedding ceremony.

All in all, everything seemed to go smoothly except perhaps for when Chris got a little bit frustrated. He was told to say "I do," and he very seriously stated, "But I haven't yet." Everyone burst out laughing; even the priest smiled. However, he told us marriage is a very serious matter.

The priest then went on to say, "I have known Chris and Terri for a very long time. In their case, I haven't a doubt their marriage will be permanent. I feel so sad when I marry some couples. I can see they are ill matched and feel it won't last. I'm very happy to say I know Chris and Terri's will." After the wedding rehearsal, they had the rehearsal dinner. This would be Terri's last night as a single person. Tomorrow, she would no longer be Terri Olson; instead she would be Terri Sutton.

In bed that night, Terri tossed and turned as she was anxiously anticipating marriage. She wasn't able to go to sleep; then all the sudden, she was passionately kissing Chris. She woke up briefly, and it all seemed so real. Her pillow had lipstick marks were all over, for she had been making love to it.

Terri's mother woke her up in the morning, saying, "Come on, honey, breakfast is ready. Terri, you had better eat because it is going to be a long day." Next, they went to the beauty salon, and she had her hair done. Terri wanted to look perfect for Chris. The way her mother and Tatiana were fussing over her was almost overwhelming.

From there, Terri her mom and Tatiana went to the dressing room at St. Cecilia Church. There Terri put on her beautiful wedding gown. She could hear the sound of music from the organ. She could sense the noise of people entering the church. When everyone was in place, she went to the back of the church. She was beginning to feel really nervous.

First came the sound of Mendelsohn's "Wedding March." After which, her father linked his arm with Terri's. Then as he slowly walked her up the aisle, every head was turned to look at us. However, Terri had eyes for only one person—that was the guy with the grey tuxedo. Chris at the time was staring openmouthed and bug-eyed at Terri.

As Terri and her father walked slowly to the altar, her heart was beating rapidly. Chris came down the steps of the altar to meet them. The priest asked, "Who gives this woman in Holy Matrimony?" her father answered, "Her mother and I do." When he placed Terri's hand in Chris's, she could feel his hands tremble.

Chris and Terri walked hand in hand back up the steps of the altar and stood before the priest. It's not humanly possible to describe the loving looks Chris and Terri gave each other. The only part of the wedding ceremony Terri remembers clearly is when Chris said, "I do, I do, oh, I do indeed." When it came to her turn, she slowly breathed "I do."

After exchanging rings, the priest said, "I now pronounce you husband and wife, you may now kiss the bride." The priest had to break them up. Then he told the congregation, "Allow me to introduce Mr. and Mrs. Sutton." Terri glanced at her mother and Tatiana. They were both smiling and had tears in their eyes.

Chris and Terri slowly walked down the aisle she had walked up with her dad. At the back of the church, they stood while everyone in Towner shook their hands and congratulated them. Then the bride and groom walked outside to have more pictures taken. As soon as they walked out the door, Chris and Terri were showered with confetti.

But even after having pictures taken, they still were not able to be alone. There was a large reception for them downstairs in the basement of the church. The young couple had to sit at the front table while toasts were made. Then lunch was served; afterward, they had to mingle with the guests. Everyone was invited to the wedding dance, which was to be held at the Towner Hall at eight-thirty in the evening.

At three-thirty in the afternoon, both sets of parents came up to them. Terri's father observed, "You two look like you would kind of like some time alone. I will get everyone's attention, and you two can sneak off. Your rental car is very highly decorated, so I advise you to take the keys to my car."

"You don't have to worry because we won't be home as we will be setting up at the dance hall. Remember to wear the tuxedo and the wedding gown for the dance." Terri's dad immediately went to the loudspeaker at the head table. Terri could hear her dad say, "May I have it everyone's attention." Terri had no idea what else he said because Chris and she were out of there like a flash.

Chris and Terri entered the car as inconspicuously as possible and pulled out of there. Then Chris headed in the direction of their parents farms. Chris asked her, "Your place or mine?" Terri replied, "Mine of course because I used to dream of you being there with me. Now I have the chance to make my dream come true." Gravel flew as Chris hit the brakes on the car hard in front of the house. Chris threw open the doors and both of them raced inside.

They were both breathing heavily as they grabbed each other and kissed. Then Chris stated, "Let's make this slow and memorable." Terri thought to herself, "I will make this very memorable for you, my sweetheart. It will be a memory you will never forget."

Chris picked Terri up at the door of her old room, then he slowly and carefully carried Terri inside. She wrapped her arms around his neck, kissing him passionately. He gently laid her on the bed. She said, "No, wait I have thought of this moment for a long time." So saying this, she stood up very slowly; and very provocatively, she took off all her clothing. She then turned around, saying, "You like?" Chris nodded, saying, "I like very much, Terri, you are so beautiful." "Okay," Terri replied, "now it's your turn to get undressed, my dear." It didn't take very long for Chris to shed all his clothing.

He stood in front of Terri, proud and in the natural. She took one look at him and shouted, "What the hell is that? It is humongous, you could hurt somebody with that thing. Just what do you plan on doing with it?"

Chris stood petrified before her, frozen. Terri could see his lips start to quiver. He said, "Terri, honey, I would never ever hurt you. I love you far too much." She started to laugh and said, "Chris, you big teddy bear, you are just too easy to tease. I'm sorry I just couldn't help myself. Now come here, I want you as bad as you want me." If anything, Chris is very forgiving. He was back in her arms in less than a second.

Chris and Terri walked arm in arm back into the dance hall where she saw Chris's father wink at him. She instantly turned beet red, which caused all of the parents to burst out laughing. Even Chris was smiling, but all he said was, "I guess this gets us kind of even." The wedding dance was a huge success. The first dance was a slow waltz for just Chris and Terri. The next dance started with Chris and Terri, then her father cut in to dance with her while Chris danced with his mother. After that, the dance floor was open to everyone. Tatiana had a ball. Terri believed she danced every single dance.

The next day was supposed to be for opening wedding gifts; however, Chris and Terri had flown out, and not having transportation, everyone had chipped in with enough money for a honeymoon vacation. They asked where the couple planned on going on their honeymoon. Terri told everyone, "Chris and I had decided just last night we were going to Ocean Shores, Washington, for our honeymoon."

Chapter 18

So Chris and Terri wound up buying plane tickets back to Seattle, and were able to catch the same flight as Tatiana. After getting back to Bellevue, they stayed in their new apartment for the first time. They spent the night in each other's arms, whispering sweet nothings into each other's ears.

The next morning, Chris and Terri packed suitcases, getting ready to leave for Ocean Shores. After several calls, they found a last-minute cancellation at a motel. After a leisurely drive to Ocean Shores in the Monte Carlo, Chris checked them into the motel. Then they got out and walked along the ocean beach. It was such a gorgeous, sunny day. The waves were gently lapping at the beach.

They took off their sandals and walked along the shore at low tide, the soft sand squishing between their toes. Chris and Terri went back to the motel to get their beach towels. They also brought a large beach umbrella. Then walked back to the beach and planted the umbrella in the soft sand, putting the large towels underneath. Then The couple laid down on them, just watching people as they swam or strolled along the waterfront.

The next day, Chris rented a four-wheel buggy. It had bicycle wheels with a bench seat in front and one in back. It had two sets of handlebars, and you could peddle it like a bicycle. The two people in the front seat could peddle. It was a very enjoyable idea. The man they rented it from said, "Most people only rent it for a half hour because it was a lot of work to peddle it very far."

But Chris and Terri were both in great shape physically, so rented one for the whole day. Terri put an ice chest in the backseat with some soda. They were cruising along when all of a sudden, it seemed like it was a whole lot harder to pedal. Terri looked over at Chris and saw he had a huge smirk on his face. Then she looked down at his feet; he was just pretending to pedal.

Terri told Chris she would get even with him, and she did. The motel room they rented had a kitchen. That evening, she got busy preparing dinner; at the same time, Terri also put some eggs on to boil. She told Chris, "Hard-boiled eggs sounded good for breakfast. This way, they will be ready for us when we get up in the morning."

The next morning, Terri put on some coffee and made toast. Afterwards, she put the eggs on their plates. Terri told Chris, "Watch this." Taking a hard-boiled egg, she cracked it on the top of her head. Chris harrumphed and said, "Anyone can do that." Then grabbing his not-hard-boiled eggs, he cracked one on his head. Terri laughed so hard she almost fell out of her chair. The egg whites and yolks were drizzling down Chris's hair onto his face.

Chris jumped up, saying, "Now I have to take another shower." He grabbed her arm saying, "You have to come with me to wash my hair." She went into the shower with him very willingly. It must've taken longer than either of them realized. Because when they finally got back to the kitchen, they decided they wanted lunch instead.

Chris and Terri stayed at Ocean Shores for five delightful days, then headed back to their apartment in Bellevue. After the two of them had been in their apartment in Bellevue for fifteen minutes, they realized there was nothing to eat. They were about to go grocery shopping when they heard several cars pull up. In walked Tatiana and her family and around thirty of our friends. Terri was embarrassed because she had nothing to offer them. Tatiana said, "Not to worry." Suddenly, everyone went back out to their cars. When they came back in, everyone was bearing huge sacks of groceries.

Tatiana smiled, saying, "All of your friends wanted to know what they could get you for a wedding present. I told them I knew you were waiting to go shopping until you got home. So this is a wedding present from all of your friends." They had also brought everything for a barbecue, except for the barbecue grill itself. So Chris hurried off to the nearby hardware store to get one. While he was gone, Tatiana asked Terri how married life was. Terri gave her a quick grin, saying, "Even better than has ever been reported."

When Chris came back, he fired up the new grill, and soon the steaks were sizzling. Tatiana and Terri made a tossed green salad. After they were all done and everyone was sitting around visiting, Chris motioned for Terri to come over. When she complied, he promptly pulled her on his lap. With great emotion, Chris told everyone, "How lucky I am to have married my best friend. We have been buddies ever since we were babies. I can't tell you exactly when we started to love each other. I can only tell you I can't remember a time when we didn't. But just for the record, I would willingly give up my life for her."

Choked up, Terri managed to say, "I feel the same way you do, Chris, but hopefully nothing will stop us from getting old together. May we live till we both have gray hair and have great-grandchildren." Everyone laughed when Chris said, "Does this mean we need to get started right now?"

Chris and Terri spent the rest of the summer just enjoying newly married life. It just seemed to get better and better as time went on. They found a couple of desks and two office chairs, and they fixed up the third bedroom to make it into an office. Chris placed their computers on the desk and were already for college to start again.

Chapter 19

Once college started, their home got quite busy on weekends. Tatiana and several friends would come over. After they had finished their studies, they all enjoyed playing cards and board games, and they would always have snacks and something to drink. As a rule, it was just coffee and soda.

But one memorable weekend, everyone decided it was time for a party. The quarter tests were over, and they were all feeling relieved. Friends had brought over some whiskey and wine and beer. After indulging in several drinks, some of the guys decided they were among the world's greatest philosophers. The worst part was the more they drank, the more philosophical they became.

After dwelling on minor issues for hours, they decided they were ready to solve the world's greatest problems. And the wonderful thing is they solved most of them—at least in their own minds, that is. By the end of the night, they had solved all of the world's great problems, except for three. Terri likes to think if they had just one more six-pack, they would have been able to solve those also.

One day, a student selling raffle tickets came up to Chris and Terri on the campus. Now selling raffle tickets was illegal, but he needed more money to be able to finish his last semester in college. The tickets were $5 each, and they were for his old car. He admitted it was ugly, but he said it ran excellently and had a heart of gold. Out of pure sympathy, Chris and Terri each bought a ticket.

Imagine Terri's surprise when three weeks later, the student looked Terri up. He told Chris and Terri he had sold one thousand two hundred tickets, and with this, he would be able to finish college. With that, he handed Terri the title and keys to a 1979 Pinto. He told her she was the winner of this fine automobile. He had also drawn a map of where it was parked.

Later, when Chris and Terri went to look at the car, they couldn't stop giggling at this thing. She can't really call it a car for it was three different colors. However, it was hard to tell just what colors as it was also covered with rust. However, the student was right. The interior was immaculate, and it did run like a top. Chris stated, "A fine automobile like this deserves a name. I think we should christen it Hunka. That will be short for Hunka Crap." Terri agreed, so Hunka it became.

Chris asked Terri, "What exactly do you plan on doing with this venerable piece of ungodly metal? If I may offer a suggestion, how about using a shredder or a compactor on it." she replied, "No, Chris, I think it's a gallant little car, and I can use it to run errands. Also, I was thinking of getting a part-time job for work experience. I will be able to use it for that too."

One weekend, a bunch of our friends were over, and were sitting around the table playing cards and sipping coffee. Suddenly, one of our philosopher friends piped up, saying, "I think I'm going to change my major to geology. When we were philosophizing the last time we were here, my head hurt terribly for the next two days."

Chris asked, "Do you think it could possibly be from the amount of alcohol you consumed that night?" He replied, "Of course not, that was purely medicinal. It was definitely all that thinking. My brain was completely derailed for a couple of days."

Chris responded with, "Well, geology will definitely solve the problem. Geologists always sit around smoking pipes and drinking coffee. When they develop a profound thought, they take the pipe out of their mouth and say, 'Aha.' This will relieve the pressure on the brain, so you won't develop those terrible headaches." Driving Hunka proved to be quite an experience. That little car drove like a dream. But it was hard to believe the looks Terri got when she was driving it. There were several times when she would stop, and people would offer her money. For some reason unknown to her, they must've thought that she was destitute.

This part of it was easy. She would just say, "No, thank you." The bigger problem was the anonymous donors. When she would come out of a shop or a store, someone would have left an envelope with cash under her wiper blades or taped to her window. When that happened, Terri would drive around until she would see a person with a sign asking for help. She would give the money to them.

Imagine her chagrin when she had finally talked Chris into taking a ride in Hunka with her. Chris and Terri stopped at a store, and when they came back out, she discovered an envelope with $20 taped to the window. When she found the nearest person on a street corner with a sign, she stopped and tried to give him the money. It happened to be a little Asian gentleman who took one look at Hunka and said, "No, take, no, take you need." He would only not take the money. He even tried to give Terri another $5. Chris was laughing so hard Terri thought his gut would bust. She told him to stop laughing before he soiled his pants.

That just made the matter worse. Chris was laughing so hard tears were rolling down his cheeks. Terri pulled over at the nearest gas station and gassed up. It took $15. Chris just about choking said, "Terri, you have just increased Hunka's value threefold."

Chapter 20

Once again, it was April. If you want to enjoy beautiful scenery, then you need to come to the University of Washington on a sunny April day. You will enjoy walking in the quad with its brick pathways. The cherry trees are all in bloom at this time, and they look just awesome. Or Red Square where overlooking a fountain, you will be able to see Mount Rainier in the distance with a soft cloud cover surrounding it. Maybe you will get to see a small wisp of steam showing at the top.

There was an excellent exercise and workout room at the campus, and Chris and Terri went there regularly. Back in North Dakota, they burned off our calories by doing work. However, both of them really enjoyed the workout at the exercise room, so they burned off their calories there. When they would get back to their apartment, Chris would show her how much the exercises had helped.

It was now the night of June 15, and Terri was wondering if Chris was going to mention their anniversary. But so far, he had not said a word. She had a card and present ready for him. But she was worried because she had heard so many stories of husbands forgetting their wedding anniversary. Terri decided not to say a word. She didn't think Chris was the type to forget. She knew as much as they loved each other, their anniversary would not be totally missed for the first time. He just had to remember.

At seven o'clock in the evening, Chris yawned, saying, "Let's go to bed, Terri. It has been an exhausting day. I'm very tired." When they got into bed, he gave her a little peck on the cheek. He said, "Good night, sweetheart," then he rolled over and went to sleep. She laid there stewing, thinking, "If that's the way you want to be, fine." She went to sleep feeling sorry for herself.

Terri awoke to the blaring of the alarm, then soft music came on along with the light. She sat up bewildered and glanced at the clock. It was midnight, and Chris was standing beside the bed. In his hands were a dozen of the most beautiful red roses Terri had ever seen. On a cart beside him was a bottle of chilled champagne and two flutes. Chris started to say, "Happy anniversary, Terri," but before he could finish, Terri was in his arms. She said, "Forgive me, Chris, I was so afraid you would forget our anniversary. You wonderful man, I will never doubt you again." At the same time, she was covering him with kisses.

They sat on the edge of the bed sipping champagne. Sometimes women just want to be held; it's in their nature. This, however, was definitely not one of those times. Terri needed to show Chris she loved him. She thinks after she was done with him, he knew.

Chris and Terri went back to sleep in each other's arms, and they didn't wake up until nine o'clock, and then had a leisurely breakfast. Afterward, they went to the zoo. Chris was sort of persistent they take the Monte Carlo. For some strange reason, he didn't seem to want to ride in Hunka. It didn't matter to Terri. She just wanted to have an enjoyable day. Zoos have gotten so much better in the past thirty years you could enjoy watching the animals better. You were able to see the animals roaming around outside in a natural habitat rather than being cooped up in cages.

Chris and Terri walked around enjoying the monkeys and the great apes. Terri actually kind of shuddered as she was looking at the snakes. But the best part is yet to come. They walked past the giraffes and zebras, then came to the elephants. There was a huge bull elephant standing near the fence with his penis hanging down. It was huge. She poked Chris and told him, "You should show him yours." He said, "Terri, I don't have anything against that elephant. I don't want him to feel bad because he's been shorted."

Later, Terri noticed Chris's brow was furrowed, so she asked him what he was thinking about. He said, "I was just imagining you and I having a child, then taking him or her to the zoo. Wouldn't that be fun?" Terri thought about it and found herself smiling at the thought. She asked, "Chris, how soon do you think before we should have children?" He pondered the question for quite a while before he finally answered.

"Terri, my darling wife, it's really up to you." Now we are about to start our senior year in college. "For myself, I wouldn't mind if you got pregnant sometime after the start of the new year." Terri clutched him excitedly, saying, "How did you happen to read my mind?"

"I didn't, Terri, but I keep thinking we both love children, and I feel that we would both be good parents." Chris and Terri were both so intrigued with the idea they decided to go to some baby stores just to look at baby clothes and dream. The young couple found themselves ohhing and ahhing over many things. They found theirselves checking out the cribs, the bassinets, and the car seats. Both had a dreamy glow in their eyes as they left the stores.

Later in the evening, Chris took Terri to the movies. It was a love story she had been waiting to see. Of course, she cried in the middle when they broke up, then she was so happy when they got back together at the end. Afterward, Chris took her to an Italian restaurant where they both had linguine. Following that, they just went home and talked for hours. To think, Terri had been afraid Chris would forget their anniversary. May all of their anniversaries be so happy, she thought.

Chapter 21

Terri kept checking the help wanted section of the newspaper every day. She saw lots of jobs, but they were always in the wrong area, or the hours would not work for her. But she kept checking them. Anyway, Terri was in no hurry. She knew she would find the right one eventually.

Tatiana dropped in to see the Sutton's one day. She had found a great part-time job. It was with Global Airlines, which flew all over the world. Plus, it had great benefits, which included free standby flights. She would be part-time until she finished college, then she would be hired on full-time.

After talking to Tatiana, Terri was more determined than ever. She knew she would find the right job, which was suited just for her. Chris was okay with her getting a job as long as it did not interfere with their lives.

In the meantime, Chris and Terri enjoyed the rest of the summer. They would drive to some area that looked or sounded interesting. Chris would park the car and get out go for a long walk. They would always try to make their walks at least five miles. It was great exercise; plus it helped experience the local scenery up close. This way, if they saw a bird or a tree or flower, they could take their time and examine it. It was far better than watching from a car window as they were driving past.

College started once again in September. It seemed strange they were beginning their last year. It also seems strange to remember the time when Chris and Terri were beginning their freshman year. They were reminded of this every time they were stopped by bewildered freshman. The students would ask them where certain classrooms or the libraries were. This generation must not have came here early and prepared themselves in advance as Chris and Terri did when they were freshmen.

In early October, Terri spotted a help wanted ad in the newspaper. It was for a part-time job at the Felix Wells investment firm. It looked like the hours should fit right into her schedule, and the pay was supposedly good. The best part of the job advertised was it was just a few blocks from their apartment.

Chris was running errands. When he came home, Terri showed him the ad and told him she would like to apply for it. She told Chris, "This sounds like it would be a good job experience, and it will fit right into my schedule. I promise I wouldn't let it interfere with our lives. If it does, then I wouldn't hesitate to quit."

Chris thought about the job for several minutes, then he said, "Okay, Terri, it sounds legitimate to me. I like the idea, it is close to the apartment. If you happen to find another job opening like that, I would apply for it in a minute. Besides, it will give us an idea what it will be like working for a living after we have finished college." Terri jumped up and give Chris a big hug and a kiss.

The next day, Terri drove Hunka to the address at 108th Street in Bellevue where she parked in the parking garage and then took the elevator to the fifth floor. Once there, she saw a big sign, reading, Felix Wells Investment Firm. The receptionist sat behind a desk looking bored and flipping her hair. Terri informed her, "I am here to apply for the job advertised in the newspaper."

The receptionist handed Terri an application form and then went back to chewing gum, filing her nails, and flipping her hair. If Terri would have used half the sense God had given her, she would have walked out of there right then. However, she filled out the application, which she then handed back to the girl. The receptionist took the application form, telling Terri to wait. Then she walked into the door of an office behind her.

While Terri was waiting, she picked up one of the company brochures and studied it. Among other things, it stated the Felix Wells Firm was a nationally known investment firm. It also stated people who had invested in the Felix Wells Investment Firm were very satisfied. If they invested in Felix Wells, they would receive record profits on their investment.

Thirty minutes later, the door opened slightly, and Terri saw someone peering out. She ignored it and pretended to study the brochure. The door opened fully, and a balding fairly tall man walked toward her. He tried to exude a confidence in himself Terri felt did not exist. To offset some of his arrogance, she decided to stare at his protruding gut. This seemed to take some of his attitude away.

The minute he introduced himself to Terri as Russ Jacobson, Terri decided to be professional yet distant to him. He said, "Terri, please step into my office and have a seat." Meanwhile, he sat down behind his desk and studied Terri's application. After looking at it for several minutes, he remarked, "I notice you have some computer knowledge. Are you very good at it?"

For what reason she doesn't know, however, on the spur of the moment, Terri decided to play down what she knew. Terri told him, "I wasn't the greatest with computers, but I could do everyday work with them." Russ replied, "The firm is not looking for someone who is a genius. We just need someone who knows basic computer logic. We are looking for someone who is able to file incoming and outgoing reports." Terri told Russ, "I would have no trouble doing that."

Russ stood up and shook Terri's hand, saying, "Thank you very much for coming in, Terri, I will go over your application a little more. I will call your references sometime tomorrow. I will let you know if you have the job or not." On the way out, Terri noticed Miss Lotta secretary was not at her desk. However, on the desk there was a large stack of scandal tabloids and a box of chocolates. Oh well, to each his own. Terri always wondered who would ever read such trash; now she knows.

As Terri drove Hunka out of the basement parking garage, she happened to notice the parking garage attendant looking at her with a skeptical eye. I thought to myself, "Up yours, buster, this little beauty may not be a Rolls-Royce, but it is mine."

When she got home, Chris met her at the door with a chilled glass of wine. "Well, how's my hardworking wife?" he asked. Terri told Chris, "I don't even know if I have the job yet, but I have decided I will take it if it is offered to me." She also told Chris, "However, I have some trepidations, for some reason I got real bad vibes from the place. These bad vibes came from both the office and from Russ Jacobson the man who interviewed me."

Chris said, "Let's not worry about the job right now. I am going to barbecue us a couple of real nice steaks and then let's study for a couple of hours." Raising his eyebrows and staring at her, he winked. He said, "Afterward, if you are real nice, I just may let you have your way with my body." Terri tried to look real sultry, telling him, "Anywhere, anytime, big boy."

Chapter 22

The next morning, just as they were heading to the university, Terri's cell phone rang. She answered it and listened for a couple of minutes, then said, "Okay." She told Chris, "The phone call was from the Felix Wells Investment Firm. I have got the job Russ wants me to start at 3:30 p.m. today. I will be working for two hours a day during the week, and I will work for four hours on Saturday mornings."

Terri entered the Felix Wells Investment Firm promptly at 3:30 p.m. Russ greeted Terri, then showed her to her cubicle. He instructed her on what her job was and how she was to do it. Everything was very simple. Terri would have had no problem doing this job in her sophomore year at high school.

Russ said, "Terri, come let me introduce you to the rest of the people in the office." The first office, they stopped at had a sign on it, saying, Human Resources. Russ told her, "This is Rodney Crowder." Rodney's handshake was very warm and friendly. He was a short, stocky man with a full head of hair starting to get gray at the temples. When he smiled, his whole face lit up, and he had little crinkles appearing by his eyes.

When Rodney spoke, even his voice exuded warmth. He said, "Terri, welcome to the company. If you ever need anything, don't hesitate to call." The next person on the list was Lynn Anderson—an attractive tall woman in her early fifties.

Lynn Anderson had a businesslike attire and a very businesslike attitude. Maybe she had problems at home because when she smiled her eyes certainly did not. Russ introduced her to Terri, saying, "Terri, this is Lynn Anderson. Lynn is our personnel director and will be your immediate boss." They shook hands; however, Lynn seemed cold and distant.

Next, Russ took Terri into an office that had two desks and a table. Both of the desks were piled high with papers, books, and brochures. There were two men sitting at the table; apparently, they were involved in some kind of a discussion. The men stood up as they entered. Russ said, "Terri, let me introduce you to Tony Lindsay and Marvin Mueller. Tony and Marvin research market reports and statistics throughout the world. Between them, they toss ideas around back and forth to finally come up with the final result. When they finish, they give this analysis to Felix Wells.

"Felix Wells in turn will examine the results very carefully. From this Felix will decide in which companies to invest. Evidently, Felix does very well at this because the Felix Wells investment firm is highly successful." Tony Lindsay was a young man around thirty-five years old. He was very handsome and had dark curly hair. He was tall—about six feet four—and well built. Terri could see right away he had a cocky confidence in himself.

Tony was also very flirtatious. When he gave Terri a handshake, he took her hand to his lips and kissed it. He said, "Welcome aboard, Terri, I will see you around the office." Then he raised his eyebrows twice quickly. Just as quickly, Terri removed her hand from his.

Marvin Mueller happened to be very different, or should we say, indifferent. Marvin shook her hand said a quick hello, then he quickly turned back to his work. Marvin looked to be around forty years old. He was about six foot tall and had a shaved head and eyebrows. Terri might have thought he hated facial hair, except for the fact that he had a huge curling mustache. It looked to Terri like he had no time for anything except business.

There were also several cubicles where young people were answering phones. Russ must have decided they were of no consequence. At least he never introduced Terri to any of them. On the way back to her cubicle, she noticed two empty offices. One of them had Felix Wells name tag on it; the other one had nothing on it and had a combination door lock.

Terri asked Russ about Felix Wells. He replied, "Mr. Wells is a very busy man and is only here about two weeks out of every month." After that, Russ took Terri back to her cubicle. No sooner had Russ left than Lynn Anderson appeared. She went over everything, which pertained to Terri. Lynn then remarked, "This happens to be an investment firm, and it is very profitable. You will see huge cash inflows, also see large sums of investments. Your job is to log all of these transactions on your computer. We need an exact account of all transactions." Terri told her she understood perfectly.

Then Lynn continued, "You will conduct yourself in a ladylike manner. You will clock in and clock out on time. I don't want to see you hustling any of the men around here. I know how all you young women are." Terri decided then and there that she wasn't going to take any of her crap. She told Lynn, "Listen up, you. I happen to be very happily married to a very wonderful man who I love and adore. I don't happen to chase around, and I don't like your presumptions. You can take this job and shove it up your ass."

Lynn immediately did an about-face. She said, "I'm so sorry, Terri, I didn't mean that. I don't know whatever I was thinking. I've just been having a very bad day. My sister just called this morning, telling me her husband had left her for a younger woman. I guess I just took it out on you. Please stay, you will find I'm not that bad of a person." Terri reluctantly accepted, then Lynn left, and she started doing her job.

Outside of the large money transactions, where it came from, and where it went. It was just a matter of crunching numbers, and to her, it was very boring. After a period of time, Lynn stopped back with a cup of coffee for Terri. She apologized again. Maybe she's not such a bad person after all.

Chapter 23

After Terri finished work that Saturday, Tatiana stopped over. All three of them went to the Husky football game against UCLA, and the Huskies won. Soon after the game, Tatiana and several friends stopped at our apartment. All of the girls played cards while the guys were busy rehashing the game. If one would listen to the men, you would think the Huskies couldn't possibly have won it if they had not been in the audience.

Tatiana really loved her job at Global Airlines. She said, "I would be able to get standby tickets for us so we could do something fun." She thought it would be enjoyable to fly to Acapulco for a weekend, but she didn't really want to go alone. Terri told Tatiana, "I should be able to take the next Saturday off." Chris loved the idea of going anywhere to get out of the rain for a weekend.

Chris got on the computer immediately and found a condo available for the next weekend. On Friday evening, all three caught a flight to Acapulco, Mexico. The three of them checked into the condo. After leaving their bags, they all went for a walk along the beach. It was the first time any of them had ever seen palm trees. They were admiring the trees when Chris said he thought he heard a scream for help. The sound was coming from the ocean. Someone was in serious trouble, and it sounded like they were drowning.

Like a flash, Chris took to the water swimming for all his might. The girls watched him as he made it to the person in trouble. To Terri it looked like he had more than one person in tow. When they had made it back to the beach, Terri saw there was a young Mexican boy and his dog. He told Chris, "Gracias, señor, my dog Pepe, he was very tired. I don't think he could make it back."

Terri told Tatiana, "That's my hero. Chris is always rescuing someone from drowning." Tatiana asked, "What do you mean?" Terri told Tatiana how Chris had saved her from drowning years ago. Tatiana's eyes widened, and she said, "Well you are a hero, Chris." He said, "Oh, Terri is just exaggerating everything." Terri said, "I am not, Chris, you did save me from drowning, and you always will be my hero."

They really enjoyed their weekend in Acapulco. Afterwards, it was back to college and work. And of course, Terri's special times with Chris. She didn't tell Chris she absolutely couldn't stand Russ Jacobson. He was nothing but a dirty old man. One day, Russ looked at her and said, "Terri, I'd sure like to get in your pants." She looked him in the eyes and replied, "Why, did you shit yours?" Terri was able to see the anger welling up in his eyes.

Terri doesn't have any idea what would have happened next. But suddenly, she heard booming laughter coming from behind them. Then she heard a voice, saying, "Well, Russ, I guess she sure told you off." Russ slunk out of there like a dog with his tail tucked between his legs.

Terri turned around and saw a handsome man of around thirty five years old. He was around six foot tall with broad shoulders and a narrow waist. He had dark brown hair already starting to grey at the temples. He stuck out his hand, saying, "HI, Terri, I'm Felix Wells, and I've heard good things about you. They say you're doing a great job here and you are an asset to the company." Terri took an instant liking to Mr. Wells.

Mr. Wells told her, "I will have a talk to Russ Jacobson and let him know not to bother you anymore. If he does, just let me know." After that Mr. Wells went back to work. From that time on, whenever Mr. Wells was around, he would stop by to ask Terri about her work or how Chris and she were doing.

Terri was slowly getting to know the permanent staff. Rodney Crowder would stop by her desk quite often. He would ask Terri about her life, where she lived, how long they have been married. He often told her if she had any problems at work, he would be only too happy to help her with it. Rodney had a very bubbly personality.

Rodney always enjoyed talking about his family. He was forty-eight years old and had been married to his wonderful wife Tess for twenty-six years. They had twin eighteen-year-old daughters Rebecka and Sheila who had just started college. They also had a twelve-year-old son Roland.

Rodney would often regale her with stories of his family life. How their dog Pepper was so attached to his son Roland. When Roland was not in school, Roland and Pepper were inseparable. Or that his daughters had just started to date, and it was driving him nuts. Then he would start laughing.

After her initial bitchiness, Lynn Anderson slowly warmed up to Terri. She gave her the keys to the office in case she had to stay late. After she saw Terri was competent at her job, she stopped checking on her work. Lynn told her she had worked at the firm for ten years and she loved her work and had never been married. Lynn confided in Terri, "I am infatuated with Felix Wells.

He seems so intelligent and masculine." But Felix was all business around her. Terri thinks Lynn was disappointed Felix couldn't see her as a woman.

Tony Lindsay was another matter entirely. Terri thinks he was just too used to having women chasing him. Terri thinks it must've bothered Tony the fact she didn't give him any attention whatsoever. At first, Tony was very charming, but then he asked Terri out on a date. She stopped him right in his tracks. She said, "Tony I'm very happily married. I happen to love my husband with my whole heart. I am in fact so in love with him that if anything ever happened to Chris, I would never get remarried and would never ever go out with another man. I have loved Chris since we were just infants growing up in North Dakota."

Tony was so awestruck that when he finally spoke, he said, "I'm sincerely sorry, Terri. I will make sure it never happens again. You are an extremely beautiful woman, and your husband is a very lucky man. I would like very much to meet him. I would just like to be friends with both of you." Terri accepted his apology, and after this happened, he would often stop by her cubicle to visit. Tony never once tried to hit on her again.

Terri never did get to know Marvin Mueller. He was very standoffish. If she said hello, he would say hello back, but that was it. Both Lynn and Tony told her Marvin pretty much treated them the same way. Tony said, "Marvin and I discuss business issues, but that was it. Any personal life was strictly off-limits." Tony said he had worked with Marvin for over eight years and still didn't have any idea where he lived.

If Terri happened to walk past when Marvin was working on his computer, he would shield the computer and screen with his body so she couldn't see it. She thought, "Screw you, Marvin, I'm not interested in what you are doing." She would often see Marvin talking to Russ, and they would act very secretive. If she happened to walk by when the two were talking, they would stop talking till she was past.

Chris and Terri were shopping at the mall. It happened to be on a dismal, cloudy, rainy afternoon. The parking lot was totally congested. Chris found a spot and parked. Then they saw a car coming from the other way stop. The guy got out of his car and came up to Chris, whining that he wanted the spot. "I was only half a block away. I should've gotten the parking spot." Chris told him, "We were here first."

He kept persisting, telling Chris to move his car. Chris pointed to empty spaces that were three cars down. He told the guy to go park his car there. He replied, "But I want this spot." Chris finally got tired of the argument, so he told the guy to go lay by his dish like a good dog and walked off. Chris kept an eye on him, but he got into his car and left the area. Seattleites are known for being polite, but that doesn't mean everyone in Seattle is polite.

Chapter 24

On Thanksgiving Day, Tatiana and Terri, with Chris's help of course, prepared a huge dinner. Terri had bought a twenty-four-pound turkey. It was so huge it barely fit into our oven. Chris and Terri started early and prepared the dressing for the turkey. Tatiana and Terri had it in the oven by nine o'clock in the morning. Terri knew it was going to take several hours to roast that big boy.

Then, they started preparing everything else to cook later. Chris peeled the potatoes while the girls got the carrots, celery olives, and sweet potatoes ready. Terri and Tatiana had baked three pumpkin pies and two mincemeat pies the night before. Chris jokingly said he couldn't possibly eat that much food all by himself.

For the previous two weeks, Chris and Terri had invited their friends over first, but many of them were going home to spend time with their families. So Chris, Terri and Tatiana had quietly asked students they didn't know what they were doing for Thanksgiving. Most of those asked were going somewhere; however, they found several who were planning on staying on campus. They asked those if they would like to spend Thanksgiving with the three of them.

By the time Chris and Terri were done, over thirty people were coming to the party including them. At three o'clock in the afternoon, people started drifting in. Terri noticed as each one walked in, they would quietly sniff the air and smile. By now of course, the smell of the turkey and all the components were sumptuous. Chris had rented two long tables and chairs. Terri hated to say this, but they also had to rent plates and silverware. Everyone pitched in to help with putting on the tablecloths and setting up the table. By the time everything was ready, everyone was very hungry.

They all sat down and said grace, then someone said, "Why don't each one of us say one thing we are thankful for." Many of them said they were thankful for the meal and being able to be there on this special day. When it came to Terri's turn, she said, "I thank the Lord for having such wonderful company." Chris said he was thankful for Terri. Terri blew him a kiss. Tatiana remarked she was thankful for Chris and Terri. She said we were an inspiration to her.

Early in December, Felix Wells stopped by Terri's cubicle, and chatted with her for a few minutes. Then he said, "What I actually stopped by for is to extend an invitation. Every Christmas season, we have a big office party at my home. I would appreciate it very much if you and your husband could come. The party is on December the twenty-eighth." After saying this he handed her the invitation, which had the address and the driving instructions on it. Terri told him, "Thank you, Mr. Wells, I will have to talk to my husband first, but I'm sure we will be able to make it."

When Terri got home, Chris wasn't there yet, so she made some nachos with olives, jalapenos, sour cream, and some of her homemade salsa. This happened to be one of Chris's favorite snacks. When Chris got home, she handed him the nachos and a beer. They sat on the love seat and proceeded to watch *Pretty Woman* for maybe the seventeenth time.

Terri told Chris, "We are invited to a Christmas party at Felix Wells's home." He replied, "It is okay with me. I have no plans except for this." Suddenly, Chris grabbed Terri in his arms and started kissing her all over. So when she got the chance, she bit him lightly on the ear. "You shameless little hussy," he exclaimed, he gathered her up in his arms and carried her into the bedroom.

Christmas has always been a big deal to both Chris and Terri, so they went shopping for a tree. After looking around, they decided on buying a live tree. Terri called Mrs. Brown. She said she would love it if they planted it by her house when Christmas was over. Chris wound up purchasing a seven-feet-tall tree. Next, they had to go buy all the decorations because they didn't have any.

When Chris set the tree up in the apartment, there was barely any room at the top for the angel. Decorating the tree was something else. Chris would very carefully place each ornament in a very special place. Being the brat that Terri is, she would just put them on anywhere. Chris would then remove the ornament and place it where he thought it should go. After that, he would give Terri a kiss.

After tormenting him for a while, she finally did it his way. When the tree was finished, it looked fantastic. It was absolutely beautiful, no thanks to Terri. Afterward, they sat back with a glass of wine to enjoy it, Chris stood up and grabbed a box of tinsel. Chris took the tinsel out of the box very carefully, then he said, "Terri, you look more beautiful than the Christmas tree. However, I still think you need to be decorated." With that, he threw a big handful of tinsel all over Terri.

By the time Chris and Terri were finished with the big tinsel escapade, there was tinsel everywhere except on the Christmas tree of course. It took only five minutes to get everything in complete disarray. Then it took over two hours to clean it up. When they had finished, both sat down laughing. Then Chris pulled the final strand of tinsel out of Terri's hair.

Chris asked, "Terri, what would you like for Christmas?" She thought about it for a minute, then she replied, "Absolutely nothing. I feel I have everything I want right now." Chris said, "I feel the same way." He said, "Terri, I was thinking why don't we have Tatiana and some of our other friends get together. Then we could find a family that is in desperate need. We could buy food and presents for them that way we could make a great Christmas for them."

And so it all began. Chris and Terri met with Tatiana and twenty of their closest friends. Everyone said they wanted to donate, but the ideas spiraled as more and more students wanted to join in. Then someone put notices on the bulletin boards at the college campus. The idea got so large the group had to have the meetings in a large conference room at the college. The room was packed, and as soon as one group left, another one came in.

By the time it was finished, there was enough to help thirty families. They had to set up committees to help find the families, committees to find out what each family needed. And committees to buy for each separate family. The plan became both heartwarming and heartbreaking.

You could not believe just how destitute some of these people were. We bought shoes, clothing, jackets, bedding, and of course food. The plight of the little ones really touched their hearts. If you could have seen the smiles on their little faces as they received their toys, your hearts would have melted.

There was one little girl in particular. Her eyes were wide in wonder as she received a dolly. She grabbed it and held it and hugged it, then she immediately ran and gave it to her baby sister. Terri was so thankful there was a second doll for her. After they were done with the gift giving, Chris and Terri went to mass to give thanks for the great gift which they had received. This was the gift of giving to those who are in desperate need.

Chapter 25

On the evening of December 28, Chris and Terri got into the Monte Carlo and headed to Mercer Island. When they arrived, Terri was very surprised because she knew Mr. Wells was a very successful and wealthy man. He had started investing when he was still in high school. He had got in at the beginning of many software and computer companies as well as several other cutting-edge technologies.

Felix seemed to have the knack of picking the right companies to invest in at the very beginning. When he was younger, newspapers and magazines called him the boy wonder. By the time he got out of college, he was worth in excess of $100 million. It was no wonder so many people chose his firm to invest in. The reason Terri was so surprised is she was expecting a mansion. It was a large older home maybe five thousand five hundred feet. It was a very nice home; however, she was expecting something a little more stately.

Mr. Wells himself met them at the door. He took their coats and led them into a huge room. It looked like everyone from the firm was already there. So Terri took Chris around, introducing him to everyone. Chris and Tony Lindsay hit it off right away, and soon they were swapping stories. She hoped the stories were not about her.

Felix Wells started a conversation with Chris and Terri. He wanted to show them around his home. Mr. Wells picked up this exquisite vase, saying, "It is from the Ming Dynasty." He handed the vase to Chris to examine. Chris looked it over casually, then handed it back, saying, "I'm sorry, Mr. Wells. Handling something that old and valuable makes me very nervous."

Not to be deterred, Mr. Wells showed Chris and Terri his art collection. Both were surprised at the number and value of them. There were Rembrandts, Van Goghs, Picassos, and many other paintings by masters. Mr. Wells didn't just collect paintings; he collected many other priceless objects.

He also had a weaponry section, which included antique rifles, pistols, sabers, and swords.

After Chris and Terri were finished looking at the art objects, Mr. Wells took them to a large table setup with hors d'oeuvre. Then he dismissed himself to go and visit with other guests. Terri noticed a wet bar where she ordered a white Russian, while Chris had a diet cola because he was driving.

There was a live orchestra, and a few couples already were out on the floor dancing. Terri noticed Rodney Crowder and his wife. Tony Lindsay was also out there with some lady Terri didn't know. Chris bowed to Terri, saying, "Would the lady care to dance?" They danced for a couple of lovely waltzes, then to a fast polka, then back to a two-step, then several more waltzes. It was wonderful how Chris and Terri just seemed to melt into each other's arms.

Then a large gong sounded. Felix Wells announced dinner was served. They sat down at the table and chatted with those around them. Mr. Wells certainly had not skimped on dinner. There was filet mignon, lobster, shrimp, and many other gastronomical delights. When everyone had finished eating, Mr. Wells proposed a toast, "To a happy and prosperous New Year. Although the old year wasn't bad either, by your plate you will find an envelope with your name on it that contains your Christmas bonus."

Terri picked hers up and put it in her purse. She thought it would be very gauche to open it there although other people were. All of a sudden, conversations seem to be springing up everywhere. Russ and Marvin started a conversation about guns and hunting. From what they were saying, Terri gathered Russ and Marvin haunted quite a bit.

Russ asked Chris if he did any hunting, and Chris replied no. Chris said, "I have no problem with someone else hunting, but I won't do it personally. I do happen to have a rifle and a 12-gauge shotgun back in North Dakota. I also have a .38 special Smith & Wesson pistol here, but I don't even have ammunition for it. I just can't bear the thought of hurting any living thing that has done me no harm."

Marvin Mueller went humph, then said, "I believe guns are meant for killing whether it be man or beast. It would make no difference to me. What would you do if someone attacked the pretty little lady of yours?" Terri could see this made Chris very upset.

Chris took his time before he answered, then he stared Marvin Mueller right in the eye. He said, "Maybe I didn't make myself clear. What I meant is if anything, whether it be man or mouse is doing me no harm, and I won't harm it. However, if someone ever touched Terri, God have pity on their soul because I certainly would not stop killing them." Marvin Mueller stared at the floor not saying anything.

The topic hurriedly changed to current events and home life. Chris and Terri stayed for another two enjoyable hours, dancing a couple more waltzes. Then they thanked Mr. Wells for the wonderful time, and left then headed back to their apartment. On the way back, they discussed the party. Chris said he thought Felix Wells and Tony Lindsay were very nice. "But Marvin Mueller is downright strange possibly deranged or demented. Be very careful around him. As for Russ Jacobson, I think the man is an unmitigated asshole."

This started Terri to giggling so hard Chris asked her what was so funny. She finally broke down and told Chris what she had said to Russ the first time that she had met Felix Wells. Chris laughed and said, "Good for you, honey, that was probably the best way to handle it. But if I had been there, I probably would have kicked his ass all the way to China and back."

When they got back to the apartment, Terri remembered the envelope from the party. Upon opening it, she gasped. She said, "Chris, this is a check for $1,500. We will add it to our savings. However, I will use a very tiny part of it to buy one of those vacuum sealers we have talked about. It will help us to preserve food and other things."

For New Year's Eve, Tatiana, Chris, and Terri and several other friends went to the Seattle Center. At midnight, they watched the fireworks display shot off from the top of the Space Needle. Back at the apartment afterward, Chris told Terri, "This is going to be our best year ever." Terri sure wished he was right.

After the New Year, it was time to go back to college, back to work. Terri noticed the firm was having more and more investors coming in all the time. The Felix Wells Investment Firm was worth well over $200 million. She couldn't put her finger on it, but she felt there was a problem. She felt something was dreadfully wrong.

More and more, she would see Russ and Marvin huddling together. For herself, she wouldn't have trusted those two with her car Hunka, let alone all assets that were in the firm. Terri had the bad feeling those two were plotting something. She just wished she could find out what it was.

Chapter 26

Chris and Terri really missed the snow in North Dakota, so on Valentine's Day, they decided to take a drive to Snoqualmie Pass. On the way there, they decided to stop in North Bend to get a hot cup of chocolate. As they sat at a booth, both of them were sipping their drinks. They were making small talk, holding hands and gazing into each other's eyes. Terri told Chris, "Oh, my darling, I love you so much."

When they got to the top of Snoqualmie Pass, the scenery was breathtaking. Everything was covered in fresh snow. It was so beautiful. The mountains the cold crisp air and the huge snowbanks. Terri got out of the car and lay down in the snow and made a snow angel. Chris said, "That is just what you are, my little angel."

then they decided to make a snowman. Chris and Terri rolled the balls as large as possible. When they had finished, it looked just like Frosty the Snowman. Just as Chris was putting the finishing touches on it, Terri hit him in the back of the head with a snowball.

Chris turned around and laughed, then he said, "Now you're going to get it, little girl." The couple had a terrific snowball fight, Terri thinks she was sort of winning. Because all of a sudden, Chris rushed at her, then he took her down to wash her face with snow. She looked up at him and said, "Now you've done it." "Done what?" Chris asked. Terri reached up and grabbed him by his balls and yelled, "You got me horny, my sweet, adorable husband." Chris smothered her with a kiss and said, "You are just going to have to wait till you get home because we don't want to get arrested for indecency."

Terri imagined Chris broke all the speed limits going back to Bellevue. When they got back to their apartment, they tore each other's clothes off. Then Chris picked Terri up and carried her into the bedroom. There they made tender and passionate love. Afterward as they lay wrapped in each other's arms, Terri whispered in Chris's ear, "It may just be my imagination, but I think you just got me pregnant." Chris was slow to respond, but when he did, he said, "You know I was thinking the same thing. I really hope I did," then they hugged each other even tighter.

The college years were slowly coming to an end, and at work, everything was running smoothly. Terri watched carefully, but on the computer, the incoming and outgoing always checked out. However, Terri had a feeling of dread. She just knew something was terribly wrong. But try as Terri might, she just couldn't figure out what it was.

One day, when Terri was talking to Tony, she asked him about the empty room she had noticed. She had never been in there, and you have to punch in a combination to get in. He replied, "It's just an old meeting room the firm does not use anymore. I have been in there with Russ and Marvin. There is nothing in the room but a long table, a desk, some chairs, and a computer."

Lynn Anderson would often stop by with coffee and donuts to visit. She seems so much more relaxed and happy than she had been. She had given Terri the job of opening and closing the firm on Saturdays. From a very poor start, Terri now considered her a friend and a confidante.

Terri told Lynn about her feelings of foreboding. Lynn said, "Don't worry about it. I get feelings just like that sometimes, and nothing ever happens." However, Terri said she always went over everything, and it all checked out. Lynn said, "Felix Wells is a very smart and well-educated man. If there was anything wrong, he would certainly let us know about it."

On Saturdays, Lynn Anderson would come in for two or three hours. Russ, Tony, and Marvin always come in at eight o'clock but always left before ten o'clock. Felix Wells and Rodney Crowder never came in on Saturdays. But Terri was told Felix Wells spent long hours working out of his house.

One Saturday, as Russ was walking by, he dropped a small slip of paper. Terri picked it up and handed it back to him; however, she noticed there were numbers on it. She later jotted them down and put them in her purse. It looked like they could be for combination. Terri wondered if it could be a combination for the locked door.

On the fifth of April, Chris took Terri to see a gynecologist. The doctor confirmed she was pregnant. When she came out of the room smiling, Chris grabbed her and whirled her around. He said, "I just knew it, when is the due date?" Terri told him, "November fourteenth." That night, they went out to dinner to celebrate. As they sat there, they started picking and discarding names for the baby. The couple finally decided they would name the baby Francine if it was a girl or Gavin if it was a boy.

When Terri went to work the next day, she told Lynn Anderson, "I am pregnant." Lynn congratulated her and said, "I am thrilled and happy for both of you." Then she asked if they had decided on a name for the baby yet, and Terri told her what the names were. Lynn then let everyone in the office know Terri was going to be a mommy.

Chris and Terri called their parents to let them know. Both sets of parents were so excited to know they were going to be grandparents. The parents informed the couple they were all planning to go to Seattle for their graduation from college. Chris and Terri told their parents, "We would be very happy that you will be here. We are also planning on going to vacation in North Dakota for a month in the middle of June."

Terri also informed everyone at the office. "Chris and I will be leaving for a month starting on June 20." Later the same day, Mr. Wells came to Terri, asking if he could borrow Hunka. Mr. Wells told her his car was in the shop, so Terri handed him her keys. One hour later, Mr. Wells came and handed Terri's keys back. All of her keys were still on her key ring; however, there was another set of keys with a remote control. She looked at Mr. Wells quizzically, then he said, "Terri, come with me." She followed him down to the parking garage. Mr. Wells took her keys, and pressing the remote, a horn sounded.

Sitting in her parking spot was a beautiful, brand-new Buick LeSabre with the sticker still on the window. It had a sunroof, leather seats, and individual temperature controls. It had power seats, air, cruise, remote entry; in fact it was totally loaded. Mr. Wells said, "It's all yours, Terri."

Terri told him, "Mr. Wells, I just can't accept this car. It is way too expensive." Mr. Wells replied, "I'm not married, Terri. I have no children, and you have become like a daughter to me. Please let me do this for you. I know you are expecting a little one. We can't have you driving around in an old clunker like that. The baby would grow up paranoid if it even looked at the old beast.

"This is my graduation gifts for both you and Chris. Please take it and enjoy it. Besides, if you don't accept this, you will only have Chris's car to drive. Because I told the dealership to take that rusty old hunk of junk and have it crushed right away. I was afraid someone would cut themselves on it and develop blood poisoning."

Terri couldn't help but laugh. She gave Mr. Wells a big hug, telling him, "You are the dearest man." Then she walked around the car several times. She couldn't believe it. There was only one color and no dents and no rust. Terri sat down inside admiring the new car smell. Mr. Wells had her turn on the ignition so she could listen to the fantastic sound system.

When Terri had finished looking at the car, Mr. Wells asked her to come with him to a nearby cafeteria for a cup of coffee. After they were seated, he said, "Terri, I'm going to level with you. I no longer trust Russ Jacobson. I think he has loyalty, but the loyalty is not to the firm. I plan on getting rid of him in the very near future.

Chapter 27

"Now I know you and Chris are plan on taking a long vacation this summer. But when you come back, I would like you to take Russ's place. Of course, if you do, I would expect you to work full-time." Terri told Mr. Wells that the job sounded very exciting. "I will talk to Chris. I'm sure he will see it my way. He usually does." They shook hands on it, then headed back to work.

The week of graduation arrived, and Chris and Terri are about to receive their degrees. After sixteen years of school, or seventeen if you could count kindergarten, they are finally finished, after this Chris and Terri will start working for a living. Their parents flew out from North Dakota. This was their first time in Seattle, and they were amazed at its size. Terri's father looked around and remarked, "It looks to be a couple of sizes larger than Towner, doesn't it?"

Their mothers were very eager for the young couple to take them shopping. They said, "This is what we girls do best, and this is one of the best places to do it in." Their fathers both laughed and replied, "If we could just find a mall which has comfortable benches for us to sit on, we would be satisfied." When the mothers were done with shopping, the couple took them for a ferry ride to Bremerton. They all got a cup of coffee, and went out on the deck. There was a fairly good breeze and a touch of salt air. On the left side was pod of orcas or killer whales. Off in the distance, you could see Mount Rainier.

Afterwards, they took their parents to the Seattle Center. At first, no one could talk Terri's mother into going up on the Space Needle because she is deathly afraid of heights. But Terri coaxed her until she finally gave in gripping Terri's father's arm all the way to the top. The rest of them walked around the top admiring the view. Terri would recommend the top of the Space Needle to anyone visiting Seattle. Terri's mom, though, thought the view from the ground was good enough for her. She spent all of her time at the top in the souvenir shop. Terri's dad was glad when it was time to go to back down because her mother's shopping bag was pretty full. When everyone got to the ground, Terri thought her mother would get down and kiss the sidewalk. She was so relieved.

The next day, everyone went to the farmer's market. There is so much to see there. Local artisans make various crafts and sell them there. One will see pictures painted by local artists, hand-carved jewelry, toys, and statues. There are fresh berries, cherries, and vegetables all locally grown. Parrots and cockatiels were for sale in some areas. Also, there are leather goods, meat, and best of all, fresh seafood.

For anyone coming to Seattle, the farmer's market is a must-see. To Chris and Terri, the seafood section is an art all by itself. She told Chris to buy a fresh salmon for dinner. Chris picked out a salmon, and the man that was there took the salmon and threw it through the air to the guy behind the counter. The guy behind the counter deftly caught the salmon and wrapped it. The act of throwing and catching the fish is showmanship itself.

Now it was time to get their bachelor's degrees—the big day. The day, the graduates have prepared for with endless semesters. Tatiana, Chris, and Terri put on their gowns, getting ready for the pomp and ceremony. Then everyone had to sit through an endless array of speeches. Chris whispered to Terri, "I think the way some of these people carry on, they just like the sound of their own voices." She elbowed him in the ribs, telling them to shut up. He just snickered.

Terri couldn't believe how fatigued she felt when it was all over. In a way, it was a letdown. They had prepared theirselves all these years, and suddenly, it's over in just a few hours. After they were finished, their parents took them out to find a seafood restaurant. They all relaxed and mellowed out, just enjoying the excellent food and a glass of wine.

The following day, they took their parents to SeaTac airport for the flight back to North Dakota. They all hugged and kissed. It wasn't as emotional as it would have been if Chris and Terri weren't seeing them again in a few weeks.

After their parents had left, Terri started working full-time at Felix Wells Investment Firm while Chris started filling out job applications. Chris always put down he would be available to start work in August. This way, he would have time to get back from their vacation in North Dakota.

At the Felix Wells Investment Firm, everything was business as usual. Tony told Terri there was a very big new business venture coming up which looked very promising. The investment firm was planning on investing a huge amount of capital. This must be the reason Terri's computer showed large amounts of cash on hand. She never did get a chance to ask Mr. Wells what it was all about.

Terri was so busy she forgot their wedding anniversary was coming up. At the last minute, she jumped into the car and went to an erotic store where she purchased a beautiful, sheer red negligée. She also bought a huge red bow that said Happy Anniversary. When Terri got home, she had to sneak it past Chris who was watching TV. He just said, "HI, sweetie" as she went past. He was engrossed in a baseball game. Terri doesn't think he even noticed she had brought in a bag. When she came back from bedroom, she tousled his hair as she went past. He just went "hmmm" and pinched her butt.

Terri went into the kitchen to get some ice tea. When she came back, Chris was gone. He was back in less than a minute. Terri asked him where he went. Chris answered all he had done was go to the bathroom, but she wondered if he'd sneaked in and peeked at the negligée. But when she checked the bag later, it didn't look like it been disturbed.

The couple stayed up late talking about their trip to North Dakota. Chris didn't even mention their anniversary. But Chris can be a real sly little fox when it comes to Terri. She told him, "I am going to bed." Chris said, "I'll be there in a minute, honey. I just remembered I forgot to lock the car."

In the morning, Terri jumped out of bed and rushed into the bathroom. She took a quick shower and brushed her hair, taking the time to put on the perfume Chris loved. While she was doing this, she thought she heard a lot of movement in the bedroom. So she knew Chris was awake. She put on her red negligée. Terri fastened on the giant bow that read Happy Anniversary, and stepped into the bedroom.

There stood Chris in the middle of the floor with a stupid grin on his face. He looked huge, he has put on at least four layers of clothes. And on top of that, he had on a pair of coveralls and his North Dakota parka. They both started laughing. Terri said, "You peeked at the negligée last night, didn't you?" Chris laughed and said, "Yes, I did." Terri will have to say it was a lot of fun peeling the layers of clothing off of Chris though. Later, when they went to the front room, there were a dozen red roses and a card on the table. The card from Chris said how much he loved Terri and couldn't live without her. What a sweetie.

On the nineteenth of June, everyone at work were stopping by Terri's desk. They were all telling her to have a nice trip. This put her way behind, so she decided to stay late to finish up her work. Everyone else had already left, so Lynn told her to lock everything up when she left. It took Terri over an hour to finish up, she put everything away and opened her purse to get her keys. When she did, a piece of paper fell out. It was the same piece of paper she had copied the numbers on which Russ Jacobson had dropped.

She went to try the numbers on the door, which had a combination lock. To her total surprise, it opened. There was not a lot in the office, but when she looked at the computer, Terri thought, "What the heck." She went back to her cubicle and got a couple of floppy disks. She copied everything on the computer twice. She didn't dare take the time to see what was on the computer. Because there was always a chance someone could come back to the office.

Terri didn't have time to look at them on her computer when she got home either. So she vacuum sealed them for safety and labeled them with her name and the date. Then she started packing the suitcases for their trip. She had almost finished with packing when the phone rang. It was Chris; he sounded very agitated. He said, "Terri, I got a call to go to Everett to check out a job. When I got to the address which was given to me, it turned out to be a vacant lot. I called the phone number the man had given me, and it rang and rang. When someone finally answered, he asked me why I was calling a pay phone.

"I do not understand why someone would want to pull a prank like this. Anyway, now I'm stuck in traffic, and I have no idea when I will be getting home. Will you pack the suitcases and put them in your car? That way we can get an early start in the morning." After she had finished talking to Chris, she went back to finish the packing of the suitcases. Then she loaded everything in the car, including her computer and the floppy disks.

Terri remembered it was hard to find motels in Montana in the summer months. It took her several tries, but she finally reserved a room for them in Billings, Montana. Just as she had finished on the phone, Chris walked through the door. Chris said, "It was so weird because someone had called me this morning, saying he heard I was looking for a job. The guy on the phone told me if I could make it to Everett by five o'clock, I would have a good chance at a very high-paying job. I told him I was interested.

"I had him repeat the address twice to make sure I had the address down right. Then this person gave me a phone number I could call after I got there. When I got to the address in Everett, I found out it was a vacant lot. That's when I called the phone number and discovered it belonged to a pay phone. I realized then I had been pranked." Terri gave Chris a hug and told him not to worry about it. She told him, "You will be able to find a job when we get back. For now, let's just enjoy our vacation."

They had dinner, but Terri could see Chris was still upset, so she tried talking to him to calm him down. After they had finished eating, she went behind his chair. Terri gently massaged his neck and back muscles. This definitely relaxed him; in fact, it relaxed him so much he almost fell asleep. His head started slowly nodding up and down, and then all a sudden, it would jerk back up. Chris looked around and said, "We better get some sleep. We will have to be up by three-thirty in the morning if we want to make it to Billings, Montana, by tomorrow night."

Chapter 28

It seems like Terri had just barely got to sleep when she awoke to a kiss and Chris saying, "Rise and shine, sleepyhead." The car was already packed, so all they had to do was shower and get dressed. Terri jumped in the car. Chris was already in the driver's seat. They stopped at a gas station and picked up a couple cups of coffee. Chris also filled their thermos with coffee while they were there.

Chris turned on to I-90 and headed east. They were almost to Ellensburg, Washington, before the sun began peeking over the horizon. When they went through the Columbia River Gorge, it was really windy. The windsock on the bridge was standing straight out. Chris did not stop until they got to Ritzville. By that time, both of them were famished. They ate a leisurely meal, then it was Terri's turn to drive. They went past Spokane, Washington, and stopped in Coeur d'Alene, Idaho, to gas up.

After Terri took off again, she drove slowly as they passed Lake Coeur d'Alene because the view is truly breathtaking. This is an absolutely gorgeous area. First, the shimmering lake with the sun glistening off of the waves. The lake is nestled among the mountains all covered with tall evergreens. One could see cabins here and there along the shore and a lone fisherman casting from his boat out on the lake.

The freeway winds up going through the upper part of Idaho to the top of Lookout Pass. At the very top of Lookout Pass is the boundary between Idaho and Montana. From there, the car will go winding downhill into Montana. Terri always enjoyed this long car trip. This one is extra special because she could enjoy long conversation with her best friend, her lover, her husband, Chris.

As Terri was driving, they would talk seriously for a while; then all of a sudden, one of them would start teasing the other one. Chris was teasing Terri real hard one time, trying to get the better of her. She told him, "You better straighten out or else." "Or else what?" asked Chris. "Or so help me, I will rape you when we get to Billings." Chris shrugged his shoulders, saying, "So rape me, and I will help you." This sent both of them off into a fit of laughter.

They gassed up again in Bozeman, Montana, then it was Chris's turn to drive again. As it was getting late in the day, they began to notice deer and antelope grazing in the fields. The first clue they were getting close to Missoula was the pungent smell of the oil refinery. Then Chris saw the sign for mile marker 446, which is their exit, so he pulled off the freeway and found their motel.

After settling into their motel, they found a nice restaurant along the strip. The jukebox was loudly playing country-western songs. As Chris and Terri were waiting for their order, they noticed most of the men and some women were wearing Western attire. Most of the men had on Western shirts, Levi's, and cowboy boots. Terri took a look at Chris with his T-shirt and sneakers. She told Chris, "Look at what all of the men are wearing. You don't fit in." Chris just took another bite of steak, then he said, "Well, I know exactly where I do fit in." So she kicked his shin under the table.

When they got back to their room, she asked Chris, "You know what I've been waiting for all day?" But Chris decided to play dumb, saying, "I haven't got the foggiest idea." So being very rational, Terri hit him alongside of the head with a pillow. Chris picked up a pillow, and the fight was on; but after a while, he cheated. Chris grabbed Terri and picked her up, then very carefully placed her on the bed. She told him, "This is more like it." Then they slowly and gently made love.

The next morning, they got up early and had breakfast. After finishing eating, they took a leisurely drive on the freeway. Chris left the freeway at Glendive, Montana, heading north to Sydney. Then it was on into Williston, North Dakota. They started to notice a lot of oil rigs dotting the landscape. When Chris turned right toward Williston, they were on Highway 2, which took them into Towner, North Dakota.

They arrived at Terri's parents' farm at six o'clock in the evening. Both sets of parents as well as several friends were there waiting for them. Everyone was excited, and of course, the topic of Terri's pregnancy came up. Chris and Terri were asked if they had picked out any names yet. Terri told them, "Yes, it would be Francine if is a girl, and Gavin if it is a boy, but whatever the gender is, we know we will love our baby very much."

The couple were so glad to be home with their parents, and the parents just wanted the couple to relax and take it easy. However, neither Chris nor Terri can sit still. It just wasn't in their nature. So they helped their parents around the farms. Chris worked a lot harder than Terri did. Whenever she started doing something, one of their mothers would say, "You shouldn't be doing that because you're pregnant." This would make her really exasperated.

She would say, "Mom, I am being very careful. I am not due until the middle of November. It drives me crazy not to be able to help you." After this, Chris and Terri's mother would pick small tasks for Terri to do, but they still insisted she take it very easy. All of their parents were all tickled pink at the idea of being grandparents. Terri thinks they will love to spoil the little one.

Chris and Terri and their parents drove up to a friend's cabin on Lake Metagoshe for a week. The lake is on the border between Canada and the United States. While they were there, they visited the International Peace Garden. It is also partly in the United States and partly in Canada. The International Peace Garden is a sign of the great friendship between the two countries. It is so beautiful and tranquil walking among the floral displays. It is hard to imagine the amount of landscaping which is done there. Flowers of every type and shape are planted and blended in to make the most beautiful patterns.

The parent's rented a pontoon boat and everyone enjoyed cruising around the lake. They got out the fishing poles, and all of them did some fishing. Terri would love to say, "I had caught the biggest fish, but alas I didn't even get a bite." Everyone else did though, catching their limit of walleye and perch.

Even though the pontoon boat had a large canopy over it, which they all sat under, they still got a little sunburned. The sun was exceedingly hot that day, and when they got back to shore, the men cleaned and filleted the fish. Afterward, they had a fish fry. Terri had forgotten how good fresh caught fish tasted.

Terri couldn't believe their vacation was almost over. The month had just seemed to fly by. On the weekend before they left, they decided to visit some old friends who lived in Knox, North Dakota. Chris's parents drove their own car while Chris and Terri followed in their car with her parents sitting in the backseat. They were about five hundred yards behind Chris's parents as they neared Rugby, North Dakota. At Rugby, Highway 2 and Highway 3 intersect. The traffic on Highway 2 goes straight thru, but traffic on Highway 3 has to stop.

Suddenly, Terri's father yelled, "Oh my God, no." They all stared transfixed, for heading north on Highway 3 was a big 18-wheeler. They were able to hear the Jake brake as it tried to slow the semi down. Its air horn was blaring, and every one of its wheels was locked up, and smoke was rolling off all of the tires. They could plainly see the semi wasn't going to be able to stop in time.

The semi must have still been going over thirty miles an hour when it hit Chris's parents car dead center. There was a horrendous crash. They could hear the sound of tearing metal, the sound of breaking glass, then dead silence. When the dust had cleared, the car was a twisted mass of tangled metal. It looked like there was absolutely no hope for survival. The Buick slid to a stop, and all four of them jumped out, running up to Chris's parent's car. Terri wishes they hadn't, for one look confirmed their worst fears. Chris kept repeating, "Mom, Dad," but he could tell they had both died instantly.

Chris and Terri were crying uncontrollably, so her father and mother took control of the situation. Terri's parents hugged the couple and gently guided both of them back to the car. They told the couple there was nothing they could do for Chris's parents now. Ambulance and police cars arrived within three minutes. The semi driver was alive but very badly injured. Medics put him in the ambulance and were gone right away.

The police came and took their statements, then left immediately. The police didn't want to bother them in their time of grief. Besides, there were at least twenty other witnesses to the accident. Of course, there was a large crowd gathered around as there always is after an accident. Terri's father said, "Chris and Terri, I have something to tell you about what happened just before you came home for vacation. I took at it with a grain of salt at the time, but this accident changes everything. Chris, your mother and father came over to visit us one night. They told us your mom had a premonition. She said something is going to happen, and they would both die very soon.

"Your parents said there was more to the premonition, but they wouldn't tell us exactly what. They did say you two would love each other always as you do now. But something dreadful would happen through no fault of your own. Because of this, you would be torn apart for a long period of time. But in the end, your son would be able to solve the puzzle. After your son solved the problem, Terri would take care of the problem, then both of you would be together always."

This part scared Chris and Terri very bad. Then her dad continued, "Your parents had drawn up their will, which name both of you as co-beneficiaries, and then they gave it to us. They also said you both should always trust one another in the times ahead and place yourselves in the hands of God. Also, your parents said to have total faith in each other." Chris was hurting something awful. Terri was too, but she had to remain somewhat strong for him. She took and held him in her arms while they both cried. She told Chris, "You had such strong, wonderful parents. They have always been my second parents too from way back, long before we were married."

Chris said, "Terri, what hurts me the most of all is they won't be able to see their grandchild. They were so looking forward to being grandparents.

Our son or daughter will never get to know their second set of grandparents. Thank God, your parents decided at the last moment to ride with us instead of them. Otherwise, there would be no grandparents."

Terri's mom heard this and spoke up from the backseat. She said, "You know what is weird. We were planning on riding with Chris's parents. We had started to get in their car when your mother got a strange look on her face. All of a sudden, she insisted we ride with you. She said you can't stop destiny, but you have to ride with Chris and Terri. They will need you in the time ahead. At the time, I was surprised, and I wondered at her strange remark."

It was overwhelming, and Terri was so worried about Chris for he was and always will be the love of her life. Terri was hurting and aching for herself, but the biggest part of the ache was for Chris. She kept hugging and holding him. They decided to go talk to the parish priest to decide what would be the best time to have the funeral. It was a good move as he had known Chris's parents very well. He was able to calm Chris down, telling him what wonderful parents he had. He told them, Chris's parents had talked to him, and they were prepared to go. He added, "They are in a better place now."

Chris made arrangements for the funeral to be in four days. The next three days seemed like they would last forever. On the afternoon of the third day, the caskets were brought to the Towner funeral chapel for viewing. Actually, viewing the bodies helped Chris to accept the fact his parents were really gone.

The funeral was held to the same church where Chris and Terri had been married. It was a large church, and it was packed. When the funeral was over, the caskets were placed in the hearse, then the funeral procession went east to the cemetery. The caskets were lowered into the ground, and then they each threw a single rose on the caskets.

Afterward, Chris and Terri went back to the basement of the church for the funeral reception. There they were surrounded by friends and family who hugged them and offered them sympathy. It seemed so unreal that only two years earlier, one of their happiest times had happened right there in the same church. Now they were here for one of the saddest times of their lives. For the next few days, they were gloomy and sad. Finally, Terri's parents told them they would have to snap out of it. Terri's father said Chris had business to take care of, and Chris's mom and dad would not want them to be sad. Life must go on.

Terri's parents took us to Rugby to see Chris's parents' attorney Michael Connor who read the will to them. The will left the farm and all of its assets and all of the bank accounts to Chris and or Terri Sutton. Mr. Connor said,

"There would also be a very large sum of money coming from an insurance settlement in the very near future." At the moment, they didn't care. They would have gladly given it all back just to be able to have Chris's parents alive and well.

Mr. Connor asked, "Do you want me to handle the case of the accident with the truck driver's insurance company?" He said the driver had driven for way too many hours, and he had admitted to the police he was taking drugs to stay awake." Chris told Mr. Connor to go ahead and take the case. Mr. Conner gave them some more information about the accident, but they were not interested in it at the time.

Later as they talked to Terri's parents, Terri's father asked the couple, "What would you like to do about Chris's parents' farm?" Chris told him,"somehow we would like to be able to keep it. Perhaps sometime in the future, we would like to live there. But for right now, we would like to go back to Seattle. We plan on working there for maybe ten years. After that, we might come back to live on the farm."

Terri's father said, "If that's what you want, I can work the farm on shares with you. Then it will be ready if and when you decide to come back here." Terri looked at Chris, and he replied, "We would love it if you could do that for us." The couple wound up staying in North Dakota for three more weeks. There were a lot of loose ends to clear up on the farm. The loss of Chris's parents still hurt, but they realized only time would be able to make the pain go away. But Terri told Chris, "We still have many wonderful memories of your parents."

Chapter 29

Chris and Terri decided finally the time had come for them to head back to Seattle. They hugged and kissed Terri's parents good-bye and thanked them for all they had done for them. On the trip back to Seattle, they had long discussions. Terri kept telling Chris how much she loved him. Chris put his hand on her knees, saying, "I love you too, sweetheart. Do you realize how much harder this would've been if you had not been there for me?"

When they were somewhere between Bozeman and Butte, Montana, Terri suddenly exclaimed, "Chris, I forgot to bring my computer back from North Dakota." Chris thought about it for a moment, then he shrugged his shoulders, telling her, "Don't worry about it. We will buy you a newer model when we get back to Seattle."

Chris and Terri didn't stop until they made it to Missoula, and they were pretty tired by that time. Luckily, they were able to find a nice motel with a swimming pool. They decided they should spend three days there just to relax before leaving for Seattle. They went right to bed and fell asleep in each other's arms. When they woke up in the morning, Chris put his hands on Terri's stomach. "Yeah," he said," I thought so. I could feel the baby moving during the night. Is it always that active"? Terri laughed and said, "Yes, the baby takes after you, it's always moving around." Chris tenderly kissed her, saying, "I can't wait for us to be parents, Terri. I hope it's a girl who looks just like you." Terri said, "Chris, my love, I think it's going to be a boy."

They drove around Missoula, then stopped and had breakfast at a restaurant which had a creek running under it. Afterwards, just for something different to do, they went to watch the livestock auction. Terri heard there was a fire in the Bitterroot Valley. They drove out to the airport to watch the smoke jumpers planes come in and land, then take off again.

Chris and Terri went back to the motel and put swimming suits on. Then swam and enjoyed themselves for a couple of hours. Next they went back to their room and just relaxed. Terri sat on Chris's lap as they watched TV together. They did things like this for three days, just mellowing out. On the evening of the third day, Chris said, "I'm finally beginning to feel like I'm alive again. I'm ready to head back to Seattle and start looking for a job." Terri told Chris, "I'm ready if you are."

They left early the next morning. As Chris drove, they talked about how nice it would be to get home. Chris drove slowly, enjoying each other's company. They parked at their apartment, then took our suitcases and walked in the door. The second Chris and Terri stepped through the door, they knew immediately something was wrong. They just stood and stared at each other in amazement. Their apartment was in total disarray. Everything had been moved. There were cushions from the couch on the floor. Drawers had been pulled out and emptied. Nothing was as they had left it. Chris checked all rooms to make sure no one was still there.

Picking up the phone, Chris dialed 911. Terri heard him tell the dispatcher their home had been burglarized. The dispatcher told them, "The police will be there right away." Within minutes, several squad cars rolled up lights flashing and sirens blaring.

The police rushed in the door with their pistols drawn. The police told the couple face the wall, put your hands on the wall, and stand spread-eagled. Then the police frisked them. Chris asked, "What the hell do you think you are doing? This is our apartment which has been burglarized." A burly policeman told Chris to shut up, he asked him if his name was Chris Sutton. He answered, "Yes."

A plain-clothed detective put handcuffs on Chris and told him, "Chris Sutton, you are being arrested for the murder of Felix Wells." Then he read Chris his Miranda rights and asked Chris, "Do you understand them?" Flabbergasted, Chris stuttered, "That-that's Terri's boss, but I hardly knew the man." The detective answered, "But you evidently knew him well enough to kill him."

The police put Chris and Terri in squad cars and took them down to the booking station to interview them. Before they were separated, Terri told Chris, "Don't talk to the police about anything. I will get a hold of a lawyer to clear this up." At the station, Terri asked for a phone. She looked at the phone book and located a criminal defense lawyer named Arlen Blankenship. After she had talked with him, he told her he would be there right away.

Mr. Blankenship was as good as his word. When he got to the holding station, he demanded to speak to both of them. First of all, Mr. Blankenship asked, "Chris, tell me, what do you know about the charge?" Chris told Mr. Blankenship, "I don't have a clue of what the police are talking about. We left

Bellevue on the morning of the twentieth of June. We have been to North Dakota for seven weeks and had just gotten back to Bellevue."

Chris told Mr. Blankenship, "The second we had walked into the apartment, the place looked like it had been ransacked. So we called the police right away, but instead of checking out the robbery, the police had arrested Chris, then charged him with murdering Terri's boss, Mr. Wells. We hadn't even realized Mr. Wells was dead."

Mr. Blankenship said, "I will talk to Vern Wilson who is the lead detective on this case." Mr. Blankenship was gone for a very long time. During the time he was gone, Chris and Terri talked to each other, thinking when the police realize their mistake, Chris will be released. When Mr. Blankenship returned, he looked very grim.

When Mr. Blankenship spoke, he told them, "There is a reason that your apartment looked like it had been burglarized. The police had found probable cause and obtained a search warrant for the apartment. When Felix Wells had not returned to the office for three days nor had he answered his phone calls or returned messages, Russ Jacobson had gone to his house.

"Russ had a key to Felix Wells house and let himself in after no one answered the door. The first thing he had noticed was much of the artwork was missing. He called out Felix's name several times, and no one answered. As he was walking through the house, he saw a massive amount of blood on the floor and had called the police.

"When the police arrived at Felix Wells's home, the police discovered high velocity blood splatter on the wall. They found a bullet hole in the wall and extracted a bullet. From the enormous amount of blood on the floor, they determined someone had died violently.

"The police detectives found a hair they thought came from the suspect. They also found bloody shoe prints on the floor leading to a table, then to the dishwasher. There was a glass on the table which had Felix Wells's fingerprints on it. In the dishwasher was a matching glass with Chris Sutton's fingerprints on. The police also found an antique vase with Chris's fingerprints on it.

"Two days later, a neighbor of Felix Wells found a .38-caliber Smith & Wesson pistol by some bushes in his yard. It had been wiped clean and thrown in the bushes. There were no prints on it; however, it was registered to Chris Sutton. When they test fired it, detectives found the ballistics from the slug matched the ballistics of the slug which police had dug out of the wall.

"On this evidence, the police obtained a search warrant for your apartment. There they found shoes which had blood on the soles. The soles of the shoes matched the bloody shoe prints found at Felix Wells's home.

Detectives also found a shirt in the laundry, which had high velocity blood splatter on it.

"The police did DNA testing on all of the blood evidence, which they found at the house. Because of all of his business dealings, Mr. Wells had his DNA tested. It was on file, so they had a DNA profile to be able to check out. It all matched Felix Wells's DNA. As if this wasn't enough, on the evening of June nineteenth, a neighbor of Mr. Wells claimed he saw a black Monte Carlo matching Chris's parked at Mr. Wells's home. The neighbor was put under hypnosis because they wanted to see if he could give them the numbers on the license plate. He was able to recall the vehicle vividly; however, the car had no license plates at all.

"Still, because of this the police figure the time of the murder was between 5:00 p.m. and 8:00 p.m. on the night of June nineteenth. Chris, do you have an alibi for this time? If you can prove with 100 percent accuracy you were somewhere else, maybe we will have a chance."

Chris was visibly shocked. He said, "My God, I have been set up beyond belief. I am innocent. There is no way I could hurt an animal, let alone take a human life. June 19 was the day someone called me with a job offer in Everett. It turned out to be hocus-pocus. There was nothing at the address, let alone a business. I was somewhere between Everett and Seattle on the freeway at that time."

Then came a knock on the door. Detective Wilson was there with a warrant for sample of Chris's blood. He had a lab technician with him, so Chris had no choice but to roll up his sleeves and allow them to draw his blood. His face looked ashen, and Terri was sure hers was too. After the technician had finished drawing Chris's blood, Terri asked Detective Wilson if she might be able to have a look at the shirt and shoes. Detective Wilson hemmed and hawed. Finally, at Mr. Blankenship's insistence, he said, "Okay. But that is all you will be allowed to do is look at them, you can't touch them in any way."

Detective Wilson made a call, and ten minutes later, policemen brought the shoes and shirt up from the evidence locker. The shoes were an old pair Terri had been after Chris to throw away. The shoes had been sitting by the bed, and the shirt was Chris's for sure. She remembered he had worn it three days before they left.

Terri asked Detective Wilson, "Doesn't it mean something that the Monte Carlo didn't have a license plates on it? There are probably hundreds of that year black Monte Carlos." Detective Wilson said, "With all the other evidence, it just helps prove the case. Besides, how long does it take for someone to remove a license plate?"

After he was finished talking, Detective Wilson and two other policemen handcuffed Chris. Terri told Chris, "I love you." Then they took him away. Presumably, the police were planning to book him and place him in a cell. Mr. Blankenship told him before he left, "Under no circumstances talk to the police without me present."

After the police left, Terri asked Mr. Blankenship, "What is going to happen to Chris now?" Mr. Blankenship stated, "It looks very bad for Chris. I've never been on a case, or for that matter heard of a case which had this much forensic evidence. The only thing we have going for us is the fact there is no body. Judges and juries are reluctant to give a life sentence or a death sentence without a body. Also, I think the fact the artwork is missing and cannot contribute it to Chris is a plus. Of course the police will just say Chris must have had an accomplice."

Terri wailed, "But Chris is innocent. He wouldn't even go deer hunting. The only reason he kept a pistol in the house was in case of a burglar breaking in. Even then, all he would have been able to do was scare them with the pistol. Chris didn't even keep bullets for the pistol. I don't even know where it was because I haven't seen it for over a year. What about the cell phone call Chris made to me on the night of June 19? Wouldn't the police be able to use triangulation to prove he was on the freeway?"

Mr. Blankenship immediately called Detective Wilson and asked, "Have the police found any .38-caliber bullets at the apartment?" Mr. Blankenship also asked if they would be able to triangulate the call from Chris, which he had made to Terri. It will show Chris was on the freeway at that time. Detective Wilson said, "Yes, we could prove where the phone call came from; however, it could just be Chris dumping the body." He also said, "No .38-caliber bullets were found in the apartment. But it doesn't prove anything. Chris could have bought them anywhere."

After Detective Wilson got off the phone, Mr. Blankenship told Terri, "I can use the fact there were no license plates on the car. Also, no bullets were found in the apartment. It is not much, but it's all we have. Maybe we can use that to make a plea bargain." Again, Terri cried, "But Chris is totally innocent." Mr. Blankenship replied, "Which would you rather have, Chris facing life imprisonment or the death penalty? Or have him receive twenty years imprisonment, with the chance of being paroled early for good behavior?"

Mr. Blankenship said, "I know it's a tough decision, but we don't have to face this just yet. You never know, maybe something good will come up yet. But innocent or not, right now the police have all of the evidence in their favor. I hate to say this, but our justice system is the best in the world. But even so on occasion, an innocent person is put in prison for a crime they didn't commit.

"My advice to you for now is to go home, then call a friend. You need someone with you at this very trying time. Then try to get some sleep, which I know will be hard. We will talk to Chris tomorrow, then we will decide where to go from there." Terri called Tatiana from the holding station, and told her, "I need you." But she was crying so hard Tatiana could barely understand her. Tatiana asked, "Where are you?" When she finally figured out where Terri was, Tatiana came down to the holding station right away. She drove Terri back to her apartment where Tatiana held her while she cried her eyes out.

Chapter 30

When Terri was partly coherent, she explained to Tatiana what had happened. Tatiana said, "I just can't understand what the police are talking about. Chris couldn't even harm a mouse. He just doesn't have the killer instinct in him. So the only thing that can explain this is someone has framed him big time. If worse comes to worse and your lawyer is right, it would be way better for Chris to take a plea deal than for him to have to face something worse. As much as you and Chris love each other, he will know you will wait for him. It will be a lot better to have him back sometime in the future than to not have Chris back at all."

Tatiana said, "Now I think it's time for you to get some sleep. I will fix you some warm milk. You need to be alert for tomorrow." Terri drank the milk and lay down in bed. Tatiana was terrific. She tucked Terri in the bed, then she sang a soft, low melody. It was just as if Terri was a child, and it worked. Even as stressed out as she was, she fell asleep.

Terri was overwrought and exhausted when she went to bed. To her surprise, she slept for twelve hours. However, after waking up, she was refreshed but sad. She felt the need to do something, being extremely angry at whoever framed Chris. If Terri could've gotten a hold of whoever did this at this time, she would have dragged his bleeding body to the police station.

However, Tatiana and Terri were at her apartment where Tatiana made a late breakfast for her. As they were eating, she told Terri, "Mr. Blankenship called. He said he is busy working on Chris's case and he wouldn't be able to meet with you today. But he did make arrangements for you to meet Chris at the holding station at 3:00 p.m. Mr. Blankenship suggested you try to remain calm and upbeat while you are there. There is no sense in making Chris any more upset than he already is."

Tatiana and Terri were at the holding station waiting for the meeting with Chris at three in the afternoon. After getting it okayed with the police,

Terri asked Tatiana if she would come to the visiting room with her for moral support. She was so excited to be able to see her husband, Terri wanted to hold Chris in her arms, but the police wouldn't let her. They were told to sit at opposite sides of the table. The police told them they would be able to talk to each other but not to touch each other. The police said they would be watching them through the window.

The first thing out of Chris's mouth was, "They don't cook as well here as you do, honey. If I ever get out of this place, I don't think I will ever be taking you here for dinner. In fact, I don't think they will ever attain a five-star-restaurant status." This kind of lightened up the mood. Terri thought she would be the one who would be cheering Chris up. Instead, just seeing Chris and hearing him cheered her up.

Chris told Terri Mr. Blankenship had talked to him that morning. "Mr. Blankenship explained everything to me, and it wasn't good. Mr. Blankenship told me no matter how innocent I was, the law was the law. I may have to serve time in prison for a crime, which I did not commit. If worse comes to worse. will you wait for me? It will mean so much to me knowing you will be there for me when I get out."

Terri told Chris, "You don't even have to even ask. I will wait for you forever. I am not some fickle female who jumps up and is gone at the first sign of trouble. According to my parents, your mom said we would be separated for a long time. But she also said in the end we would be back together forever. This is enough for me, Chris. We have had a little over two happy years together. If you have to go to prison, I will be very sad. But during this time, I will raise our child, and when the day comes when you get out, we will both be waiting there for you with open arms."

Chris went on to say, "Mr. Blankenship is going to be doing the very best that he can. But he also told me he was pretty positive if all else failed he was sure he could get me a plea deal. I'm very glad Mr. Blankenship was upfront with us. It would be much worse if he kept telling us he would be able to get me off. Then only to find out he was wrong."

As the visit ended, Terri told Chris, "I will be back every time I get the chance." After leaving, Tatiana and Terri went back to the apartment. She hadn't even noticed Tatiana had straightened up the apartment before she got up. Tatiana made some coffee and sat down for some serious talk. After sitting down with their coffee, Tatiana said, "Terri, we have not been thinking straight. We have been so busy thinking about Chris we forgot there is someone who had to have done this to him." Tatiana asked Terri, "Do you have any idea of who could have killed Mr. Wells and framed Chris?" Terri realized she definitely did have two people in mind. "At the firm where she worked, there were two sleaze balls, Russ Jacobson and Marvin Mueller."

Terri told Tatiana, "There are these two creeps who have been assholes ever since I started working at the firm. They were always talking and whispering to each other. In fact, Russ Jacobson is the person who had turned everything over to the Bellevue Police Department." Tatiana remarked, "Well, there you go, let's try following them to see where they live. The artwork which was taken from the house has to have gone somewhere. Maybe we can find a way to screw them up. There is always the possibility Russ and Marvin will screw up and make some kind of mistake. If we can find the mistake, maybe we can keep Chris from going to prison."

Tatiana went on, "If we can't find anything and Chris does go to prison, we will keep trying. If worse comes to worse and Chris does go to prison, we will keep trying to see if we can get him out. Even if we don't figure it out until Chris is ready to get out of prison, we will at least try to clear his name. I am thinking it will take us a long time. But I just had a vision that we will triumph in the end."

Chapter 31

And so it started, Terri and Tatiana following Russ and Marvin. Terri would not be able to use the Buick or the Monte Carlo because Russ and Marvin might be able to recognize the cars. So instead, they used some of Tatiana's family's cars. Terri and Tatiana would use a different car every night. The girls would follow Russ Jacobson partway home one night. Then would follow Marvin Mueller partway home the next night. Then they would switch cars waiting at the spot where they had left off the last time. When the one they were following passed by, Tatiana would pull out and follow them from that point.

It took almost two weeks, but at last, the girls located both of their homes. The best part of it was both Russ and Marvin lived in an area where there were no other homes close to them. The ladies started surveillance, but nothing seemed to be happening. After that, they started thinking of breaking into their homes.

Mr. Blankenship called Terri, saying, "I want to meet you at the holding station." After Terri got there, he sat down with Chris and her. Mr. Blankenship said, "Mr. and Mrs. Sutton, I have tried every avenue. I have talked to the prosecutors until I'm blue in the face. I mentioned the lack of a license plate on the Monte Carlo, plus the absence of a body. Also the fact the police were not able to find any .38-caliber bullets at your apartment. Also the fact neither of you have ever had so much as a parking ticket."

Mr. Blankenship said, "Our only hope is for a plea deal, and my advice to you is the sooner you take it, the better. The police are expecting DNA results back from the hair they found at the crime scene. If they find it belongs to Chris, it will be the last straw, so we have to make it soon." Chris asked Terri, "What do you think of making a plea deal?" Terri told Chris, "It really sucks, but what choice do we have? If this is what we have to do, then let's do it. You know you are the love of my life, Chris, and I will wait for you forever."

Chris asked Mr. Blankenship if he could talk to the prosecutor to see what kind of a plea deal they could make. When Mr. Blankenship came back, he told them, "The prosecutor would not make any kind of a deal. Not unless both of them agreed to take a lie detector test first." Both Chris and Terri said, "We are ready to take the lie detector test right way." Mr. Blankenship warned us sometimes cops would lie about the results of the test. The police were famous for telling people they have failed the test when they had actually passed.

When it was Terri's turn to take the test, the police placed some sensors on her. At first, the policeman administrating the lie detector test just asked questions about everyday life. Then he started asking her all of the bad questions like, "Did you know Chris killed Felix Wells?" "Was Chris wearing the shirt, which had the blood evidence on the fatal day?" "Did you know where Chris hid the artwork?"

When the lie detector test was finished, the police started grilling Terri. He told her, "The test shows you are lying, and you flunked the test." Terri looked straight in the lie detector administrator's eye and asked him, "Did your mother teach you to make bald-faced lies like this? You realize you are plump full of shit. It only makes sense they would put a liar in charge of the lie detector. They probably use you for an example of how to beat a lie detector test."

His face immediately went from a pasty white to a brilliant beet red. Terri thinks she must've gotten to him, for he said, "Get the hell out of here and don't ever come back." Later, Mr. Blankenship told us we had both passed our tests with flying colors. Terri still thinks the vast majority of the police force are upstanding citizens and do their jobs properly. She doesn't count the lie detector administer as one of them.

Terri found out later the police gave Chris an even worse time. They made him take a lie detector test three different times. Then the police tried to tell him he had failed every time. Chris told them both, "The only reason you made take me take the test more than once is you could not believe you are about to send an innocent man to prison." When this didn't work, the police told him, "Your wife has confessed." Chris laughed in their faces and said, "Confessed to what? Loving me."

When Mr. Blankenship went to talk to the prosecutor about making a plea deal this time, the prosecutor said, "I can't believe how those two learned how to beat the polygraph test, but they did." Mr. Blankenship told the prosecutor, "Perhaps it's because Chris is innocent." The prosecutor said, "That's not even possible. We have overwhelming evidence that Chris did it. But if he will take the Alford plea for manslaughter, I will see that he will receive the maximum of twenty years in prison. There will be the possibility of parole in fifteen years for good behavior."

When Mr. Blankenship came to talk to us, he told us, "Chris would be smart to accept the deal right away. If the police would happen to find the body and there's more evidence, then it will become really bad. But if you accept the deal now and it is finalized, there will be no more that can happen to him."

Terri's heart sank when she heard Chris say, "Let's do it," even though she knew Chris had no other choice. She told Chris, "I will go back to work at the investment firm. But I will try to do everything possible to try and find out who framed you, even if it takes till you got out of prison."

Before Chris was taken way, they managed to kiss, then he was taken back to the holding cell. When Terri left, she had Tatiana take her to the investment firm. When the girls got there, she told Tatiana, "Wait here for me." As soon as Terri walked through the door of the investment firm, she was immediately confronted by Russ Jacobson. He sarcastically told her to leave, saying, "You will never set foot on the property again."

Even though Terri was halfway expecting something like this to happen on top of everything else she had gone through, she was shocked. But it did not make her feel despondent or in despair; rather it invigorated her and made her angry. Terri was thinking, "You bastard, you and Marvin were the cause for all of this to happen. Before I'm finished, I will see you both in prison instead of Chris if it's the last thing I ever do."

Terri went back to Tatiana's car, slamming the doors. When she sat down, Tatiana asked, "What is wrong?" Terri replied, "Let's go back to the apartment. There we will have some coffee and put on our thinking caps." While they were on the way, Terri filled her in about what had happened at Felix Wells Investment Firm. Tatiana reacted with shock and surprise in her voice, saying, "That's awful bold. There is definitely something very fishy going on where you used to work. Someone in the investment firm committed this crime, most likely it is Russ or Marvin, but let's not rule out anyone else."

Tatiana said, "Whoever committed this crime decided they needed Felix Wells out of the way. So they killed him and framed Chris. Also, there must be a reason the police never found the body. I think it probably would have proved Chris didn't kill Mr. Wells."

As the girls sat over their coffee, Tatiana said, "You mark my words. I believe we are going to be hearing more about the Felix Wells Investment Firm very soon. Is there anyone who works at the investment firm you might be able to talk to?" Terri replied, "Yes, there are three. There is Lynn Anderson who is the personnel director. Then there is Rodney Crowder, the human resources manager. Also, Tony Lindsay who does market research and works in close proximity to Marvin Mueller."

Tatiana said, "I think we should hold off on talking to them. They could be friends with Russ and Marvin. One or more of them could possibly be involved in this. Let's stick with our original plan for now. Let's see if we can find anything in Russ's or Marvin's homes, which will incriminate one or the other of them. If nothing, then maybe we can scare them into making a move."

Tatiana suggested, "I can put you in for a position at Global Airlines." So Terri applied and was accepted for a job at Global Airlines, which flew everywhere in the world. This job had fantastic benefits, health insurance, sick leave, vacation pay, and a 401k. Plus, she could fly anywhere for free, although it had be on standby.

Once Terri started working, Tatiana and Terri also started their surveillance of Russ and Marvin. Tatiana had talked to a friend of hers who was a locksmith. He would not go with them, but he gave them lock-picking tools and showed them how to use them. Now the girls just had to wait for a chance when Russ and Marvin were not at home.

Chris took the Alford plea, and like he was promised, he received twenty years at the Monroe Correctional Complex. The Suttons found out Chris had taken the Alford plea just in time, for the very next day, the DNA results from the hair came back. It matched Chris's DNA, which Terri figured it would. Whoever had done this had gone all out. They knew if whoever had figured everything else out, he would have figured a way to get one of Chris's hairs.

Terri was able to visit Chris for the last time at the holding station. Chris said he was told the Monroe Correctional Complex was better than the Bellevue police holding station. The visiting facilities were supposed to be much better than most prison facilities. There were also possible conjugal visitation rights. If this were true, it would mean the whole world to Chris and Terri.

Chapter 32

One day at work, Tatiana excitedly showed Terri a slip of paper. The tickets were for a trip to Las Vegas. Better yet, the tickets were for Russ Jacobson and Marvin Mueller. They would be leaving Friday evening and would not come back until Sunday night. This would be their big chance. Tatiana and Terri would watch at the airport terminal to make sure the men left.

Tatiana and Terri were at the airport Friday evening. Terri stayed hidden. She didn't want Russ or Marvin to see her. They didn't know where Tatiana was sitting, so she waited in the area where she would be able see the plane take off ahead of time. Tatiana found Terri, telling her, "Russ and Marvin's plane has already left." Terri gave her a large smirk and said, "Let's go for it."

Tatiana and Terri went to Russ Jacobson's house first. Tatiana stopped at a parking space which they had found where Russ lived earlier. The two of them casually walked up to the house and brazenly used the lock picks as they were instructed. The door opened immediately. After Terri walked into the room, she turned on her flashlight. Tatiana, however, reached for the light switch and flipped it on. She said, "This way it looks like we belong here, whereas if someone sees the light from a flashlight, they will call the police."

As they searched, Tatiana remained cool. Terri, however, was very nervous. Her heart was in her throat. Every step she took, every little creak of the floor made her jump. Just when she had started to settle down to business, Terri heard a voice, saying, "Who's there?" She had to admit she almost pissed her pants.

Tatiana started laughing and pointed to a large macaw parrot in the corner. She admitted she would've been scared too; however, she had already seen the bird. After Terri got over the scare, the girls searched the house from top to bottom. They had the foresight to wear rubber gloves and weren't afraid to touch things.

Terri and Tatiana searched the house from the basement all the way to the top floor, and the only thing they found were hundreds of pornography pictures. Quite a few of them were of very young children. Terri said, "On top of being a crooked SOB, Russ Jacobson is also a pervert." They did not find any guns, ammunition, or artwork. They did, however, find a large safe.

This intrigued them to no end. When Terri says it was a large safe, she means it was the size that you would find in a business, not a home. Alas, whatever was in there was beyond them, for the girls had no way of opening the safe. So while they stood there thinking, an idea came to Terri. She told Tatiana the thought which came to her. Tatiana said, "Wow, that's a great idea. It will scare Russ right out of his hide." Again, they searched the house; only this time, they were searching for something specific. Tatiana found what they were looking for in a room fixed up as an office.

What the girls needed was simple. Just a large sheet of white paper and a marking pen. On the paper, Terri wrote, "We were here. We know what you are doing. We will be back. BEWARE." Tatiana and Terri thought Russ's imagination would fill in the rest. Tatiana said, "If Russ had anything at all to do with Felix Wells's murder, this will scare the crap out of him."

As they were leaving, Terri flipped off the lights, but Tatiana flipped the lights right back on. Terri asked Tatiana why did she do that. Tatiana answered, "Russ will know soon enough when he sees a sign on the safe someone has been here. But when he sees the lights on, he will already be apprehensive. He will know someone was here, and they don't care if he knew it. The note will make Russ so scared his imagination will run wild. It will probably scare him more than if someone was in front of him with a weapon. He will never imagine a couple of women were capable of doing this."

As the girls left for Marvin's home, their spirits were quite high. This time, as there were no homes close to Marvin's home, Tatiana pulled right into the driveway and parked like she owned the place. Once again, the lock picks worked, and they walked right in and turned on the lights. Tatiana said, "Uh-oh." Standing right in front of them stood a large growling Rottweiler. Tatiana was petrified, saying, "What do we do?"

Terri, on the other hand, had been around animals all of her life. She knew you could not show fear; plus she really loves dogs. Terri got to her knees and put out her hand, making a kissing noise, saying, "Come to me, big boy." Instead of attacking when he came near her, it started trying to lick her to death. Following her lead, Tatiana did the same thing and received her share of slobber.

Marvin Mueller's place was immaculate. There was not a pen out of place. Terri always thought Marvin was anal compulsive. As the girls searched the house, the Rottweiler followed them every step of the way, begging for attention. Tatiana thinks the dog would have probably given them everything in the house if he had the chance. Terri figured he was just starving for love seeing as how Marvin didn't have any.

At first, no one found anything of interest until they got to the spare bedroom. There again everything was neatly in place. The masks and whips were hung neatly on the wall. The bed was built so sturdily it looked like it was indestructible. The handcuffs were placed very carefully on the headboard along with other torture paraphernalia.

The table near the bed was spread out in a very special order. Marvin had devices which would screw down on the thumb and fingers, also brass knuckles. There were some sort of electrical probes. There were torture instruments of every kind. Some of them Tatiana and Terri had not even seen in horror movies. Terri pitied anyone who might have been in the room.

Amazingly, once again, Terri found a large business type of safe. She really wished they could have opened it. But again with what was found in the spare bedroom, maybe Tatiana and Terri would not have wanted to see what was in the safe. This time, the girls had taken some paper and a marker pen with them from Russ's home. Tatiana said, "I want to write the message this time."

Tatiana said she was positive Russ and Marvin would talk to each other after they had been to their homes. Terri agreed with her wholeheartedly. Taking the marker pen in hand, she simply wrote, "This goes double for you, asshole." Then she said, "I think that will get the message across. I would love to see Russ's and Marvin's faces when they get home."

Terri and Tatiana had already agreed to leave the lights on at Marvin's place too. As soon as Tatiana opened the door, the dog started whining pathetically. He looked so forlorn that Terri wondered out loud, "What could we do for him?" Tatiana answered, "You know, my mom has been looking for a dog just like this one to keep her company. Since she's retired, she'd been looking for some company, so why don't we just take him along with us?" Terri said, "Come on, boy, you have a new home." The way the dog bounded out, you could tell it he was overjoyed. The second Terri opened the rear door on the car, he jumped in like a flash. Tatiana said, "That's a good name for him. Let's just call him Flash."

On the way back to Bellevue, Flash had his tongue out and was looking at them like they were his new best friends. Whenever one of them would say something, he would stare at the one who was talking. It was late when the girls got back to Bellevue, but they went straight to Mrs. Brown's house. When Mrs. Brown opened the door for them, Flash bounded in. She looked at him, saying, "Well, who's pretty boy are you?" Flash rushed to her, and she started petting him, and that's all it took.

Tatiana told her mother, "The dogs name is Flash, and he belongs to you, Mom, if you want him. I'm not positive, but I don't think he's had a very nice life." Mrs. Brown got down on her knees, hugging him. She said, "You poor puppy, of course, I'll take you. I've been looking for a dog preferably a Rottweiler just like you. And you won't ever have to worry about being mistreated again." Flash acted just like he understood. He started thumping his tail and wiggling all over while looking at Mrs. Brown's face.

All day Monday while Tatiana and Terri were at work, they kept wondering how Russ and Marvin were doing. Terri was so curious she drove by the Felix Wells Investment Firm on their way home. The firm must have closed early as there was no one visible. Tuesday was a repeat of the day before. However, there were problems when Terri went past the investment firm on Wednesday. Terri saw a whole slew of police cars and some federal cars parked there.

When the girls got up Thursday morning, Tatiana and Terri quickly scanned the paper, carefully watching for anything about the Felix Wells Investment Firm. They watched the early morning news on TV, but there was nothing there either. On the way home that night, Terri and Tatiana once again saw cars parked by the investment firm. This time, all of the cars parked there had federal license plates on them.

When Tatiana and Terri got home that evening, no sooner did Terri turned the TV on when she heard the announcer say, "We interrupt this program to bring you breaking news." The announcer exclaimed, "The Felix Wells Investment Firm whose founder was murdered in June is now insolvent. Over $200 million of the firm's and investors' money has vanished."

The announcer continued, "The local police and the FBI are searching for two persons of interest in the case. If anyone knows the whereabouts of Russ Jacobson or Marvin Mueller, please contact the Bellevue Police Department." The police emphasize they are not suspects. They just want to talk to them as they are probably innocent victims."

Terri jumped out of her chair and yelled, "Innocent victims, my ass. The only innocent victim is my husband Chris, and he is serving time at Monroe Correctional Complex. These SOBs killed Mr. Wells and framed Chris all because Russ and Marvin wanted to steal the firm's money."

Tatiana stood up and encircled Terri in her arms, saying, "Terri, you have to calm down because you could make the baby come early, and you won't be helping Chris this way." Terri took Tatiana at her word and calmed down, then she started to smile. Terri said, "If nothing else, I guess we got those jerks on the run. Russ and Marvin probably weren't expecting to take the money quite this fast. I am willing to bet we spoiled their little plan."

Tatiana asked Terri, "Why don't you call Mr. Blankenship. Maybe this could help get Chris out of prison?" When Terri talked to Mr. Blankenship, he had already seen the news on TV. He said, "I will talk to Detective Vernon Wilson and then call you back right away." When he got a hold of Terri two hours later, Mr. Blankenship said, "Vern Wilson was adamant this has nothing to do with Felix Wells's murder. He said the disappearance of the firm's money is one crime, the murder of Felix Wells is another."

Meanwhile, Chris in Monroe prison. At first, Chris couldn't believe what had happened to him. He had wound up in a cell, which only had one other prisoner. Chris was so devastated he sat down on his bunk and started to cry. The wonderful new life with Terri had seemed to have just begun, and now it was finished.

Chris thought, "Now here I am in prison, accused of killing a man I just barely knew—a man with whom I had no problem with whatsoever. In fact, he seemed to be a pretty decent guy." All of a sudden, Chris heard a gravelly voice, saying, "Why don't you quit sniveling and face the music like a man?" Chris looked up the voice came from a silvery-haired man with gapping teeth. He was an old con who looked to be older than Mount Rainier but three years younger than the Big Dipper. Chris told the old geezer, "It's easy for you to say, but I happen to be here for crime I did not commit."

"I would imagine so," the old timer replied. "I have not met anyone here at Monroe prison who is guilty." "But I really am innocent," Chris shouted. "Sonny, it doesn't matter," the old man said. "If you are innocent or not against your better wishes, you are not likely to get out of here anytime soon. I have been in every prison in Washington State and several prisons in other states. I'm telling you, the Monroe Correctional Complex isn't that bad."

The old con continued on, "Now you can do one of two things. You can sit around feeling sorry for yourself and eating your heart and your brains out. Or you can make the best of things, my boy. Attitude is everything when you are in prison. If you keep on the way you are going, you will drive yourself crazy or maybe even to suicide. However, if you take the attitude that being here is not so bad or you won't be here forever, the time will just roll along. You may be able to find something which suits your talents. You will also find you will get out of prison sooner because of good behavior.

"Now, sonny, if you want, you can tell me your story." The old man was a very good listener, and he made no comments until Chris was finished. After Chris was done, the old fellow started by telling him, "Monroe has an excellent education plan. As a convict, the prison will not let you be a teacher. But with your education, maybe you can help as an assistant teacher. Also, there are always young convicts who are trying for their GED. Maybe you can volunteer to help them.

"Monroe also has an excellent visitation plan. The prison encourages inmates to interact with their families. It helps to ensure convicts will not reoffend when they are released. There is also a conjugal visitation plan. If you are on good behavior, the prison will allow your wife or girlfriend to visit you. The best part of it is it's not just for a short couple of hours, but for up to two days. This may not seem like much, but it beats the hell out of nothing."

Back to Terri in Bellevue. Her mother called to inform Terri she was flying out to Seattle soon. She plans on staying for at least three months after the baby is born. Seeing as how Tatiana has moved in with her, Terri was glad she has a three-bedroom apartment.

It was now Terri's first chance to visit Chris at the Monroe Correctional Complex, and she was so excited. She asked Tatiana, "Would you drive me there because I don't want to be by myself as I don't know what to expect." Terri knew Tatiana would be able to calm her down if she ran into trouble. After the girls had entered Monroe, they had to go through a metal detector, and their handbags were x-rayed.

As Terri and Tatiana were walking to the visitation room, they could hear the gate slamming shut behind them. Just the sound made them cringe, and Terri could just imagine how Chris must have felt. Because when he went through those gates, Chris knew he would not be getting out in the foreseeable future. When Tatiana and Terri walked into the visitation room, they had a pleasant surprise. Terri was expecting to see something dark and dreary; instead it was a very pleasant and spacious room.

The visitation room had large tables and chairs, there were soda machines and snacks vending machines. Terri could see other inmates who were visiting with their loved ones. She even saw families with children. Terri wondered how a man who had little children could possibly commit a crime. But then she thought of Chris and realized she shouldn't be too hasty to make judgment. There's no way to know the individual circumstances in each case.

Terri had been very scared of what Chris's attitude would be like, but she needn't have worried. When the guards brought Chris into the room, she was so thrilled just to see his face. Terri threw herself into his arms. The guards allowed them to hug and kiss briefly. Then they went and sat at the table across from each other, holding hands over the top of the table. Terri could feel the depth of Chris's love in his hands and in his deep blue eyes.

The first question Terri asked Chris was, "How bad is it here?" Chris shrugged his shoulders and said, "Well, it's definitely not home. At the same time, it's not nearly as bad as I thought it would be. It beats the hell out of the holding cell in Bellevue."

Chris said, "I am lucky in one way. My cellmate is an old codger named Ben Rogers. He has been around the block a time or two. When I first got here, it was totally devastating, and it depressed me beyond belief. But then Ben sat me down and explained the facts of prison life to me. I cannot say I like being in here. But after I talked with Ben Rogers, I am able to deal with it."

Chris told Terri and Tatiana, "There's the fact to be able to make it in prison life, I have to learn how to adjust to it. Prison certainly will not adjust to my specifications. Ben got me interested in using my education to help young convicts. Even at this time, I am helping some young men studying for their GED. Ben Rogers is an eccentric old fart. He claims when he was young, he was hell on wheels with a furry tail. Ben says when he was back in the old days, he robbed banks and chased the ladies. Ben maintains in those days when people saw him coming, they better get the hell out of his path. But old age and sore bones have mellowed him out."

Terri excitedly started telling Chris what had happened at the Felix Wells Investment Firm. She told him how Tatiana and her have forced the issue by going into Russ's and Marvin's homes. Terri told him how Russ and Marvin had fled with over $200 million of the firm's money. Then she said, "We are going to start tracking bus and airline flights. We are planning to track these hoodlums down, and when we do, we will bring them back."

At this point, Chris held up his hand, saying, "Whoa, hold up a minute, sweetheart. Terri, I know you want to get me out of prison; however, when I do get out, I would like to be able to see you all in one piece. For now before you get too involved, remember you are going to have our baby pretty soon. Yes, you can start checking records for the bus, train, and airlines for now. It would be wonderful if you could find out where Russ and Marvin went. You can probably do this as you are the smartest person I know. From past experience, you are a bloodhound when you get started on something. You are also like a bulldog because once you get your teeth into something, you won't let go.

"But please, Terri, for now just try to find the paper trail. Don't do anything else for a while. If you try to find Russ and Marvin and catch them, at least wait until the baby is one year old. If Tatiana's is planning to help you, which I am sure she will, I would like for both of you to enroll in a self-defense course. Just in case you need to kick Russ and Marvin's butts."

Chris said, "Now I have a nice surprise for you. I told you I had heard the prison allows conjugal visits. We both thought these visits would just be for a couple of hours. Since then, I have found out they allow a full two days every two months. Of course, that's if you remain on good behavior, so now I have a reason to be very good."

Terri was so thrilled when Chris told her this she squeezed his hand so hard he flinched. She told Chris, "It is almost time to leave, but at least we are leaving on a good note." Chris looked at Tatiana and said, "Thank you for taking care of Terri, please continue to do so." Tatiana answered, "Of course I will. I love both of you for you are my two favorite people." Chris and Terri were allowed to have one short kiss and a hug before the girls left. As Tatiana and Terri walked back to the car, her spirit was free and soaring once more.

Chapter 33

On the way back to Bellevue, Tatiana and Terri decided to start working different shifts once the baby was born. This way, one of them would always be there for the baby, until Terri could find a reliable babysitter. When the girls went back to work, they started checking bookings for flights, buses, and trains in earnest.

Tatiana decided to check the bookings from this time forward in case they were hiding somewhere in the area. Also back to the time from just before Russ Jacobson and Marvin Mueller disappeared. Terri was sure the culprits were no longer in the country, but of course, she couldn't be positive. Right now, she was just searching for clues. "Russ and Marvin, you don't know it yet, but I'm about to become your worst nightmare," Terri said.

Well, this is the day of reckoning, because the baby is due, and Terri's mother flew into Seattle yesterday. Today, her mother and Tatiana took Terri to the hospital because she started having contractions. The nurses put her in a wheelchair and rolled her to a bed (as if she couldn't have walked there). The doctor kept checking on Terri. Finally, the doctor told her, "Mrs. Sutton, it looks like it's time for us to get to work."

The doctor kept telling Terri, "Push, push," as if she wasn't pushing hard enough. At the time, she would've liked to have pushed his face in. Having a baby is not Terri's idea of the most fun thing in the world. She could feel little beads of preparation on her forehead, and she wished Chris was here to hold her hand. However, Terri was thankful Tatiana and her mom were there for that.

Suddenly, Terri heard a loud cry. Her baby had been born, and boy, did it have a good set of lungs. The baby was determined to let the world hear about his frustration. Suddenly, Terri's thoughts changed too. She has the very best doctor in the whole wide world. A nurse cleaned the baby, then the doctor handed it to her, saying, "Congratulations. You have a beautiful, healthy baby boy. He is twenty-one inches long and weighs eight pounds, six ounces."

Terri wrapped the baby in her arms and loved him. She checked him out from head to toe. It was amazing that she had given life to this tiny man. Of course, her mom and Tatiana crowded around to admire him. Her mom said, "Terri, the baby is the spitting image of Chris when he was born."

Tatiana and Terri agreed except for two things. The baby had Terri's dark hair and green eyes. A nurse came up and asked, "What his name would be for the birth certificate." Terri proudly told her, "His name is Gavin Christopher Sutton." A name for which she was going to make sure he was proud of. Because she had every intention of clearing his daddy's name, and she didn't care how long it took to clear it.

Terri got a chuckle out of how Gavin's face would follow hers as she talked and sang to him. She thinks Gavin must have recognized her voice because she had always talked to him and sang to him while she was pregnant. She couldn't believe the expressions Gavin would make when he screwed up his face and got ready to cry. She was ahead of the thought and fed him.

The hospitals don't keep a person very long after a normal delivery these days. Terri was home the same evening. As soon as she got home, she put Gavin in the bassinet. Then Terri called Chris at the prison. She said, "Guess what, honey? You are the proud father of Gavin Christopher Sutton. And you know what, Chris? Your son looks just like you." Chris wanted to hear every last detail, so Terri wound up telling him everything again and again. She promised Chris, "I will bring Gavin up to see you as soon as possible."

Terri had just finished the phone call to Chris when she received another call from Lynn Anderson. Lynn asked, "Would be all right if I could come over, and would be all right to bring along some company?" Terri told her, "Go ahead." When Lynn arrived, she had Rodney Crowder and Tony Lindsay with her. They all gave Terri a hug and then had to take a look at little Gavin. Then they asked if they could sit down with Terri and have a talk.

Terri's mom fixed them a large pot of coffee. Then Lynn Anderson asked Terri, "Why didn't you ever stop by the office to see us? We were worried about you." Terri told her, "I did stop at the office, and Russ stopped me at the door. He told me I was not welcome at the Felix Wells Investment Firm and to never come back." Lynn said, "Why, the dirty little piece of crap. You should've seen the last morning he was at the firm. Russ and Marvin were both bustling around just getting in each other's way. They kept looking over their shoulders at the door. I had no idea what was wrong, but I have never seen anyone look so scared in my life."

Tatiana and Terri looked at each other then burst out laughing. They gave each other high fives, yelling, "It worked." The rest of the group all looked at the girls like, "What in heaven's name is going on?" Tatiana told them what they had done and how they had burglarized Russ's and Marvin's homes. Terri said, "I think the bastards figured out someone had figured out what they had done. Then Russ and Marvin went back to the firm and stole the money."

Lynn said, "Terri, I was on the computer all day long when Russ and Marvin disappeared. After both of them had left, all of a sudden within a period of three hours, all of our accounts were liquidated and turned into cash in the investment firm's bank account. No sooner than all of the accounts were in the bank when the money just disappeared. I called the bank, but it had already been electronically transferred. I was able to trace it to the Cayman Islands, and from there, it was dispersed in many directions."

Rodney Crowder spoke up, saying, "Terri, we all know Chris was framed. We just don't have any idea as to how it was done. We are all positive it has something to do with the money disappearing. However, we were not able to convince the police. We thought if we all got together, somehow we might be able to figure out what happened. I do know for every question, there has to be an answer."

Rodney said, "I believe there are two ways to solve the answer to the problem. One is to follow the money trail and see where it went. The other is to find out where Russ Jacobson and Marvin Mueller have disappeared. As far as the money trail goes, it was first sent to the Cayman Islands; and from there, I am sure it was split and sent to several different offshore banks. Offshore banks are very slick, and will never give up the names of their depositors. I think the only hope of getting anything from them is slim to none.

"One idea I had was to make deposits in several of different offshore banks in person. Maybe if you had a smooth line of talk, plus maybe you could meet a disgruntled employee at that specific bank, maybe, and I do mean maybe, you might be able to get some employee to talk. However, that's a shot in the dark."

Tony Lindsay spoke of one day when Marvin Mueller happened to drop an airline ticket. Tony said, "I picked it up and handed it back to him. Marvin acted kind of huffy like it wasn't any of my business. It wasn't, but I was just being polite. Anyway, I saw the ticket was to Costa Rica and had someone else's name on it. I don't remember what the name was. Of course, the ticket could have been for someone else. But again, there's a possibility Marvin Mueller has a passport in another name. Even if they fled to Costa Rica, there's no guarantee they are still there."

Terri said, "But at least, it's a starting point, and every journey begins with the first step, so they say. Costa Rica could well be our first step. But how long the journey will be afterward is hard to say. I sincerely hope it's not too long. As for Marvin Mueller, he's not very hard to describe. If anyone at all who has ever seen Marvin, he/she will surely remember him."

Now it was Lynn Anderson's turn to speak up. She said, "Well, descriptions of a person are one thing, pictures are another. I was always turned off by those two hooligans, they always gave me the creeps. I always thought those sneaky bastards were up to something. So whenever Russ and Marvin were not aware of it, I would take pictures of them. Here are the pictures. You can pick out the best ones."

Tatiana suddenly jumped up and hugged Lynn, exclaiming, "Lynn, that's the best part of everything. Terri and I now work for Global Airlines. We will have thousands of duplicates of these pictures made. We will distribute these pictures to every pilot, stewardess, baggage handler, and anyone else who works for Global Airlines.

"We will ask anyone who sees either of them to contact us. Global is a very big airline. At the same time, it's like a close-knit family unit. When people who work for Global find out what these guys have done to a fellow employee, I'm sure they will be on the lookout for them."

Terry said, "I will wait till baby Gavin gets old enough to leave with the babysitter. If anyone spots Russ and Marvin anywhere in the world, Tatiana and I will be on the first flight out to find them, and we will take them down."

Tony Lindsay stated dryly, "You may have to call me if you find them. Because I don't think the two of you ladies would be able to get them under control by yourselves. In fact, I think both of you should sign up for a self-defense course. Just in case they spot you before you spot them." That's when Terri chimed in, "Tatiana and I are already planning on taking a self-defense course. Chris suggested it already. Ron, Tony, Lynn, I really appreciate you stopping by and what you have done. It will be about a year before I can actually do anything. In the meantime, if you find out any more information about Russ and Marvin, will you please give it to me. It will really help."

As the group were leaving, Terri thanked them again. Lynn, Rodney and Tony all said they would stay in touch. Rodney Crowder said, "I will try to keep following the money trail. But I don't think it will come to much. The United States government does not have much luck tracing drug money."

Chapter 34

The very next day, Terri and Tatiana drove to the Monroe Correctional Complex to see Chris. Terri started to get goose bumps on her as she was getting close to the prison facility. Just the looks of the concertina wire on the top of the fences and the cold gray prison walls, the guard towers all gave her the heebie-jeebies. The whole prison looked dreary and bleak.

When Terri entered the prison this time, as soon as she heard the prison gates slam behind them, Terri jumped. From the gates, they were escorted to the prison visitation room where Chris was already waiting for them. He gave Terri and Tatiana a big hug, saving the biggest hug and kiss for Gavin.

Then carefully opening the blanket, Chris looked with wonder at his newborn son. He very cautiously put his finger toward him. Gavin put his little hand out and wrapped it around Chris's finger and tried to suck on it. Chris asked the guard for permission to hold his son. The guard said, "Okay, but only for five minutes."

Chris spent his five minutes sitting at the table, hugging and kissing Gavin again and again. Then Chris said, "I can hardly believe Gavin is a part of you and me. You cannot believe what a treat it is for me to have you and Gavin here. It's much better than being around a bunch of convicts." The five minutes were up, so Chris handed Gavin back to Terri, saying, "Terri, as Ben told me, it's not as bad here as I thought it would be. Having graduated from the University of Washington has helped me tremendously. The instructors have asked if I would help assisting with a couple of educational learning classes, and I jumped at the chance.

"Helping with the classes really gives me a purpose in life. This way, I have a chance to talk to the inmates going to these classes. I told the convicts if they wanted to take the GED or sign up for any type of correspondence course, I would be glad to instruct them. Also, in one month, Terri, you will be able to spend two days with me in a trailer inside the prison. That is, if you want to, of course." Terri told him, "Chris, of course, I want to spend time with you, not only in one month, but every time we have the chance. With my job, the baby, and the distance, I can only get up here to visit you once a week. But any time we have the chance to spend forty-eight hours together, I will be there."

The next week, Tatiana and Terri signed up for a self-defense course. The girls would both take the course at the same time while Terri's mom was still here. After her mother left, they would be working different shifts. When the time came, Tatiana and Terri would have to take the self-defense course at different times.

The first day of the self-defense course was just verbal instructions. The instructor told the class, "Anything can be used as a weapon—hands, fists, fingers, feet, head, and knees. If you need more, just look around you for weapons are everywhere. For instance, a sock filled with sand, rocks, or gravel makes a good equalizer. The heavy cup you are drinking from, a hot coffee, or tea in the face makes your attacker stop for a moment. Then use the coffee cup itself alongside the temple, not on the head for the skull is too hard to do much damage.

"Remember, you don't ever use these techniques for fun. If you have to use them, the person facing you will not be a friend. Also, a well-placed knee to the groin has changed many a person's mind. The belt is a good weapon especially if it has a large buckle, or a five-foot section of garden hose will work wonders. Bricks, rocks, lamps, your purse, all of these will work. Also, with a phone, you can hit someone with it. Most people don't think of all the options, which are in plain sight right in front of them. The object is to put them out of commission before they have a chance to harm you."

The instructor continued, "This is not your average self-defense class. We use a combination of several different fighting techniques. We teach you to use anything from karate and tae kwon do to judo to street fighting. We have developed a technique designed to utterly demoralize your attacker. If you are attacked, go on the offensive right away. Go into the attack mode. Turn, stomp your feet, yell hai this alone will startle them and give you a second to plan your attack."

He said, "Have you ever heard the adage, 'Always wrestle a boxer or box a wrestler'? This is very true. We teach you to come up with the unexpected, not the routine." Thus, they started a schedule Tatiana and Terri would maintain for a long, long time. It involved work, the baby, and the self-defense courses. As time went on, the girls became experts at self-defense. One day, the instructor told Tatiana and Terri they were by far the best students he had ever had. They told the instructor, "We have to be. We have a motive." Instead of quitting the course like most everyone else, the Terri and Tatiana just worked at it harder.

Terri sent pictures of Russ Jacobson and Marvin Mueller to everyone who worked for Global Airlines. She offered a reward of $1,000. This would apply to anyone who gave them information which would lead to the capture of the two men.

Terri contacted the Monroe Correctional Complex applying for her first forty-eight-hour visitation with Chris. While she was at it, Terri sent money to the prison phone plan. This way, Chris would be able to call her direct instead of having to make a collect call. Everyone whom Terri dealt with at the prison turned out to be extremely courteous. The prison encouraged family participation. The prison felt the more families who were involved with the programs, the less chance that inmates would go back to their old ways when they were released. Plus, the inmates wouldn't cause as many problems while they were still in prison.

There were many rules for anyone visiting the prison, but to Terri, they all seem logical. Everyone had to dress respectably. There could be no holes in the clothing, no tattered jeans, and shirts and blouses had to be buttoned. If someone brought a baby, they were allowed to bring one diaper for every hour they planned on being there.

A person could wear jewelry but not something which would conceal contraband. In the visitation room, there were vending machines. There visitors were able to buy their loved ones soda, candy, and other goodies. The good Lord knows the inmates didn't have money to buy it for themselves.

There was no smoking allowed, which didn't bother Chris or Terri because neither one of them smoked. However, it was a shock to the system for new inmates who were heavy smokers. It probably drove them bonkers at first. One wonders how many of them started back to smoking when they got out of prison.

Terri counted the days and hours until at last the big day came. She was at the prison early as she didn't want to miss one second of time alone with Chris. Even though she was excited, she managed somehow to obey the speed limit. Terri did not have time for a ticket right now.

Terri carefully parked in the designated parking area. It is funny how you lose track of things when you are excited. She took Gavin out of his car seat and started to head in. Thirty feet later, Terri had to go back and get his diaper bag. This time, she even remembered to lock the car.

Terri took a few deep breaths to calm herself down. It worked. She finally had her head on straight. Then she walked into the prison. They ran the diaper bag and her purse through the X-ray machine. Next, she walked through the metal detector with Gavin. Terri had done it. They were in.

The guard handed everything back to Terri, then another guard took mom and baby to the trailer where Chris was waiting for them. Terri laid Gavin down carefully in a bassinet, then Chris and Terri just fell into each other's arms. Just about this time, Gavin decided enough was enough and started screaming. Terri had to sit down and let him suckle until he calmed down.

When Terri had finished feeding Gavin, she handed him to Chris. Terri told Gavin, "This is your daddy." Gavin promptly put his little hands on Chris's nose. Chris gazed lovingly at his son. Gavin stared back at him and then smiled. Chris commented, "It look looks like Gavin has grown quite a bit in the short time since I've seen him last." Terri told Chris, "The doctor said he was in the ninety-eighth percentile group for his height."

After Gavin went to sleep, all Chris and Terri could do was hold hands and stare with love in their eyes at each other. Suddenly, Chris cleared his throat and then said, "Terri, if you want me to, I will let you divorce me so you can have a life." Terri took Gavin and placed him in the bassinet. Then she went and sat on Chris's lap, running her fingers through his hair and kissed him. Terri said "Sweetheart, I have waited all for my life for you. What's another twenty years. Anyway, somehow I'm going to prove your innocence for all of the world to see. I will prove your innocence even if it takes me every minute of those twenty years."

Terri told Chris, "There is only one man in the world for me, and you are it, Chris Sutton. If you had gotten killed instead of being sent to prison, I would have never looked at another man. We are in this prison together, so be on good behavior while you are in here. That way, you may be able to get out early. Gavin and I need you, and we will be waiting for you no matter how long it takes."

Chris put his arms round Terri, hugging her and began kissing her passionately. He whispered in her ear, "I was hoping you would say something like that. I don't know what I would do without your support and your love. You and Gavin are the whole world to me."

Chris and Terri spent hours just holding each other and talking. When Gavin was awake, both of them would take turns holding him. They both had to laugh at some of the facial expressions, which Gavin would make. She showed Chris how to change him. Chris was very proud to be able to do this. It made him feel like a father.

The young couple talked about some of Terri's plans and things she had done. Chris had a good laugh when she told him what they had done to Russ and Marvin. Chris was very intrigued about the self-defense course. He had Terri show him some of the things Tatiana and she had been taught. Terri told Chris the instructor thought Tatiana and she were starting to excel at self-defense. Of course, the girls have a reason. If they ever catch up with Russ and Marvin, Terri and Tatiana may have to use everything they have been taught.

Chris said, "Terri, I want you to be very careful and always take Tatiana with you when you follow up on any of those leads. Russ and Marvin are not going to want to be caught. I am sure those two hooligans will always be on guard. I would never forgive myself if something was to happen to you." Terri promised Chris she would be very careful both for his sake and for Gavin's. "Besides, I won't be able to start anything until Gavin is old enough to leave with the babysitter. I think that will be in about a year. Even then, I won't be able to leave Gavin for more than four or five days at a time at first."

Oh, it was just so fantastic to be able to hold Chris and to make love to him again. Terri had to laugh out loud when Gavin started to cry at two o'clock in the morning. Chris got excited and jumped out of bed. He picked up Gavin cradling him in his arms and rocked him back and forth. He said, "Terri, what's the matter with Gavin? He won't stop crying." She took Gavin from Chris, saying, "He is just hungry and wants to be fed." With that, she put Gavin on her breast, and he stopped crying immediately.

Chris and Terri enjoyed being together as a family at last even if it is just for a short time. The two of them were able to do what every normal family did. The couple ate, slept, watched TV, and made love. The only thing Terri could not do was leave the prison and take Chris home with her. Chris and Terri were very sorry when the forty-eight hours was ending, but they were already looking forward to the next time. At the very least, it had given them the feeling of being a family again.

Chapter 35

The following year passed quickly. Gavin started crawling. He started to get teeth and was a little fussy at the time but not bad. But at the same time, Terri was very careful when she had to put her fingers into his mouth. Gavin started to walk when he was ten months old. Terri had to put everything up; however, this did not deter him.

Terri would hear banging in the kitchen. When she went in there, she would discover her pots and pans on the floor. Gavin also had a fascination with the phone. When Chris and Terri were talking, she would put the phone to his ear, and Gavin would listen to Chris's voice and smile. He learned to say "daddy" and "mommy." Chris was overjoyed during our forty-eight-hour visitation when Gavin would say "daddy" and toddle to him.

Tatiana and Terri continued with their self-defense course. Both of them worked at it rigorously. The instructor had nothing but praise for both of them. Of course, he didn't know they would probably need to know self-defense sometime in the future. The idea of facing men in perhaps mortal combat gave the girls all they needed to stay on with the course.

Terri hadn't received any reports back from the pictures of Russ and Marvin she had sent to Global Airlines personnel around the world. Maybe the brazen thieves were remaining stationary somewhere. Terri and Tatiana decided to take five days and go to Costa Rica. The girls decided to go there because of Tony Lindsay, saying Marvin Mueller had an airline ticket to Costa Rica, which Marvin had dropped.

Terri was racking her brains trying to find a reliable babysitter. Out of the blue, she received a phone call from Lynn Anderson. Terri told Lynn what she and Tatiana had planned, then Terri asked her if she knew of anyone who would be a good babysitter for Gavin for five days. Lynn answered, "As a matter-of-fact I do. How about letting me do the babysitting?"

Lynn said, I'm not doing anything, and I would love to watch Gavin, not only this time but any time you go searching for those assholes." So now that Terri had a babysitter, all the girls had left to do was to plan for the trip. Tatiana had a good idea. She said, "Let's book a room in Costa Rica where the pilots and stewardesses all stay. Maybe if we talk to them in person, they will remember something." Terri and Tatiana decided to leave on December the fifteenth. This would be around the time of the start of the Costa Rica dry season, or what Costa Ricans call their summer.

Both of The girls packed their suitcases, making sure they included sunglasses, sandals, camera, bright colored T-shirts, blouses, shorts, and swimsuits. At the last moment, Terri remembered sunscreen, which was not needed in Seattle at this time of year. Lynn Anderson was staying at Terri's home. Terri figured it would be better for Gavin that way.

On the plane to Costa Rica, Tatiana asked the stewardess what would be the best place to meet some airline personnel. The stewardess told her, "You should go to the bar in the hotel where you will be staying. Everyone from all of the airlines stayed at that hotel. Inevitably, everyone all stopped at the bar every evening. Even the people who don't drink alcohol come to the bar. Many of them came just to talk and exchange stories."

Tatiana and Terri arrived at the Juan Santamaria International Airport in San Jose, Costa Rica, at 2:30 p.m. The girls took a taxi straight to our hotel and checked in. After taking their luggage to their room, Terri and Tatiana went outside to check things out. When Tatiana and Terri had left Seattle, it was raining. Here in San Jose, Costa Rica, it was a balmy eighty-seven degrees Fahrenheit with a slight breeze.

Tatiana and Terri were pleasantly surprised at the surroundings, for San Jose was a beautiful and very modern city. Everyone the girls passed would nod to them and smile. Most of the Costa Ricans they saw looked to be of European heritage and spoke mainly Spanish. As Tatiana and Terri were walking along the sidewalk, they did meet some Afro Costa Ricans who spoke a type of Creole English.

After wandering around for an hour, they went back to the restaurant at their hotel and ordered lunch. Both of them wanted coffee with their meal. No sooner than each of them had taken one sip when both said, "Wow." Tatiana called the waiter over and told him, "This is a great tasting coffee." The waiter replied, "Yes, everyone comments on it. This coffee is called Costa Rica Tarrazu, one of the finest Arabica coffee beans in the world." With that, the waiter refilled our cups.

As they were enjoying their meal, a couple of airline pilots walked up to the table and asked if they could join us. Tatiana waved them to the extra chairs. After introducing themselves to the girls, the pilots asked them if they happened to be airline stewardesses." The man said, "The only reason why we are asking is because we haven't seen you here before." Terri told them, "No, we are not airline stewardess although we do work for Global Airlines. We happened to be here for both sightseeing and an errand."

The airline pilots told us, "Our names are Joe and Fred, and we have been flying into San Jose for five years." Fred and Joe both loved Costa Rica and had both purchased retirement homes there. Fred commented that many Americans had retirement or vacation homes in Costa Rica. Next, both Fred and Joe had took out their wallets to show us pictures of their wives and children. Terri took out her pictures of Chris and Gavin to show them. The pilots were shocked to see the picture of Chris in his prison uniform.

Tatiana and Terri explained the situation, ending up by telling the men why both of them were in Costa Rica. Terri said, "I realize it's been over a year since these crooks disappeared. But I was hoping someone from the airlines might recognize Russ's and Marvin's pictures. I also thought someone might have other information including hopefully where Russ and Marvin have disappeared to."

Joe asked, "Can I see their pictures?" So Terri pulled them out of her purse. She told Joe, "This picture is of Russ Jacobson, the other one is of Marvin Mueller." Joe and Fred stared at the pictures for what seemed like a long time. Fred finally asked, "Can I borrow the pictures for five minutes?" Terri told him, "Keep the pictures. I have hundreds of them." She also gave pictures to Joe, asking, "Maybe you can show the pictures around."

Fred left, saying, "I will be right back." Meanwhile, Joe stated Russ and Marvin had flown into San Jose on their plane the previous year. The men were on a flight from Los Angeles and stayed at this very hotel for seven days. Joe and Fred had actually had a drink with Russ and Marvin at the bar.

Fred returned to the table a few minutes later, saying, "It's nice to know all of the hotel staff. I found out Russ Jacobson is now going under the name Tom Jackson. Marvin Mueller's alias is Hank Devlin. They also both have passports under those names. The men only stayed at this hotel for seven days, and no one seems to know where the men have gone from here. The best idea I have for you ladies is to come to the bar tonight. Have one hundred or so of these pictures with you. Because all of the flight crews from all of the airlines which fly to Costa Rica will be there."

At 8:00 p.m. local time, Tatiana and Terri went to the hotel bar and lounge. It was packed with airline personnel, many still wearing their uniforms. Fred went to the microphone at the bar and called for attention. Then he called Terri up to the microphone, saying, "This little lady needs your help. Her husband of only two years has been framed for murder and was sent to prison. The culprits who did this then absconded with an enormous amount of money. They were right here in San Jose, Costa Rica, just a little over a year ago, after which they disappeared."

Fred said, "Joe and I met them in this lounge a year ago. I have already found out the men are using different names than their own. Where the men have gone from here is what we would like to find out. If either of these guys ever fly on one of your planes, whether it is now or years from now, please contact Terri Sutton.

"Now Terri and her friend Tatiana have pictures of the men who did this which they will now hand out. The pictures have their names and aliases and also how Terri can be reached. Terri really loves her husband and they have a young son. Any way you can help will be greatly appreciated."

Tatiana and Terri were busy handing out photographs. Many of the airline personnel had actually seen Russ and Marvin there in Costa Rica. But no one knew where the men had gone from there. Everyone promised to notify Terri right away if they ever spotted Russ and Marvin again.

Chapter 36

The next day, Tatiana and Terri decided there was nothing more to find in San Jose. The girls still had over three and a half days before they had to fly home, so Terri and Tatiana decided to do some sightseeing. Terri ended up renting a car so they could check out this beautiful country while they were still there. The girls made sure that they had plenty of film for their cameras because both of them wanted to take lots of pictures. Terri knew Chris would want to know all about Costa Rica. And as they say a picture is worth a thousand words.

Tatiana and Terri were totally impressed with Costa Rica. Tatiana couldn't believe how the flowers are so perfect they seemed almost unreal. The flowers appeared so vibrant Terri had to go up again and again to look at different groups of them. She just could not believe the vivid hues, brilliant reds, oranges, yellows, and purple. She just couldn't get enough of inhaling their lovely fragrances.

Tatiana and Terri kept taking pictures of everything so Terri would be able to show them to Chris. She really liked the picture of the beautiful church which had a stark black volcano looming in the background. Both also enjoyed visiting with the Costa Rican people who all seemed highly educated and also were very friendly.

On the first day of the journey, Terri and Tatiana went to a coffee plantation where they toured the grounds. There the girls found out coffee beans actually thrive on higher ground in mountainous areas. The trees are kept short by the growers on purpose so the beans can be easily picked. Coffee beans can only be grown on or near the equator. Coffee beans need hot temperatures and lots of rain. The beans are picked at the farms, which are family owned rather than being owned by brokers. Then brokers from different coffee makers will come to bid on them. After Tatiana and Terri had finished the tour, they were given a savory cup of coffee brewed from freshly roasted coffee beans.

Next, Terri drove to a butterfly garden where they saw thousands of brilliantly colored butterflies. Tatiana and Terri were amazed not only at the variety of butterflies but also their colors. A guide told them depending on the species, a butterfly can live anywhere from one month to a year. Some butterflies including the monarch make migrations of up to two thousand five hundred miles. Some butterflies have what looks like eyes on their wings to deter enemies. The butterflies feed mostly on nectar from flowers and sip water from the flowers' leaves.

As it was getting late, the girls found a hotel room and had dinner, then went outside by the pool to sit in chaise lounges. It was totally relaxing as both sat watching darkness starting to close in on them. The sunset seemed to explode in a vision of tremendous colors. Then the night descended around them. This gave them a view of the quarter moon coming up on the horizon. The stars seemed like they were magically appearing one by one, sparkling and twinkling in the sky overhead. Terri could make out all the constellations with a clarity she had not seen since leaving North Dakota.

In the morning after finishing breakfast, Tatiana and Terri set out for Tortagero Park. Upon arriving, they found out there was a canal cruise, which both of them immediately signed up for, but it wasn't leaving until 2:00 p.m. Tatiana and Terri spent their time walking through the rainforest where there was a symphony of sound.

There were the calls of hundreds of birds and the chattering howls of the monkeys. One bold, impudent little monkey ran up and stole a banana right out of Tatiana's hand. After grabbing the banana, he had the audacity to run up a tree. The little rascal sat on a branch eating the banana, all the while staring at them defiantly. The girls watched the little monkey for a while finally bursting out into laughter. The monkey acted like he was insulted. He gave them a final disgusted look and left like he was in a huff.

Having bought a pamphlet, which showed pictures of many of the birds and animals in the park, Terri and Tatiana tried their best to try and identify some of them, but it was pretty hard. There are over three hundred species of birds in Tortagero Park. So the two concentrated on the ones which seems more familiar. Terri was surprised to see kingfishers as they are very common in North Dakota.

Tatiana and Terri spotted several toucans. Terri just loved looking at those long-billed birds. Tatiana exclaimed, "There is a green macaw parrot." There were also spotted several green iguanas. Finally, it was time to run to catch the cruise. They just barely made it on time. The cruise was fantastic. The boat went leisurely down the canal. Their tour guide pointed out things in both Spanish and English. One of the first things he noted was a band of Capuchin monkeys. The monkeys were dark on the bottom and cream colored on top. The tour guide stated, "Early explorers named them because they thought the monkeys looked like Capuchin friars."

Next, there were some black spider monkeys and the small South American squirrel monkey. The South American squirrel monkey has orange on the back and a white with a black face. The South American squirrel monkey is an endangered species, probably because of deforestation.

When the guide told us to come and see the American crocodile, the girls rushed to look over the side. The American crocodile is larger than most crocodiles. Some males can reach twenty feet in length, and have longer narrower snouts than African crocodiles.

Tatiana and Terri thoroughly enjoyed the time in Tortuguero Park, which is full of turtles. They were able to see all sorts of turtles. After leaving, it was with a feeling of sadness and gratitude. Sadness because they were leaving such a lovely place gratitude for the fact of having been able to see it. There was still one day left. Tatiana said, "I still want to see the Poas Volcano." After driving a little over halfway there, Terri found a hotel room for the night.

The next morning after arriving at Poas Volcano at 10:00 a.m., Terri and Tatiana were able to take a tour. Poas Volcano has two crater lakes near its summit. As you look at the huge crater near its summit, you see a vast opening with Lake Laguna Caliente, which is three hundred feet deep in the center. It is one of the most acidic lakes in the world.

Both of them enjoyed the southern crater better. It developed because of a blast which erupted around nine thousand years ago. Lake Bolos is located in this crater. It is very picturesque and is surrounded by a lush tropical rainforests. The ladies arrived back in San Jose very tired but with a lot of pictures and memories. Tatiana and Terri had both fallen in love with Costa Rica, both with the land and its people. In the morning, they woke up refreshed and ready to head back to Seattle.

Chapter 37

When they arrived home, Gavin came running, yelling, "Mommy, Mommy, Auntie Tati." Terri picked him up and hugged him. She had so missed him. Lynn Anderson said, "Gavin has been a good boy." When the TV was turned on to the local news the announcer said, "A body had been found. Authorities thought at first it was Felix Wells's body, which had been discovered. However, upon further examination, authorities found out it was a doctor who had been missing from around the same time frame."

Terri thanked Lynn and told her all about the trip. Lynn said, "I would be glad to watch Gavin again anytime you need to take off." She also said, "I think Rodney and Tony are working on some new ideas. They will let me know if something came up with anything solid."

The next weekend, Gavin and Terri went to Monroe to visit Chris at the prison. After he had finished hugging Gavin, both sat down. Terri told Chris about their trip to Costa Rica. Chris wanted to know about every detail and poured over the pictures. She told Chris about what the airline personnel said how they would keep a watch out for Russ and Marvin. She filled him in on their new aliases.

After Chris had contemplated this fact for a moment, he said, "I'm sure Russ and Marvin are hiding in a country which has no extradition treaty with the United States. It also means those two could be very dangerous. Terri, maybe you should just back off. I don't want you getting hurt. I can deal with the time I'm spending here in Monroe prison, but if anything were to ever to happen to you, I don't think I could go on."

Terri said, "Chris, listen to me, those bastards did this to you. I am going to find them eventually, no matter where they are. Believe me, I will be careful. When I find Russ and Marvin, I will get the help I need to apprehend them. After all, my darling, you wouldn't hurt a flea. You deserve to have your name cleared both for your own sake and for Gavin and me.

"Don't you see I have to do this, Chris? After all, it's at least partly my fault. If I had not gone to work for the Felix Wells Investment Firm, none of this would have happened. If I hadn't been working there, they would have had to find some other scapegoat. Russ Jacobson hated me already especially because Felix Wells was being nice to me. Russ was probably worried about his job and figured he would even the score. He might've done this anyway, and I was the last straw."

Chris finally agreed. "It wouldn't hurt if Tatiana and you kept looking. But you promise if you ever do find them, don't try to catch them by yourselves, get help." Terri promised she would.

The next month, Lynn Anderson, Rodney Crowder, Toni Lindsay, Tatiana, and Terri held another meeting. Rodney thought Terri should plan a trip to Grand Cayman Island, because that's where the money was first sent. He said, "I know it's doubtful you will find any information there. However, Grand Cayman Island is loaded to the hilt with offshore banks. This would give you the feeling of how offshore banking works."

Rodney said, "Tony and I are working on a couple of different angles right now. Another one of them is checking on phone records. We happen to have inside help with the phone company. We are trying to find any record of phone calls to Russ's and Marvin's families. There's a possibility this could pan out."

Rodney explained to us offshore banks have greater privacy and security. The offshore banks also have lower or no taxation. Some of them offer higher interest rates. United States citizens or anyone subject to United States income tax are required to report their earnings under penalty of perjury. But this doesn't prevent shady characters from ignoring this, as some of the offshore banks offer numbered or anonymous accounts.

Chris at Monroe prison. Chris feels he has made a small effort in getting young inmates to sign up for education classes. He's also tutoring some of them for their GED. It is hard enough for these young men to make it on the outside when they are released. It will be even harder for them if they don't have a high school diploma or a GED.

Chris can actually say he enjoys helping these young men and some of the older ones as well. Outside of this fact it also gives him stability, meaning, and purpose to his life in there. Chris is trying to get more convicts involved in education classes. His goal right at the moment is to get one very sullen young man to enroll. At the moment, one young convict Brian Edward is pissed off at the world. Chris is getting ready to have a talk with Brian right now. He said, "Brian, you always look like you are walking around with a chip on your shoulder. If you would like to talk about it, you will find I am a good listener."

At first, Brian was very reluctant to talk. When Chris persisted, he suddenly broke down crying. Brian said, "All my life, I have done everything possible to please my father. However, for whatever reason, it was just never good enough. So I finally rebelled, I dropped out of high school in my junior year. After that, I started running with a rough crowd.

"However, I never did anything really bad, but my father was furious. My father is a very successful businessman. One morning, while I was sleeping, I was awakened to loud noise. My own father had brought cops into my bedroom. He told the police to search my bedroom. I knew there was nothing in there; however, they still searched for drugs, and the bad thing is the police found some. I knew I had not put them there. I may have been running with a bad crowd. But I don't use drugs, and I don't sell them."

Brian said, "I think my father planted the drugs in my room. He has always acted like he hated me, possible because my grandmother on my mother's side has always sided with me. My mother passed away when I was very young. My life has been living hell ever since then. My grandmother has always said she plans on leaving everything to me, and she is very wealthy.

"When it was time to go to court both the judge and prosecutor wanted to let me go with a warning. But my father insisted I was bad to the core. He asked that I be put in prison to teach me a lesson. The judge finally agreed and sentenced me to one year and one day in the Monroe Correctional Complex. However, the judge also stated once the sentence had been served everything must be stricken from the record. My father was furious, and he has never come to see me, but my grandmother comes to see me every week."

Chris told Brian, "I am truly sorry to hear this. I know what is like to be sent to prison for a crime you did not commit. But at least you will get out long before I do." Chris then told him his own story. Brian listened with his mouth open. When Chris was finished, Brian asked him, "How could you stand being cooped up in prison for something that you didn't commit?"

Chris told him, "It is because the most beautiful woman in the world has faith in me and is standing by me." He told Brian, "Terri will be there for me when I get out of prison. The second reason I can stand to be in prison is to be able to help young guys like you to somehow straighten out their lives. I sincerely hope you will let me help you."

Having told Brian his story, Chris added, "I think the best and only way to get even with your father is become a better man than he is. Grab yourself by the bootstraps and turn your life around. Become a better and more successful man than your father ever thought of being. I would also advise you to live with your grandmother when you get out.

"Let me help you to get your GED, then the next thing I would recommend is you finish college after you get out of prison. If your grandmother is as wealthy as you say she is, then I am sure she would be glad to help pay for your college. Completely ignore your father as he would just try to screw you up. Do this for yourself, not for anyone else. It will give you a chance to realize your full potential, Brian. If you do all of this, you will find life is truly worth living. You will become your own man, answering only to yourself. Or possibly sometime in the future, answering to a good woman like mine. Please, Brian, let me help you to make this the first day of the rest of your life."

Brian jumped up and gave Chris a big hug, saying, "Thank you, Chris, let's start today. You have saved my life. I was planning on hanging myself today. Instead, you have given me a brand-new lease on life. Chris, somehow, someday, I may be able to help you." So it began. Brian proved to be an apt pupil, and Chris was very impressed by him. Except for Terri, Brian proved to be the most intelligent person Chris had ever met. Chris never had to go over anything with him more than once. It didn't take long for Brian to reach his goal. He took and passed his GED.

But Brian didn't want to stop there. Chris started him on some college correspondence courses. Brian told Chris he had decided his ultimate goal in life was to become a lawyer. Thank God for the judge who was wise enough to have everything stricken from Brian's record.

Chris asked Brian, "Could you arrange a meeting for me with your grandmother." Sometime later, Chris met with her at the visitor center. Brian's grandmother said, "Brian had told me many good things about you." In return, Chris told her how much Brian had changed. Brian is determined to become an attorney, not for the sake of making money, but for serving justice for the poor and illiterate. Brian wanted to help the underdog. When he was positive someone was innocent, he would fight for their rights whether they could pay are not.

Chris told Brian's grandmother, "What Brian needs from you right now is financial help for Brian so he can go to college. I know Brian will make you proud. Also, it would help if you could keep him away from his father. I have never met the man, but he sounds like a real scumbag." Brian's grandmother grabbed my hand and thanked me. She said, "Don't worry, Brian will get all the help he needs. Once Brian gets out of prison, I will have him live with me, and I will not allow his father to come anywhere near him.

"As for my ex son-in-law, if you will excuse my expression, he is lower than rat crap. The only reason he ever married my daughter was because of my money. He knew she was an only child. He figured he would be able to get his hands on the money. However, he was such a brute and a jerk, and I'm sure it contributed to her early death. Brian's father knows now he will not ever benefit in any way from the inheritance. But he is so twisted in his mind he doesn't want his own son to get anything either. Chris, I am very thankful to you. If I can ever be of help, all you have to do is ask."

Chris was very happy for Brian when he was released from Monroe prison later in the year. Brian comes to visit Chris quite often and calls him regularly. Brian entered college as soon as he got out of prison and plans on going year round until he finishes.

Chapter 38

Two months after Tatiana and Terri got back from Costa Rica, they were off to the Grand Cayman Island. The girls landed at Owen Roberts International Airport. When Terri registered at the hotel where they were staying in, Terri showed the clerks pictures of Russ Jacobson and Marvin Mueller, alias Tom and Hank. She told everyone the men were her brothers-in-law.

To make it seem believable, Terri had made up a story the family had not seen them for quite some time. Russ and Marvin didn't realize they had inherited a substantial sum. No one at the hotel or any of the bars Terri and Tatiana went to recognized them. Maybe Russ and Marvin were never in the Grand Cayman Islands, or they may have transferred the money over the Internet.

Next, Terri went to the bank to which the money was first transferred to. While she was there, Terri set up a numbered account for herself, and deposited $5,000, then she asked to see the bank manager. Using the same story, which she had told at the hotel and in the bars, the manager looked at the pictures, shook his head no. However, Terri thought she saw a fleeting flash of recognition on his face. All of the tellers at the bank said they did not recognize Russ or Marvin either.

Terri went to another bank to open another numbered account. It may be a just wishful thinking on her part, but she had an idea. Terri plans on opening accounts in several offshore banks because there is always the slim chance she can get the information about the stolen money. If this should happen, maybe she would have a chance of obtaining it and then a way of hiding it for the investors from whom it was stolen.

Chris and Terri are not wealthy by any means, but with the money coming in from the farm and a very substantial amount they had received from the insurance settlement, they are not hurting either. So with this, Terri is able to afford to search for Russ and Marvin and open a few numbered offshore bank accounts.

Having finished what they came to the place for, Tatiana and Terri set off to explore Grand Cayman Island. It is the largest of the three Cayman Islands. Grand Cayman encompasses seventy square miles and the capital Georgetown. There are fifty-five thousand permanent residents on Grand Cayman Island. What is amazing is the fact there are more businesses registered on Grand Cayman Island than there are people.

The weather is fairly hot, but you will find the residents very friendly. Blue iguanas are everywhere, but don't ever hurt or kill one or even accidentally run over one with your car. The blue iguanas are protected by the law. Anyone injuring one of them will soon have a date with police.

One of the first things Tatiana and Terri decided to do was go to see the turtle farm in the West Bay district. The turtle farm has several huge round opened tanks. Inside each of these tanks contain green sea turtles, which they raise. There are hundreds of green sea turtles in each tank. Each tank will hold turtles only of a certain age. Tatiana and Terri got to hold one which was ten months old. It was approximately the size of a very large dinner plate. The adult turtles are very huge almost as large as the Galapagos turtles.

The majority of the green sea turtles are raised for meat. You will find it on the menu of most Grand Cayman restaurants. However, the turtle farm also releases quite a few of the turtles to the wild. You can find them throughout the Caribbean. Before the girls left, they bought ceramic turtles from the souvenir shop. Terri will take one to give to Chris on her next visit with him.

Terri and Tatiana also stopped in "hell," a souvenir activity from the past. It too had a souvenir shop of course. Behind the shop was an area which showed volcanic activity. There was jagged lava all over the place. It looked like what Teri imagined the moon would look like or maybe better yet hell itself.

The girls still had time to go to Seven Mile Beach, known for its snorkeling and scuba diving. Tatiana and Terri preferred to sit on a beach blanket laid out on the soft, warm sand. It was wonderful just listening to the waves washing up on the beach. When both of them got tired of this, they walked along the beach gathering up seashells.

Grand Cayman Island was a very warm and friendly place and it was with a touch of sadness they left for the airport. One of Terri's greatest hopes is someday Chris will be able to walk along the beach in Grand Cayman Island with her.

After that, it was back to Seattle and the daily grind and the day-to-day work at Sea-Tac airport. Terri worked the counter every chance she had. She was hoping against hope someday she would be able to catch a glimpse of those scoundrels. As unlikely as it seems because Seattle is probably the last place Russ and Marvin would be likely to be seen. But perhaps business or family would bring them back.

Terri always took Gavin with her every chance she had when she went to see Chris. Oh, how Terri looked forward to those forty-eight hours with Chris every two months. It was the only time she ever felt truly alive. Terri yearned to be with her darling constantly. It seemed like Chris was the one who was always cheering her up instead of the other way around.

By the time Gavin was four years old, Terri started taking him to baseball games. The little rascal really enjoyed going to these outings. But Terri didn't realize how much until the one time she went to visit Chris, and Gavin suddenly told his daddy, "Guess what? When I get big, I'm going to be a baseball player." Chris said, "That's wonderful, son. Can I come and watch?" Gavin replied, "Yes, if you have tickets."

As Gavin was getting older and would soon be entering kindergarten, Terri started thinking of a more permanent place than the apartment. She talked to Chris about the idea of buying a house. Chris was all for the idea. Terri decided she still wanted to stay in Bellevue because it has some of the best schools in the state of Washington.

When Terri spoke to Tatiana about buying a house, Tatiana told her about a place which was two doors down from her mother's house on South 108th Street. Terri decided to take a look at it. It was a beautiful four-bedroom with a nice lawn with a fenced backyard. The home was in immaculate shape and belonged to a young man from Newark, New Jersey. He had inherited it when his mother had recently passed away. The owner was willing to sell the house cheap as he wanted to get back to his home and family on the East Coast.

Terri talked to her bank and was able to get a loan, Tatiana, Terri, and Gavin moved in forty-five days later. Although the house was in fantastic shape, Terri and Tatiana repainted the whole interior because the colors didn't happen to agree with Terri. When they were finished painting, one of the first things Terri did was put up a swing set for Gavin in the backyard.

A real plus to moving here was to find Tatiana's mother would love to babysit Gavin. Flash the Rottweiler and Gavin became instant buddies. To Terri's delight, Gavin started calling Mrs. Brown, Grandma Brown. If anything, she spoiled the child worse than Terri did.

Tatiana and Terri still worked every day at their self-defense course. The instructor asked the girls if they would like to be part-time instructors. He said it would be for just during the time they usually practiced. Terri and Tatiana agreed to do this because it will help to still keep them in shape.

This arrangement was perfect until one day, an arrogant man enrolled in the self-defense course. He was huge, and looked at Terri with contempt when the owner told him Terri would be his instructor. He snarled, saying, "What in the hell can she teach me?" However, he said those last few words flat on his back with his arm pinned behind him and Terri's foot on his neck. She could see the anger welling in his face as he got up. Terri knew he was about to try something.

Terri decided to let him have his chance; otherwise, he would always say he was unprepared the first time. This was no problem because Terri could see the anger coursing through his body. In self-defense as in anything else, anger makes you lose your sense of judgment. This didn't stop this guy. He had lost his rationalization, and he was totally angry. Although he was big enough, Terri could tell he wouldn't try anything until he thought he had an advantage.

Terri thought she would give him the chance. She turned her back on him purposely walking away. She kept her ears finely tuned. Within a second, she could hear him rushing at her. Terri waited till the last second, then whirling around, she grabbed his arm ducking as she flipped his body over the top of her. His body made a pretty large thud when he hit the floor. Even though there was a mat to fall on, Terri was a little bit afraid she had really injured him this time.

But the man got up quickly with a scowl on his face. Terri thought, "Oh boy, I'm going to have put him down again." Just as fast his scowl turned into a huge grin. He walked up to Terri and said, "That's what I'm talking about. You are the instructor I need. I will admit I had my doubts about you when I first saw you; however, you made a believer out of me. I can actually say I saw the light. Well, maybe it wasn't really light. I think maybe it was stars that I was seeing."

Terri had no more trouble with him from that moment on. He turned out to be a good student and learned rapidly. He told Terri later he had been hired as a bouncer at a very tough bar. He said his size didn't intimidate some of the customers. He said, "Many of the customers were even bigger than I am. After I started the self-defense course, they have finally started to show some respect."

Chapter 39

Time was rolling by so fast, and Terri had not yet accomplished anything to help Chris. To make matters worse, a reporter from a scandal magazine brought up the fifth year anniversary of Chris's trial. The reporter said in the article Chris should have received the death sentence. Evidently, the reporter must have thought he needed to do a follow-up for his article. The reporter started following Terri around trying to get her to talk to him. This all ended the day he was walking beside her down a flight of stairs. He kept holding a microphone by Terri's face trying to get her to say something. Terri doesn't know exactly what happened; just to be nice, let's say he tripped.

Regardless, Terri sure must have felt terrible seeing him tumbling down the steps. He lay unconscious at the bottom until an ambulance took him to the hospital where he remained for three months. Somehow in the confusion of the moment, his microphone and recorder disappeared. Terri is sure what she felt about that too. One thing she didn't feel bad about was the reporter never bothered her again.

Terri enrolled Gavin in kindergarten. He was so excited to be going to school and finding lots of new friends. However, this brought up a small problem. One day, he asked his mommy why his daddy couldn't be home with them. All of his little friends had daddies who were home with them. Terri explained to Gavin, "Some men I work with had done a very bad thing, and the bad men had fixed it so Daddy would get the blame. It is just like the time when little Joe pushed Bobby on the ground. You were just standing there. However, Joe told the teacher you did it so you got the blame." After telling him this, Gavin understood and was okay with Terri's explanation. She also told Gavin when he got old enough, she would tell him the whole story. Terri knew Gavin was tall for his age, but when she saw him playing with his friends, she realized he was almost a head taller. Anyways, this isn't always for the best as it makes other parents think Gavin is older than he is.

Grandma Brown was a real jewel and a lifesaver. She would watch Gavin after he got home from school. She would always give him some healthy snacks and make sure he did his homework the first thing after he got home from school. When Gavin was finished Grandma Brown would play games with him, or they would watch television.

Gavin came up to Terri one day, saying, "Mom, you know what Grandma Brown is a real honey cake." Mrs. Brown was delighted when Terri told her that. She said, "Terri, Gavin is one very special boy, and I love him to pieces. He is very polite and very intelligent. I know he will go far. I just love children. None of my children have given me any grandchildren as they are too busy with their careers. But hopefully one of these days, they will all settle down and get married."

The next time Terri had her forty-eight-hour visit with Chris, they had an awesome time. This was the only time they had family time together. Terri knows forty-eight hours don't seem like much, but it sure beats the hell out of nothing. Chris and Terri really appreciated the fact Monroe prison allows this time for them. At first, the three of them would watch television while they played board games. But when it got close to Gavin's bedtime, Chris would have Gavin read a story to him. After Gavin was finished, Chris would read Gavin a story. Gavin usually would fall asleep right in the middle of the story. Chris would then pick Gavin up and put him to bed. Chris considered this to be a great privilege.

After Gavin was tucked in bed, Terri told Chris, "Now it is my turn to get the attention." She grabbed his head, kissing him hungrily. She reached down and felt the front of his trousers, saying, "Chris, are you glad to see me, or is that just a banana in your pants." Leading me into the bedroom, Chris responded, "I think it will be better if I just show you."

Afterward as they lay in each other's arms, Terri looked deep into Chris's eyes. She told him, "Chris, I feel so guilty. You have been in prison for over five years now. No matter how hard I have tried, I have not even started to find Russ or Marvin. Starting next summer, I plan to have Gavin spend a month with my parents in North Dakota every year. During that time, Tatiana and I will search for them, if it's okay with you.

"I have already talked to my mom and dad, and they love the idea of Gavin spending a month with them. While he is gone, I will try to be a big-time detective. I feel like God gave me a brain for a reason. Now I am going to try to use it. I will use it both by searching the Internet, also by flying to any country we have the slightest suspicion where Russ and Marvin will be.

"I don't think Russ and Marvin would dare come back to the United States. If they did, it would just be for very short periods of time. Also, the money which was taken from the Felix Wells Investment Firm had to have gone somewhere. Finding it, however, might be a bit of a problem."

Chris said, "Terri, you will need to be very careful. I know you and Tatiana have become experts in the art of self-defense. I was thinking about one of the first things your instructor told you when you started the course. You told me at the time a sock filled with sand pebbles or gravel makes a good weapon. I want you to promise me from now on whenever you go searching for Russ or Marvin, you will both keep a pair of men's socks in your purse.

"You never know you might meet up with Russ and Marvin when you least expect it. So whenever you fly to someplace, even if the evidence is not that strong, I would like you to fill the socks as soon as you get the chance. Then put them back in your purse. You will never know when you might need them."

Once again, Gavin and Terri hugged and kissed Chris good-bye. Terri still yearned for the time when they will be able to take Chris home with them. Then they can once again be a family permanently. Terri had made up her mind—whatever it takes, wherever it takes her, somehow, someway, she will clear Chris's name.

Gavin was becoming quite a character was always on good behavior. He had good manners and a very pleasant personality. But Gavin loved to tease, and he was always coming up with some off-the-wall statement. For instance like the time a stranger saw him holding a Winnie the Pooh DVD. The stranger asked Gavin if he had ever watched the movie. Gavin told him he used to watch the movie every day when he was a kid.

Gavin was set to get out of school. During the middle of June, Terri had all of his bags packed. Tatiana and Terri were about to take him to her parents' farm in North Dakota. Gavin was very excited about the trip. He asked Terri all kinds of questions about the farm. Gavin wanted to know if his grandpa would teach him how to milk the cows and asked if he would be able to learn how to ride a horse.

Tatiana and Terri were unsure of where they would start. There were a couple of options which didn't look like they held very much promise. The girls were almost ready to walk out the door when the telephone rang. Terri picked up the phone, and male voice asked, "Is this Terri Sutton?" She answered, "Yes, it is." He went on to say, "Hi, my name is Richard. I'm a pilot for Global Airlines. I am not positive, but I just flew two men to Saint Maartins in the Caribbean.

Chapter 40

"These two guys happened to look like the two men in the pictures you handed out. I engaged them in conversation because I thought you might like to know their plans. The guy's said they plan on staying in Saint Maartins from now until the end of July." Terri thanked Richard for the information, then she asked Richard for his address in case she was successful. He told Terri he wasn't doing this for money then wished her good luck, and hung up.

The phone conversation made their decision for Terri she knew she and Tatiana would be going to Saint Maartins. First, Terri took Gavin to her parents' farm in North Dakota. He was so thrilled to be with Grandpa and Grandma Olson. Gavin was giving them hugs and asking them a million questions. He wanted to be shown all around the farm. Gavin was in seventh heaven, and Grandpa and Grandma just doted on him. Terri realized leaving would be no problem, so they hastily left.

Tatiana and Terri flew from Minot, North Dakota, to Minneapolis, Minnesota, and from there, they caught the next available flight to Saint Maartins. They landed at Princess Juliana International Airport at seven o'clock in the morning. Terri immediately got a rental car, then checked into a hotel. Yes, they did remember to fill the socks with sand first.

There was no doubt that sand is an abundant commodity in Saint Maartins. There are many absolutely beautiful beaches in Saint Maartins, which is divided by two countries. The larger side of Saint Maartins is French and occupies 60 percent of the island. The largest city on the French side is Maigot. The French section is renowned for clothing, shopping, outdoor markets, and its nude beaches. The 40 percent of the island which is Dutch occupying the south side of Saint Maartins. Their main city is Philipsburg where huge cruise ships dock, unloading thousands of passengers. Philipsburg is also known for its wild and festive nightlife. It is also known for its beaches and for its alcoholic drinks made from guavaberry-based native rum.

A local dialect is spoken informally on both sides of the island, but English is the dominant language. The total population of Saint Maartins is around seventy-five thousand. Slightly more than half the population live on the smaller Dutch side of the island. Once again everywhere the girls went, they would find nothing but friendly people.

Every time Terri stopped somewhere, she would show people pictures of Russ and Marvin. However, Terri called them Tom Jackson and Frank Devlin. Terri told anyone who would listen they were her brothers-in-law. Terri said she really needed to find them because there's a huge family emergency.

From time to time Terri and Tatiana interrupted their searching by doing some shopping. They enjoyed the outdoor markets in Maigot. It was so much fun haggling over the prices. The girls don't get to do that in Seattle. As they walked along, every time there was a booth, someone would call out to them. "Hey, ladies, I think this necklace made just for you. Oh, beautiful ladies, I have these fabulous leather purses. I have been hiding them for two years till you got here."

Terri had to be very careful when she drove because some of the roads are very narrow, and some of the residents and other tourists were very careless drivers. There were several narrow misses. But it was nothing compared to the time they drove past the Princess Juliana International Airport. Terri could not believe it she got stuck in a traffic jam. There are only seventy-five thousand residents on the entire island, and Terri believed there was not a single person who was not stuck in the traffic jam.

The worst part of being stuck in the traffic jam is when Terri had rented a car, the only one available was of indiscriminate ancestry. Tatiana and Terri sat stationary sweltering in the heat because it had no air-conditioning. Terri has heard somewhere, there are people in this world who actually buy these cars. She doesn't have the slightest clue why they would do such a thing.

When Terri and Tatiana finally got out of the traffic jam several hours later, they decided to check out the bars in Philipsburg. This was definitely where all the action was. Everyone seemed to be just hanging loose and enjoying themselves. The girls listened to the sound of friendly conversation. All of the bars stopped at were very upbeat, and it was easy to get into the swing of things.

Terri understands why people love the Caribbean—in all of the Philipsburg bars, the Caribbean and Calypso music just seem to flow. Terri ordered drinks for Tatiana and her. She asked the bartender to make the drinks very weak. Even so they sipped them very slowly as they wanted to maintain their cool. It definitely wouldn't be good if Terri got tipsy and Marvin and Russ walked in and recognized her.

This time when Terri started to show pictures of Russ and Marvin, several people recognized them. "Oh yes, we saw them at Orient Beach yesterday. The men are there almost every day." There was a steady stream of men coming to the table to ask us to dance. Terri laughingly turned all of them down, pointing to her wedding ring. Now if Chris had been there with her, they would've danced up a storm.

Listening to the music caused a stirring within Terri. It made her want to come here with Chris sometime in the future. Tatiana, however, was enjoying it here and now. She was dancing every dance, going from one partner to the next. After a while, Terri noticed Tatiana had started dancing with just one man. They seemed to be having a wonderful time.

After one dance ended, they headed for their table. Tatiana introduced him to Terri. His name was LaShawn Williams. He was a tall muscular African-American man. LaShawn was a very handsome guy with an engaging smile and a quick wit. Terri could tell Tatiana was attracted to him. He sat down at our table and immediately began telling us about his life. LaShawn was a pilot for large worldwide corporation based in Seattle. He flew their top executives all over the world in a Gulfstream jet. He had been here in Saint Maartins for just three days.

LaShawn happened to be a good listener. He looked at the pictures of Russ and Marvin. Then he listened to the story of how they were Terri's brothers-in-law and she needed to find them because of a family emergency. He glanced at Terri, then at Tatiana, then back at Terri. LaShawn then shook his head, saying, "Don't hand me that line of bull crap. I can tell there's a lot more going on here than looking for a relative. If you want to tell me, I can listen. I'm good at keeping it secret. If not, it won't bother me."

Between Tatiana and Terri, they filled him in on the whole story. After they had finished, LaShawn asked, "What are you going to do if you do find these men?" Terri told him, "I don't know for sure. We are planning to handle the problem when we come to it. We are hoping we can spot Russ and Marvin without them knowing it then following them to see where they go. Somehow we hope to find a paper trail, which will probably mean burglarizing their place when we find it."

LaShawn shrugged, saying, "Well, I certainly hope it all works out for you, but be very careful. If you ever need help, get hold of me. I happen to know a lot of powerful people, both very high and also very low, the absolute scum of the earth. They are able to get things done when no one else can. I really wish I could stay and help you, but alas, I'm already scheduled to take off in the morning."

LaShawn gave the girls his phone number in Seattle telling them to call if they had any trouble. He said, "It will be passed through to me, and I will send help." Then looking at Tatiana, LaShawn asked, "Would be all right with you if I called on you when I get back to Seattle?" Tatiana fluttered her long eyelashes at him, saying, "I would be terribly disappointed if you didn't."

After LaShawn left, Terri looked at Tatiana and smiled. Terri asked her, "Do you think LaShawn might be the guy you have been searching for?" Tatiana answered, "I certainly hope so, he looks like he has great potential. I've been searching for the right man for a long time. So far it looks like LaShawn could be the one." Tatiana and Terri finally decided to call it a night. They went back to the hotel and slept till noon. The girls had already decided to spend the day at Orient Beach. Everyone had told them Russ and Marvin had been there yesterday. Also they were spotted there quite frequently. Tatiana and Terri were excited and filled with nervous anticipation.

Terri and Tatiana put beach towels and sunscreen in their bags, and the last thing put in the bag was socks filled with sand on the very top. They then put on our bikinis and drove to Orient Beach, which is on the east side of the island. Orient Beach was spectacular and had beautiful pure white sand. There were chaise lounges with umbrellas on the beach which they could rent.

After Terri had paid for the chaise lounges, she asked about the different colored umbrellas located several hundred yards to the south. Terri was told it was a nude beach, and you are not allowed to go over there unless you were in the nude. So both of them went and laid on their chaise lounges. The girls slathered themselves liberally with sunscreen as they had no desire to get sunburned.

It was great just lying there on the chaise lounges, which they did for quite some time just watching for Russ or Marvin. However, the water looked so tempting as if it was calling to them, and they just had to accept, so the girls gave in and went for a swim. The water was so crystal clear you were able to see the bottom for a long way out. It was also nice warm and deliciously refreshing. You could walk out for a long way, then drop into the water, and the waves from the Caribbean ocean would bodysurf you back to shore. They enjoyed doing this for quite some time.

Terri and Tatiana finally went back to the chaise lounges just relaxing and catching the sun. They noticed several nude couples coming from the south. Later, the couples would walk back to the nude beach. Some of the couples were completely nude, but some of the women were topless but would have on bikini bottoms.

Around four o'clock, Tatiana popped up, saying, "Terri, let's go down to the nude beach." Terri asked her, "What are you out of your mind? We can't go down there with our clothes on." Tatiana replied, "What if it just happens that is where Russ and Marvin are hanging out? It may be our only chance to catch them." Terri said, "But, Tatiana, you have to be nude to be able to go down there. I just can't do it."

Tatiana replied, "Terri, you will have to do it. Remember this is for Chris. We will only take our tops off like some of those ladies we have seen walking past us. So how about it? Let's take our tops off and saunter on down there. We can hold hands, then everyone will think we are an item."

Terri was really embarrassed, but she knew Tatiana was right. Terri whispered to her, "We are never going to tell Chris about this, are we?" Tatiana and Terri took their tops off, and holding hands, the girls walked very slowly across about five hundred yards of sand, which separated them from the nude beach. No sooner than they had got to the nude beach, when Terri gasped, "That's Russ and Marvin over there." Terri didn't want Russ and Marvin to see her, so she ran and hid in the ladies' room and peeked out.

Tatiana went to the concession stand and ordered two lemonades. Then she slowly walked back, making sure she would walk right past them. Terri couldn't believe Tatiana actually stopped and talked to them for about five minutes. Of course, it was all right because neither Russ nor Marvin had ever seen Tatiana.

Terri slipped farther into her hiding place. Her heart was beating rapidly. After searching for Russ and Marvin for so long, she wasn't sure what to do next. Suddenly, Tatiana was at her side, saying, "What did you find out?" Terri gulped. Tatiana smiled sadly, saying, "I don't think it's them, Terri."

"What do you mean?" Terri asked. "Just what I said," she replied. "They do look almost like in the pictures, but not quite. Also, they speak German for one thing. When I talked to them in English, they answered in English but with a heavy German accent. This would be very hard to do for a person with English as their first language. It would be hard to imitate. Also the one who looks like Marvin Mueller is only about five feet seven inches tall. That's a long way from the over six feet tall you told me about."

After observing the men for some time, Terri realized Tatiana was right. So they walked over, and Terri started talking to them. She told them they looked like some people she knew. Terri took out the pictures of Russ and Marvin and showed them to these men. The Germans both jumped up extremely agitated, then started jabbering to each other in German. The men threw the pictures on the ground and spat on them. Then taking their feet, they ground the pictures into the ground. In heavily accented English, they angrily asked us, "Do these pieces of excrement happen to be your friends? If they are, then we would like you to leave. We don't want anything to do with anyone who has friends like this. We almost got in very much trouble just because of the fact we looked like them."

Tatiana and Terri hastily told them, "No, nein, these are not our friends. In fact, they are our mortal enemies. The reason we have the pictures is they did something very bad." After the Germans had learned the girls were looking for them not because Russ and Marvin were their friends, but the girls were looking for them because they were their enemies. The men agreed to tell the girls everything they knew.

Our German friends told us they had first learned of Russ and Marvin when they were in Jamaica. They were driving when the windows of their car got shot out. The Germans took off driving very fast. Two cars with very rough-looking men in them followed their car while shooting at them at the same time. One of the guys said, "We were very scared for our lives, we turned left, we turned right, but no matter what we did, we couldn't lose them.

"Just when we thought the end was at hand, we heard police sirens. One police car came from the opposite direction, and the policeman looked right at us. We can see the policeman talking on the radio. The men who were shooting at us took off rapidly in different directions. We thought the police would follow them, but no. The police turned around and chased us. We immediately pulled over.

"Five squad cars of policemen surrounded us. The police jumped out of their cars with their pistols drawn and pointed them at us. They told us to throw down our weapons, even though we didn't have any weapons. Then The policemen dragged us out of our car and made us lay on the ground. After that they frisked us.

"The police told us, 'You are under arrest, Tom Jackson and Hank Devlin, we have finally caught you.' We tried to tell the police that's not who we are, but they didn't believe us. The police were not about to listen to us; instead, they took us to the nearest police station. When we got there, they fingerprinted us. We tried to show them our passports. The police just said they see fake passports all the time.

"After sitting in a squalid jail cell for three days with lousy food and flea-infested criminals, we were finally taken to an office. This time, we were treated with dignity and respect. A police sergeant who was at the police station told us, 'We apologize for all that has happened to you. Your fingerprints proved to us you are not Tom Jackson or Hank Devlin.

"'The men who look like you are very notorious men. They have been trafficking in young women and drugs. Other gangs who do the same thing are out to get them as you have seen. The gangs don't want any competition, and this has started a turf war.' The police captain said, 'We want to catch them, not only for what they do, but we don't want to see the turf war escalating.'

"The captain then asked us what we were doing in Jamaica. We told the captain we had done very well in Germany and had retired early. We told him we wanted to see the world, so we were stopping for a month at a time in different countries just vacationing. The captain recommended we vacation elsewhere. He said it was too dangerous for us in Jamaica. Recommending Saint Maartins, he handed us plane tickets complimentary of Jamaica.

"The captain give us a police escort to our hotel to collect our baggage. Then another escorted us to the airport. We are only too happy to be here in Saint Maartins. We enjoy looking at the girls, and I must say you two look very fine." Tatiana and Terri hurriedly crossed their arms. Then Tatiana told the Germans, "The reason we had our tops off is because we had heard Tom Jackson and Hank Devlin are on the island." The two men told the girls, "We will escort you back to your chaise lounges." As soon as the girls left the nudist area, they put their tops back on.

The two Germans were very friendly. They asked if the girls had watched when their plane had landed at Princess Juliana International Airport. Tatiana told them, "No, we had been asleep at the time." The men told the girls, "You should have watched. It's pretty scary. You come in very low across the Caribbean ocean, right over the top of the bathers at the beach. Before you leave Saint Maartins, you should go on the ocean side of the airport and watch. What you see will surprise you."

After they got back to their own chaise lounges, Terri explained to them the real reason she wanted to find Russ and Marvin. Terri thought she owed them that much anyway. The Germans expressed their sympathy, then told the girls they spent their retirement visiting exotic places. The men asked for their phone numbers just in case they ever heard of or ran into Russ and Marvin again. If they did, they said they would let the girls know immediately.

When the girls arrived back at the hotel, they called the airline for tickets to Jamaica and found out they would not be able to leave until late the next afternoon. The next morning, they took the two Germans advice. Terri and Tatiana went to the beach on the ocean side of Princess Juliana International Airport. What they saw was hilarious. It was definitely worth watching, and Terri would recommend it to anyone who visits Saint Maartins.

First, you see the airplanes coming in for a landing. The planes came in very low and close to the Caribbean ocean. When the airplanes came in, they are not over forty feet above the beach. The planes would touch down just past the airport fence. The fence itself is the closest to the runway of any airport in the world. Then when the jets would take off, their backend would be very near the fence.

Saint Maartins is a wonderful place. If you ever get the chance to go there, make sure you take in everything. One thing you will want to do is take time to go to the beach behind the airport. Tatiana and Terri watched as macho young men lined up along the fence. A 747 was just about to take off. It turned around with its backend toward the fence.

The macho young men gripped the fence as hard as they could. The 747's powerful jets started to roar, then went to full force for the takeoff. The backlash from the jet's engines made some of the macho young men's legs fly straight back in the air. One young man lost his grip on the fence, and he flew fifty feet in the air and landed in the ocean. Luckily, no one was badly injured this time.

After watching this for several more times, Terri told Tatiana, "This is evidently a case where a young man's fancy turns to stupidity." Tatiana answered, "Yes, did you observe the young ladies in bathing suits watching them? I hope this isn't interpreted as a process of natural selection. I am afraid if it is, we will wind up with a future generation of strong bodies and weak minds." Terri laughed and told Tatiana, "Yes, and the feeble brain shall inherit the earth."

Before they left Saint Maartins, Terri opened another numbered account at another offshore bank. As their plane took off for Jamaica, Terri couldn't help but wonder how many young men had got blown into the ocean this time.

Jamaica is an island nation in the Greater Antilles. In the 1600s, it was a haven for pirates. It was here that Captain Morgan was empowered by Great Britain to prey on Spanish ships. Jamaica is 145 miles in length. It is 50 miles wide and 90 miles south of Cuba.

Jamaica has three international airports. The girls had decided to fly into the Norman Manley International Airport in Kingston. They did this mainly because it is where they were told Russ and Marvin were last seen. Because Kingston is the capital of Jamaica, a lot of illegal activity can be found around the city. Russ and Marvin seemed to thrive on illegal activity.

When they landed, it was very hot and humid, so Terri went straight to the rental car center to pick up a car. She got pretty spooked because a couple of very decrepit young men followed them and kept asking if they wanted to buy marijuana. The girls politely refused, but the ruffians insisted on following them. The girls notified a security guard, and they took off. Terri and Tatiana were certainly pleased after getting into the rental car and taking off. Tatiana said, "I hope we never see those creeps again," and Terri agreed.

Terri told Tatiana, "Let's go to the nearest beach and fill a couple of socks with sand. Those derelicts really scared me." They did this immediately because those two guys gave them the creeps. Then the girls took off heading into the main part of Kingston. Tatiana was driving, and Terri noticed she made several left-hand turns and a couple of right-hand turns. Terri asked her, "What is this all about?"

Tatiana replied, "Terri, check it out. There's an old blue car which has been following us." Terri turned her head to look back. It was those same two creeps who had bothered them at the airport. The worst part about it was it was starting to get dark. Terri asked Tatiana to head for the hotel where Terri had reserved a room before leaving St. Maartins. Terri said, "Maybe there will be people around, and it will scare them off."

It took them quite a while, but Tatiana finally located the street the hotel was on. As Tatiana swung into the parking lot, their worst fears were realized. There was not a soul in sight. That wasn't the worst part. It was also a dead-end, and the blue car quickly moved to block us in. When the girls got out of the car, they had the socks hid behind their backs. They tried to act very, very scared and had no problem doing because they were scared.

The two creeps came menacingly toward them. The taller one said, "I think you work for us now, mon. You very pretty ladies make as much money. We try you first, see if you are any good." Terri shuddered at the thought. It was absolutely disgusting. She wasn't about to let them lay their filthy hands on either one of them.

The hoods evidently had been used to women who could not or did not put up much of a resistance. The dirtbags were totally unprepared for anything. Not that it would have made much of a difference anyhow. Terri and Tatiana have been preparing for a situation like this for years. When the two thugs reached out to grab them, they both slammed their socks as hard as they could right alongside of the jerks temples. The single blow knocked them both out cold. They were out cold and flatter than a chicken stealing coyote which has been run over by a Mack truck.

Terri and Tatiana almost jumped out of their skins when they heard a familiar voice behind them. It said, "Good job, girls, I saw you at the airport and tried to catch up with you there. When you got away, I had to run to get my car. By the time I caught up with you, I saw these two guys following you, and I knew you were in serious trouble. When I got here, I was tempted to step in right away, but then I remembered in Saint Maartins, you claimed you could handle yourselves.

"As I waited, I saw these two punks thought they didn't need a weapon. You handled the situation by yourselves, and I have got to admit you are as good at self-defense as you said." They looked at LaShawn Williams in surprise. Tatiana said, "What are you doing here?" LaShawn replied, "Didn't I tell you in Saint Maartins I was flying to Jamaica? When I first saw you at the airport, I thought you had come here to see me." "In your wildest dreams," Tatiana retorted, "but seeing you are here, you may possibly be of some use."

The two supposed gang members were still out cold, so Tatiana got some plastic ties out of her purse and tied them up. Then for the first time, everyone went and looked inside of the blue car. A good-looking blonde lady was in the car. She was tied up and had duct tape across her mouth. When LaShawn cut her loose and removed the duct tape from her mouth, she said, "Oh, thank God, I need your help."

The blonde lady told us her name was Judy, and she and two of her friends had been kidnapped a week ago. Judy said, "We all had been raped repeatedly by these two punks. They had been forced to work as prostitutes. Please help me to free my friends. I know exactly where their house is." Before they left, LaShawn moved the blue car to the side. Then he opened the hood and pulled off every wire he could find and destroyed them. After finishing with the car's motor, LaShawn pulled out his knife and slashed all four of the tires, flattening them.

The girls decided it would be better to take LaShawn's vehicle because it was a van. They piled the two thugs on top of each other behind the last seat. Uncomfortable is good when it comes to those two assholes. LaShawn asked Judy if there were any more men at the house. She replied, "No, my two friends are the only ones there, but they are tied up and gagged. These two jerks did that so they could not run away or scream for help."

With Judy guiding us, we quickly found the place. It was located in the seediest part of Kingston. You would have to look for a long time before you would be able to find another shack as rundown as this one was. After taking the house keys from the pants pockets of the two perverts, LaShawn yanked them out of the van. After unlocking the front door, he pushed them through the door first, just in case anyone else had come while they were gone. But Judy was right; no one else was in there except for her two friends.

LaShawn made short work of freeing the girls. They were crying tears of joy and thanked us over and over again. The other girls told us their names were Wanda and Gail and all three of them had come to Jamaica from Dallas Texas for a vacation. They had all been captured within three hours of arriving in Kingston. Then all three had been raped and forced into prostitution.

The two gang members had always kept one of them tied up at the house the other two would have to work the streets. The women were very carefully watched and were told if they were gone too long with a John, if they talked to the police, their friend who was tied up at the house would be killed.

Terri asked the ladies if they wanted to talk to the police. All three ladies said, "No, it would just mean we would have to stay in Jamaica that much longer. The police would make us answer questions, and maybe we would have to stay for a trial. We just want to get the hell out of here; however, those two creeps have taken all of our credit cards, cash, and passports. We will probably have to call our parents to wire us money to get home."

LaShawn thought about this for a moment, then told everyone, "We need to search the house. It has all got to be here somewhere." They searched everywhere, including in the hoodlums wallets. They searched every nook and cranny and wound up finding all of the girls credit cards and ID. Additionally, they found a huge amount of marijuana, methamphetamines, and cocaine. Also a large stash of firearms plus a huge amount of cash.

The girls all wanted us to dump the drugs down the toilet. But LaShawn said, "Not so fast, I have a much better idea." First, he took his knife and made holes all the way through the back of the couch in four places. Then he did the same with the bottom of the couch. After that, he ran some rope from one hole to the next at the top of couch. Then taking another piece of rope, he did the same thing to the other two holes at the top of the couch. LaShawn then took two more pieces of rope and did the same thing at the bottom of the couch.

Next, LaShawn took a couple of gallons of turpentine, which he had found when searching the house. He doused the seat cushions with the turpentine. He took the two would be criminals who by now were wide-awake and begging for mercy. LaShawn left the plastic ties on them but placed one on either end of the couch. He then proceeded to tie the upper ropes around their chests and the lower ones around their upper legs so they would not be able to move.

LaShawn piled all the guns, ammunition, and drugs in front of them. Everyone was already able to hear them screaming as they walked out the door. However, shutting the door cut off the sound of their voices. Then LaShawn had all of us pile into his van, first making sure he had the correct address for the house. Then LaShawn drove back to the hotel where the girls had left the rental car. Tatiana and Terri got into the rental car and followed LaShawn back to the airport.

They all went into the airport making sure Judy, Wanda, and Gail got tickets back to Dallas. LaShawn handed them $60,000, which he had found while searching the house. At first, the girls were reluctant to take the money saying it had come from drugs and prostitution. Tatiana told the ladies, "If you don't deserve to have it after all you have gone through, then who did?" When put that way, the ladies accepted the money gladly.

Just before the girls left, LaShawn called the Kingston police from a payphone in the airport. When the police answered, LaShawn told them, "We have captured a couple of dealers of drugs and weapons. We have tied them up." The police asked for their names, but LaShawn just gave them the culprits address and hung up.

When the girls were safely in the air and on their way to Dallas, LaShawn asked what the girls wanted to do next. Tatiana and Terri filled him in on what had happened in Saint Maartins. Terri told LaShawn, "We found out Russ and Marvin were or had been in Jamaica. Also, we would like to be able to make a search for them."

LaShawn thought about the idea for a while, then he said he didn't like the idea of Tatiana and Terri staying alone. He said, "This would just make you too vulnerable. There are many other gangs here in Kingston who traffic in women. So why don't you let me help you? I have a very nice apartment in a better part of Kingston. It has two extra bedrooms. I think you might be smart to stay with me. That way, I will be able to help you search for Russ and Marvin. Plus, nobody will be as apt to try something when they see you with me. At the same time, people are more willing to open up to two beautiful women."

Terri turned in the rental car at the airport, and as it was late in the day, Terri and Tatiana went straight to LaShawn's apartment. It was an awesome apartment complete with cathedral ceilings. It had large windows overlooking the Caribbean ocean with a wraparound patio out front. They sat on the patio and drank ice-cold Red Stripe beer. Red Stripe beer is brewed locally here in Jamaica.

Terri could hear the beat of Caribbean music coming from somewhere close. It just gives her such a sense of belonging here. As the threesome listened to the music being played, they watched the clouds turn into beautiful red and orange hues, then it slowly sank into the Caribbean.

LaShawn then showed the girls to their rooms on the second floor. Each of them had its own private patio outside. LaShawn explained to the girls the apartment was actually owned by the corporation for which he worked. He said the corporation owns apartments in several different cities, which their executives visit frequently. LaShawn said his most private desire is to own his own jet someday and start his own business.

Terri sank thankfully into the bed and contemplated the day's events. Terri had left the window open, and the soft balmy breeze had a soothing effect. From the distance, she could hear the sound of Calypso music. As she lay there, she thought there's definitely a strong current flowing between Tatiana and LaShawn. Tatiana is her best friend, and Terri would love to see her hook up with a good man. As far as she is concerned, it looked to Terri like LaShawn certainly fit the bill.

Terri woke up the next morning to the delightful sound of laughter. Also to the delicious aroma of freshly brewed coffee and bacon and eggs frying.

She hurriedly took a shower, got dressed, and went downstairs. There she found LaShawn and Tatiana engaged in conversation. LaShawn told her to sit down at the table. Tatiana and Terri sat down while LaShawn served breakfast to them.

Later, the three decided to just drive around showing pictures of Russ and Marvin to everyone they saw. LaShawn would frequently stop and ask if anyone had seen them. Several people said, "We have but not recently."

As they were driving along, suddenly Tatiana yelled for LaShawn pull over and stop. LaShawn hit the brakes, thinking something was wrong. Tatiana asked LaShawn to back up fifty feet and stop again. Then pointing at something, Tatiana laughingly inquired, "What in hell is that supposed to be?" They were looking at several carved nude statues of men. They were about five feet tall with erections standing up which were three and half feet long.

"Oh, that's ready Freddy," chuckled LaShawn. "Several Jamaicans carve them to sell to tourists." "Well, I certainly hope you are not endowed quite so well," Tatiana said. Then she put her hand over her mouth, realizing what she had said.

After everyone finally stopped laughing, LaShawn took off again. After driving around for several hours, they found a nice beach house by the ocean. The second they stepped out of the air-conditioned van, the heat suddenly seemed unbearable to them. They went into the beach house where they quickly changed into swimsuits, and they raced into the Caribbean ocean. The Caribbean waters were so warm and relaxing. After just a few minutes, everyone felt totally refreshed. They stayed for a couple of hours just enjoying themselves. Even though Terri felt guilty because Chris was not there enjoying this with her.

Everybody piled back into the van and went back to LaShawn's air-conditioned apartment. There Tatiana and Terri relaxed while LaShawn prepared dinner. He told them he was making a genuine Jamaican dish. The dinner would be spiced jerk chicken, corn on the cob, fresh hot buns straight from the oven, and again red stripe beer.

The spiced jerk chicken was as appetizing as it sounded. As Tatiana and Terri were relaxing on some comfortable chairs afterward, LaShawn announced, "I'm am going to make some telephone calls." He said, "Remember I told you I had connections both in real high places and also with the scum of the earth. In this particular case, the scum of the earth will do us much more good." After making several telephone calls, LaShawn returned to the girls and said, "Well, I started the network. If Russ and Marvin happen to be anywhere in Jamaica, we will know it sometime tomorrow."

Terri went to bed early because she was really missing Chris and Gavin. All her heart yearned for them. She also longed for the future when Chris would once more be by her side. At least, Terri would be able to see Gavin again soon. Just before drifting off to sleep, she heard LaShawn and Tatiana talking downstairs.

The next morning, Terri happened to be the first one up. She brewed coffee and started breakfast. It wasn't very long before LaShawn appeared followed a little later by Tatiana. After finishing breakfast, LaShawn walked out to the driveway to pick up the newspaper.

LaShawn had no sooner sat down to read the paper than he burst out laughing. He said, "Listen up, you two, you have to hear this. It's from a column in the local newspaper. It says the police in Kingston received an anonymous tip yesterday. The police were told about two local thugs who were dealing in arms and drugs. After the police were given the address to the place, they went there immediately. There the police discovered two men who were all trussed up sitting on a rickety couch. There was a huge stack of arms and drugs piled in front of them.

"A spokesman for the police told us we have been trying to find a reason to arrest these two thugs for a long time. But we could never find enough evidence to put them in jail where they belong. He said when the police got there the two felons were tickled to see them. In fact, they begged the police to take them to the hospital. Once they arrived at the hospital, the thugs were treated for large boils on their buttocks. The rogues informed the police, 'Don't mess with these two women, they very bad news.' The police in Kingston have not been able to figure out what they were talking about."

All three had a good chuckle over the newspaper article. They had just started talking about what they were going to do today when the telephone rang. LaShawn picked up the phone and listened for a few minutes. Terri and Tatiana heard him say "okay," then he hung up. As LaShawn turned around, he said, "The phone call was from one of my network in Kingston. They have found where Russ and Marvin were living."

LaShawn said, "My contact told me no one was living there anymore, and it looks like they left in a hurry. It looks like Russ and Marvin have left Jamaica for good; however, I do have an address for where they were living. I think it would be wise if we were to go and check it out for ourselves."

As LaShawn approached the area, they noticed it was in a middle-class neighborhood. This surprised them as Terri thought it would be in the slums. When the threesome pulled up in front of the house, even LaShawn thought it wasn't bad. It wasn't nearly as nice as LaShawn's apartment, but it was definitely upscale for Kingston. The lawn was well manicured, the house was freshly painted, and it even had a nice patio. There was a man standing by the door who unlocked it for us and then left.

As soon as the three entered, they could tell Russ and Marvin had left in a hurry for on the table were a couple of sandwiches, which were half eaten. The sandwiches appeared to be a little over a day old. A glass of milk had been spilled, leaving a stain on the table and on the floor. The telephone receiver was lying on the floor, and the phone was still beeping. It looked to them like someone apparently had to get their ass out of Dodge fast.

Terri looked the place over carefully for any trace of evidence, showing where Russ and Marvin may have gone. She did find a paper which had some handwriting on it. Terri recognized the handwriting as belonging to Russ Jacobson. From some power bills Tatiana found, they surmised Russ and Marvin must have lived here for around two years.

LaShawn went into the first bedroom where he found it was very cluttered up. There were enormous amounts of pornographic material which was strewn around the room. They found pornographic materials everywhere on the bed, the floor, and even on the dresser. The group searched the whole room from top to bottom, but didn't find anything that would be of value to help them find where Russ and Marvin had disappeared to.

After entering the second bedroom, they discovered it was immaculate. Everything was in its proper place; the bed was neatly made. Terri remarked, "This has to be Marvin Mueller's room. The first bedroom, which looks like a pig sty, had to belong to Russ Jacobson."

When they entered the third bedroom, it was like a blast from the past from when Terri and Tatiana entered Marvin's home in Seattle. For there they saw all types of weapons, handcuffs, and torture devices of every kind. When Terri looked closely at all the torture devices, She was able to see faint specks of blood at the ends of the whips. In a file cabinet in the corner of the room, Terri found pictures of women in shackles. Also found were some papers with names and dollar amounts on them.

Then Tatiana found an eight-by-ten picture with very good-looking women in shackles all chained together. In the background, there appeared to be some Arab-looking men checking them out. Neither Russ nor Marvin appeared anywhere in the picture. LaShawn snapped his fingers. He said, "You know what we are looking at? It's a slave auction." Tatiana and Terri both said, "Oh, those poor girls." LaShawn said, "I'm going to keep this picture. I'm going to have it duplicated. Then I'm going to see it sent it to police and news agencies all around the world.

"Every face in that picture stands out enough, so when the news agencies receive it, I hope they will put it on television and in newspapers. The people in this picture will be found, and maybe will be forced to set the girls free."

After seeing everything in the house, Everyone came to the conclusion Russ and Marvin were into the slave trade. From what they were able to figure out from everything seen in the house, Russ and Marvin must have been capturing women in one country and selling them in another.

Further study of everything, which was found seemed to bear this out. Not only that, but this must be an extremely profitable business. LaShawn and the girls wound up searching the house for hours. They dumped all of the drawers and moved every piece of furniture. Terri even looked at the bottom of every conceivable surface to see if it had anything taped to it. Tatiana tapped on all the walls to check for secret hiding places or passages but found nothing.

By the time everyone walked out of the house, plenty of evidence had been found. But unfortunately, not a trace of where Russ and Marvin had disappeared. Terri checked with the nearest neighbors to see if they knew anything. The nearest neighbor said, "All I knew was both of the men kept to theirselves. I had seen them bring many women to the house. But it was always too dark to see if there were any problems." The neighbor said, "When Russ and Marvin left almost two days ago, they tore out of there very fast." When Terri showed him pictures of Russ and Marvin, he confirmed they were the ones who had lived there.

The group left and went back to LaShawn's apartment. Terri felt tormented by the fact she had come within two days of catching Russ and Marvin. Terri had been hoping she would find something which would help her to free Chris and clear his name. Tatiana and LaShawn, sensing her disappointment, tried to cheer her up. They told Terri, "Just because we didn't find Russ and Marvin this time, doesn't mean we will never win."

Chapter 41

Tatiana and Terri decided they had done all which could be done in Jamaica, and it was time to return home. After checking at the airport Terri found there was a flight out that night, and they would be on it. Tatiana and Terri said their good-byes to LaShawn. He told the girls he would be seeing them in Seattle. Terri told him, "We look forward to seeing you there, especially Tatiana."

Terri and Tatiana had a long flight ahead of them, first from Jamaica to Fort Lauderdale, Florida. Afterwards, they would have a three-hour layover before they caught a flight to Minneapolis, Minnesota. When the girls arrived in Minneapolis, they planned to get a room and would be able to rest up. The next day, they would fly to Minot, North Dakota, where Terri's parents would pick them up. The girls would stay in Towner for two days, then Tatiana and Terri would drive her car back to Seattle.

On the flight back, Tatiana kept talking about LaShawn. She told her, "Terri, I really think that he is the one for whom I have been waiting. LaShawn asked me if we could start seeing each other when he comes back to Seattle. Of course I told him yes." Terri acknowledged to Tatiana she thought he would be a great catch. She wished Tatiana the best of luck and told her, "LaShawn is a wonderful man. I think the two of you would make a great couple."

When they arrived in Minneapolis, Minnesota, both of them were exhausted and barely had the strength to find a room. After getting a room, they flopped down on the beds and were asleep instantly. When they woke up the next morning, the two barely had enough time to take a shower and get to the airport on time to catch their flight. When Terri walked into the Minot terminal, her parents were there to meet them.

A five-year-old cyclone flew into Terri's arms. Gavin had to tell his mom everything which had happened while she was gone. "Mom, Mom, guess what? Grandpa taught me how to milk the cows. He said I was better than you were when you were my age." Terri tweaked his nose. Gavin said, "And guess what, Mom. Grandpa and Grandma bought me a Shetland pony and taught me how to ride it. I will show you how when we get there."

Gavin had more to say. "Mom, Grandma and Grandpa took me fishing. Grandpa showed me how to bait the hook and put on the bobber. Then Grandpa threw the line in the water 'cause I'm too little yet, he said. Then you have to wait till the bobber goes under the water. When you see it go under, you give a little jerk and reel the fish in.

"I got three fish, but Grandma got the biggest one. Me and Grandpa cleaned them, and Grandma cooked them up for dinner. The fish were really good. Grandma baked a chocolate cake, then she put frosting on it, and I helped." "Yes," Grandma added, "he helped by licking out the frosting bowl. Gavin has been a very good boy. We kept him so busy he didn't have any time to miss you."

By this time, Terri's parents had already put the luggage in the trunk and were in the car. Terri asked her parents if they could stop at a restaurant. She said, "Tatiana and I are famished. We hadn't had time to eat before we left Minneapolis." At the restaurant, Terri was bombarded by questions, both by her parents and Gavin. Terri can say for a five-year-old, he could come up with some very intelligent questions.

First of all, Gavin asked her, "Mom, where did you go?" Terri told him, "I went to two different islands both Saint Maartins and Jamaica. They are very beautiful islands in the Caribbean ocean." Then he asked, "Mom, how big is the ocean?" Terri said, "Well, honey, the ocean is huge. If you are in the ocean, you would not be able to see land anywhere you looked." Then Gavin asked, "What is an island?" She told him, "It is a piece of land surrounded on all sides by the ocean."

Then Gavin asked, "Did you catch the bad guys who made Daddy go to jail?" She said, "No, son, we didn't get the bad guys, but we did find the place where they had been living. But we were two days too late. The bad guys had left before we got there. But Tatiana found a boyfriend while we were there."

This brought us to a new line of questioning. Gavin asked, "Auntie Tati, do you like him?" She replied, "He would not be my boyfriend if I didn't like him." "How big is he, Auntie Tati?" Tatiana answered, "He's about the same size as your daddy is Gavin." Then he asked her, "Does your boyfriend have a mustache?" Tatiana said, "No, he is clean-shaven." "What does he do, Auntie Tati?" "He flies jet airplanes all over the world, and he will be coming to Seattle, so you will be able to meet him."

Almost the minute we got back into the car, Gavin fell asleep. But the second we got back to the farm, he woke back up. He had to show us his

Shetland pony and how he was able to ride it. Later, as we were watching television, Gavin startled all of us. He said, "Mom, while I was sleeping in the car, I had a dream. I dreamt when I am bigger than I am now, when I am almost as big as Daddy is, at that time I will be able to find out where the bad guys are." My parents and Tatiana looked at each other in amazement. Could it be possible? Chris's mother had said almost the same thing before she passed away. Regardless, Terri wasn't about to stop looking for them.

The girls stayed at Terri's parents' farm for two more days. During this time, Gavin kept the girls busy by showing them everything he had learned during the summer. Then after a tearful farewell, they took off for Seattle. Gavin told his mom, "I sure hope you let me stay with Grandpa and Grandma again next year. I had a lot of fun." Terri gave him a hug and told Gavin, "I certainly will let you stay there next summer."

Terri and Tatiana were happy to get home and back to work. Terri went to visit Chris immediately, of course. Gavin was all excited. He had to tell his daddy all about his trip to the farm. Then two weeks later, it was time for a forty-eight-hour conjugal visit.

This time, it seemed like forever since Chris and Terri had spent forty-eight hours together. So much had happened in the last two months. But first, it was Gavin's turn to spend time with his daddy. Chris had Gavin tell him once again about his trip to North Dakota. Gavin told his dad Grandpa had taught him how to play checkers. Chris got the checkerboard, and he and Gavin proceeded to play. Terri could see her husband and her son were really enjoying the game. As they played checkers, they kept up a running conversation. Gavin blurted out, "Mom said she almost caught the bad guys this time, Daddy. Wouldn't that have been something?" Chris looked quizzically at Terri. She gave him a nervous smile and mouthed "later." She thought, "Maybe later Chris would forget about it."

After the checker game, which ended up with Gavin being the undisputed champion of course, he did a little victory dance as Chris and Terri laughed. But it still wasn't bedtime yet, so they had to make some popcorn. Gavin sat between them, eating popcorn as his parents watched television. But it wasn't very long before his head began to nod. When he fell asleep, Chris tucked him into his bed.

It felt so great to have Chris's arms around her again, his lips pressing hers. But if Terri thought Chris had forgotten what Gavin had said, think again. Chris said, "All right, Terri, we have always been able to tell each other everything. So tell me what's this about you almost catching the bad guys?" First, Terri said, "Chris, I was planning on telling you. I was just waiting until after Gavin was asleep."

Terri proceeded to tell him the whole story. The only part she left out was going topless in Saint Maartins. She really believed Chris would've frowned at that. He clutched her tightly when she told him all about the two punks following them in Jamaica. Chris held his breath as Terri told him about getting out of the car. But he breathed a sigh of relief when he found out Tatiana and she were able to take care of theirselves.

Chris felt terrible about the ordeal the three girls must have went through before LaShawn Tatiana and Terri had rescued them. But Chris almost woke Gavin up with his laughter when Terri told him what LaShawn had done to the bad guys. After she was finished telling the story, he asked her all sorts of questions about LaShawn. In the end, he agreed LaShawn would make a good match for Tatiana.

When Terri had finished telling Chris about the story of Tatiana and her adventures and then answered all the questions Chris had for her, Chris took Terri in his arms and kissed her ever so tenderly. He said, "Terri, you and Gavin are all that I hold dear. You two are the light beckoning me at the end of the tunnel. The tunnel is the prison sentence I am now serving."

Chris said, "Here in Monroe prison, I have a separate life. Every day, I concentrate on what I can do to help educate the convicts who are willing to learn. Terri, there are a lot of men in here who just need an education and another chance. It is what fulfills my life here and keeps me from going berserk. It helps to make the time go by much faster.

"But I also see the other side of the coin here at Monroe. I see robbers, murderers, and rapists. They are the scum of the world, and they have no desire to change their ways. They enjoy being criminals. If they get out of here, they will continue committing their crimes. Terri, in your travels, you will be bound to meet some men such as these. They may pop up at a time when you least expect it.

"Terri, you and Gavin are the love of my life, you are all I have. I would be totally destroyed if anything were to happen to either of you. I know there is no way to stop you from doing what you are doing. It has become the goal and purpose in your life. I just ask you again to be very careful. I think you have found a good guy in this LaShawn. Please take him and Tatiana with you when you go from now on." Terri kissed Chris and thanked him for caring so much. She also promised she would do what he asked.

Chapter 42

It was hard to believe their little boy would be starting the first grade in the fall. Terri was very thankful Gavin enjoyed school. Every day when he came home, he would tell his mom what he had learned during the day. Terri was in the habit of reading stories to him. She had even read stories aloud to him while she was still pregnant with him. Terri always made sure to read him a story every night. Now that he was old enough, she would have Gavin read a story to her when she had finished.

Terri believes one of the most important things in a child's life is to have his parents read to them. It sets a goal and a standard. It gives them a yearning to learn more—a yearning to learn and to be able to read for themselves. Of course, a child also needs playtime. They need physical activity to be able to burn up some of the excess energy which they have.

Consequently, Terri started searching for healthy outside activities. She needn't have bothered. One day, Gavin came home and told his mom he wanted to play basketball. "Basketball? Aren't we jumping the years?" Terri always thought boys started playing basketball around the six, seventh, and eighth grades. But they certainly did not play basketball in the first grade.

Gavin was right about this though. Mom just didn't have a clue. They did have a basketball team he could join called the Wildcats. Terri went to a sporting goods store and found him shoes, trunks, tops, and a gym bag. For these young basketball teams, the basketball hoops had been lowered, and the kids would play just half-court. It was so much fun to watch these little guys play. They made many mistakes, but they were just learning. They will be the basketball champions of tomorrow. When the parents would go to the games, all of the parents would cheer for both teams.

One day out of the blue, LaShawn showed up at their door, holding a dozen red roses. Tatiana was flustered and said, "I thought you would call first?" LaShawn said he was sorry, but the corporation had kept him so busy this was the first time back in Seattle. He said, "I didn't have time to waste on a phone call. I just had to see you again."

After that, it was a whirlwind romance. LaShawn would be in and out of Seattle constantly. Every time he was there, he would take Tatiana out for the evening. They would go out on dinner dates or out to the movies and to see the opera or plays. Terri had never seen Tatiana so happy. One night, Tatiana came home with a radiant smile. The way she acted Terri knew something was up. Tatiana held out her hand for Terri to look at. On it was a magnificent diamond engagement ring. Terri immediately jumped up, giving her a big hug. She said, "Oh, Tatiana, I am so happy for you."

Terri asked her, "When will the wedding date be?" Tatiana said, "Well, you see, April showers may bring May flowers. However, this time it will bring a wedding, and it will be on April 17." Tatiana asked Terri if she would be the maid of honor. Terri told her, "Of course, I will, Tatiana. It will be so much fun, and I wish you all the happiness in the world. I am really going to miss you." "Not as much if you think," Tatiana replied. "The house two doors down was for sale. So we bought it. Now we have my mother sandwiched in. You live on one side of her and I on the other side."

Tatiana assured her, "Terri, you don't have to worry about be going it alone. I had a long talk with LaShawn, and he agreed. It's just too dangerous for you to go on these trips all by yourself. We won't let you do it. Not by yourself, that is. From now on, both LaShawn and I will go with you." Terri was thrilled, and she told Tatiana, "With LaShawn along, it will make everything so much safer. We sadly discovered when we were in Jamaica Russ and Marvin may not be the only ones we have to worry about. Right at the moment, I have no idea where we will be searching next. Hopefully, we will have some more information before summer."

Life was again a whirlwind of other activities. Terri was helping Tatiana prepare for her wedding. Doing this and keeping up with Gavin was a chore in itself. Plus, they still had to go to work every day. Then there were her special times with Chris to which she always looked forward to.

One day, Lynn Anderson called with some disturbing news. She had been trying to get in touch with Tony Lindsay for several months. It seemed like he had just dropped off the edge of the earth. Lynn had stopped by his house. It was vacant, and every stick of furniture was gone. It was like he had just disappeared.

Lynn said she talked to the neighbors on either side of Tony and across the street from him. Everyone said the same thing. They had seen him come home one night, but the next day Tony was gone. Lynn then went and talked to the place where he had worked. His boss said, "One morning, Tony just didn't show up. Tony had not notified us beforehand, and he never called back later. He never even showed up to pick up his paycheck."

Terri asked Lynn, "Do you think it could have anything to do with Russ Jacobson or Marvin Mueller?" After she asked, Lynn replied, "I don't have any idea, I guess it's possible. Tony Lindsay has always kept in touch with Rodney Crowder and me. It's just not like Tony to not let us know about some big event in his life. I even did a search for him on my computer, but nothing came up."

April arrived, and with it Tatiana's wedding, Terri was the maid of honor while Gavin was the ring bearer. The wedding was very elegant as LaShawn and Tatiana had spared no expense. Tatiana looked absolutely elegant in her floor-length wedding gown. After the wedding, Terri hugged them both, telling them how lucky she was to have them for friends.

At the reception, Terri asked LaShawn and Tatiana if they had finally decided where they were going on their honeymoon. Tatiana replied, "We will be island hopping to several different places in the Caribbean." Terri asked her if they would be stopping in Jamaica or Saint Maartins. Tatiana answered, "We probably will be stopping in Saint Maartins. LaShawn has already said we won't be going to the nude beach. As for Jamaica, we are definitely not going there.

"Two other places I'm sure we will be going to are Costa Rica and Aruba. I have already decided I am going to locate the banana-stealing monkey. Only this time, I will have a whole bundle of bananas for him."

While LaShawn and Tatiana were on their honeymoon, Terri was busy doing some research. Terri was racking her brain trying to figure out where Russ and Marvin had disappeared. She used their alias of Tom Jackson and Hank Devlin. Terri searched the Internet constantly but had no luck. At work, she checked all the flights, which had left Jamaica from the time period from just before they left to a month afterward. Terri had no luck and realized Russ and Marvin could have left by boat.

After she had racked her brain, Terri suddenly thought, "Why don't I just try the Jamaican police." It took her several calls before Terri finally got hold of a detective who would listen to her. After she explaining the situation to him, Terri told him she needed to locate Tom Jackson and Hank Devlin. The detective told Terri he would try to find anything which might help, and said he would call her back. After what seemed like forever, the Jamaican detective called, saying, "Why don't you try Rio de Janeiro in Brazil. We have reports of several women disappearing from there."

Chapter 43

Chris at the Monroe Correction Complex. It has given Chris a lot of satisfaction from the fact several of his students have received their GEDs. There are already some who have been released from prison and have returned to civilian life. The inmates who have been released write to him from time to time to tell him how they are doing. The one thing they have in common is they all said how much having a GED has made a difference in the type of job they had gotten.

Brian Edwards would call Chris once in a while. More often, Brian would stop by the prison to see Chris in person. Brian was doing exceptionally well in college. He was already on the dean's list. Brian has been living with his grandmother ever since he got out of prison. His grandmother told Brian she should have tried to get custody of him when his mother passed away. She said she should have gotten a private detective to prove his father was an unfit parent.

Brian said his father had tried to call him several times by phone, but as soon as Brian would hear his father's voice, he would hang up on him. Brian told me he had received enough of his father's bull crap to last a lifetime. Without a whipping boy, his father seemed to be lost. Brian was determined he would never be a whipping boy ever again.

All in all, Brian seemed to have gotten his life back together again. No longer did he walk around with a sullen hangdog look. Chris was very proud of Brian. Whenever one of Chris other students was about to give up, Chris would use Brian as an example.

Prison personnel have noticed what Chris was doing and approved of it. Sometimes, they will even recommend to a young troubled convict he should come to see Chris. Prison life here is not like being at home, but Chris has adapted to it. Visitations from Terri and Gavin are what have really helped. They helped make Chris realize he is still a member of the human race.

Not long after Tatiana and LaShawn got back from their honeymoon, they were huddled with Terri together planning a trip to Brazil. Terri asked LaShawn if he had any contacts in Brazil. LaShawn said he was sure he did, but he would need to send out feelers first. He said, "I will start putting feelers out right away."

LaShawn told us, "Brazil is a beautiful and very modern country. At the same time, there are some criminal elements there which are among the most dangerous in the world. There are some areas that are known as favelas, or slums as we know them. Most of these favelas are controlled by drug lords, and residents of the favelas are protected by the drug lords as long as they conform to the drug lord's demands.

"Any stranger who enters into the favelas are at once suspect and in danger. If Russ and Marvin happened to be in one of these areas, we will have a hard time getting anywhere near them. But at the same time and for the same reason, I don't think I would expect them to be anywhere near a favela. Unless of course they have a very powerful contact; otherwise, they would be in more danger than anyone else.

"I'm afraid even my contacts would not be able to find anyone in a favela. But the good thing is, so far Marvin and Russ have not been inclined to live in slums. I will check with my contacts and see what they can find. Hopefully, if Russ and Marvin are in Brazil, they will be in an area which is not quite as dangerous."

To make the most of their time, Terri got airline tickets for her mom. This way, Terri's mother could come to Seattle to pick up Gavin. She would then return with him to North Dakota. Gavin was really looking forward to another visit to the farm. He loved his grandpa and grandma, and he was afraid his pony might have forgotten him. He had all sorts of plans for what he intended to do this year.

Terri was definitely looking forward to going to Brazil. It was a strange and exotic country, which she had always been interested in. The idea of seeing the mighty Amazon excited her. As LaShawn had been there on several locations, Terri asked him to tell her more about it. She was surprised when he told her, "Brazil is larger than the continental limits of the United States. However, there is a huge area of Brazil which is uninhabitable.

"The northern area of Brazil as mostly made up of the Amazon basin. But I don't believe we will be going anywhere near there. We will be flying into the Galeao Antonio Carlos Johim International Airport. This is located in Rio de Janeiro in the southern part of Brazil. It was just our luck when the group landed it turned out to be a rainy and bleak day in Rio de Janeiro. Tatiana and Terri got room at a hotel while LaShawn was busy making phone calls. It was their first day in paradise, and they couldn't see crap.

The next morning, Terri was awakened by the sun shining through her window. She jumped up to look out the window. It was absolutely fantastic. There were large cumulus clouds, and palm trees were swaying in the breeze. Terri hurriedly showered and dressed, then called LaShawn and Tatiana. LaShawn said his contacts had not found anything yet, so the three decided to spend the day exploring Rio de Janeiro.

Although Terri had a rental car, they decided to walk. The first place they went was Centro, which is the historic center of Rio de Janeiro. Portuguese is the official language of Brazil and is second to Portugal in the number of Portuguese people living there. However, they were able to find many who could speak English.

Next, the group strolled along Guanabaro Bay. From there, Terri was able to see Sugarloaf Mountain. She had heard so much about Sugarloaf Mountain Terri was expecting to see something on the order of Mount Rainier. But instead, Sugarloaf Mountain is a monolith of granite. It is shaped something like an upside-down ice cream cone rising from the water's edge.

Having seen the cable cars going to the top of Sugarloaf Mountain, all three decided there was nothing for them to do but try it for themselves. Terri took a taxi asking the driver to take them to the cable cars. After arriving there, they found the cable cars run a one-thousand-four-hundred-meter route. The threesome started at Moro de Acucar. There they got on a cable car, which holds up to sixty-five people. This took us to Pao de Acucar where everyone boarded a second cable car to the top of Sugarloaf Mountain.

The ride was entrancing, and the view was breathtaking, but Terri will admit to being a little bit scared. Terri laughed to herself as she watched Tatiana clutching LaShawn very tightly. When Terri asked Tatiana if she was scared, she replied, "Well, maybe just a little bit. But at the same time, I would not want to miss this experience for the whole world."

The end of the ride at the top of Sugarloaf Mountain was worth it. From there, one was able to see for miles. From there a person was able to watch all the activity in Guanabaro Bay. Terri was able to see the ships, sailboat and, people waterskiing. In the distance, she was able to see the Christ the Redeemer statue. It rises from the very summit of Corcovado Mountain. All three of them said they would have to go there before they left Brazil.

The next day, was spent just relaxing in the sun. During this time, LaShawn must have made at least thirty phone calls. He told us his contacts had not been able to find anything definite yet. But his contacts had found out Russ and Marvin were definitely somewhere in Rio de Janeiro. LaShawn's contacts said the contacts thought they were close to a breakthrough.

The next morning as the three of them were walking along, they happened to stop in a store which sold slingshots. Tatiana suggested they each buy one, so everyone did, along with a sack of marbles each. Farther down the street, they ran into a carnival parade. Just the sound of the drums and the other percussion instruments made them stop to watch. Not to mention the throngs of people crowding the sidewalks.

Terri mentioned to LaShawn and Tatiana, "To me, this is what Rio de Janeiro is all about—festivity." Terri Tatiana and LaShawn were enthralled by all of the costumes and the floats. The participants were from different Samba schools, which teach different types of dancing. There was one incredible float, which had long feather like streamers. The feathers were floating ever so delicately in the air. In the very center were very fabulous, handcrafted purple flowers.

It is hard to imagine all of the colorful costumes worn by everyone in the parade. There were vivid oranges, pinks, reds, yellows, silver, and blue. There were organized dancers. All along the way were white-costumed ladies with their intricate dance steps. Tatiana and Terri were impressed by the women in skimpy halters and bikini bottoms with elaborate high headdresses.

They were enthralled by the parade and disappointed when it was over. Afterward, LaShawn stopped at an open-air café where he bought us a cup of Brazilian coffee and planned their day. LaShawn and the girls finally decided to go to Copacabana beach. It was such a hot day, and everyone wanted to spend at least part of the time in the water. Rather than drive theirselves, Terri decided to take a taxi. Luckily, lockers were found where they were able to put their belongings.

One of the first things they did upon arriving at Copacabana beach was to admire the mosaics. The mosaics were all done in blues and grays. The blues made up the water at the top and the bottom of the mosaics. In the middle were the grays making up huge waves. They laid down some beach blankets and then ran into the water. Terri couldn't believe the ocean water could be this warm. After tiring themselves out swimming, the group retired to the beach and sunned theirselves.

Lying on their beach blankets, Tatiana observed the surfers farther down the beach. She said, "You know surfing is something I always wanted to try." Terri said, "Me to, let's go for it." "Personally, I think you are both nuts," replied LaShawn. "However, if you want to try, we could wander on down and see what they have for beginners." Gathering up their beach blankets, all three sauntered on down to where surfers had been seen.

After walking in that direction, the group found out they were now on Arpoador beach, known for its perfect waves for surfers. LaShawn managed to find a surf shop complete with instructors. After several attempts and a lot of mistakes, the surf instructors taught them how to surf a little. Surfing was such great fun. They didn't leave until it was almost dusk.

As everyone was walking back along the beach to where the threesome had left their belongings in a locker, it became dark, and streetlights came on. When you talk about a million-dollar view, this was it. The streetlights highlighted the waves coming in with the mountains looming in the background and dark clouds hovering overhead. A quarter moon was peeking through the clouds, leaving its reflection on the water in the bay.

LaShawn caught a taxi for us to a restaurant near their hotel. They were all famished having eaten nothing since breakfast. Then to top it all off, there was all the exercise they had from swimming and surfing. They ate a hearty meal. Such a pleasant ending to such a perfect day. When everyone had finished dinner, they went strolling back to their rooms when suddenly were heard fast footsteps coming from behind them. A grubby-looking man dressed in dark clothing grabbed Tatiana's purse and tried to take it. But Tatiana had a firm grip on it. LaShawn whirled around, striking him in the face.

It was a hard blow, and the perpetrator flipped over backward end over end twice. He got up and started to flee, but by this time, all three had all plucked out their slingshots. The potential thief was hit with marbles several times before he rounded the corner and got away. Terri said, "I will bet he will be more careful next time he tries to steal a purse." Tatiana laughed, saying, "Sometimes it just doesn't pay to be a crook."

The next day, LaShawn said he still doesn't have anything solid from his contacts. But the contacts had told him they had narrowed the place where Russ and Marvin were living to a certain neighborhood. Terri suggested, "This would be a good time to take in Rio de Janeiro's cultural scene." LaShawn and Tatiana agreed this seemed like a good idea. Tatiana added, "Then maybe this evening, we can take in some of the nightlife in Rio about which we have heard raved about."

During all of the morning and afternoon, they once again explored the Centro district. This time going to a couple of Rio de Janeiro's museums. Afterward, they checked out some outdoor stalls for locally handcrafted goods. Terri bought a necklace and a beautiful shawl for her mother. Also a Portuguese children's book, which had English translations for Gavin. Terri thought he might get a kick out of it. One thing had always bothered her ever since Chris was in prison. This was the fact she was never able to give him anything for Christmas, their anniversary, or even on his birthday.

After everyone had finished shopping, they went back to their rooms and prepared for a big night out. Tatiana and Terri were in evening gowns, and LaShawn looked outstanding in a black tuxedo. LaShawn decided to take the car this time as they would be going to more than one place.

First, LaShawn found a nice restaurant in the Centro district. When the waiter appeared, Tatiana asked him if he could recommend a typical Brazilian dish. He said, "But of course, you need to try *feijoada*. It is considered our national dish. It is made with pork, rice, black beans, collard greens, cassava flour, and oranges." They all tried it and agreed it was very savory and satisfying.

Next, the three went to a bar where they took a long time sipping on a beer. From their booth, one could hear conversations in English, Portuguese, Spanish, and a half dozen other languages. (Terri thinks from hearing so many languages over half of the customers were tourists.) LaShawn asked the bartender, "Where is a good place to dance?" The bartender recommended them to a large *fieras*, or dance hall. He said, "It is only ten blocks from here. It is a very lively place, and you will enjoy it."

It was very enjoyable. LaShawn was very lucky in being able to find a table with four chairs. It was so crowded. The music was lively, and couples jammed the dance floor, which was enormous. Everyone ordered a caipirinha, which is the Brazilian national drink. Its main ingredient is cachaça. It is a rum made from fermented sugarcane. It differs from other rums in that they are derived from molasses.

LaShawn and Tatiana were quick to join the other dancers on the floor. The newlyweds danced the sambas, salsa, tango, and the bossa nova. Terri was super glad to see them enjoying themselves so completely. For herself, Terri would never be totally happy until Chris was back by her side. Yet she still enjoyed the scene. While she was sitting there, several young men stopped and asked her for a dance. Terri just smiled and showed them her wedding ring, showing the men she was taken.

When a couple who looked to be in their thirties abruptly sat down at the table, Terri tried to tell them the seats were taken. But the couple told her, "Just listen to us, you need to hear us out." The man introduced himself by saying, "My name is Clark Evanston, and this is my wife June." He then proceeded to pull out his wallet showing her a badge and an identification card. Clark said, "We are both detectives with the Miami, Florida, vice squad.

"We happen to be here as tourists on vacation, which we assume you are too. From now on, whatever you do, please do not turn around. As soon as we entered the fieras, we noticed a man sitting at the bar from a wanted picture we had received on an Interpol poster. This man is wanted in many countries. He is one of the heads of a ring which kidnaps young women and sells them as sex slaves.

"After we saw him, we tried to be as inconspicuous as possible. After watching him covertly for a time, we noticed he was concentrating on one thing. It took us a while, but we finally realized he was watching your every move. He was oblivious to everything else, and is the reason we came to talk to you."

Clark said, "Now what I would like you to do is get up and dance with me. This way, you can get a good look at him without him realizing it." Clark immediately stood up and took Terri out onto the dance floor. As they were dancing, he said, "Now if you glance over toward the end of the bar, you will see him. He is a bald tall man wearing a gray sport coat. Just glance quickly as I whirl you around, for he is still staring at you."

Clark whirled Terri around a couple of times. She was careful not to meet the tall man's eyes. Clark had to hold Terri up as her knees almost gave away, but she quickly regained her composure. Terri told Clark, "I know that bastard, take me back to the table so we can talk." As soon as they got back to the table, Terri told Clark and June the whole story. She didn't hold anything back, including what had happened to Chris.

Terri ended up by telling them how Tatiana and she had broken into Marvin's home, where they had found masks and various torture devices. She told Clark and June this had happened not just once, but twice. She said, "We also found torture devices in his home in Jamaica. We were searching for Russ and Marvin and have been for years. The one you see standing by the bar is Marvin Mueller, his alias is Hank Devlin."

Terri showed Clark and June the pictures, explaining the other one's name is Russ Jacobson, and the alias he goes by is Tom Jackson. Clark and June stated, "This is more information than Interpol has." Terri told them, "Seeing he is here, I want to capture Marvin." The Evanstons told Terri, "Not on your life. It is just way too dangerous. Why don't you let Interpol handle it. We need to give them this new information anyway when we get back to Florida."

Terri told the Evanstons, "No, I have been searching for Russ and Marvin for far too long. Interpol is far away, and Marvin is here and now. My husband has been in prison for a long time for a crime he did not commit. Maybe I cannot capture Marvin, but at least I have to try." Terri went on to tell them about Tatiana and herself, how they had practiced for years at a self-defense course, and now Terri is an instructor herself.

Clark and June reluctantly agreed to help. First of all, they got Terri's cell phone number; then Clark and June gave her their phone numbers. June reached in her purse and handed Terri a small metallic device, saying, "This is a tracking bug. Every time it passes a cell phone tower, it will emit a signal. This bug will track anywhere, it also has a magnetic base. This way, it can be attached to anything metallic. Keep this with you at all times. If something does go wrong, we will be able to trace you."

Clark said, "Now let's see if we can come up with some type of a plan." At this time, LaShawn and Tatiana came back to the table. LaShawn pulled up an extra chair and sat down. Terri explained to them about everything that was happening. She told everyone, "I want to walk out the front door alone. I will be the bait. Then we will see if the mouse falls in the trap." LaShawn strongly objected to the idea. But Tatiana held up her hand, saying, "I think Terri has the right idea. She has been preparing for something like this for years."

Tatiana said, "I think we need to give Terri a chance; besides, I have watched her practice. I know she can kick Marvin's butt." What they finally decided was LaShawn and Tatiana would go out the door first. Then Terri would walk down the street a little way to the right. Tatiana would go to the left to get the rental car. Then when Terri came out, she would start walking to the right. LaShawn would then start walking about twenty-five feet in front of her. The Evanstons would wait until Marvin left, and then trail behind him as he followed Terri.

So it was settled. LaShawn and Tatiana sauntered out the door. Around six minutes later, Clark and June whispered good luck to Terri. She was immediately on her way out of the door. Terri's heart was hammering in her chest. Terri knew she would be able to do this. A sideways glance at a store window told her Marvin was following her. She started to walk fairly fast, but she could hear rapid footsteps coming up behind her. Terri kept glancing at the store windows to see how close Marvin was. Terri could not believe her ears when she heard Marvin shout, "Hey, Terri." Then she heard running footsteps as he rushed to grab her.

Terri whirled around, grabbing Marvin's outstretched arm, throwing him over her head. As he flew the air, Terri whirled around, giving him a flying kick as he flew past. Marvin hit the sidewalk hard; unfortunately, Terri wasn't able to nab him as her high heel broke and sent her to the ground. At the same time, a black limousine came to a screeching halt. The door was flung open, and Marvin scrambled into it. The door slammed shut just as LaShawn made a huge lunge for it. Terri was just barely able to hobble to the rear wheel well of the limousine in time to plant the bug before it roared off.

Chapter 44

Just as the limousine pulled out, Tatiana pulled up in the rental car. LaShawn told Tatiana, "Move over because I will drive." Terri jumped into the rear seat as they left. Terri yelled out to the Evanstons, "We will call you. Can you track the bug? I planted it on the limousine." From there on out, the chase was fast, furious, and just insane. As much as they wanted to capture Russ and Marvin, they had the same urge to escape. LaShawn roared round corners on two wheels, the tires screeching in protest. He went the wrong way on one-way streets. LaShawn ran red lights. People were scattering out of our way to the left and right. Where are the police when you really need them?

LaShawn was able to keep up with Russ and Marvin as long as they stayed on the city streets. However, the limousine had a much more powerful engine than the rental car. The limo was able to pull away from LaShawn when it hit the straightaway. Up ahead, LaShawn saw the limo take a left-hand turn as he followed. Terri, Tatiana and LaShawn did not realize at the time, but they had just entered into the favela da Rocinha. This was one of the worst slums in Rio de Janeiro. At the same time, LaShawn had totally lost track of the limousine. LaShawn drove around the maze trying to find our way out.

It was around this time Terri noticed there was a car following them. It was not the limousine, but whoever was in it, the three were not very fond of the idea. LaShawn drove around several blocks trying to find other way out of the favela. The houses in this area were the worst of the worst. They were nothing but ramshackle shanties. That's when LaShawn shouted, "Thank God, there is a opening to the freeway. Let's get the hell out of here before we get shot."

The good thing was they were finally on the freeway, and yet the bad thing was LaShawn had found out he was going up the mountain. Even worse is the fact the car, which had been following them in the favela, was still following them. At first, the car following seemed to be satisfied with just following them; however, after a few miles red and blue lights came on. Realizing it was the police everyone was relieved and LaShawn pulled over.

Two policemen with flashlights came up to our car and asked LaShawn to provide his driver's license and the registration of the car. After the police had examined the documents, one of the policemen asked us what our business was in the favela da Rocinha. LaShawn explained, "We had simply taken a wrong turn and were not able to find our way out of the area."

The police probably suspected them of belonging to a gang or maybe even drug dealers. Regardless, the police called for a K-9 unit to come and check them out. The police made the three get out of the car, had the dog sniff everywhere. The K-9 handler had the dog check the front seat and the backseat, under the hood, and then in the trunk. The police must've finally been satisfied the three didn't have any drugs. LaShawn asked the policeman, "How do we find our way back to our hotel?" The policeman drew them a map and apologized for the inconvenience. He told them they needed to be more careful in the future. "Don't go near any favelas." LaShawn, Tatiana, and Terri all agreed with him wholeheartedly.

When Terri and the Williams finally made it back to their hotel rooms, they decided to get some much-needed rest. In the morning, Terri was awakened to the sound of the telephone ringing. It was from Clark Evanston. He was very worried about how she had fared last night. Terri invited Clark and June to meet them in the lobby of their hotel at 10:00 a.m. When Terri finished talking to the Evanstons, she immediately called LaShawn and Tatiana to inform them of their meeting.

Upon meeting with the Evanstons, everyone decided they were in the need of two things—breakfast and a quiet place where the group could talk and not be overheard. After Terri had talked to the manager of the hotel, he suggested, "We use a small conference room. There you would be able to order your breakfast and have it delivered to you." This turned out to be the ideal solution. Even as their meal was delivered, they had already started to plan.

LaShawn told Clark and June everything which had happened to us after leaving the fieiras. This included losing sight of the limousine in the favela da Rocinha. Then being followed by the police who had thought the three were hoodlums. Clark commented dryly, "It is very lucky for you it was the police who were following your car. All of the favelas in Rio de Janerio are controlled by drug lords. If it had been one of them or one of their gang members who had followed you, the end result would have probably been much different."

Clark said, "By the way, Terri, when you flipped Marvin on the sidewalk, you caused him to drop his cell phone. I picked the cell phone up, but I have an obligation to turn it over to Interpol. However, I will show you what I found on it." Terri hastily scribbled down the phone numbers, which were basically all to one number. Terri assumed this number belonged to Russ Jacobson and that it was also a cell phone number.

What startled them most of all were the pictures, which were on the cell phone. They were mostly of Terri sitting alone by the table at the fieras. The one which scared Terri the most was one of her coming back from the powder room. In the background looking like he was trying to grab Terri was Russ Jacobson. There were no pictures of LaShawn and Tatiana. But there was one of Clark and June Evanston sitting at the table with Terri.

By the time Terri had finished looking at the pictures, she was livid. Terri shouted, "Those miserable bastards, I should have let Russ and Marvin capture me. I had the bug which the Evanstons had given me. Clark, you and June could have caught up with them by tracing it. I'm sure by the time you had caught up with us that in the meantime, Russ and Marvin would have bragged about their exploits. I am sure they would have had to brag to me about how they had framed Chris. If I ever gotten the chance, I would have whipped their ass. Then maybe I would have been able to free Chris from prison."

At this point, Terri broke down in tears at the thought of failing so miserably. Clark said, "Buck up, Terri, I'm very glad you didn't decide to do that. It would've been way too dangerous. The creeps could have gone directly to an airplane and caught a flight. There are no cell phone towers in the air. Or they might have taken the boat or even gone into the mountains. There are many places where there are no cell phone towers. You could've been lost to us forever.

"Now, however, we do have a chance. Russ and Marvin will think they have gotten away free. The chances are both of them will leave the place where they are living now. Russ and Marvin have just had a big scare and will think this area is too hot for them. They also know having lost Marvin's cell phone the police may try to triangulate it. The call would probably lead to the place where they are living. I will start tracing the bug and see where it leads us."

It was at that time LaShawn's cell phone rang. He put up his hand to silence the group. As LaShawn listened to the phone, he grabbed a pen and paper and began to write. After he had put his phone down, LaShawn said, "My contacts have found the place where Russ and Marvin were living. Unfortunately for us, they have already left. According to my contacts, the two of them pulled out about two hours ago. Why don't we go to their house and see if they left any clues to what they were doing or to their new whereabouts?"

Clark said, "In the meantime, June and I will start tracing the bug. We will call to let you know in which direction Russ and Marvin are heading." Before LaShawn and the girls left, they all exchanged home addresses and phone numbers. Clark and June promised, "If we did not catch up with Russ and Marvin now, we will monitor Interpol to let us know of any further developments."

After LaShawn, Tatiana and Terri had checked out of the hotel and were placing their bags in the car, Terri glanced up at Corcovado Mountain. There at the very top stood Christ the Redeemer. Today, there was a thick cloud cover above the statue. Through a break in the clouds, the sun sent down a beam of light right on Christ's head and outstretched arms. To Terri, it seemed like an omen. Terri silently gave thanks to the Lord, promising, "Someday, she would come back with Chris and go up there."

LaShawn quickly drove to the house, which Russ and Marvin had occupied, in a medium-class neighborhood. As the door was standing open, LaShawn just walked right in. Outside of the furnishings, there was not a clue to be found anywhere. The three searched everywhere, but Russ and Marvin must've been ready to leave at a moment's notice. The only thing to be found was a picture on the wall.

Evidently, Russ had also taken pictures of Terri at the dance hall table. This one was a picture of her taken from a different angle. The assholes had blown the picture up to an eight-by-ten, then had taken a knife and pinned it to the wall with the knife through her heart. Terri thought, "This seemed extremely appropriate, as I have had a knife through my heart ever since you bastards got my husband sent to prison."

Tatiana called Clark to see if he had found out anything. Clark said, "Russ and Marvin are heading toward Brasilia." Tatiana then asked Clark if he was able to tell them how far Brasilia was from Rio de Janerio, After looking it up, Clark replied, "About 720 miles." LaShawn went to a gas station to gas up and get a map, and from there, he planned out their route. LaShawn was on the road within ten minutes after stopping. The drive was very scenic, and very enjoyable, but at the same time it was very long and wearisome.

By the time the three had found a hotel on the far side of Paronoa Lake, it was two o'clock in the morning. By that time, Everyone was exhausted; and when Terri got to her room, she just plopped down on her bed and passed out. After a nice shower the next morning, she felt renewed. Terri wandered outside to take a look at Paronoa Lake. It is a large man-made lake built to increase the amount of fresh water to Brasilia.

The city of Brasilia itself didn't even exist until 1960. Rio de Janerio had been the capital of Brazil from 1763 to 1960. But Brazilians wanted a more central location for their national capital. In 1956, they went to work building a brand-new capital from scratch. Brasilia was dedicated on April 21, 1960. When the architects started building Brasilia, they anticipated a city of around a half million people. Today, the population of Brasilia is over two and a half million.

As soon as LaShawn and Tatiana were awake, Terri called Clark Evanston. Clark told them, "When Russ and Marvin started moving this morning, they immediately went to the center of Brasilia. There the bug had sat in one place for over two and a half hours. Now they seemed to be headed for Sao Paulo, Brazil, which is 630 miles to the south of Brasilia."

After talking it over, LaShawn, Tatiana, and Terri decided to take a chance Russ and Marvin were not going to turn off. Terri turned in the rental car at the Brasilia airport and got airline tickets for Sao Paulo. Terri thought in this way, they would be able to pick up another rental car in Sao Paulo and be there ahead of Russ and Marvin. After picking up the car and getting rooms in Sao Paulo, they waited for a phone call from Clark and June Evanston.

as the three of them were waiting, they tried to figure out why Russ and Marvin had gone to Brasilia first. It just didn't seem to make any sense. Sao Paulo was much closer to Rio de Janerio than it was to Brasilia. Terri was sure they would probably never know. It probably had something to do with bribing some politician. They also thought Russ and Marvin were probably coming to Sao Paulo in order to leave Brazil. Clark finally called, saying, "The limo is getting close to Sao Paulo, and it looks like Russ and Marvin are heading for the airport."

LaShawn and the girls scrambled for the airport, and after they got there, they waited and waited. The phone finally rang again. Clark said, "I have been trying to reach you for over thirty minutes, but I was not able to get through. Russ and Marvin changed directions and instead went to Ocean Terminal 21."

LaShawn took off immediately for Ocean Terminal 21, hoping to catch Russ and Marvin before they left. But the traffic was as bad as it gets on Highway 405 at rush hour in Seattle. When LaShawn and the girls finally got there, they discovered the limousine. It was the same one because Terri was able to recover the bug from the right rear wheel well. The limousine was sitting there empty, and the keys were in it. A sure sign the limousine had been left to be stolen, and a good sign Russ and Marvin had fled Brazil. Once more, Terri was a day late and a dollar short.

With no more leads and a heavy heart, there were left with no alternatives but to go home. Terri called Clark and June, telling the Evanstons thanks for all they had done and to let her know if the Evanstons find out anything else. With that, they headed for the airport and home.

Chapter 45

Chris in Monroe. It always seems like when everything is going smoothly, something always comes along to upset the apple cart. Chris had his hands full with the educational courses being taught at Monroe. He was also helping anywhere from two to eight prisoners at any one time with their GED. Chris really loved doing this. It filled his days and made the time seem to go by much faster.

But it seems no matter what you try to do in life, there is always someone else who takes exception. The exception in this case was an unwashed, uneducated big convict whose nickname was Butch. No one there at Monroe, not even the guards, seemed to know what his real name was. Butch seemed to be full of hatred toward everyone. Somehow he had decided the thing to do was to direct his vile temper toward Chris.

At first, it was all just verbal. Butch would call Chris professor in a sneering manner. After he realized the verbal abuse didn't bother Chris, Butch decided to try something else. He started bumping into Chris every chance he got. One day, when Chris's back was turned, Butch grabbed him from behind. Some of the other inmates saw this and pulled him off immediately. "What's the matter?" asked Butch. "Are you afraid to fight your own battles?"

Chris told him, "No, Butch, I'm not in the least little bit afraid of you. If you are able to set it up with the guards, I will fight you. But I will not fight you unless it is sanctioned by prison personnel. Even then, I will only fight you under one condition. Which is, if I win fair and square, you will let me help you to get an education." Butch said, "Okay, I promise. Because after I get finished with you, you will be in no condition to teach me anything."

The guards at the prison were asked if Butch and Chris could have a match. Always eager for some cheap entertainment, they passed the request up the chain of command. The word came down from the higher echelon the fight was a go. Everyone wanted to see Butch defeated. Because he had hurt other convicts so badly they ended up in the infirmary.

What Butch didn't realize is Chris has always been in great physical shape. He did a lot of workouts to keep it that way. Also, every time Terri came for their forty-eight-hour visitation, she had always taught Chris various moves from her self-defense course. Terri had always been afraid something like this would eventually happen, and she wanted him to be prepared for it.

When the time for the fight began, Butch tried to simply overpower Chris. Brute strength had always worked for him in the past. When Butch tried to rush Chris, he simply stepped aside, at the same time hammering Butch in the back of his head and in the kidneys. After that, Chris simply used every trick which Terri had taught him. No matter what Butch did, he was not able to catch Chris in his death grip. Butch may have been a big boy, but he had finally met his match. By the time Chris had thrown him several times and then pinned him to the mat, Butch knew without a doubt he was finished.

Chris was also surprised because amazingly Butch kept his word about coming to him for lessons. When they first started the lessons, Chris could not believe it. Butch did not even know how to sign his name, nor did he know the ABCs. Chris could now understand his anger. Butch wasn't able to read, and he could not write. Butch had always used his immense strength to keep anyone from questioning his intelligence. Chris would bet he had a very hard time as a child. Everyone must have thought he was a dummy.

But slowly and very painfully at first, Butch pursued his lessons. He sometimes became very frustrated and would walk away. At that time, Chris would go to Butch, saying, "Butch, you can do it, you know you can." The light finally came on when Butch read his first book without faltering. This book happened to be the first of a series, and Butch wanted to find out what happened in the rest of the series. Butch had just crossed the threshold. The little bit of knowledge he had absorbed had given him a tremendous appetite for more. They have both made a stupendous discovery. Chris was not a bad guy, and Butch certainly wasn't dumb.

As a matter-of-fact, once Butch got started on the right path, he was downright brilliant. Chris realized now Butch never had a proper childhood. His parents were both drug abusers. Somehow they had gotten away with never once sending him to school. The parents had moved around so much, authorities never even realized he was not enrolled in school anywhere. His parents made sure Butch was fed, clothed, and had a place to sleep, which was about it.

Of course, with this type of upbringing, it did not take long for Butch to wind up in trouble. One man made the mistake of mocking Butch. He wound up in intensive care. And Butch found himself staring through the windows of the Monroe Correctional Complex.

Butch's new education started him on the path to discovery. He found out he wanted to know everything from very simple things, all way up to Einstein's theory of relativity. But it was not just an education which Butch needed. He asked Chris for help with his manners. It took a long time, but eventually, Butch did get his GED. From that time on, when he was not working on a college correspondence course, you would always be able to find him in the prison library.

Chris was also able to find out his real name. It was Reginald White. Butch told Chris he thought Reginald sounded so prissy he was not able to stand it. Chris thought about this for about half a second. Then Chris asked him, "Why don't you tell everyone to call you Reggie?" Butch rolled the name over his tongue a few times repeating it. A great big smile appeared on his face, and he said, "Okay, from now on Reggie it is."

Reggie really cleaned up his act. He started to act like a gentleman. He was kind and courteous to everyone. Even the prison guards were impressed. Reggie was serving time for assault and battery and had been denied parole three times. Every time he had come up for parole, everyone on the parole board had voted no every time. After Reggie had cleaned up his act and completely turned around. The next time he faced a parole board, they were completely astounded. All the members of the parole board voted to release him. After the parole hearing, the members of the parole board asked him what had caused the change. Reggie simply said, "Chris Sutton showed me the light."

After Reggie's release from prison, he wrote to Chris and told him he had found a good job. Reggie also said he had signed up for night school and was planning to earn a college degree. In closing, he told Chris he was the only man in his life who had ever beaten him in a fight. Reggie went on to say, "If I had known what would happen to me after losing my first fight well, I would've lost that fight years ago. Instead of it being an end, it was the start of a new beginning. Chris, there is no way in the world I can ever thank you enough. Whenever it is your turn to be paroled let me know so I can send them a letter on your behalf."

Chapter 46

Where has the time gone? Chris has now been in prison for over twelve years. To Terri, it seems like fifty years. Since the time they nearly caught Marvin in Brazil, LaShawn, Tatiana, and Terri have been on a bunch of wild goose chases. They have been to Aruba, Puerto Rico, Peru, Morocco, and South Africa. But sadly, it was all for nothing. Terri has not seen so much as a hair of Russ Jacobson or Marvin Mueller since she left Rio de Janeiro.

Terri knows Interpol is also after Russ and Marvin, especially now Interpol has both their real names and their aliases. Clark and June Evanston give Terri a call every now and then to give her an update. The only thing Interpol knows for sure is Russ and Marvin are still in business. Due to the fact beautiful young women keep disappearing. Every so often, one of the women will reappear; but by this time, they have been badly abused. It is hard to believe such things can exist in the modern world.

Gavin still looks forward to visiting Terri's parents every summer. However, he outgrew the Shetland pony quite a while ago. Of course, when that happened, Grandpa and Grandma had to get him a big horse. Gavin rides in the Fourth of July parade in Towner every year. Next year, he wants to enter the rodeo. He plans on being a saddle bronc contestant. Terri is not very fond of the idea.

Gavin is a very big boy for his age and is heavily into sports. He started playing basketball when he was in the first grade and continues to excel at that. Gavin started playing softball when he was in the second grade. Now he has moved up to baseball. However, Gavin's first love is football, which he started playing when he was in the third grade. At first, Gavin looked so funny in a helmet and shoulder pads. But now when he puts them on he, is starting to look downright masculine. Whenever Terri has a chance to watch a game, she's always afraid he will get hurt. However, when Terri tells Gavin she worries about him, Gavin always says, "Mom, quit worrying about me. I'm a big boy now."

At least for now, Gavin has not set his goal on professional football. In his own mind, he has set his goal much higher. Gavin wants to go to Bellevue High School and be on their football team. Yes, he wants to be among the elite. Gavin wants to become a Bellevue Wolverine. He told his mom, "Mom, you have got to come and watch them. The Bellevue Wolverines are awesome."

And the Wolverines are awesome. They train hard, and they play hard. Terri will admit they are amazing. They have won the class AAA state football championship in Washington several years in a row. Aside from football, Terri is very glad Gavin will be going to Bellevue High School. They are also great academically, along with all of the other high schools in the Bellevue School District. They have always been placed in the top one hundred schools in the United States for several years in a row.

Gavin came to Terri one day and asked, "Mom, why is my dad in prison? I really enjoy visiting him, and I wish he was at home with us like all of my friend's dads. I know Dad is in prison for manslaughter, but what happened? I have gotten to know my dad, and I don't see how he could ever hurt anyone." Terri told him, "Gavin, you are right. Your dad has not got a mean bone in his body. He loves you and me very much and would love to be here with us. But he was framed for a murder, I do not know how he was framed, but I do know who did it."

Terri realized Gavin had forgotten what little she had told him about his dad being in prison when he was young. So she sat down with him to tell him the bare essentials. Terri told Gavin about the Felix Wells Investment Firm. Terri told about the money disappearing from the firm and Russ and Marvin disappearing on the same day. Terri told Gavin how she had been trying to catch Russ and Marvin for years. How close they had been to capturing Marvin in Brazil and how at the time she had broken her high heel, and he got away. Terri told him about the chase from Rio de Janeiro, to Brasilia, to Sao Paulo.

Gavin sat there thinking about this. After Terri had finished, he looked at her and said, "Gee-whiz, Mom, I didn't realize you were that tough." Terri tousled his hair and said, "Don't you forget it, buddy. Just try not doing your homework, and I will show you how tough I am." They both started laughing because Gavin always did his homework, and Terri had never treated him rough.

Gavin was also a perfect gentleman for his age. He was wise beyond his years. He loved his father and wanted to visit him every chance he got. But one day, he came to Terri. He was kind of hesitant at first. Gavin said, "Mom, I have come to a very hard decision. I still want to go with you to visit Dad every chance I get during normal visiting hours. But from now on, I will not come with you when you get a forty-eight-hour pass."

When Terri asked him "But why not, Gavin?" He replied, "Mom, this is not because I don't love Dad, because I do with all of my heart. But you and Dad are husband and wife. You need forty-eight hours together all by yourselves. I admit I will miss it, but I'm very confident Dad will be paroled early."

Of course, Chris was disappointed he would not be able to see Gavin for longer periods of time. He was surprised a twelve-year-old was so understanding. Chris admitted to Terri, "We do need more alone time." Terri told him, "Chris, your son takes after you. Like you, he does not have a mean bone in his body. Gavin is sacrificing his own time with you, for us. It is his decision because he loves both of us. Let's honor Gavin's decision and make the most of it."

So they did. On top of all else, Chris and Terri were able to talk aloud and make plans. If an idea or topic came up, they were able to talk about it right away. Chris told Terri, "The time I spend with you is my quality time. When you are not here, that is my work time. It may surprise you if I were not locked up here every night, if I had my freedom to come and go as I choose, to be able to come home every night, the actual work that I'm doing here is by my own choice. This part of prison life is not bad.

"This is the type of work I would like to do when I am released. However, with this manslaughter conviction on my record, I doubt a job like this will ever happen. Unless somehow we can get my conviction reversed by proving I never did it.

"Terri, I have to tell you, just knowing you and Gavin will be here for me when I am released is what has made all the difference in the world to me. Without you, I probably would have gone insane. But you have been with me every step of the way. Not only that, but you have actually put yourself in harm's way trying to prove my innocence."

Chris went on to say, "It is hard for me to believe I have made it over twelve years of the twenty-year sentence. I have a little surprise for you, but please don't let it get your hopes up. Nothing has ever gone right for us ever since my parents were killed in the car accident in North Dakota. Prison authorities let me know yesterday that my first parole hearing will be a few months after I have served fifteen years in prison. But at the same time, the authorities also said it is very seldom a prisoner is ever released on the first try."

Terri threw her arms around Chris, giving him a fierce hug. She told him, "My darling husband, you shouldn't have had to serve one second of the sentence. The part which is really killing me, though, is the fact even though I have tried as hard as I could I have never been able to clear your name. I do know without a doubt, somehow, someway, it will happen by the time you are released from prison. Or at the very most, it will happen shortly thereafter." Chris said, "Don't worry yourself, Terri there is no one who could have tried harder than you have. You have just had bad luck."

Terri said, "I know, Chris, I just have to try harder. I have not had a decent lead since we left Rio de Janeiro. It's as if Russ and Marvin have disappeared off the face of the earth. Even Interpol with all of its connections has been unable to find them. But I'll keep on searching." Chris's face suddenly lit up, saying, "Maybe you have been looking for ideas in the wrong places.

"I just thought of some new ideas. First, why don't you try to find what areas the young women have been disappearing from. Russ and Marvin must have a certain method. Check with the Evanstons to see if you can figure it out. The second idea I have, I do not have a clue of how it could be done, but you told me there were women who have disappeared and then reappeared much later. If you were able to get a hold of some of those women maybe they would be able to tell you how it happened.

"A third idea is, Russ and Marvin can't have been successful every time. There has to have been women who were almost captured. The chances of it happening are slim to none, but there's always the chance it could have happened. If it did, I am sure they would be able to give you a lot of information."

Chapter 47

Those ideas became a new plan for Terri. She first contacted the Evanstons and asked them if they would be able to figure out Russ and Marvin's method of operation. Also, if there was a method, where is it happening now. Clark and June gracefully said, "We would try, but it would most likely take a long time."

The next thing Terri did was go to her computer to set up a new website. She named the website Lost and Exploited Women of the World. In it, Terri asked for any woman who had been captured and held as sex slaves. If any woman who thought someone tried to capture her, any woman who had been captured and escaped soon afterward, she asked if any woman ever had any of these things happen to her, to please contact Terri Sutton.

From the first day Teri started the website, she was swamped with nuisance e-mails. Terri doesn't even think they were all from women. She learned there were a lot of sick people in this world. There were a lot of women who were just angry at their husbands or boyfriends. Some women got on the website just to let off steam. Then there were the weird ones who thought the idea of sex slavery was a terrific idea. The only reason they replied was they were looking for a place to enlist.

After a period of time, Terri got very frustrated. She started checking her e-mails infrequently just in order to delete them. For months on end, Terri did not receive even one e-mail, which would help her. Then just as she was about to delete one message, Terri stopped and read it. All the e-mail said was, "Please help me." Then it gave Terri a physical address. Next, it said, "Please don't reply by computer. My life would be in great danger." She ended it by signing, "Trapped in Tacoma."

After Terri had read the e-mail, she looked up the address. It was in the hilltop area of Tacoma. From what she had heard on the news, the hilltop area was a very dangerous place. It was notorious for shootings and muggings.

She thought to herself, "Terri, you would have to be crazy to go there." But dangerous area or not, this girl definitely needed help, and that meant her because no one else even knew about it.

Terri talked to Tatiana. LaShawn happened to be away on business at this time. Terri and Tatiana decided they wouldn't be able to wait until he came back. This girl, whoever she was, needed help right now, not ten days from now. Tacoma was not far away, so the girls decided to drive down just to take a look at what they were getting into. Still, the very idea of going to the hilltop area scared them to death.

It was just starting to get dark as Tatiana slowly drove by the address. Lo and behold, right at this very time, a young woman was being forced into a car. The clothes she was wearing said she was a prostitute. But her looks, her bearing, and her tears told them she was not one.

The pimply-faced punk who was forcing her into the car fit Terri's idea of a gang banger. The arrogant look on his face said, "I can whip any man around. I can have any woman I want, anytime, anyplace." Terri looked at Tatiana, saying, "This little shit looks like he is just dying to have his ass whipped by a woman." Tatiana wholeheartedly agreed with Terri.

Tatiana followed him until he dropped the lady off at a street corner. He then pulled into a parking lot across the street to keep a tab on her. Tatiana immediately stopped their car right alongside of the girl. Terri got out of the car and told her, "Get in the car." But she was terrified. "Get out of here before you get all of us killed," she screamed. Terri simply told her, "You asked for help, and this is all there is. Now I need you to get in the car, leave it to me to take care of this piss-complected little runt."

The woman said, "You don't understand me. He is able to kill us with his bare hands." Terri told her, "This may be what he thinks he can do in his world. However, there is an awful lot of difference between his world and reality." Terri kept half turned away from him as he came running up.

"Get out!" Terri doesn't know what else he was going to say, for you should not use words when action is needed. Terri whirled around and kicked him in the crotch with every ounce of strength in her body. She thinks this may have been the first wake-up call the little punk ever had in his life, for he immediately bent over and began to throw up. She told him, "Oh, but, little lady, the show is not over yet." Terri grabbed him by the arm and swung him around, so his face kissed a light pole.

This seemed to give the punk a brand-new insight into life. He fell backward onto the sidewalk. The punk's whimpering and sniveling did absolutely nothing for Terri. She grabbed him by the hair and told him, "You are not about to pull anything like this again, are you?" Through his busted and splintered teeth, he managed to splutter, "No, ma'am." Terri went on,

"And you are going to get a job at a grocery store as a checkout boy, aren't you?" The punk managed to nod his head yes.

Terri reached into his pockets and pulled out his wallet and car keys. Then she asked him, "You are planning on turning your life around, aren't you?" He again nodded yes, so Terri went on, "We will see you in church this Sunday then?" He blubbered, "Of course." Terri said, "You better be. I will get your name and address from your wallet." Just before she was about to leave, she said, "And you better put something in the collection plate."

This time, when Terri asked her, the young lady had no trouble getting in the car all the time staring at her in wide-eyed wonder. Tatiana, however, was doubled over laughing. When she was finished, she took off like the car was on fire. When they were back on the I-5 freeway heading north toward Seattle, Terri took the keys and threw them in the ditch. Terri was lucky she wasn't picked up for littering. She is just joking. Terri actually threw the car keys in a dumpster like any responsible citizen would.

Tatiana asked the young lady what her name was and how she had gotten into this situation. She told us her name was Dawn Hendrickson. Dawn said she had been waiting at a bus stop when this creep pulled up beside her. At first, he was nice and told her he was willing to take her to anyplace she wanted to go. Dawn said, "I immediately had reservation's just looking at him, so I told him no, I will just wait for the bus. This was when he pulled a gun on me and made me jump into the car.

"He then took me to his home where raped me repeatedly. He told me he was training me to become his first whore. When he was tired and wanted to go to sleep, he locked me into a room, but the idiot forgot there was a computer in there. That is when I found your website and sent an e-mail to you. Today was supposed to be my first day to start working the streets."

At this time, Dawn broke down and started to cry. Tatiana asked her, "Don't you think we should go to the police?" She said, "No, no, no, I do not ever want to see the ugly creep again. I don't want to have to live this ordeal all over." Terri suggested, "We will first take you to my house, then later we could take you to a battered women's shelter. They would know how to take care of you better than Tatiana and I would."

When they got home, Terri remembered the wallet and opened it. There was over $2,500 in there. Terri handed this to Dawn, saying, "At least take the money. You may need it." Dawn asked Terri, "Why did you set up the website in the first place?" Terri explained it to her along with the reason she had set the website up.

Dawn wanted to know much more, so Terri told her about Chris and her marriage and how happy they had been." Terri told her how Chris had been framed for murder and had been sent to prison. She told her about Russ

Jacobson and Marvin Mueller and how they disappeared along with all the money from the Felix Wells Investment Firm. Terri also told Dawn of her long search for them, of the many places LaShawn, Tatiana, and she had gone and about trying to capture Marvin in Brazil and failing.

Terri wound up telling Dawn how she had set up the website after Chris thought she might be searching in the wrong places. Dawn laughed when Terri told her about some of the ridiculous e-mails she have received. Terri ended up by telling her she was about to shut the website down. Dawn, however, was intrigued, saying, "Please don't give up on the website. If you can save only one woman, it will be worth it."

Dawn said, "Listen, I am just about to finish up on getting a master's degree in psychology. I only have two more weeks to go, and I already have a good job lined up. Terri, why don't you let me take over the website? I would have no trouble being able to deal with the crackpot cases. There may be others out there like me who have gotten into trouble and need help. I would be able to help them, and if I find anything which pertains to you, I will let you know."

Now with the website off Terri's shoulders, she had some time to catch up with old friends. She had not heard from Lynn Anderson in ages. After she dialed the phone, Lynn picked up the receiver just as it was about to ring. As she said hello, Lynn said, "Terri, is that you? I had just picked up my phone to call you. Something crazy just happened, and I wanted your input on it. You will remember I told you years ago Tony Lindsay had disappeared? Well, I never saw or heard from him again, neither had Rodney Crowder. Anyway, Rodney received a fairly large inheritance and seeing as how all of their children had already flown the nest, Rodney and his wife decided this was a good time to see the world. Lord knows they deserve it.

"Rodney's wife has always had a desire to visit Australia." (Terri thought Lynn is a great lady, but she sure knows how to draw a story out. But Terri will just let her tell the story in her own way.) Lynn continued on, "Well, Rodney and his wife really loved Sydney, Australia, the people were so nice, and they just adored the Great Barrier Reef.

"When they arrived in Perth, one of the first things they noticed was a man parking a Ferrari. Rodney said this man was dressed like an English gentleman. Then Rodney put it out of his mind until he got a little closer; then he got his wife's attention and said, 'Look, isn't that Tony Lindsay?' His wife agreed with him, so Rodney walked up and said, 'Hi, Tony. Where have you been? We have all been wondering what happened to you.'

"The man looked like he was in shock for a time, then after a moment, he seemed to regain his composure. He immediately replied, 'Pardon me, you must have mistaken me for someone else. My name is not Tony, it is Percival.'

Then he scurried away, and a short time later, the Ferrari was gone. Rodney is positive that it was Tony. He said the man's voice even sounded like Tony. What do you think, Terri?"

Terri took her time answering because she was very skeptical of the story. She told Lynn, "There are many people in the world who look like someone else. I was shopping in a store one day, when I happened to see a man who looked exactly like Chris. When he was talking to a clerk, he even sounded like Chris. However, when I got closer, I noticed many little subtle differences. I am sure this was the case in Australia too."

Lynn said, "You are probably right, Terri, but the only difference in your case is you knew it couldn't possibly be Chris. Because you know where Chris was and it couldn't possibly have been him. In Tony's case, however, no one has seen or heard from him in years. We don't have a clue as to whether he is alive or dead. In this case, it could have been Tony. I agree with you the chances of it being Tony are very small."

Terri was trying to figure out what she should do this summer for she had no leads on Russ or Marvin at all. This was the first summer since Chris had been in prison Terri didn't know where she was going to go. When Gavin figured out his mom didn't have her summer planned out, he got very excited. Gavin said, "Mom, how about spending the summer with me? We can go to North Dakota to visit Grandpa and Grandma. Having no other plans, I decided to give them a call. They were very excited about the idea.

Chapter 48

After arriving at Terri's parents' farm, Gavin had to show her all around the farm. Gavin took great delight in showing her every little detail. He must not have realized, Terri had lived there for eighteen years. Terri will say Gavin knew a lot more about the outdoor chores than she did. She really got a kick out of the how he treated his horse. Gavin would curry it for hours on end. Nothing was too good for Buck, which is the name he had given his horse.

If Gavin paid too much attention to Buck, the little Shetland pony would come up and nudge him. Then Gavin would have to pay just as much attention to the pony. As soon as Gavin would step out of the house in the morning, Buck and the Shetland pony would whinny and nicker until he went over to them.

Terri told Gavin, "I thought you said you had the horses trained. It looks to me as if they have you trained." Gavin laughed and told his mom he had trained them both. He said the horses could do tricks. Gavin proudly told me, "Buck is a quarter horse." Terri teasingly asked him what the other three quarters were. Gavin explained to her a quarter horse was supposed to be exceptionally fast for a quarter of a mile.

Next, Gavin related to Terri Buck was a really good cutting horse, and he had trained Buck himself. He proudly told his mom what a cutting horse was. "When you are working with a herd of cattle and you want to cut one out of the herd, you just point Buck at the critter, and Buck will cut the cow of the herd. When you rope that critter, you just fasten your rope on the saddle horn, then Buck will keep backing up, and you will be able to flip the critter and hogtie it." Terri's father told her, "You know, Gavin is just as handy around the farm as Chris was at his age. I don't know if Gavin has told you about this, but he is thinking about taking agribusiness when he goes to college. He is also interested in going to the University of North Dakota."

Terri told her father, "This is all a surprise to me. I guess it's time to have a long talk with Gavin. I think I have been too busy with everything else, I have not asked him what he wants to do. Chris and I do not want to ever hold him back. Whatever Gavin wants to do, we will be behind him 100 percent."

Terri's dad said, "I'm glad to hear that, Terri, I think Gavin has one more surprise for you. But I will let him deal with that himself. Gavin did ask me to approach you on the subject of college. Also, the courses Gavin plans to take, he was afraid you would be upset.

"There's also something else I wanted to talk to you. Your mother and I are getting older. Now you and Chris already own his parents farm. By the time Gavin finishes college, we will be ready to retire. We would like Gavin to take over our farm. Gavin already knew most of what's needed. He doesn't go around with his head in the clouds. We are very proud of him."

Terri gave her dad a big hug, and told him, "Personally, I would love to see Gavin have the farm. I will talk to Chris, but I know he will be just as thrilled as I am with the idea. Besides, Chris and I are not positive about what we are going to do when he gets out of prison. A lot will depend on if Chris can get a decent job.

"Chris and I know we plan on staying in Bellevue until Gavin graduates from high school. After that, we are not sure of anything. I guess if Gavin does go to college in North Dakota, it will make a big difference. If he does, we will probably come back to live on Chris's parents' farm. This is something we have talked about. We just haven't come to a final decision yet."

Terri had always loved Towner, but being there was really hard on her this time. It was just so nostalgic being there without Chris. Everything and everyone Terri met brought back a memory of Chris. Terri purposely pulled up good memories to remember. She drove past the high school. She would've gone in, but it was closed for the summer. Just seeing the school calmed her down with loving thoughts of Chris. Terri drove to that old oak tree where Chris had proposed to her. At first she cried, but then the memory of him all nervous and funny kicked in. Terri started to laugh and realized Chris was not gone forever. Just thinking about this did wonder for her spirits. Chris may not have been here in person, but he certainly was here in her heart.

On the evening of the third of July, her parents, Gavin, and Terri went to the annual street dance held in Towner. It was wonderful seeing old friends, renewing old acquaintances, and visiting with them. Towner was a small community, so everyone there knew about Chris. The people who knew him knew how kind and gentle he was. No one harbored the slightest notion about Chris being guilty. Everyone being very supportive, telling Terri to say hi to Chris the next time she sees him.

In the midst of all the excitement, Terri had momentarily lost track of Gavin. She was not very worried because he probably knew everyone in town. Then Terri happened to notice something across the street, Gavin was holding hands with a very pretty, dark-haired girl. Gavin must have noticed his mom because he tried to hide in the crowd; however, Terri just smiled and waved nonchalantly.

After his mother waved, Gavin must have decided everything was all right, for he quit trying to duck from Terri in the crowd. Instead, he crossed the street bringing the girl along with him. Gavin said, "Hi, Mom, I would like you to meet my friend Becky." Even in the dark, Terri was able to see his face turn flame red. Then Gavin said, "Becky, this is my mother, Terri Sutton."

Terri was able to keep her composure even though she had a hard time to keep from laughing. Terri told her, "I am very glad for the chance to meet you, Becky." She smiled sweetly, saying, "I'm very glad to meet you too, Mrs. Sutton, Gavin has been telling me so much about you for years." After Gavin had introduced his mom to Becky, Terri did not think his face could get any redder. But thanks to Becky's remark, he somehow managed it.

It was almost like a throwback in time. Chris and Terri had always hung out together. To see their son Gavin, who resembled Chris so much, hanging out with a pretty, dark-haired girl was quite a shock. Gavin was definitely starting to grow up. It was almost like Gavin and Becky were Chris and Terri years ago. If they happen to follow in their footsteps, Terri certainly hope Gavin and Becky wouldn't have the sad part.

Later, Terri asked her dad and mom, "How long has this been going on?" Her mom thought about it for a while, then said, "I think Gavin met Becky the very first time he stayed for the summer." Terri broke out laughing, saying, "Like parents, like son. Well, I will say our son really knows how to pick them. Becky is a very pretty girl." Her mother said, "She is also a very smart and proper girl. We like her very much."

Terri guessed she would've found out about Becky the next day anyhow. Gavin and Terri's father loaded Buck into the horse trailer. Afterwards, everyone got into her dad's pickup and headed into Towner for the Fourth of July parade. When they arrived, Gavin took Buck out of the trailer and joined the rest of the parade.

At the beginning of the parade were a number of veterans of the armed services. They proudly bore the United States flag. The veterans were followed by a marching band. Behind the marching band came several floats followed by the horseback riders. Among them were Gavin and Becky all decked out in western gear and cowboy hats. They were riding side by side. As the pair rode past Terri, both doffed their hats and bowed.

When the parade was finished, Terri and her parents drove out to the Towner rodeo arena. Gavin and Becky came later riding their horses. The kids ground tied them to enable the horses to munch on fresh green grass. Then Becky and Gavinn removed the saddles and saddle blankets. Gavin and Becky proceeded to rub their horses down, also giving them water and oats. It looked like they were very responsible kids.

Terri's dad had made a set of steps, which he placed in the back of the pickup. After he had parked, Terri's father placed two large umbrellas in the holes drilled in them. From there, everyone had an instant place to sit in the shade. Terri's mother had packed a large picnic lunch. The whole family munched on fried chicken and German potato salad. Thus sitting in comfort while enjoying the rodeo. They cheered the contestants on. It was hard to believe some of the spills the riders took and just jumped up and walked away.

In most local rodeos, there are usually several contestants from the surrounding area. For most of these, the Towner rodeo will be the only rodeo they will compete in. The local cowboys look forward to the rodeo every year. There are also contestants who travel long distance and enter as many rodeos as possible. Gavin knew many of the local contestants. However, Becky having lived there all year long all of her life knew all of the contestants from the Towner area.

It was fun watching Gavin and Becky together. It was like being regressed to when Chris and Terri were the same age. Even her mom and dad made a comment about it. Terri made sure to take a lot of pictures of them together. She had already taken pictures of Gavin and Becky in the parade. Terri knew Chris would be dying to see the pictures. She could hardly wait to see what he would have to say.

When Terri finally had a chance to speak to Becky by herself, Terri asked her if she had any plans for the future. Becky replied, "Oh yes, I am going to go to high school here in Towner. After I graduate from high school, I plan on going to college at the University of North Dakota. As of now, I plan on taking agribusiness courses just like Gavin. Because farmer's and rancher's wives need to know all about the business too."

Terri will admit she was a bit taken aback by this. She said, "Oh, do you plan on being a farmer's wife?" "Yes, I do," Becky replied, "after we have finished college, I plan on marrying Gavin. Please don't say anything to him, Mrs. Sutton, Gavin doesn't have any idea about that yet." Terri gave Becky a hug, telling her, "Don't worry, Becky, I won't say a word. Terri told her, "I had this same feeling for my husband when we were your age,

I knew I was going to marry Gavin's father from a very early age. Chris didn't have a clue. He thought we were just best buddies. Chris finally asked me for a real date after he received his driver's license. After that, we were inseparable. Anyhow us girls have to stick together, don't we? Sometimes guys are just so clueless." Becky hugged Terri back, saying, "Thank you, Mrs. Sutton I somehow just knew you would understand."

Becky said, "Mrs. Sutton, you are so wonderful. Now I can understand why Gavin is always talking about you and his dad. Is it true Gavin's dad has been in prison since before he was born?" Terri simply told her, "Yes, Becky, if you care as much about Gavin as you say you do, you will realize how hard it is on both of us to be apart." Becky answered, "Yes, I do understand, Mrs. Sutton. I hate not having Gavin around for eleven months every year."

For the rest of the time Terri and Gavin spent on the farm during the summer, Becky was almost always around. When she was not there, neither was Gavin. Terri was not very worried about them because they were both good kids, and as of now, Becky and Gavin seem to be in the hand-holding stage. If Gavin takes after his father in this way, which of course he does in everything else, they will just remain best buddies until the pair are in high school.

One night not long before Terri was to go back to Seattle, her dad said, "Terri, there's something I have been wanting to talk to you about. First of all, let me begin by saying I have no doubt about Chris's innocence. There is no possible way he could have committed the crime, which sent him to prison. One definitely does not have the ability to kill a man when you are not even able to do something as simple like butchering a chicken.

"I don't know what is wrong with the police department out there. Chris is not even a possible suspect. Why, I'd suspect you before I would suspect Chris. Now don't get upset, Terri, I'm just theorizing. I know you did not commit this crime either. What I am talking about or rather asking, are there any other possible suspects besides Russ and Marvin? I know all the evidence points toward the two whom you have been chasing as being the best possible suspects. Everything points toward them, and from what you have said, they certainly aren't living very saintly lives now.

"But maybe you shouldn't put all of your eggs in one basket. Just imagine, maybe there is someone else behind the scene. Someone who would be smart enough to frame Chris the way they did. Someone like this might be smart enough to go even farther. If he was smart enough to frame Chris, he might be smart enough to frame those two for something else. Not for the murder, he would've already pinned it on Chris. But what if someone did something to make those two take off at the exact time the money disappeared?

"If someone was able to scare the two of them badly enough they probably would have taken off instantly. Then everyone would think they had gotten away with millions from the investment firm. I think anyone who was smart enough to do something of this sort would also be smart enough to just keep on doing what he/she was doing and laying low for a period of time. The reason I am saying this is if these two whom you are chasing have all those millions, then why are they pulling the crap they are doing to raise money?"

Terri went to place her arm around her dad's shoulder. She said, "Dad, in the first place, Russ and Marvin have been bad from the very beginning. Tatiana and I found all sorts of torture devices in Marvin's apartment. Russ and Marvin are probably doing all the bad stuff because they enjoy doing it. Dad, you have to quit watching all of those murder mysteries. These two are as guilty as sin. Maybe in the movies which you watch, there will be a third party as ingenious as you say. However, in this case, we are talking about a real-life mystery.

"After all, why else would Marvin and Russ try to capture me in Brazil? They would not have done this except to stop the one person who knows what they have done." Her dad responded with, "Terri, there could be one of two reasons. The first is evident—to catch you and sell you as a sex slave. The second reason is, they might've wanted to let you know what really happened."

Chapter 49

On the plane trip back to Seattle, Terri told Gavin he had a very nice girlfriend. Gavin replied, "Becky is not my girlfriend. She's just a very special friend. We happen to have a lot of things we enjoy doing together. For instance Becky can ride horses just as well as I can she also plays baseball with me. Becky would like me to come to North Dakota in the winter some time. Becky said she would love to teach me how to ice-skate.

"No, Mom, Becky is not my girlfriend, but she is my best friend, and we do a whole bunch of things together. I think she is real neat, and I look forward to seeing her every summer." Terri thought to herself, "So, Gavin, you have a best friend who is a girl. To me it makes her a girlfriend."

As soon as Terri and Gavin got back to Seattle, they headed up to Monroe prison to see Chris. After the family had talked for a while, Terri handed the pictures to Gavin so he could show them to his father. Chris was really enjoying looking at the pictures and Terri was watching Chris carefully to see if he caught on. He certainly did. Chris asked Gavin, "Who is this good-looking girl?" Gavin told him, "She is my best friend Becky. She's a lot of fun." When Gavin wasn't looking, Chris looked at me and smiled then he raised his eyebrows questioningly.

Terri mouthed back to him "later" and grinned at him, so Chris immediately changed the subject. He said, "Why, that's some horse you have, Gavin. What's his name?" Gavin said, "His name is Buck. It's short for Buckskin because that's the color he is. Buck can run really fast, even faster than Sunshine, Becky's horse. But Buck and I, let Becky and Sunshine win a race once in a while. We don't want them to feel bad."

Two days later, it was time for Terri's forty-eight-hour visitation with Chris. Just as soon as the couple entered the trailer, Chris and Terri fell into each other's arms. When you don't get to be with each other for two months, you look so forward to those forty-eight hours, and you want to make the most of them. Forty-eight hours may not seem like very much to most people, but to the Chris and Terri, it meant the world, and the two of them would talk for hours on end.

This time, they spent a lot of time talking about Gavin. Chris wanted to know all about Gavin's relationship with Becky. Terri told Chris, "Gavin and Becky's relationship is no different than yours and mine was when we were the same age. I watched Gavin very carefully, and he is just as protective of Becky as you were with me. But Gavin still says Becky is his best friend and not his girlfriend."

Chris grinned, saying, "How little do we men know." Terri said, "You got it figured out right, buster. I happened to have a chance to talk to Becky all by myself. She told me Gavin doesn't know it yet, but he is going to marry Becky when they are adults. Becky and Gavin are also planning to attend the same college in North Dakota." Chris chuckled, saying, "Is this the same way you felt about me at the same age, you little vixen?" Terri winked at him and said, "Of course, you don't think for a moment women would leave anything to chance, do you? I was very carefully adjusting your mind all of the time we were growing up.

"Did you think you're proposing to me was purely inspirational on your part? I was busy brainwashing you all the time we were growing up. As they say, the proof is in the pudding. I got you, didn't I?" Chris said, "Well, I'll show you who's brainwashed." Chris picked Terri up and started carrying her to the bedroom. She whispered into his ear, "See, it worked again, didn't it?" Chris started laughing so hard he almost dropped Terri. But there's one thing Terri has to say about Chris. He's definitely not a quitter.

During their forty-eight-hour visitation, it was not unusual to wake up, only to find the other one of us staring at the other one. This usually ends up in a long conversation, which it did this time. Only this time, it started with Terri waking up and kissing Chris gently on the shoulder. Chris rolled over and said, "What is it, babe?" Terri told him, "I forgot to tell you about the conversation I had with my father. He had asked me if there are any other possible suspects who could have framed you.

"I told Dad he had been watching too many murder mysteries on TV. I have been giving his idea a lot of thought, but I can't possibly see who else could have possibly done it. Also, how could Russ and Marvin have obtained false identifications so fast? They had to have had them in advance. Plus, the only other ones who might have had access to the money were Tony, Lynn, and Rodney.

"I don't think any of them would've been smart enough or ruthless enough to be able to pull something like this crime off." Chris said, "You can never know what is on someone else's mind honey. If someone else was actually intelligent enough to figure something like this out, they would've also been smart enough to hide that very intelligence. Just because someone seems good and kindhearted to you does not necessarily mean it is the way they are in their hearts and in their minds. However, I do agree with you. It has to be Russ and Marvin."

Chris said, "Thinking about all of the others, I don't see how they could have managed to pull off something of that magnitude. Besides, Lynn, Rodney, and Tony were all on our side. They even tried to help you find Russ and Marvin. Besides, they are all right here in Seattle, except Tony of course. I think Russ and Marvin may have had something to do with his disappearance. Maybe he knew too much or found out where they went. Then Russ and Marvin would've had to dispose of him." The very idea Tony may be dead made Terri really sad and shed some tears for him.

After Terri composed myself, she said, "Chris, there something else I want to talk to you about. Gavin happens to be very involved with my parents' farm. He loves the work, and he loves North Dakota. Gavin and Becky are already planning to take agribusiness courses in college. Dad told me my parents plan on turning their farm over to Gavin when he graduates from college.

"Dad asked me if it would be all right with us. I told him it was fine with me. I was positive it would be okay with you, but I told him I would have to talk to you about it first." Chris gave Terri a kiss, saying, "Of course, it's all right with me. I absolutely love the idea.

Just think of all the advantages if Gavin takes over your parents' farm. We already have a farm almost next door. Maybe sometime in the future, we will be able to move back there. Then we could be neighbors with our son. Maybe in time, Gavin would get married, and we would have grandchildren, and we would be able to spoil them." Terri and Chris lay in each other's arms dreaming about those times. Then both fell back to sleep at all the wonderful dreams.

Shortly after Gavin's thirteenth birthday, Terri received a call from Dawn Hendrickson. She told me she had gotten an e-mail from a girl who had been captured and then escaped. But Dawn was not sure if the men who captured her were Russ and Marvin. Terri asked Dawn, "Where is this girl located now?" Dawn replied, "You may find this hard to believe, but she lives right here in Seattle; in fact, she is here with me now."

Terri asked Dawn if it was possible she could talk with the girl. Dawn said, "Okay, Terri, I will bring her over right now." Within forty-five minutes, they arrived at Terri's home. She saw a very good-looking, red-haired lady of around twenty years old. After they were introduced, Terri asked the red head where it happened and what happened to her. She told Terri, "I had gone to a fashionable nightclub in Mexico City. This was located in a very exclusive part of the city, and felt perfectly safe knowing there wouldn't be any problems. The joint was really hopping, so I had a few drinks and danced with several different men. Each and every one of them seemed like perfect gentleman.

"Sometime after midnight, I stepped outside to get a fresh breath of air; then just as I was about to go back inside, someone clapped a hand over my mouth to stop me from screaming. What felt like a pistol was pressed against the back of my neck. Then I heard a voice, saying, 'I will take my hand away from your mouth, but if you scream, you will die.' Nod your head yes if you will obey. The hand was quickly replaced with duct tape, and then I was blindfolded."

The lady then said, "I was placed in a car and driven to a location which took about forty-five minutes to get to. I could tell there were two men because I could hear them talking. We ended up at a house or apartment, I could not tell which. The creeps took turns raping me for three consecutive days. The pair told me they were training me to become a prostitute. The gangsters said if I did not do exactly as I was told, they would kill me.

"I was so petrified with terror. I was willing to do anything I was told. I wasn't ready to die. I am way too young, and I figured at some point I may have the opportunity to escape. All of the time I was with them, both of them wore masks, and there is no way I would be able to identify them. On the fourth day, they told me it was time to start making them some money. They took me to a street in a better part of Mexico City. I could see several hookers already working there.

"When I got out of the car, I was ready to do whatever was wanted of me as long as I was under their control. I was simply scared to death. Luckily, the first car which came along happened to be a police car. The police pulled over and demanded I get in their car. The police questioned me, saying they had not seen me on the street before. I told the policemen I had no desire to be a prostitute. I was being forced into it.

"The police believed me and asked me where those men were. I told them I saw them take off as soon as the police car pulled up. The police wanted to know where these men lived, but I was not able to tell them that either. I had been blindfolded when I got there and when I left. The police were nice enough to take me to the American Embassy, and here I am."

Terri started by asking her some questions. "Was the house the men lived in fairly decent and in a good neighborhood?" She stated, "It was totally rundown and smelled bad inside, and I don't know about the neighborhood. But from the sounds and smells, I believe it was in a slum." Terri thought, "It doesn't sound like the type of place Marvin or Russ would live."

Next Terri asked her if the men used any handcuffs, shackles, or any torture devices. Again, she answered no. Terri asked, "If you would ever see them again, would you be able to identify the man who abducted you?" She replied, "No, because they were wearing masks all the time I was with them." Terri got out her pictures of Russ and Marvin and asked, "If there was any way you could identify them as the two, would you?" She looked at pictures and immediately said, "Those are not the ones who did it." "How can you be so sure that it isn't them," Terri asked. "You said they were wearing masks all the time." "Yes," she replied, "but they were both black."

Dawn said, "Terri, I am so sorry for wasting your time." Terri said, "No, Dawn, it's never time wasted when anything like this comes up. We definitely have to check it out. I guess I just never realized how many sleazy criminals there are who prey on innocent women. It will just make it that much harder to be able to find Russ and Marvin. But let me know if anything else comes up because you never know the next time it might be them."

One thing Terri was able to do for Gavin was to put both of them on a two-thousand-minute family cell phone plan. This way, Gavin had his own personal cell phone. Terri told him, "You can only text Becky on weekdays, but you will be able to talk to her on weekends." Becky's parents had gotten her a cell phone too. The best part of it was it turned out to be from the same cell phone company. This way, Gavin and Becky were able to talk to each other for free. Terri can tell you for a fact those two cell phones were very busy on weekends. Gavin's usual excuse was, "I have to see how Buck is doing."

Gavin was always up early and ready for school. He was also always there to finish his homework or to help with the dishes. Although the home did have a dishwasher, but Terri seldom used it. Hard as it is to believe, washing dishes was Gavin's and her special time together. One time mother and son would talk about school. Another time would talk about sports. Sometimes they would talk about her job and Terri's quest to clear Chris's name.

In the spring of the year as it is now, Gavin is busy playing baseball. Terri loved going to the games to watch his team play. It is at this time she really wishes Chris was there to see it. Chris would have loved to see his son playing sports. Like everything else, Gavin puts his whole heart into baseball. In one game, the team was down by two runs. It was their turn at bat, and the bases were loaded. There were already two outs when Gavin stepped up to the plate. It was do or die. If Gavin struck out, his team would lose the game. He already had two strikes when the next ball was thrown. By the sound you heard when the bat hit the ball you knew this was a good one.

The baseball flew fast and far. It cleared the fence. You couldn't hear anything because of all the noise the crowd was making. But maybe all the shouting was just Terri. When Gavin passed home plate, his teammates hoisted him onto their shoulders; then carried him to the water bucket where the team doused him. Then everyone had a good laugh. On the way home, Terri told Gavin, "He was the hero of the game." He said, "Oh, Mom, I didn't do anything any of the other guys couldn't have done. I just happened to tap the baseball a little bit harder."

It was getting very close to June, and Terri was getting nervous about doing their annual search for Russ and Marvin. Again, Terri did not have a clue about where to begin. She had not even made a search the year before. So she decided she needed to make some phone calls. The first call she made was to Dawn Hendrickson. She said, "Dawn, do have anything new on our e-mails." Dawn said, "Wait a minute, let me quickly check my computer for single women missing around the world."

Dawn called her back a short time later, saying, "I noticed one area where several women have disappeared lately." Dawn said the bad thing was it was happening in Medellin, Colombia. Terri had heard a lot about Medellin during the '90s, about all of the people being murdered there. The idea of going to Colombia simply scared the hell out of her.

The next thing Terri did was place a call to Clark and June Evanston. Clark confirmed, "Quite a few women had gone missing in Medellin lately." Clark said, "Let me check with Interpol on the computer. I will let you know what I find out in a few minutes." When Clark came back online, he said, "Interpol shows several women have disappeared in Medellin, Colombia, in the last three months. This is higher than the number of women who have disappeared there in the last three years."

The final verification came when Rodney Crowder called Terri out of the blue. Rodney said, "Terri, do you remember years ago, at the time I told you about a friend of mine who is high up in the phone company? He has been monitoring the phone of Russ Jacobson's sister for all these years. He had never come up with anything until just last week. Last Wednesday, she received two long-distance telephone calls from Medellin, Colombia. It took him a few days, but my friend did come up with an address and the phone number." Rodney gave the information to Terri, which she immediately wrote down.

Next, she went to see Tatiana and LaShawn. Like Terri, Tatiana had a lot of misgivings. They have both heard many things about Medellin, and none of it was good. LaShawn, however, waived away our fears, saying, "Medellin has tamed down a lot in the past several years. I have flown there myself several times. In fact, the corporation I work for has a large condominium there, which by the way we will be able to use."

After this forthcoming, LaShawn asked for the address of Russ and Marvin. After looking at it, he said, "Well, at least it's in a decent neighborhood, which helps a lot. Ladies, we have a lot of planning to do to get ready for this trip. Hopefully, we won't screw this one up like we did in Brazil." The very first thing they decided was in Colombia all of them were going to take their time. It was decided not to rush in and blow the chances of catching the two.

Terri decided she would rent a different car every day, then all of them would drive past the address to check it out once in the morning and once in the evening. The threesome would not make a move until everyone had agreed the time was right. Terri suggested, "We should bring both regular cameras and movie cameras. Also, we need plenty of socks, which we could fill with sand and some plastic ties with which to cuff Russ and Marvin with after we catch them."

Tatiana came up with the idea, saying, "Even with the different cars we will be driving, Russ and Marvin could still become wise to us. We need to have different clothes to wear each time. We should also think about wearing different disguises. I'm thinking of different hats, lots of wigs, sunglasses, and maybe a mustache and a beard or two for LaShawn."

Everyone agreed this time they were going to do everything different. For once, the crew knew beforehand exactly where the bastards live. No one had caught as much as a glimpse of them in the past seven years. The three friends were all ready for a little celebration. Tatiana got out a bottle of California's celebrated sparkling wine. She poured us each a glass. Tatiana raised her glass, saying, "To the hunt and success." Terri had not been so excited in years, for she knew this time was it.

Chapter 50

There were a few things that Terri had to do first, like getting Gavin ready for the trip to North Dakota. Terri told him, "Give your grandmother and grandfather a hug for me." She also told Gavin, "Give Becky a hug for me." Terri thought of telling him "give her a kiss for me," but she figured this would be pushing things a bit. Terri thought the kiss could definitely wait for couple of years.

For the first time, Gavin will be flying to North Dakota all by himself. He is pretty excited about the idea, but as a mom, Terri worries about everything. She told Gavin, "Give me a call after you have arrived in Minot." After Gavin left, she was still worried that he wouldn't be able to find the right terminal when he arrived in Minneapolis. Terri was worried because Gavin had to change planes when he got there.

However, her fears were groundless. Gavin called her right on time, and told her his grandfather and grandmother were waiting in Minot to pick him up. And he said, "Guess what? Becky came along with them." At least it looked like Gavin's summer will be filled with fun. Now all Terri had to worry about was her trip.

LaShawn, Tatiana, and Terri boarded the plane in Seattle where they caught a flight to Fort Lauderdale, Florida. In Fort Lauderdale, there was a three-hour layover. All the time she was there, Terri was filled with the jitters. She was still pretty worried about Colombia. While on the plane, LaShawn assured Terri her worries were groundless.

The threesome were able to board a flight straight through. After arriving at the José Maria Cordova International Airport around 7:30 p.m. local time, the weather was a delightful sixty-nine degrees. Terri had been afraid being so close to the equator the temperature would be a scorcher. She looked around and discovered skyscrapers highlighted by mountains in the background.

As soon as the group had picked up their baggage, they headed for the car rental agency. There Terri explained to the lady behind the desk, "We would like to exchange our vehicles every day. Each day, we will want a different make, model, and color." But no matter how hard Terri tried, the rental agent just couldn't understand what she wanted. Terri finally asked for the manager. At first, he seemed very confused as to why she wanted to do this. But amazingly, the injection of a $100 bill into his hand changed everything. He said, "You want a different type of car every day, different make, different color." He was satisfied. Terri was satisfied.

The next item on the agenda was driving to the corporation's condominium. The corporation LaShawn worked for must have believed in treating their executives right. For it was a palatial three-story condo with wraparound decks on every floor. As soon as you walk through the door, you experienced the feeling of vastness. LaShawn told us this condominium was over five thousand five hundred square feet.

In the front room, was a three-piece, soft leather couch, with a sixty-inch LCD TV and a wet bar set over to one side. Terri loved the kitchen. It was spacious, but it was the island in the kitchen, which was her favorite. Terri went and sat down in one of the plush stools and told Tatiana, "I could sit there forever."

But LaShawn interrupted Terri's moment of bliss. He stated, "There is a grocery store nearby. This condo is completely stocked with food, but I would like to get some fresh food we don't have to thaw out." Everyone went to the grocery store and picked up some prime rib steaks for LaShawn to barbecue. Tatiana picked up some greens, tomatoes and other ingredients for a salad. Terri found some freshly baked French bread, which smelled heavenly. Tatiana also got some eggs and bacon for breakfast in the morning.

As he was barbecuing steaks, LaShawn started to tell the girls about the more recent history of Medellin. He said, "The first problems in Colombia started with the murder of presidential candidate Jorge Eliecer Gaitanin in 1948. The murder itself was actually committed in Bogotá, Colombia. However, the resulting political violence spread to every section of the country.

"This violence caused small farmers to flee for the comparative safety of the large cities. The farmers were not very wealthy people and weren't able to afford homes in a nice neighborhood. Instead, they started to build shacks on the side of the mountains with whatever material they could find. These areas soon became slums, and the slums became rampant. You will find the slums in every city in Colombia."

As dinner was being enjoyed, LaShawn continued on with his story, "Coal and hydroelectric plants made Medellin a highly industrialized city. Soon, there were plenty of jobs; however, the pay scale was very low. As in Brazil and other South American countries, the slums slowly gravitated toward the slopes of the mountains. Crimes in these areas increased substantially.

"Then just when the government seemed to have the crime partly under control, the drug lords began to roll in. By the late 1980s, Medellin became known as the most violent city in the world. This was mainly caused by drug cartels fighting over turf. It was set off by a drug organization headed by Escobar. However, with the death of Escobar, Medellin's crime rate began to decrease."

LaShawn said, "We are located in an area of Medellin known as El Poblado. This happens to be a very good area. There are almost no murders in this section. However, if you leave this area, you will begin to find some violence. Once a person starts to travel farther from this area, one will begin to see more and more violence. If one is stupid enough to go far enough, it starts to get downright dangerous. In some places, there have been pitched gun battles in broad daylight in the middle of the street. Fortunately for us, the address we have for Russ and Marvin is also in El Poblado."

After waking up the next morning, LaShawn and the girls decided to go past Russ and Marvin's address. First of all, everyone put on disguises and sunglasses. Russ and Marvin know Terri, so she has to be especially careful. But they might have also seen LaShawn and Tatiana from the dance hall in Brazil. They didn't have any idea if Russ and Marvin were early risers. So it was decided LaShawn would drive by now, and if the shades were pulled down and there was no one outside, then he might drive up by once more later in the day.

As they looked at a map, LaShawn figured out the house would be on the right side of the road as he drove past it. As Terri was the most recognizable to Russ and Marvin, she sat in the back of the car on the left-hand side. Terri didn't want to take any unnecessary chances of being seen by them. Their efforts were fruitless the first time LaShawn drove past their house. About the only thing they learned is Russ and Marvin must be making money. It only made sense it was dirty money.

The house was in an exclusive part of the city, and it looked expensive even by this standard. Terri was sure Russ and Marvin hadn't purchased a house. Not if they were still committing crimes in this area. However, even a renting a place like the one the cost had to be astronomical.

As soon as all of them were back to the condo, Terri got busy on a computer. She started by looking up the statistics of colleges in Medellin. Terri discovered there were over thirty colleges in and around the city. The main ones being the University of Antigua the Medellin branch of the University of Colombia, and the Universidad Pontifica Bolivariana. After checking all of the statistics, Terri then started to check to see if any girls had disappeared from them. Bingo, there happened to be four girls missing from each of the main colleges. Not only were girls missing, but all of these girls had disappeared within the last three months. An addition to this there were six more girls missing from some of the smaller colleges.

In the meantime, LaShawn was busy trying to locate some of his contacts. After LaShawn located two of them, he asked if they would conduct a quiet surveillance of Russ and Marvin's address." He also asked the contacts if they could find out what time there was movement around there. LaShawn wanted to know what type of vehicle Russ and Marvin were driving. If possible without being noticed, he asked them if they would be able to follow Russ and Marvin to see what the two were up to. In ending, LaShawn told them some pictures would really help him.

Around five in the afternoon, the threesome made another trip past their house. The only change was the front shades were now open. There were no lights on inside the house, and no one was able to detect any movement. Terri asked LaShawn, "Is there a chance of planting a bug? Or maybe you're contacts could put a tap on their phone line with a recorder which we could listen to." LaShawn said, "That would be an excellent idea. I will get a hold of my contacts, and I will ask them if they can do it."

Terri and Tatiana were surprised at what a beautiful and modern city Medellin actually is. It is a city of three million inhabitants situated in the Abura Valley on 237 square miles. The Medellin River flows through the city of Medellin. The fact Medellin is five thousand feet above sea level makes it cooler than most cities near the equator. In fact, its nickname is the city of eternal spring.

LaShawn's contacts called, saying, "We have some information for you. We were able to take some pictures of Russ and Marvin." The contacts said, "Russ and Marvin left at night around 11:00 p.m. They drove a large van and liked to cruise around college campuses. Whenever they saw women walking along the sidewalk, the van would always slow down. Sometimes the creeps would stop and ask some woman if she needed a ride. Thus far, none of the women would get in the van."

LaShawn then asked if his contacts could bring the pictures of the vehicle and of Russ and Marvin to the condominium. When they had arrived, LaShawn placed the pictures in his pocket. Then he asked if the men had the ability to tap into the phone line. Also if they would be able to attach a recorder to it. The men said, "We would be able to do it, but it would cost a lot of money." Terri gave them $2,000, and the men assured her, "It will be done tonight after Russ and Marvin have left for the evening."

After the men had left, LaShawn brought out the pictures for the girls to look at. It was Russ and Marvin without a doubt. They still looked like assholes to Terri. She thought to herself, "It's been fourteen years. It may take another one or two weeks, but I'm going to get you two SOBs." Terri remarked to LaShawn and Tatiana, "I have an idea, but we may have to wait a couple of weeks to be sure of the pattern. If you notice, it is always pitch-black here long before eleven, except for the moon and stars. So we wait for a night with heavy cloud cover, then we strike under the cover of darkness.

"Remember when we drove past the house? Do you remember those huge bushes on either side of the front door? I think one night when it gets pitch-dark, we can hide behind the bushes. From there, they won't be able to spot us. When Russ and Marvin open the door and walk past us, at that time we will club them in the back of the head with socks filled with gravel. Then we will handcuff them with plastic ties and take them back into the house."

LaShawn and Tatiana agreed it sounded like a feasible plan. Tatiana said, "Hopefully, we can hear some of their phone conversations first. If we hear them talking, it may give us some idea of what their plans are." Terri decided when she got a different car tomorrow, LaShawn would drive by the house and Tatiana and Terri would take still pictures and moving pictures of it. Of course it all depended on if the shades were closed. Then after the pictures were developed, the group would be able to study them and figure out exactly how they could sneak up to the house when the time comes.

The next day, LaShawn drove slowly past the house while Tatiana took still pictures and Terri was running a movie camera of the whole block. When everyone looked at the pictures later, Terri realized they were in luck. Three spaces down from the house was a parking lot, LaShawn would be able to park the car there. Then the three would casually walk up pretending they were going into the house. At the last minute, all of them would be able to hide in the bushes.

As LaShawn's contacts had his cell phone number, they were now free to explore the city. Having heard stories for years in the media about the violence in Colombia, with Medellin always being in the forefront, Terri and Tatiana were once again surprised. They discovered what a modern and friendly city Medellin actually is; however, the United States warns its citizens. If you are planning on traveling from one city in Colombia to another, avoid the roads and go by air or train.

The fact Medellin is the second biggest industrial city in Colombia, surpassed only by Bogota, has contributed to getting on top of the drug crisis in the '80s and '90s. In 2002, President Uribe ordered the Colombian military to take undertake operation onion. Its main purpose was the end of FARC and AMC two large drug organizations.

Although the military was only partially successful in ending both organizations, it got some surprising help from an unusual source. Some of the drug dealers started a new smaller organization; evidently, it was to keep some of the pressure off of them. The new organization actually ordered a curfew for teenagers. They also instituted a program for prostitutes in which they would have regular checkups by doctors. Terri would imagine the idea behind this was even the bad are not completely bad.

The Medellin LaShawn and The girls found had beautiful parks, and it had places for the arts, poetry, and drama. They were impressed by the many modern libraries and museums. Although Tatiana did notice traffic could get quite congested at times. But you could bypass this by taking one of the two modern metro systems, or you can travel by bus. They also found tourism is on the rise in Medellin, though this was mainly due to business corporations.

However, Medellin also has much to offer the average tourist. You can find many guided tours including but not limited to rowing, sailing, camping, swimming, fishing, kayaking, trekking, and biking. You may enjoy bike tours of the city or of the country.

LaShawn, Tatiana, and Terri stuck mainly to the museums, although the threesome did take in a couple poetry recitals even though their knowledge of Spanish was limited. everyone enjoyed the lilt of their voices, their facial expressions, as these could convey sadness, love, or excitement. As for the theater, if you enjoy Shakespeare, it doesn't matter what language it is in. It is still enjoyable.

Chapter 51

Gavin in North Dakota. When Gavin got off of the airplane in Minneapolis, Minnesota, he was a little scared at first. Gavin needed to know how to find the gate where he was to catch his next flight to Minot, North Dakota. After being a little unsure of himself at first, he thought to himself, "You're a big boy now. You have watched Mom do this several times. You just need to do the same thing."

Gavin simply looked at his airline ticket and saw the actual flight number. Then he went to the reader board, which showed him what gate he needed to go to. After that, it was just follow the signs. Sure enough, there was his flight, and it was just getting ready to board. The second he stepped into the Minot airport terminal, Gavin saw his grandpa and grandma standing on the other side waiting for him. He almost stopped in his tracks. Becky was there with them. He cannot believe what has happened in the past year. Becky has turned into a girl and a very pretty one at that.

Gavin hurried out and gave his grandpa and grandma a hug; then Becky smiled and said, "What about me?" Gavin told Becky she had gone and become a girl. Becky laughed delightedly, "Gavin, I have always been a girl, but I am still the same Becky you have always known. Now come here and give me a hug, or I will whip you at arm wrestling." Those words convinced him. Gavin gave her a hug. Becky sure did smell nice.

Everyone started to talk at once after Gavin got in his grandpa's car. He asked his grandpa, "How is the haying going this year?" Grandpa said, "All right. I have a good hired hand to help me. But we will finish a lot faster now that you are here to help us." His grandma said, "I am going to make your favorite dinner—fried chicken, spring potatoes with gravy, and corn on the cob. If you still have some room left after that, I have some fresh apple pie."

Becky said, "I told Buck you are coming home. I kind of think he understood, for Buck started galloping around the corral, kicking up his heels in the air. Buck was acting just like he was a colt. Your Shetland pony was following him acting just as goofy as Buck was. I can't say I really blame them for acting that way very much. Because I feel very much that way myself."

It was such a relief coming back to North Dakota. Gavin's parents and many others have left the place for somewhere else; however, Gavin looks forward to the day when he will be able to live in North Dakota. The first thing he did when he got here was put on his denim pants and a western shirt. Then Gavin asked his grandma if he could have a couple of apples. She chuckled, and handed them to him, saying, "So you're ready to spoil them already?"

Gavin hurried out to the barnyard, hiding apples behind his back. Buck and the Shetland pony were already at the fence nickering. Putting both of the apples in his left hand and keeping them behind his back. Gavin walked into the pasture and rubbed the horses foreheads with his right hand. Buck and the Shetland nuzzled his hand, but they weren't dumb. Buck kept trying to get behind Gavin's back no matter how much he had turned the other way. Finally laughing at them, he gave into Buck and the Shetland pony giving them each an apple. When they had finished eating the apples, the horses kept nodding their heads up and down as if in appreciation.

When grandpa, Tom the hired hand, and Gavin got ready to head for the hayfield the next morning, grandpa first filled several jugs with water. Grandpa said, "Always remember to drink plenty of water so you don't dehydrate. Today will get quite hot, and dehydration can lead to sunstroke. I remember when I was a teenager working in the hayfield. My older brother had to go to town to get some parts for the mower. He left me in the hayfield, and there wasn't any place anywhere within miles to get a drink. My brother had forgotten to leave me the water jugs. By the time he came back, I was very close to getting sunstroke."

Within ten days, grandpa and his crew had finished with the haying, but there is always work to be done around the farm. Grandpa and Gavin had to milk the cows every morning and evening. Cows like to be on a fixed schedule, or will slowly stop giving milk. So the cows were always milked at the same time every day. The beef cattle were not so much of a problem. Grandpa and Gavin just had to make sure there was plenty of water and grazing for the animals.

Grandpa says, "A farmer has to be a gambler. They gamble the rain will hold off during the haying season, because the farmers don't want the hay getting wet after it has been cut. At the same time, they want rain in the spring so their grain fields yield a good harvest. Then you gamble that both cattle and grain prices will be up in the fall, so you don't lose money on your investment."

Every evening, Gavin would spend some time with Becky. True to her word, she was same old Becky she had always been. Becky and Gavin still enjoyed playing baseball and riding their horses. Quite often, they would ride to the Mouse River to go fishing. At least, Becky was not one of those sissy girls who would not bait her own hook. However, she didn't seem to mind it when Gavin did it for her though.

One afternoon, his grandma asked, "Gavin, are you and Becky going to go to the street dance with us tonight?" Gavin was surprised as he had been planning on going to the Fourth of July parade and rodeo. However, he had completely forgotten about the street dance. Becky was standing right there smiling. Gavin wondered if she had put his grandma up to this. Of course he said yes he was going to the dance.

What Gavin means is everyone goes to the street dance every year, why should this year be any different? When Becky, Gavin and his grandparents got to the street dance, the band was just starting to warm up. So Becky and Gavin just started to mingle with the crowd. Becky introduced Gavin to a few people that he didn't know. By now, the music was starting to rock, and quite a few couples were already out on the street dancing.

Becky turned to Gavin and asked, "Gavin, would you like to dance with me?" He sort of hung his head and admitted, "I do not know how to dance." Becky said, "Gavin, it is easy, and I will teach you how to dance." Reluctantly, he let her lead him out into the street. Becky told him, "It's easy, just let your feet follow the music." After a while, Gavin was starting to get the hang of this thing. Dancing with Becky began to feel like it was so normal, and he will have to admit holding her in his arms was kind of nice.

After several dances, they finally went back to the sidewalk to take a breather. Gavin told Becky, "Wait right here for me. I'm going to grab a couple of sodas, I will be right back." Getting the sodas took a little longer than he had planned on, and when Gavin got back, Becky wasn't there. He scanned the crowd, but was not able to see her anywhere. Then Gavin looked at the people dancing in the street, and there she was.

Gavin started to get a little jealous at first. He thought, "How come would Becky be dancing with anybody but me?" Then Becky caught his eyes with a pleading look, which said, "Come help me, Gavin." He realized then Becky was not out there dancing because she wanted to be. The jerk who was dancing with her looked like he was a couple of years older than they were. He was unkempt and did not look very respectable. Gavin thought to himself, "This dude may be older than I am, but I happen to be a lot bigger than he is." Gavin decided he was not about to let the jerk force his girl to dance with the other guy.

Gavin walked up and tapped him on the shoulder, saying, "Pardon me I believe you are dancing with my girlfriend." The jerk snarled, "Shove off, piss ant, she's my girlfriend now." Gavin took that to be fighting words. The words made Gavin more than just a little bit angry. However, he kept his cool. With one hand, Gavin grabbed him by the back of his shirt collar; with the other hand, he reached far between The guys legs and grabbed his crotch area. This must not have felt very good for The creep let go of Becky right away.

The intruder did try to turn around; however, Gavin squeezed real hard, and he screamed. Gavin slowly walked him back to the sidewalk. The jerk walked sort of bowlegged it seemed to Gavin. Before Gavin let him go, he gave his crotch a little squeeze, and asked him, "You're not going to try to bother Becky ever again, are you?" After the guy replied no, Gavin released him it turned out to be the wrong thing for him to do. He turned around swinging and hit Gavin on the head, knocking him to the ground. Gavin came up off of the sidewalk, swinging with every ounce of strength he had. The one blow knocked the intruder out cold. Gavin felt real bad seeing him lying there. But then again, he shouldn't have ever tried to mess with Becky.

Immediately, Becky was all over him, asking, "Gavin, are you hurt?" He told her, "Not as much as that jerk is." Then Gavin took his soda and poured it over his head. The soda woke him up. When he got to his feet, Gavin yelled, "Boo!" this must have scared the dude somewhat for he took off running as if his life depended on it. He was really picking up his feet and putting them down. Gavin was astounded at how fast he was. The way he was running, Gavin figured he must've been some sort of Olympic track star.

Becky was busy feeling Gavin's head where he had been hit. She asked if he was hurt. After he told her no, she asked, "Gavin, did you mean what you said?" Her eyes were shining excitedly. Gavin told her, "I don't understand what you are talking about, Becky? Do you mean what I said when I was walking him back to the sidewalk? I happened to say quite a few different things, and most of them weren't very nice."

Becky said, "No, I'm talking about the very first thing you said to the jerk. You told him I was your girlfriend. Did you really mean that? Or were you just trying to help me out of a very bad situation?" This question really flustered Gavin. He had never been tongue-tied before. He finally managed to stammer, "Becky, I was trying to help you, not just because you needed me to. I mean, I really hope you are my girlfriend." Becky hugged him and kissed him on the cheek. She said, "I always have and always will be your girlfriend, Gavin." He put his fingers to his cheek where she had kissed him. Gavin doesn't plan to ever wash that spot. He will treasure it forever.

The night was still young, and Becky and Gavin didn't want to miss a second of it. He asked Becky if she would teach him some more about dancing. This time, Gavin took it seriously trying to learn everything he could. He even played dumb, pretending not to be able to get the hang of the slow dances. Gavin kept asking Becky to show him how to do them again. One thing about Becky she's not stupid. She caught on right away. She said, "Gavin, if you like the slow dances, it's okay with me. I like being close to you too." He was glad to hear that, and danced many slow dances during the night.

The next morning, Gavin woke up before his grandpa and grandma did. He got up very quietly, then got dressed and went out to the barn. Gavin was determined to do the milking all by himself. He wanted his grandpa to have a chance to relax and enjoy himself for a change. Just as he was finishing up with chores, Gavin saw his grandpa standing there. He told his grandpa, "I really wanted you to be able to take the morning off."

Grandpa said, "Gavin, I really appreciate the thought, but I am so used to doing it by myself I will have a hard time not doing it when I retire. However, I enjoyed watching you to make sure you did everything which was needed. I enjoyed watching you, and you did everything exactly right. Someday, you will make a good farmer if it is what you still desire when the time comes."

Gavin and his grandpa went back to the house and ate a hearty breakfast, then loaded Buck into the horse trailer. By the time this was finished, grandma was ready with a picnic lunch. After arriving in Towner Gavin realised Becky was already there with Sunshine. The Fourth of July parade was getting ready to start, so Gavin unloaded Buck. Once again, Becky and Gavin rode side by side in the parade. Directly in front of them was a brightly decorated wagon pulled by a pair of Belgian draft horses. There were a bunch of teenage girls in the back of the wagon, throwing candy out into the crowd.

Everything seemed to be going smoothly as the parade went down the main street of Towner. Suddenly, some ignorant person set off a Fourth of July rocket. Theoretically, the rocket should have gone straight up into the sky. Instead, it toppled over and went between the draft horses' legs where it exploded. The terrified horses reared up in the air, then took off at a gallop. The draft horses and wagon almost went into the crowd, then veered off at the very last second.

Becky yelled to me, "Gavin, it's up to us because no other riders are close enough." Immediately, both Buck and Sunshine were off like a shot. Later, some people would say they had thought it was all staged. Buck and Gavin passed the wagon on the right side, while Becky and Sunshine went to the left. They both leaned over and grabbed the runaway team's reins. Sunshine and Buck slowed down finally, bringing the terrified team to a halt.

After a few agonizing minutes, the band started to play again, and the parade continued on. Becky and Gavin waited for the rest of the parade to catch up to them then rejoined it. The girls of the wagon, although they were very shook up, commenced throwing candy again. When the parade had ended, they found grandpa and grandma Olson. Gavin told his grandparents Becky and he were riding out to the rodeo grounds, and would meet them there.

Grandma said, "I can't believe how you two always manage to be in the middle of some excitement." Gavin told her, "Grandma, we certainly weren't looking for excitement. I just think trouble keeps looking for us. Now we just want to get out of here. I'm afraid people will come around asking us a bunch of stupid questions." Grandpa spoke up, saying, "No one would be asking stupid questions. People would just like to thank you and Becky for what you did." Gavin said, "Nevertheless, we don't want to be bothered."

The ride out of the rodeo grounds was relaxing; however, Becky and Gavin did notice a lot of cars were slowing down pointing at them and waving. Gavin was very glad when he saw his grandpa and grandma go past them in the pickup. Gavin hoped his grandparents would park toward the back of the rodeo grounds where no one would be able to spot them. As soon as Gavin found the pickup, he hid Buck and Sunshine behind the horse trailer. Gavin wasn't able to put them inside because it would have been too hot.

Grandpa told the kids, "Everyone wants to see you two. You are the heroes of the day." Gavin said, "Grandpa, Becky and I didn't do anything anyone else wouldn't have done. We just happened to be at the right place at the right time." "And you two wound up doing the right thing," his grandma added. "I agree with you, anyone else probably would have done the same thing. The only thing is, they might not have been able to do it on time. I am very proud of both of you. Now if anyone comes around, just accept their praise gracefully."

All at once, his grandpa got up and started walking to the rodeo arena. Just as he got to the announcer's stand, they heard the rodeo announcer speaking into the microphone. He said, "Ladies and gentlemen, we all saw a very brave thing which happened during the parade this morning. A couple of young riders were able to stop a runaway team before it went crashing into the crowd. Would Becky and Gavin please come up to the announcer's booth."

Then Gavin saw his grandpa talking to the rodeo announcer. The next thing you know they were able to hear his voice over the loudspeaker. Grandpa said, "Becky and Gavin were the ones who stopped the runaways this morning. However, they are very shy and take no credit for being heroes.

Both say anyone else would have done the same thing, Becky and Gavin just happened to be there. The kids would prefer to be left alone and don't want to be asked any questions. However, if you were to give them a round of applause, I assume it would be appreciated." His grandpa had no sooner finished talking when the crowd stood up and gave the two a standing ovation.

Later in the day as people walked past Becky and Gavin, they would give them a thumbs-up. The only ones who came over to talk to them were the girls who had been in the back of the wagon. The girls thanked them over and over for maybe saving their lives. Becky told them, "It wasn't really us. It was Buck and Sunshine who had done all of the work." After Becky told the girls who the real heroes were, the girls had to go and pet Buck and Sunshine. Becky gave the girls a couple of apples to feed the horses. Buck and Sunshine acted like it was the best thing that ever happened to them.

The rest of the summer passed all too quickly. Most of the time, Gavin spent with his grandpa and grandma Olson and Becky of course. He also looked forward to seeing his mom and dad and his friends in Bellevue. This year, Gavin will be playing football as he will now be in eighth grade. Even as he looks forward to all of this, Gavin will still miss North Dakota. He looks forward to coming back next summer. Every year, it gets harder for him to leave.

Chapter 52

Back in Medellin, LaShawn's contacts had successfully placed a tap on Russ and Marvin's phone line. The tap was complete with a recorder and remote control device. The contacts brought the remote listening device to the condominium. Now all, LaShawn and the girls have to do is monitor the conversations to see what Russ and Marvin's plans are. Or more correctly, to see what they're up against. It never pays to underestimate the enemy.

After a week of listening to the monitor, they had not heard anything at all. Terri began to wonder if Russ and Marvin ever used the phone. All of them were just about to give up on the idea of listening to the phone and pursuing different avenues. In fact, Terri hadn't even checked the recording device for two days when Terri picked it up and discovered there was a message on the answering machine. A heavily accented voice asked, "When will the merchandise be ready to be picked up? I want at least twenty prime specimens, but more would be acceptable."

The message went on to say, "I would be willing to pay top dollar as long as the merchandise is good. I would pay even more for prime specimens. He ended up by asking Russ and Marvin to call back the following night. The phone call had evidently been made the night before as there was no answering message. Whoever had left the message must have been well-known to Russ and Marvin for whoever had called did not leave a name or a phone number. Just a thought of what this message had to be about made Terri sick to her stomach. How could anyone in their right mind treat women like they were animals?

After everyone had listened to the message several times, they sat there dumbfounded. They sat and tried to absorb everything they had heard for about twenty minutes. LaShawn was the first one to give voice to his thoughts. He said, "This looks like white slavery in action. Now we need to figure out what to do about it. What are your thoughts about the country this character who is speaking is from?" Tatiana and Terri both said, "He sounded like he was Chinese." However, LaShawn who had traveled all over the world was sure he was Cambodian.

LaShawn Tatiana and Terri were tormented worrying about what would happen to these poor girls. The women were being treated like they were livestock and could be purchased at a sales ring. Terri remarked, "We need to capture Russ and Marvin, even at the expense of clearing Chris's name. The first thing Chris would want us to do would be to free these poor girls."

Tatiana said, "I know Chris, and I agree the girls would be his first priority. But there must be a way we can do both. First, let us wait and see how these creeps answer this message. This looks like it would be too big to handle by ourselves. I think we will have to contact the authorities. Maybe we can get a package deal. Like maybe we get the buyers, sellers, and the girls all at one time."

Terri placed a phone call to Clark Evanston to let him know what the threesome had found out. She told him, "We need help." Clark said he would inform Interpol. He was sure they would want to be there. The reason for Interpol wanting to be there is because this is a crime, which involves the whole world. I will have Interpol get in touch with you. I will also ask them to look for anything, which could help clear your husband's name."

Clark called Terri back two hours later after he had talked to Interpol. Clark said, "Interpol was very interested and was getting everything ready to leave at a moment's notice. The person I talked to at Interpol said they will have to contact the Medellin police; after all, it is their city. However, Interpol plans on doing this at the last moment in case there are any inside informants. In the meantime, can you keep monitoring the phone? We need to know what their plans are."

Tatiana set their alarm for three o'clock in the morning, as she thought the last phone call must have been made around this time. They did not want to listen continuously in case it made some change in the phone tone. After everyone got up, Terri put the listening device on speakerphone so all would be able to hear what it said. What they heard was bone chilling, and the first voice heard was Russ Jacobson.

Terri listened to Russ's voice, saying, "We have twenty of our product ready for you. The women are all fine specimens, and all of them are handpicked and in their prime." The voice on the other end of the line said, "Excellent, I happen to be in Caracas, Venezuela, right now. I can be in Medellin, Colombia, with my plane by tonight. I already have your home address. I will let you know when I'm on the way to your house. You can expect a call from me tonight between 11:00 and 11:15 p.m."

LaShawn, Tatiana, and Terri stared at each other in horror. The three had not been expecting something to happen this soon. Terri called Clark, saying, "I am sorry I had to wake you up at this time, but it is very important." After Terri had relayed what they had just heard, he cursed. Clark said, "Give me a moment to call Interpol and I will get right back to you."

Fifteen minutes later, Terri's phone rang. It was Clark on the other end. Clark said, "Terri, I just got done speaking to Interpol. Everything is all right because they decided to take off yesterday. The heads of Interpol were afraid something like this might happen. Interpol didn't want to take a chance. They might miss this opportunity. The bad thing is Interpols plane don't expect to arrive in Medellin until eleven o'clock tonight. This will cut the time they have to stop this transaction to a minimum. If worse comes to worse, try to think of a way to delay the action at the last minute."

Before hanging up, Terri gave Clark the address of Russ and Marvin. She also gave him her own address plus all of their phone numbers. She asked Clark to give all of this information to Interpol. Terri said, "LaShawn, Tatiana and I will try to come up with some kind of an idea. If anything involves us, have Interpol give us a call, and in the meantime, we will try to think of something on our end." Then Terri said, "Hold on a minute, Clark, I have an idea."

Terri told Clark, "As we were listening to the message on the answering machine, we heard the man say he is flying from Caracas, Venezuela. While the leader was talking, he mentioned he would be calling between 11:00 and 11:15 p.m. This probably means he will call as soon as the plane lands. Maybe Interpol can check all planes from Caracas to Medellin, which will land close to this time. If they did, then maybe Interpol would be able to stop them from taking off again." Clark said, "Terri, your idea is brilliant. I'm sure Interpol will find a way to do it."

Meanwhile, LaShawn, Tatiana, and Terri just sat around the condo. Sleeping was not a possibility. They drank cup after cup of coffee as all of them tried to think up some type of strategy. The group came up with one idea after another, only after analyzing each one, they would discard them as fast as they thought of them. At 8:30 p.m., Clark Evanston called. He said, "The Interpol plane had managed to catch a tailwind, and would be here forty-five minutes early." All three sank back into their chairs. This was such a relief because it took a load off all of their minds.

At exactly 10:35 p.m., Terri received a call from Sean McCluskey. He told her, "I am the head of the Interpol task force, which had just arrived. I am sending my men to stake out the address you had given us. The Interpol task force will remain hidden while Sean's task force waited for the people flying in from Venezuela to arrive. After the slave traders had gone into the house, the task force would wait another fifteen minutes for the deal to be transacted."

Sean said, "During the time the task force are waiting, I will contact the Medellin police so they can be in on the bust. Interpol had already made contact with the higher authorities in Medellin. After the fifteen-minute interval, the Interpol task force would storm the house. Once inside, the task force would take everyone inside the house into custody."

Sean said, "While my men are doing this, I will stop by your condo to pick you up. I want you along mainly to identify Russ Jacobson and Marvin Mueller. You will not be allowed inside until everything is secured." When Sean arrived at the condo, LaShawn, Tatiana and Terri piled into his vehicle, and promptly left.

As Sean was driving, he told them he had just been notified his team was in place and a Medellin SWAT team was on its way. The Asian boss and his five accomplices had also just arrived in a large bus. The next thing heard was on Sean's radio, the Medellin SWAT team has just pulled up and are going into the house. Sean was almost at the address when he received the next message. Suspects are apprehended. Everything is under control. Sean asked, "How many suspects do you have?" The voice of the radio replied, "There is the Asian boss and five of his accomplices. At this time, we have them all in handcuffs."

At this point, Terri got excited and yelled, "What about the other two? They are the ones who captured the girls." Sean picked up the microphone and asked, "What about two Americans? Is there any sign of them?" A voice answered, saying, "We are searching the house room by room now, sir. We have seen no sign of them yet. But the house is completely surrounded, so there is absolutely no chance they can get away." Terri said to Sean, "I know you're men are carefully handpicked, but what about the Medellin police? Do you think one of them could have warned Russ and Marvin? Sean said, I don't think they would've had enough time."

Once the group arrived, there were flashing lights all around the area. There was a solid ring of police surrounding the whole house. Sean pulled out his badge and escorted LaShawn and the girls into the house. There everyone saw the Asian ringleader and his men all in handcuffs. The leader was yelling at his cohorts in a foreign language. Sean took us into another room. There he told us one of his men could understand every word the leader was saying. Sean said, "He will tell me later what they were saying."

After the main floor had been thoroughly searched, LaShawn, Tatiana and Terri were able to follow the squad to the basement. The task force had discovered twenty girls who were all handcuffed and chained up. It looked like the girls were of all colors and nationalities. The one thing all had in common was they were all young and beautiful. Sean told the ladies they were all safe now and began freeing them from their fetters. As the shackles came off, most of them cried; however, some laughed in relief. As Sean freed each one, he asked them if anyone had seen what happened to the two Americans?

When Sean mentioned Russ and Marvin, several of the girls spat on the floor; however, none of them knew where the men had disappeared to. When Sean got to the eleventh and twelfth girls, both knew what had happened. The girls both said, "At first, Russ and Marvin came down here with a man who examined us in every way. Then the Asian leader handed Russ and Marvin a suitcase full of money. The Asian man then went back upstairs to get his men. The Asians were planning to take us someplace.

"The two who had captured us stayed down here, when we all heard a big commotion upstairs. We heard a door being broken open, then a voice saying, 'Police, drop your weapons.' The two bad guys were startled at first, but then laughed and headed for the left side of the basement. One of them pressed something in the middle of the wall, and the cement wall swiveled around. The bad guys entered into what appeared to be a tunnel. Next the whole section closed behind them. I think this was maybe twenty minutes ago."

Sean yelled for two of his men to go check the wall out. It took another twenty minutes of pressing on the wall before it swiveled open again. Both Interpol and the Medellin SWAT team entered the tunnel. Sean found a light switch, and when he flipped it on, the tunnel became illuminated. Sean told us, "Wait right here while I go with my team to check the tunnel out."

Everyone came back forty minutes later empty-handed. Sean told us the tunnel had ended a block away inside a garage. The garage door was wide-open, and there were signs a vehicle had been parked inside until recently. There was no sign of Russ Jacobson or Marvin Mueller. Terri couldn't believe Russ and Marvin had gotten away once again. The bastards had even gotten paid for the girls before they left.

Sean told us, "You should head back to the condominium and get some sleep. The task force will be busy interviewing the girls and will be interrogating the people who came to pick the girls up. When we finish interrogating everyone, the task force will be inventorying everything in the house. We will be searching for anything, which may give us a clue to where Russ and Marvin went.

We will also try to find anything, which might enable you to prove your husband was framed. This whole process will probably take several days. When we are finished, I will come over to your condominium to fill you in on everything."

The idea of going back to the condominium sounded terrific. The three friends had all been up for well over twenty-four hours and felt sleep deprived. Everyone was ready for a good night's sleep. It gets hard to think straight when you are overtired. As soon as Terri hit the bed, she went to sleep immediately. She had a wonderful dream about Chris out of prison. Along with Gavin and Becky, they were playing volleyball on a beach. The dream was so relaxing and peaceful however she awoke to the harsh reality. Terri realized this dream could come true, but not for at least another year and a half.

The next four days were as boring as they come. Terri kept wondering if Interpol would find anything at all. The girls and LaShawn played cards to while away the time. Terri went to a nearby store and purchased every board game she could find. After a while, even the board games became monotonous, but they continued with them. But now everyone agreed they would try to cheat at them. The idea wasn't so much the cheating. They all had to try to catch the one who was cheating and prove who was cheating. At least this livened the games up a little bit.

While the group were playing the games, they kept waiting for a phone to ring. All three checked their phones periodically to see if the phones were still working. For Terri, waiting was the height of futility. Finally, on the fifth day, her phone rang. Terri stared at it in amazement before she answered. It was Sean. The long waiting period was over at last. Sean McCluskey said he was coming over to the condominium to see them.

After arriving, Sean started to fill them in on the details of everything which had happened. Sean said when he came back to the main floor, his Interpol agent who understood Cambodian had intercepted him. His agent had listened very carefully, never once giving a clue he understood what was being said. He told me the Asian crime boss mentioned there were fifteen more girls being held captive on their airplane. There were two guards and a pilot aboard the plane. Sean immediately informed the Medellin SWAT team with this information. The SWAT team was able to board the plane, freeing the girls and taking three more prisoners.

The Cambodian crime boss had a lot of nerve. He informed Sean he had bought and paid for the girls who were in the basement. The girls were now his property. The women should be given to him, and then he would leave. Sean said, "I told him the only place he was going was to a Colombian prison for the rest of his life. I also told him since he liked the idea of forced prostitution so much, he would very likely find out what being on the receiving end was like."

Sean said, "I then tried to find out from the Asian crime boss how we would be able to contact Russ and Marvin. I could tell by the look of contempt in his eyes I would not get very far with that idea. Either he didn't know or he wasn't speaking anyway. I'm sure he will enjoy his years in a Colombian prison. We made a deal with the Colombian authorities they could have him as long as they gave him life in prison with no chance of parole.

"We checked every square inch of the house, searching to try to find a paper trail. We did not find as much as one single scrap of paper. Every stick of furniture including televisions, cooking utensils, and dishes and silverware had all been rented. The rent for all of these items and the rent for the house itself had all been paid for in cash. Russ and Marvin had not left any identification at either place.

"The only information we received, which was even a little bit of helpful, came from two of the girls. Evidently, Russ and Marvin had the hots for these two. They asked the girls if they would agree to be their personal slaves. In return, Russ and Marvin would take them to their permanent location. However, the men would not tell them where it was located. The only clue the girls got was it was a mansion and was in a warm climate and was located on the beach. The girls sincerely hated them as Russ and Marvin were the ones who had taken them captive, and the girls refused."

Sean continued, "I think wherever this permanent house is located, Russ and Marvin would not want to commit any crimes in the area. So it would probably be in an area where few, if any, women had disappeared recently. My guess is it could be anywhere in the world where there is a warm climate, very possibly somewhere English is spoken as the main language."

Terri thanked Sean profusely for all the help and the information he had given them. Then asked him to contact her if he ever found out anything else. Before Sean walked out, he turned to Terri, saying, "You have a friend in Interpol who is working hard on your case." Sean would not tell her who it was. Terri figured it was Clark. Even though Clark was with the police department in Florida, he seemed to have a lot to do with Interpol.

As there was nothing more anyone could do in Colombia, the three of them decided to head back to Seattle. Terri was very depressed. Everyone had tried so hard to do everything right this time. Yet with all of the hard work, Russ and Marvin had managed to escape once again. Time was not on Terri's side. She would be very lucky to find a place to search in the year and a half Terri had left before Chris hopefully got out of prison.

Chris will be having his first parole hearing in about a year and a half. With all the good he had done, Terri would be very surprised if he were not patrolled at that time. At the same time, Terri was bitterly disappointed in herself. Terri had promised Chris and herself years ago by the time he was out of prison, she would be able to clear his name. Now it looks like everyone will think he was guilty for the rest of his life.

LaShawn and Tatiana tried to cheer Terri up. Tatiana gave her a great big hug, saying, "Terri, anyone who knows Chris also knows he could never have murdered Felix Wells. Anyone who thinks Chris committed this crime, well they do not make any difference for us. Someone like that can just sit and wallow in their stupidity. Both you and Chris have been through one hell of an ordeal. Now you're just going to put your faith in God and justice. I have a very deep belief the truth will come out in the end. Somehow, someway, the answer will come suddenly, out of the blue. However, it might not come from you, but it will come at a time when you least expect it."

Terri told Tatiana, "Thank you, I guess I just get depressed from coming so close and then failing. I think I will put all of my resources into trying to find Russ and Marvin's permanent home. I promise to not get upset if I am not able to find it, but I will try. You have made me realize it may not come from me. At the moment, I don't have a clue where to start. I will check with Dawn Hendrickson and maybe Clark and June Evanston. Perhaps at the very least, they will steer me in the right direction. It's worth a shot anyway."

Chapter 53

Clark and June suggested maybe it was time to put everything out into the open. Put everything where thousands of people will be able to see it every day. After the Evanstons suggestion, Terri placed Russ and Marvin's pictures on the Internet. There were many sites devoted to searches for missing persons. Terri entered the names and aliases of Hank Devlin and Tom Jackson. She put all of the information and their pictures on every site she could find.

On her next forty-eight-hour visitation with Chris, Terri broke down and cried. In all of the time Chris had been in prison, this was the first time he had seen her like this. Chris asked, "Terri, what is the matter?" Terri was sobbing so hard she could barely talk. She said, "Oh, Chris, my sweetheart, I have failed you so miserably. I had set my hopes so high I thought for sure we would be able to catch Russ and Marvin this time. I was certain LaShawn, Tatiana, and I would be able to get the evidence, which would prove your innocence. Then we could have got you out of here and home where you belong."

Chris picked Terri up and sat her on his lap on the couch, putting his arm around her and holding her tightly. With his other hand, he gently stroked her hair as he told her, "Terri, please don't feel like you haven't done anything. At the very least, you scared the dickens out of them. There are twenty girls from the house in Medellin and fifteen more from the airplane who are free now. None of those girls would be free except for you, Tatiana and LaShawn.

"You three have also put a white slavery dealer out of business and into prison where he belongs. The Asian leader will not be able to purchase any more girls and turn them into prostitutes. There's even more—he will get to spend the rest of his life in prison. Colombian prisons are not known for being gentle. The prisons are a lot harsher than here at Monroe. I don't have any idea of how many dealers Russ and Marvin have. But at least this takes one of them out of the business.

"Who knows, there is always the possibility the word will get around. It could reach other buyers of women as prostitutes. Russ and Marvin could very well be ostracized. If it works like in the drug trade, their lives could also be in jeopardy." Terri sniffled and told Chris, "I don't want Russ and Marvin killed. I want them to be captured." Chris assured Terri, "There was very little chance of them getting killed. Russ and Marvin will hide out at their permanent place until the heat had died down."

Chris said, "As for me, my parole hearing is coming up in little over a year. I have been in here a month short of fourteen years. I've always been on good behavior. When there is trouble with another convict, very often the guards will have me talk to them. I have a very good chance of being paroled, I think I can make it at the Monroe Correctional Complex for one more year."

Terri kissed him, saying, "I know you can, Chris, but I want be able to prove you didn't deserve to be in here in the first place. I don't want people talking about you behind your back. I don't want you to have to go to a parole officer all of the time." Chris said, "I can live with seeing a parole officer, Terri. It is better than being in here. At least, we would be together."

Chris turned on some music. He stood up holding out his arms to Terri. She was in them in less than a heartbeat. Terri and Chris danced slowly in the small space of the trailer. She whispered to him, "When you're free, I am taking you to some of the exotic places I have been. We will walk along the sandy beaches of Saint Maartins. We will swim in the beautiful Caribbean ocean. I want you to explore Rio de Janeiro with me." Chris replied, "I know a place I want to explore." "Where?" Terri asked. He said, "The bedroom, right now."

Chris always knows how to lighten Terri's heart. From this moment on, Terri became her old cheerful self again. For the first time in a long time, she knew in her heart everything would work out for the best. It was as if a songbird had built a nest in her heart that day. From that day on, she started looking forward. Terri stopped worrying so much. She put everything she had into her job, Gavin, and his school activities. She also renewed her searches, although she was more lighthearted about it now. Terri no longer got frustrated when nothing turned up right away.

Gavin turned fourteen years old in November of this year. You never think much about how tall someone else is, until suddenly your son is taller than you. Gavin was almost as tall as his father was now. One day, Terri was talking to him when Gavin suddenly started to laugh. She made the mistake of asking Gavin, "What is so funny?" Gavin said, "I don't know, Mom, I just started thinking how funny you look down there." Terri gave him a playful swat just to let him know she was still his mother.

One day, while Terri was talking to Gavin, she mentioned to him, "In all of the time your dad has been in prison, I have never been able to buy him a present. On all of his birthdays, Valentine's days, our wedding anniversaries, on Christmas, I have not been able to give him anything except a card. So I made sure on those holidays, I went searching for the gift I wanted to give him. When I found out what each present would have cost, I would put the amount of the present in a special savings account for him. There is a very large sum in the account now."

Terri said, "Gavin, now it won't be long before your dad is released from prison, I would like to get your dad something very special to celebrate. If you happen to think of something, please let me know." Two days later, Gavin came to Terri all excited. He said, "Mom, you need to come out to the garage with me. I want to show you something." When Terri got to the garage, she didn't see anything, which had not been there before.

She asked Gavin, "What is it I am supposedly looking at?" He replied, "Dad's Monte Carlo, Mom, it hasn't been driven for years. You always told me Dad loved his car. Why don't you have it completely restored for him? A good restoration shop can make the Monte Carlo look better than when it was new." Terri gave Gavin a hug and said, "Okay, son, I think you have come up with the perfect idea for a gift. Don't say a word to your dad. We will let it be a surprise."

Terri and Gavin searched and found a restoration shop, which had an excellent reputation. The men at the shop looked at the Monte Carlo before saying it was already in remarkable shape. The men from the shop said they would take the body down to bare metal. They would repaint it inside and out. There would be new gauges, new carpet, reupholstered leather seats and door panels. The men would replace all the tie rods, redo the steering, install four-wheel disc brakes, and put in a completely new muffler system.

While this was being done the men would send out the motor and transmission to be totally rebuilt. When everything else was finished, they would install a state-of-the-art sound system. The boss of the shop told Terri he would have it all completed before Christ's parole hearing came up.

Chris at Monroe. Chris worries more about Terri's search to prove his innocence than he is worried about himself. For he knows he is innocent. Terri and Gavin know this too. Which is enough for him. Chris worries Terri will be disappointed when she won't be able to find a way to prove he is innocent. Yes, Chris would love to be able to prove to the world he had nothing whatsoever to do with the crime.

Being innocent and proving it are two different things. Russ and Marvin are just too slick. He doesn't think the two have left one stone unturned. Since Chris has been imprisoned, he has watched countless forensic shows. He has had many convicts watch them with him. Still, Chris has no idea how Russ and Marvin were able to pull this crime off.

Chris will admit he has figured part of it out. Russ and Marvin had to break into their apartment not once but twice. The first time was to steal his pistol, shirt, and shoes. The second time would have been to bring the shirt and shoes back. This time with the forensic evidence which would eventually put Chris in prison.

All the time Russ and Marvin had Chris's shirt and shoes, they would've had to be careful not to get any of their own DNA on it. This might have involved wrapping their bodies in sterile cellophane with which they also would have had to be very careful. Then one of them would have had to shoot Felix Wells at close range all the while wearing Chris's clothes. As if this wasn't enough, one of them had to purposely walk through the blood wearing his shoes.

This is the only way high-velocity blood splatter from Felix Wells could've gotten onto his clothes. Chris certainly doesn't want to dash Terri's hope. Because unless there is something the crooks did wrong or if Terri can find out about the pistol or the Monte Carlo, Chris doesn't think there's any hope of solving this case. Chris knew for a fact Russ and Marvin were not using his Monte Carlo, because he was driving it to Everett. There happens to be hundreds of Monte Carlos, which are almost identical to his. So Russ and Marvin must have purposely bought one which looked exactly like it.

Maybe, just maybe, Terri's not so far off the track after all. There may be some possibility the outlaws have the Monte Carlo in storage somewhere. This would explain why Felix Wells body has never been found. Chris bets it is in the trunk of the other Monte Carlo to this day. If Terri ever catches up with those crooks, he will ask her to look for storage receipt.

To think Chris was about to tell Terri she would never be able to prove his innocence. Convicts there at Monroe have told him many crooks like to keep a trophy. So there's no way of telling they may have kept some other evidence as well. He believes there was some artwork taken at the same time. Anyway, Chris has changed his mind. He believes Terri still has a chance of proving his innocence.

In the process of trying to find out what has really happened to put Chris in prison, Terri and her friends have done an enormous amount of good. They have saved several women from an utterly horrible fate. Just the search itself has given a meaning and purpose to her life. In the same way helping young convicts get an education has helped Chris immensely. It has given him a reason to live for. That plus a very good woman and their son waiting for him when he gets out.

Chris is hoping against hope he gets paroled on his very first try. He has heard this is highly unusual, but it does happen from time to time. He will have quite a few references from the guards, many who have already told him they will write letters to the parole board on his behalf. Then there are all the convicts Chris has helped to get an education. Several of them have been paroled and are leading a good life. They have all told him they will go to bat for him when his parole hearing comes up.

Chris yearns to be a full-time husband once more. He misses the wonderful life he had with Terri. Chris also wants to be a full-time father for the first time. He has missed so much of his son's life. If he gets out of prison, he will still be able to be there for the last three and a half years of his high school life. He knows Gavin loves sports, and wants to be there cheering for him at football and basketball games. There is so much in life Chris has missed.

Chris has to hand it to Terri. One could not ask for a better wife. Terri has been there every step of the way for him. He has really missed all wedding anniversaries and will have to plan a party and a very good one for the first year when he gets out. It will have to be something very special for a very special lady.

Chapter 54

This year seemed like it was filled with activity. In late March, Gavin informed Terri there would be a program for next year's freshman and their parents. It was to be held at Bellevue High School where Gavin would be starting school in the fall. Every student who would be a freshman and their parents were urged to attend. Terri doesn't think any parent who loves their child would want to miss out on this opportunity.

Terri could not believe their baby boy was about to start high school. It seemed like it was just yesterday she had enrolled him in kindergarten. Gavin and Terri went to Bellevue High School where they were joined by around 350 other students and their parents. Bellevue High School is a huge class AAA school and is very modern, having just been rebuilt. Almost all of the old school has been torn down, so it was pretty much a brand-new school.

After Terri and Gavin arrived, the students and their parents were instructed to go to the gym where the principal would speak. There the principal instructed everyone about the big picture—what Bellevue High School could do for you. "One can take courses, which would simply enable you to graduate. But we at Bellevue High School hope you will set your goal much higher. We would like you to aim for college and your goal in life. We want your high school days to be filled with fun and good memories. To really succeed it is a good idea to enroll in the harder courses."

The principal said, "Besides the required courses, we also have sports, football, basketball, baseball, tennis, golf, soccer to name a few. If you are interested in writing, you can join the staff of the *Barque*, our school newspaper. We have a great art and photography department. We have superb teachers in science, math, world history, music, English, and band. In fact, at Bellevue High School, we have no teachers who are not superb.

When Terri and Gavin were finished in the gym, everyone was split into smaller groups. From there, they were able to spend fifteen minutes with each department. At this point, Terri helped Gavin pick his tentative classes. When Gavin went to the athletic department, he signed up for football and baseball. In fact, Terri had a hard time prying him out of the athletic department.

Next mother and son went to presentations from English, math, computers, art, and band. Gavin got real excited about the science program where he signed up for freshman biology. Gavin seemed to know most of the kids. Of course, he had gone to school with most of them since he was in kindergarten.

Terri still had not made up her mind about what she was planning to do this summer. Of course, Gavin will be going to help her parents in North Dakota. He keeps telling his mom she should come with him, but Terri told him, "I am not sure yet of what I will be doing." In the back of her mind, she kept thinking, "This might be my last chance." So Terri told Gavin, "I probably won't know what I am doing until the very last minute."

Terri was toying with the idea of making a whirlwind tour of several countries. They would all be in countries with a warm climate. The thing these countries would have in common would be there would have few or no missing women. Terri knows the idea of finding Russ and Marvin this way was a long shot. But again, she still needed to try. Terri would not stop in any country for more than two or three days at the most.

She approached Tatiana with the idea. Tatiana said she was willing and ready to go. Tatiana told Terri LaShawn would not be able to come with them this time. The corporation he was working for was expanding, and would be keeping LaShawn busy flying them all over the world for the next three months. Terri decided in every country visited she would use both Russ and Marvin's real names and aliases. In each country went to, Terri would search for their records. If Russ and Marvin were in any of these countries, there must be some type of paperwork.

As soon as school got out for the summer, Terri put Gavin on the plane to North Dakota. After he left, she went to see Tatiana to figure out their itinerary. Terri and Tatiana were having a problem deciding where to go. Suddenly, Tatiana had a brainstorm. She said, "Seeing we have no idea of where we want to search, let's tackle it as if we are playing Russian roulette." Terri got out a large map of the world and a set of darts.

The only rule set for the game was you couldn't aim you could only throw the dart. The first country hit in the tropical zone was where the girls would go first. It was a great idea, but it still took several tries. Terri somehow did not think Russ and Marvin would be in Antarctica, Iceland or Nova Scotia. Terri's next dart struck the Seychelles islands. Tatiana said, "Where in the hell is that?"

Neither of them had ever heard of the place. It was in the middle of the Indian Ocean. It was one thousand miles from anywhere. Tatiana remarked, "Are you sure we want to go there? The place is very secluded." Terri said, "What better place for Russ and Marvin to hide; besides, it is where the dart hit."

Tatiana and Terri started off on a whirlwind tour, but had no idea of how it would end up. Or what might be discovered for that matter. The flight to Victoria the capital of the Seychelles was a very long, boring, and weary trip. When Terri and Tatiana finally arrived, the two were dried out and bone tired. The girls went to the nearest hotel. There Terri got a room and both of them slept for more than twelve hours.

As soon as Terri and Tatiana got up, they ate breakfast and headed for the capitol building. There Terri found out there were 115 islands, which comprise the Seychelles. The total population of these islands number was just under eighty-seven thousand people. Terri entered the names Russ Jacobson, Marvin Mueller, Hank Devlin and Tom Jackson into the computer. The computer came up with no information. There was no one by any of these names in the Seychelles.

Tatiana looked at Terri and said, "Well, that didn't take very long. Now what we do?" Terri told her, "We need to recuperate before we head to our next destination because we don't even know where it is yet." The two walked around Victoria for a couple of hours then headed for a restaurant. While there Terri asked the waitress for an idea of what a person might do for entertainment. The waitress suggested, "Why don't you try snorkeling."

After leaving the restaurant, Terri suggested they find a place to rent snorkeling gear. Tatiana said, "Don't be foolish. Snorkeling gear is not expensive nor is it very big. Let's buy it because we may find other places where we want to snorkel." After purchasing the snorkeling gear, the girls headed to the beach. Both of them were very impressed with the beach for neither had ever encountered such soft, powdery sand. With so few inhabitants in the Seychelles, there were few other people on the beach.

As Terri looked around, she saw lush tropical rain forest in the background. Closer to the beach were large palm trees. Among them, were found a few blackbirds looking similar to parrots. Later on, Tatiana found out the birds were in fact Seychelles black parrots, the islands national bird.

The temperature in the Seychelles was a decent eighty degrees; however, the humidity was very high. Terri and Tatiana were very grateful to enter the water, which was tantalizingly refreshing. Once both of them had put on their masks and breathing tubes, they were amazed at the variety of fish. There were some fish, which were absolutely huge, and some were no bigger than a dime. The fish came in all colors, shapes, and sizes. Terri just loved watching them flit around. Some even came up and stared into the facemasks. The fish probably wondered what species of fish the girls were.

Later, Terri and Tatiana were told there were over one thousand species of fish in and around the Seychelles islands. They did find see some coral reefs, but the coral was mostly bleached out. In another area, Tatiana discovered coral reefs, which were beginning to recover. The girls eventually got out of the water before starting to look like they were bleached out too. As they walked along the beach, Terri could see other islands in the distance. Tatiana came upon a giant Aldabra tortoise. It didn't look as if it had a care in the world. It didn't even bother to tuck his head into his shell. He even allowed the girls to pat his head. Then he acted just like he deserved this. As they traveled farther down the beach, the sand suddenly stopped. From there on, it was rocky with waves lapping over the top of them.

As the girls turned around and headed back to their hotel, they ran into a local woman who fell in step with them. She turned out to be a wealth of information about the Seychelles. She told them there was no one who is actually native to the islands. There were people of all nationalities who had emigrated here from somewhere else in the world. The people who lived here now were all their descendants. The two official languages are French and English. Tourism accounts for a large portion of the gross national product.

The most astounding fact is this is a matriarchal society. Mothers were the dominant parents in the family. The mothers were the ones mainly in charge of the children and the money. Terri thinks she will tease Chris about this fact when she gets home. In actuality in Chris and Terri's marriage, they have always made major decisions together. Terri thinks this holds true in most American families.

Tatiana and Terri decided they needed one more day of rest before resuming their journey. The next morning, Tatiana discovered a tour which went out into the ocean on a glass bottom boat. This sounded like an excellent way to observe underwater scenery. The water was so crystal clear one could see schools of many types of fish. Terri asked the guide if there were any sharks in these waters.

This made the tour guide laugh. He said, "Sister, there are sharks in every ocean in the world. There is no barrier anywhere. There is no barrier to keep sharks from going wherever they want to go. If there is a food supply, a shark will be there. Even here in paradise, however, I have never heard of a shark attack in these waters. Our guide told them, "Even though there are 115 islands listed in the Seychelles, there are actually 150 islands. Of course some of them are only a pile of rocks jutting out of the ocean."

Later in the evening after having dinner, Terri got out the world map and the darts. Terri handed the first dart to Tatiana. Her first try landed right in the middle of Afghanistan. Tatiana promptly pulled the dart out, saying, "Uh-uh, we're not going there." Terri agreed wholeheartedly; however, she didn't do any better. She stuck her dart in the middle of the Pacific Ocean with no land in sight. Tatiana did better on her next throw, so they were off to New Zealand.

Terri and Tatiana arrived in Wellington, New Zealand, on a beautiful Saturday evening. All the government offices would be closed until Monday morning. Terri found a room where they could relax. Next had dinner; and next after which they went to a nightclub to relax. Terri and Tatiana sipped their drinks, listened to music and the conversations around them. Both were asked to dance several times, but the girls just smiled simply, showing the men their rings and politely refusing.

As the girls were starting to leave, they heard a man swearing at a lady. Just as Tatiana was about to walk past them, the man grabbed lady by the hair and hit her. Then he pulled back his arm to hit her again when Tatiana grabbed his arm. He turned around to swing at Tatiana; instead, he found himself lying on his back on the floor.

The angry man jumped up embarrassed and madder than a swarm of African bees. It didn't help the way the crowd laughed and booed him. He evidently thought he had just tripped and fell on the floor. Anyhow, he tried to take another swing at Tatiana. This was not a good thing for him to do for him to do, for he wound up on the floor once again. This time, Tatiana took a chair and placed it over his head.

The bottom rung of the chair was just above his neck, and Tatiana promptly sat down on the chair so he couldn't get up. He twisted, squirmed, and kicked his feet in every direction. He also had a supreme case of potty mouth. Tatiana paid no attention to him. Terri pulled up an empty table and chair over and sat down. When the barmaid came over, Tatiana and Terri both ordered a drink.

Tatiana asked the barmaid if she had called the police. She said, "The police are on the way." The man kept cursing at Tatiana and screaming at her to let him up. She sweetly asked him if he was going to be good and behave himself. This just set off another round of swearing. Tatiana told him, "If your mother were here, she would probably wash your mouth out with soap." He must've been a bad one to raise, for this set him off on a tirade about his mother.

The lady who had been slapped finally joined us at the table. She told us she didn't even know who this person was. She had never before seen him in her life. He had come to the table and asked her to dance. When she refused, he started badgering her. This then turned into the violence the girls had seen.

When the police officers arrived, they immediately handcuffed him. Two of the officers led him away while the last officer stayed long enough to inform them the police had been looking for him. He had escaped from a mental institution was very violent, and had killed before. The officer said, "Psychologists say he is very likely to kill again."

After the officer had left, the lady told the girls, "My name is Earlene. I am very grateful for what you have done." She asked them what they were doing in Wellington, New Zealand. After Terri told her the reason for being here, Earlene said, "I can help you with this on Monday. I happen to work for the New Zealand government. I can find out quickly if any of those people can be found in New Zealand." She also volunteered to show us around the Wellington area the next day.

Earlene was as good as her word, for she knocked on the door at nine in the morning. Everyone went to her car, and then Earlene took them to her favorite restaurant. While they were dining, Earlene told them a little about New Zealand. "It is actually two islands, North Island and South Island. The islands are separated by Cook Strait, and the closest distance between them is fourteen miles. English is the dominant language, but Maori is the official language.

"The Maoris are of Polynesian descent and were already in New Zealand when the Europeans first arrived. The Maoris make great artwork, which I hope to show you later. The Maoris are having a festival today, so hopefully we will be able to stop and see the festival. South Island is the larger of the two islands and is home to the Southern Alps. There are eighteen mountain peaks over nine thousand eight hundred feet high. North island although the smaller of the two islands has over 76 percent of the population. Even though Wellington is the capital, Auckland is the largest city in New Zealand."

After finishing breakfast, Terri and Tatiana got into Earlene's car. She took them to the suburbs so they could enjoy the scenery. There were many farms, and it looked like the majority of them raised sheep. Terri loved watching the lambs frolicking with each other. The lambs looked so cute and cuddly Terri had to laugh when they ran. If one of the lambs jumped in one spot, all the rest of them would jump when they came to the same place.

Earlene stopped so Terri and Tatiana could and take in the Maori celebration which had at least fifty dancers all of them were young and extremely good-looking. The dancers look a lot like one would imagine the Hawaiian dancers looked. Of course, both places were originally settled by the Polynesians along with several other islands in the Pacific Ocean. After getting back to Wellington, Earlene took them to an arts and crafts fair. There were many booths selling local art, and much of it made by the Maoris. Terri purchased a statue with a natural-looking head and was amazed at the intricate details, and it looked so lifelike she couldn't resist it. Tatiana also bought a carved statue, but this one had a really grotesque head. She said, "It is so ugly it is cute." They also both purchased greenstone necklaces with earrings to match.

Before Earlene dropped them off, she told them where to find her at the government building the next day. Terri and Tatiana once again got out their map of the world. If it turned out Russ and Marvin were not in New Zealand, they would be taking off the very next day. On the very first try, Tatiana's dart hit the Falkland Islands. Tatiana and Terri decided they would make this the next stop on their journey. Seeing how close Argentina was, the girls decided they would stop there after visiting the Falklands.

By the time the government building opened the next morning, the two friends were there to see Earlene. Within an hour, Terri found out everything she needed to know. Russ and Marvin did not live anywhere in New Zealand. Terri thanked Earlene for all of her help and headed for the airport. Within four hours, they were headed for the Falkland Islands.

The second Terri stepped into the Port Stanley Airport in the Falklands, she realized they had made a big mistake by coming here. The Falklands were not a place where Russ and Marvin would be able to hide. The first person talked to verified this fact. He said, "The total population of the islands was only three thousand one hundred people." Terry showed him the pictures of Russ and Marvin. The Falkland Islander said he knew everyone on islands, and they were not here.

Because of the fact there was an eight-hour wait for a flight to Buenos Aires, Argentina, Terri and Tatiana checked out the status of the Falkland Islands. The Falklands are an archipelago consisting of the East Island and the West Island, with 776 lesser islands. It is around 280 miles to the South American mainland. Stanley the capital of the Falklands is on the East Island.

The Falklands are considered to be a part of the United Kingdom; however, Argentina disputes this fact. Argentina has always claimed them, calling them the Malvinas. Falkland islanders themselves always rejected this claim. This dispute came to a head in 1982 when the militaristic government of Argentina at the time invaded the Falklands. This was mainly done to distract Argentinian's mind off of their economic problems at home. British forces were dispatched to the Falklands on April 2, 1982. By June 14, 1982, Argentina withdrew from the Falklands.

Both of the larger Falkland Islands are used mainly as a pasture for sheep, although reindeer have been introduced recently. Tourism is steadily growing mainly due to the fact the Falklands became a household name after the 1982 war.

Chapter 55

The flight to Buenos Aires, Argentina, was quick and uneventful. Tatiana and Terri were looking forward to their time there. Buenos Aires is the capital and largest city in Argentina. It also happens to be the second largest city in South America, second only to Sao Paulo in Brazil. Buenos Aires is like Sao Paulo in the fact it is the political, financial, commercial, agricultural hub of Argentina.

The population of Buenos Aires proper hovers around three million people ever since the late '40s. However, its suburbs have grown to ten million in this time. To the west of Buenos Aires is the Pampa Humeda, which is the most productive region of Argentina. It is a great agricultural area producing wheat, soybeans, and corn.

Buenos Aires is sometimes referred to as the Paris of South America. Its museums, art production, theaters, and orchestras have gained worldwide fame. It is also the home of the tango. Terri hopes someday in the future she would be able to bring Chris there and do the tango with him.

Soon after finding a hotel, Tatiana and Terri were off to the government building where records were kept. They went from one government official after another. Terri doesn't have any idea if the people she talked to were lazy, unknowing, or unwilling. Because she had a hard time finding someone who would check the records for them. Terri was finally able to locate a lady who spoke excellent English. She was willing to do a search of the records for a slight nominal fee, of course.

Terri gave the lady $100 and the names Russ Jacobson, Marvin Mueller, Tom Jackson, and Hank Devlin. The lady was on the computer for over an hour after which she handed Terri a sheet of paper with names and addresses on it. It seems there were two Hank Devlins and three Tom Jacksons living in Argentina. The only good thing was all of them lived in or around Buenos Aires.

The girls decided to check on Hank Devlin number one first as he lived the closest. As soon as Terri and Tatiana entered the neighborhood, there were doubts this was the right one. The houses in this part of the city did not look rundown. However, it looked to be on the lower end of the middle class part of Buenos Aires. Terri still needed to check it out, so she drove past the house. In the front yard, there were bicycles and children's toys.

This certainly didn't mean it was not our Hank Devlin, but it lowered the chances by several notches. The girls went to the nearest restaurant where they had coffee and a pastry. While sitting there, Tatiana said, "I'm sure this is not him. When we go back there, we will pull in the driveway, and I will try knocking on the door. Then we will know for certain it is not the right Hank Devlin." Terri was a little hesitant at first, but then said, "Okay, let's go for it."

They were in luck because this time as there was a car in the driveway, which hadn't been there before. Terri parked their car behind it, and Tatiana headed for the door. Almost as soon as she knocked, a man answered. Terri knew it was not Marvin immediately. This man was a short Afro-American. She saw Tatiana start up a conversation with him when he started to talk. Then both started laughing.

When Tatiana got back in the car, she was still laughing. Terri said, "Okay, how about sharing with me what is so funny." This just started more giggling. Tatiana said, "Oh, Terri, how was I to know this Hank's wife had passed away three years ago. He recently decided it was time he needed a mother for his children. So he sent away for a mail-order bride, and she is supposed to show up today. When I showed up on the doorstep, he thought I was the one. I did ask him if he happened to know the other Hank Devlin? Of course, he didn't."

It was getting late in the day, so they headed back to the hotel room. Once there, Terri checked out a map of Buenos Aires. Terri and Tatiana wanted to know which one of the men they would check next. This one was one of the Tom Jacksons. Tatiana marked him down as Tom Jackson number one, and Terri told Tatiana, "I hope one of these Tom Jacksons or Hank Devlins is the right one. It's too bad we don't know how long each of these men has lived in this area. It would give us an idea of who the right one might be."

Early the next morning, Tatiana drove past Tom Jackson number one's house. It was definitely in a trendier part of Buenos Aires. However, it was not the mansion the girls in Colombia had been told about. (Of course, one can always lie. Plus, Russ and Marvin are great at lying.) No one seemed to be home when they went past. However, there was a neighbor out watering his grass, so Tatiana stopped and talked to him. she asked, "How long has your neighbor lived next door?" He said, "I don't know. I've lived here for eight years, and my next-door neighbor was already living here when I moved in."

The neighbor told them he didn't really know the man. They waved to each other when they met, but that was about it. He did mention his neighbor was frequently gone for extended periods of time. When he described Tom Jackson number one, the description was not exact, but it could possibly be Russ Jacobson. Terri asked for the time he left for work and the time he came home. The neighbor said, "I see him leave at six-thirty in the morning and got home at four-thirty in the afternoon."

This information boosted their hopes up a little as there was nothing more they could do today. The girls were just going to have to wait until tomorrow morning. Tatiana observed, "Now would've been a good time to be in touch with some of LaShawn's contacts. Sadly, the only one who can get in touch with them was LaShawn."

Terri and Tatiana were back at Tom Jackson's house in time to follow him at six-thirty the next morning. Tatiana didn't get too close, so they didn't get a good look at him. Instead, she kept several car lengths behind him because she didn't want him to get suspicious. It looked as if he is heading for the center of Buenos Aires. Tatiana happened to get stopped at a red light at an intersection, but Tom Jackson kept on driving. Terri was able to follow keep him in sight for the next few blocks while waiting at the light.

Tatiana went to the last place they had seen him and noted there was a parking lot there where they could park and wait for him the next time he drove past. As the girls sat watching for him the next morning, Terri got a good glimpse of him as he went by. Tatiana pulled out to follow, but Terri told Tatiana, "I don't think it is Russ. But keep on following him anyway. I want to be positive."

Tatiana followed him into a parking garage at a high-rise in the center of Buenos Aires. She parked ten cars away. Then both of them watched carefully as he got out of his car and made his way toward an elevator. They hurried to be right behind him as he entered the elevator. As they entered the elevator, he asked the girls, "What floor please?" Terri told him, "The tenth floor," but her heart sank for it was not Russ.

The next one concentrated on was Tom Jackson number two. This one lived the farthest distance from them, so they wanted to get him out of the picture quickly. Even with their map, the girls had to stop and ask for directions twice. When Tatiana drove by his house, they couldn't believe what a rundown shack he lived in. There was an old man sitting on a rocker on the porch, a nondescript dog lay at his feet. He had a pipe clamped in his almost toothless mouth and was carving on a piece of wood. Even from the car, Terri could tell the pipe wasn't lit.

Tatiana and Terri looked at each other in agreement. They had seen a string of stores about a mile back, so Tatiana swung the car around and headed for them. The ladies loaded the rental car to the max with food, clothes, dog food, warm clothes, which looked to be his size. Terri purchased blankets and anything else she thought he might need. Terri placed an envelope with $500 in there and placed it where he would be able to find it. Just when both of them thought they were through, both spotted it at the same time—some tobacco, two large cans of pipe tobacco. Terri knew tobacco is not good for you. But if it gave an old man some enjoyment, what the heck.

When Tatiana pulled into the old man's driveway, he looked like he was flabbergasted. He evidently hadn't had any visitors in a very long time. At first, Terri didn't know if he would understand English, so she asked him if his name was Tom Jackson? It turned out Terri was wrong. The old man said yes, he was Tom Jackson, and in fact, he was originally from Great Britain. Tom and his wife had moved to Buenos Aires when they were first married. But now he was all alone as his wife had passed on years ago.

Terri told him an anonymous benefactor had asked them to bring him a few things. Terri and Tatiana went to the car and started hauling everything into the house. The place was very barren, but it was super clean. When the girls had finished, Tom told them, "I would like you to stay for coffee, but unfortunately, I don't have any." Luckily, Terri had purchased some coffee, so she made a pot full. The two of them felt they just had to stay and visit with him for a while, for he was all by himself and very lonely. It is one thing to get old, but to be old and alone is something you never want to happen to you.

Before leaving the area, Tatiana scouted around and found a senior citizen center not far from his home. It was a place where senior citizens could come and visit every day. Tatiana told them about Tom Jackson, and the people at the center assured them they would be in contact with him. If he needs it, someone will go to pick him up whenever he wants to and bring him to the center to visit. Here he will be able to visit with people who are his own age. The center also has free meals every day, and the senior citizens could play cards and dominos. When Tatiana went back to inform Tom about this he was so happy, he cried.

After leaving Tom's home, the girls felt great. It is a wonderful feeling to be able to help another human being. Tatiana looked at Terri and said, "Chris and LaShawn would be proud of us." That night was spent listening to the National Symphony Orchestra. Later, they had champagne sent to their room to celebrate their good deed. The next day, was spent touring museums in Buenos Aires.

Later in the evening, Terri told Tatiana, "This still has not gotten us any closer to finding Russ or Marvin. We have struck out three times in a row. I am still hoping for a home run with one of the other two." Tatiana and Terri flipped a coin to see who would be the next one. It turned out to be Tom Jackson number three. Both of the last two lived right next to the ocean, so their hopes were very high.

It was already ten in the evening, but Terri was all hyped up and raring to go, thinking they would just take a quick drive past Tom Jackson number three's home. It was such a beautiful clear moonlight night, and both were just enjoying the drive. Terri were so close to the ocean she was able to smell the salt air. The girls were both thinking this would be just the type of area where Russ or Marvin would choose to live.

Tatiana slowed way down as she drove past the home. Suddenly, a young girl of about twelve years old came darting out of the driveway. She was holding up her hands for them to stop. She was screaming in Spanish. After stopping the car, Terri indicated to her they did not speak Spanish. The girl then reverted to English. She said, "Please help me, there are two very bad men inside our home, trying to rob my father and mother."

Terri handed the girl her cell phone, telling her to call the police. Tatiana and Terri took their socks filled with sand, which they always keep with them in a foreign country, then headed for the house. Both of them kept to the shadows as they snuck up on the house. The girls crept up to the front door, which was wide-open and peeked inside the foyer. The door must've been left open when the young girl fled.

Terri could hear loud voices coming from the interior, so both very carefully tiptoed to the room from which the voices were coming from. Peeking inside Terri could see a man and woman all tied up on a couch. The two robbers had their backs turned toward them and were yelling at them. Terri was not able to understand what they were saying. She gathered the robbers were trying to make the man or woman tell them where they kept their valuables. The room was very huge. Way too big for them to be able to sneak up on them. What was needed was some type of diversion.

Terri indicated to Tatiana a small cove in the foyer, just large enough to hide both of them. Tatiana headed for the cove while Terri peeked around the corner one more time. Both of the robber's backs were still turned. The man did notice Terri however. She indicated to him to do something, which would make them come out here. Then Terri quietly withdrew to the cove. She was able to hear the man's voice. He must've told the robbers the valuables were somewhere out here.

It wasn't very long before one of the men walked out to the foyer. As he was walking past them, Terri swung the sock as hard as she could at the back of his head. Tatiana was right there to break his fall and lowered him quietly to the floor. Tatiana handcuffed him with plastic ties on his hands and feet.

Then she put a rag in his mouth to keep him silent, next she carried him out onto the porch. Then both went back to hide once more in the cove.

After a period of time, Terri heard his partner calling for him. When his friend didn't answer, he cautiously came out into the foyer. Not seeing his friend anywhere, he moved very slowly, waving a pistol back and forth in front of him. Terri's heart was in her throat and she could feel Tatiana shaking beside her. They could hear the man's footsteps moving slowly and steadily across the floor. Terri knew this was the end, and to have it come from someone, she didn't even know.

When it was looking the worse and the robber was only a couple of steps away from the cove, Terri heard the homeowner yelling loudly. At the sound, the robber spun around turning his back to the girls. This looked like their only chance, so in unison, Tatiana and Terri struck him on either side of his head with the socks. He dropped like a rock, and Tatiana quickly handcuffed him. Then after making sure both robbers were secure, Terri and Tatiana went into the other room and released the man and woman.

The man immediately asked, "Where is my daughter?" Tatiana told him, "Your daughter is safe. She was out in the street calling the police when we came in here." The father yelled for his daughter to come back to the house. He said, "Everything is okay now." After she came in sobbing, his daughter said, "I was so scared, Daddy. I called the police, and they didn't believe me. The dispatcher told me it was a prank, and I could get in a lot of trouble for it. I didn't think these two ladies would be able to do anything."

Her dad said, "Honey, these two ladies probably handled it better than the police would have." After the father got on the phone to the police, he must have been someone with authority. For when he got off the phone, the police were there within five minutes. The police profusely apologized for the dispatcher not listening to his daughter. Then they loaded the two robbers who looked like they were suffering from bad headaches into the back of a police car. The police then took all of their statements. After which they were gone in a flash.

Tom Jackson number three insisted the girls stay for a while. He and his wife took the girls to the large formal room where they gave the girls each a glass of cognac. Then he introduced himself to them as Tom Jackson. Terri told him, "We already know who you are." When she mentioned this, Tom wanted to know how they could possibly know who he was. Terri explained to him how she was after a different Tom Jackson. When Terri had finished the story, Tom looked bewildered.

After telling Tom and his wife the whole sordid story right from the beginning, Tom said, "You two are some very remarkable ladies. You stopped to help someone who may have been the very person for whom you have been searching for. I do not understand why you would do this." Tatiana answered, "The Tom Jackson we are searching for would not want to have a family. It would only encumber his activities. It would tie him down, so to speak. When your daughter came running out to the street pleading for help, we knew immediately you weren't the same Tom Jackson we wanted."

This Tom Jackson could not thank the girls enough. He said, "You saved our lives. The reason we wouldn't tell the robbers anything is we knew who they were. We knew after the robbers got what they wanted, they would have to kill us. So we were stalling, hoping something would happen to save our lives. That it happened in the form of two beautiful young ladies defies belief.

"Now we would like to know what kind of reward you would like. Your heroism deserves something beyond the ordinary." Terri told Tom, "We do not want and would not accept a reward. The fact you and your family are alive is reward enough for us." Tom said, "I have an idea. When your husband is released from prison, I would like for both you, Tatiana, and your husband's to come here as our guests. We will give you a grand tour of Buenos Aires." The girls told Tom this was a reward they would be more than willing to accept.

The only person left now was Hank Devlin number two. The first time Tatiana drove past his home, Terri was impressed. This one was truly a mansion, at least the part of it, which they could see. It had an eight-foot rock wall enclosing it, and there was concertina wire on top of the rock wall. As if this wasn't enough, every fifty feet had a security camera mounted on it. The security cameras were constantly scanning back and forth. At the front gate, Terri saw a guard shack with a guard stationed inside. The gate looked like it was made of iron, and looking through it, Terri could see Doberman pinscher guard dogs roaming the inside area.

Terri did see a chauffeured limousine leave the estate. All she could make out was the driver. The windows in the rear were heavily tinted. Terri could not even see if there was anyone else inside the car. Tatiana drove back to their hotel to try and figure out what to do next. The first thing to come to their minds was a boat. With a boat, they would be able to see if there was a way in from the ocean. The following day, Terri rented a boat. When the girls cruised by the house on the ocean side, they saw it was just as heavily guarded as the front.

Terri discovered Buenos Aires is sometimes known as the city of books. So the girls went to the library. When Terri got there, she asked for a copy of who's who in Argentina. Terri could not find a reference to a Hank Devlin. There were some other Devlin's listed in the book but no Hank. Then the girls went back to the strategy which had been used before. Every day Terri would go to the rental agency and exchange the car for a different one.

Tatiana was worried the guard at the gate would recognize their car. This way the girls would be able to check the estate every day until they saw the limousine leave. Hopefully, Terri would be able to find out where it went. That way, maybe she can find out whether or not he was Marvin Mueller.

The next two days were very trying. Tatiana drove past the residence several times, but they weren't able to see anything. Finally, on the third day, Terri saw the limousine pull out of the gate right in front of them. Even better yet it was heading in the same direction the girls were. Tatiana was able to stay within sight of the limousine for fifteen minutes. Then the limousine pulled into a parking lot, which looked like it housed a large corporate building.

The sign on the front of the building let them know it was a large petroleum company's headquarters. Tatiana was able to find a parking spot, which was reserved for visitors. Then Terri watched as a chauffeur opened the door of the limousine. Instead of the man Terri was expecting, a very well-dressed woman stepped out.

The girls hurried to be able to enter the building before she did and immediately headed for the information desk. As the lady walked past them, Terri asked the man at the information booth who she was. He replied, "She is the CEO of our corporation, Hannah Devlin. But she will get very angry if you call her that. She prefers to be called Hank Devlin. In fact, she gets upset at the newspapers and publishers when they list her as Hannah. Now is there anything else I can help you with?" Terri had to say something, so she told him, "We are lost and need directions back to our hotel."

Terri was sort of crushed she had really thought they would be able to find Russ and Marvin in Argentina. Tatiana managed to cheer her up by saying, "Look at the bright side, Terri, we did find out where Russ and Marvin are not living." This made Terri laugh, and she said, "Well, at least we did have some remarkable adventures on this trip. We were able to help a very lonely old man and managed to save a family." Tatiana agreed then she said, "I think maybe it's time we head back to Seattle."

Thus ended an exciting, exhausting and exhilarating trip. Terri and Tatiana flew back to Seattle and home. Hopefully, this would prove to be her last summer without Chris. As soon as Terri got back, she went to see Chris and let him know she had failed once again. He told her his theory about the Monte Carlo, about it being a duplicate, and yet was probably stored somewhere maybe right here in Seattle. Chris said he thought wherever this other Monte Carlo was, it would probably have Felix Wells body in the trunk.

Chapter 56

Gavin in North Dakota. Gavin had a thoroughly enjoyable summer on his grandparents' farm. His grandpa taught both Becky and him how to drive; however, the kids only get to drive around the farm for now. Almost everyone in North Dakota who lives on a farm learns to drive very early. Gavin had already been operating tractors since he was in the sixth grade. At first, it was only when his grandpa was with him. It was not until Gavin was familiar with all of the safety features that he was allowed to drive them by himself.

Becky and Gavin had a fantastic time this summer. There were long horseback rides on Buck and Sunshine. His grandma would pack them a nice picnic lunch, and they would go fishing. One day, Becky found a tree with two hearts carved intertwined on it. The initials on the heart were CS and TO. It didn't take them very long to figure out this were his parents' initials. Gavin carved identical hearts on the tree with Becky's and his names on them.

One day, Gavin happened to mention to Becky he was sort of looking forward to the street dance on the third of July. She looked at him and asked why. Gavin stammered, "I was kind of looking forward to you teaching me some more about dancing." Becky gave him a hug, saying, "Oh, Gavin, I am looking forward to it too. Now I know you are interested in dancing, we won't have to wait so long. There happens to be a wedding dance at the hall in Towner this Saturday."

Which was how Becky and Gavin found themselves at the dance on Saturday night. As they were dancing, Gavin told Becky, "You sure do feel nice. Just like a loaf of Grandma's fresh-baked bread." Becky started laughing and said, "Gavin, sometimes you are downright goofy." It was much easier dancing on a dance floor instead of out on the street. Becky taught him how to waltz, but Gavin was not ready to try the polka just yet. Becky and Gavin admired how gracefully his grandpa and grandma were able to do the polka.

Becky admitted to him she was not very good at the polka either. However, after watching his grandpa and grandma dance, both thought they would like to learn. Becky suggested, "Maybe your grandpa and grandma could teach us the dance."

His grandpa and grandma were delighted when the kids asked them. For the next four polkas, Gavin danced with his grandma. Becky, in the meantime, was dancing with Gavin's grandpa. Gavin and Becky finally were able to do the polka together. The kids were definitely not great. Becky was a lot better at it than Gavin was; however, his grandpa and grandma assured them they did fine. They said with a little more practice the young couple would soon be as good as they were. Right at the moment, Gavin kind of had his doubts.

Gavin thinks the very best thing which happened all summer long is trouble did not find them one time. It was much better than the summer before. Gavin and Becky were able to just thoroughly enjoy themselves. Gavin didn't get into any fights, and there were no runaway team of horses for them to stop. It was just a very enjoyable summer Gavin didn't even mind it when Becky kissed him on three different occasions.

Even the best of times have to end. His mom is already home, and Gavin has to be at Bellevue High School on the twenty-sixth of August for freshman orientation. Gavin is really looking forward to high school. Of course, playing football for the Bellevue Wolverines was going to be one of the most exciting times of his life. Gavin flew back to Seattle where his mom picked him up at the Sea-Tac airport, then he went to Bellevue High School with her. There Gavin signed up for freshman English, biology, math, world history, PE, music, and of course, Wolverine Football.

Gavin started playing football the very same day. It didn't take him very long to realize why the Wolverines were almost unstoppable. The training was formidable. First the team had to go to the weight room to lift weights and work out on exercise machines. Everyone would do this for two hours every day. Afterward, the team would have football practice for another three hours. It was hard work, but Gavin loved every minute of it.

It didn't take very long to toughen up even the weakest players. The team worked hard. Everyone practiced hard. Their coaches were the very best. The team would practice every move until it was mastered, then would practice it some more. Gavin was lucky in the fact he was in great shape to start with. At least, that's what he thought. However, it didn't take Gavin very long to realize he was building muscles in places where he didn't even have muscles before. But he loved it. Why? Because he was one of the mighty Bellevue Wolverines.

The time came for the teams first freshman football game. Gavin would love to say he was the hero of the game. But it wouldn't be true. Oh, he got to play. Gavin even tackled the opposing quarterback a few times. However, the real hero of the game was the little guy everyone called PeeWee. He is only about five feet eight inches tall, but man could the kid run. Once he got a football in his hands, there was no stopping him. He wound up scoring four touchdowns.

Gavin thought the freshman football team was great. However, when he was able to watch the varsity team play, they were astounding. Every year the varsity team get to play one or two out-of-state teams. These teams were usually ranked in the top high school teams in the United States. Quite often, the Bellevue Wolverines would decimate these opponents.

Gavin loved the courses he was taking at Bellevue High, and the teachers were awesome. If you had a problem in any class, the teachers were more than happy to help. Gavin likes all of his classes and all of his teachers. But biology is probably his favorite. With his interest in farming, he wanted to know everything possible about plants and animals.

In spite of Terri's resolve, she was in a state of great despair. Chris has now been imprisoned for over fifteen years. There was going to be a parole board hearing for him in February. Don't get her wrong. Terri wanted her darling husband Chris out of prison. The problem was it was almost time for Christmas vacation, and Terri had promised herself she would find out who had actually committed this crime. She not only had not been able to find the culprits who had framed Chris, Terri had not been able to prove Chris's innocence. If she had, he would've been out of prison years ago. Chris had not done this. He had not committed any crime whatsoever. He did not have it in him to hurt anyone.

Terri was sitting in a recliner and feeling sorry for herself and Chris. She broke down and started crying. Gavin saw this and came up and wrapped his arms around his mom, giving her a hug. He asked, "What's the matter, Mom? You never let things get you down." Terri broke down and told Gavin, "I am feeling very low." Gavin patted his mother on the back, saying, "Cheer up Mom, we know Dad didn't do this, and he will probably get out of prison after his parole hearing in February."

Chapter 57

Gavin said, "Mom, I start winter break tomorrow. Why don't we both fly back to North Dakota? It will help get your mind off of all your problems. Besides, we have never had Christmas with Grandpa and Grandma Olson since I was born. I bet going back there would cheer us all up." Luckily, there were still a couple of seats left on an early morning flight to North Dakota. Terri and Gavin immediately packed their bags and headed for Sea-Tac airport.

Gavin and Terri were both able to catch some sleep on the flight to Minneapolis. Terri's father wanted to pick them up at the airport in Minot, but she told him, "No, I'm renting a car so I will have something to drive while I am in Towner." At the Minot airport, Terri went to a car rental agency and rented a four-wheel-drive SUV. Knowing how the weather is in North Dakota, she wanted to be prepared. There is always a good chance of snow in December although today the sky was clear and a balmy fifteen degrees above zero. Not bad for North Dakota at this time of the year.

When mother and son arrived at the farm, there to meet them was Terri's dad and mom and of course Becky. She was so excited. Becky had been wanting to teach Gavin how to ice-skate for years. The family sat down and had some hot spiced apple cider. Afterward, Gavin and Becky helped Terri's dad with the morning chores afterwhich the kids were on their way to go ice-skating. When Terri had first seen Becky a few short years ago, she was very cute girl. Now she was turning into a beautiful young lady. Terri's mom told her Becky reminds her a lot of Terri.

Terri stayed inside the house all day and visited with her mom and dad. Around four in the afternoon Terri heard the roar of an engine. It was Gavin coming back on the back of Becky's snowmobile. Everyone had to laugh when the kids walked in for both of their cheeks were rosy, and there was ice on their eyebrows. Becky and Gavin said it was a lot of fun ice-skating, even though Gavin fell down on the ice a few times. Becky didn't stay long for she had to get home.

After breakfast the next morning, Terri decided to drive to Minot to do some Christmas shopping. Gavin wanted to stay and help his grandpa with the chores and to visit Becky of course. He asked his mom if she would pick up a present for him to give Becky. Terri's father told her, "Maybe you should not go because there's a storm warning for this evening." Terri told her dad, "I will be home long before the storm hits." When Terri got to Minot, she got pretty involved with shopping. After Terri was finished around four-thirty, she was ready to go back to Towner. However she stepped out of the store into a full-scale blizzard, which had just moved in.

The snow and wind were almost blinding; however, Terri was able to make it to a motel a short distance away. Thankfully, there were still vacancies, so she checked in. Then Terri called her parents to let them know she was safe. Terri told them, "I will stay at the motel until the storm subsides." The trouble was the storm didn't let up for two more days. Thank God, there were some books and a TV in the motel. Plus, there was a restaurant right next door, and the crew from the restaurant was also staying at the motel, so it would be open for business.

Meanwhile, back on the farm, Gavin started to get restless. Becky was snowed in at her parents' farm so he wouldn't be able to visit with her. Grandma told Gavin, "Go down to the basement. You will probably find some books you would enjoy reading." Gavin was down in the basement browsing through the books. He started pulling them out one after another, trying to decide what he would like to read. Suddenly, a couple of vacuum-sealed packages fell out from among the books.

Gavin went back upstairs and asked his grandparents what the packages were. The grandparents informed him they were floppy disks for the computer. "Evidently, your mom or dad must've left them here years ago." Gavin asked if there was a computer around, which he would be able to use. His grandma answered, "I believe your mother left one here a long time ago. It's also in the basement."

Gavin and his grandparents went down to the basement to search for it. After grandpa found it, Gavin took it upstairs and hooked everything up. Amazingly, the computer still worked. Then Gavin took one of the floppy disks out of its vacuum-sealed bag and placed it in the computer. It worked, but it came up asking for a password.

Figuring the floppy discs must have belonged to his parents, Gavin typed in Terri. This password didn't work, so he typed in Terri Olson, then Terri Sutton. None of these passwords seemed to work. Next, he tried Chris; then he tried Chris Sutton. At last he tried Olson, then Sutton. None of these passwords worked either. Next, he tried Chris and Terri Sutton, then Terri and Chris Sutton. This was a puzzle Gavin was determined to solve.

He shut the computer down and went and got a pen and paper. Gavin started writing down all types of words to try like Towner, Bellevue, North, Dakota and Washington. He made a very long list he was planning on trying tomorrow. But for now, he was tired, so setting the pen and paper down on the nightstand. Gavin went to bed and finally fell asleep.

In his sleep, Gavin was restless and kept tossing and turning. Then came the dream. A lady appeared in his dreams and asked, "Gavin, do you know who I am?" In the dream, he answered, "I have seen pictures of you. You are my grandmother Sutton." She said, "You're right, Gavin, and I want you to get up and write down two passwords. The first password is for you, and it is #%Kn12(). The second password is for your mother, and it is F<ip91Z*. Use the first password tomorrow on the computer you found in the basement. Make sure you give the second one to your mother. She will need it later." With that, she said, "I love you Gavin."

With the dream ended, Gavin slept peacefully till morning. He woke up feeling refreshed and took up paper and pen planning to try some new passwords. When Gavin saw the writing on the paper and knowing it was his handwriting, for a time he was not able to understand. Then slowly the dream came back to him. Throwing on his clothes, he ran for the computer.

Gavin turned on the computer, then typed in #%Kn12(). It worked. He couldn't believe it the password actually worked. Gavin slowly looked the file over. He was simply flabbergasted. At first, he thought his eyes were deceiving him. Not knowing what else to do, he yelled, "Grandma and Grandpa come here quick." They came running, asking, "What's the matter, Gavin, are you hurt?" He answered, "No, I am not hurt take a look at what's on the computer."

Both his grandfather and grandmother read what was on the computer monitor and gasped. His grandma made the sign of the cross, saying, "Oh my God." His grandpa said, "Well, I'll be dipped in shit." All three of them kept reading as Gavin scrolled down. After reading everything four or five times, everyone shook their heads in complete disbelief.

Gavin's grandparents wanted to know how he had gotten the file open. Gavin told them how Grandma Sutton appeared to him in a dream. His grandma said, "Before your grandmother Sutton died, she said your parents would be apart for a long time, and it came true. Grandmother Sutton also said their son would find the answer to the puzzle, which is you, Gavin, and you did find the answer to the puzzle."

Then Gavin and his grandparents were all crying and hugging each other. Grandpa Olson stated, "I can't believe it. After all this time, all the time your mother has been searching all over the world. I can't believe during all this time the answers were right here in our house." Gavin asked, "How did these floppy discs come to be here anyway?" His grandma Olson replied, "I remember now. Your mother mentioned she suspected some sort of financial shenanigans going on at the firm where she worked. So she downloaded some secret computer for the data on them.

"But it happened just when your parents were about to go on vacation. While they were here, your grandpa and grandma Sutton got killed in a car accident. When you parents went back to Bellevue, your father was framed for Felix Wells murder and was sent to prison. Then you were born, and your mother didn't have a clue these floppy disks were the blueprint for framing your dad. I imagine she thought it was just financial records and forgot about them."

Grandma said, "Perhaps we should call your mother and let her know." Grandpa Olson spoke up, "Absolutely not, we are still in the middle of a huge storm. You know Terri, when she hears about this, she would try to get back here come hell or high water. She would try to get back no matter what. We don't need to have her ending up in a ditch just when things are about to turn around. The blizzard is supposed to subside sometime tonight, and Terri will be coming home tomorrow, which is Christmas Eve.

"I say let's not tell her anything even then because we have always opened our presents on Christmas Eve. After we have finished with the presents, Gavin can tell her he has one last present for her. It will be the present she has been waiting for over fifteen years."

Gavin said, "Grandma Sutton gave me two passwords. She said I was to give the second one to my mother. I wonder what the other one's for." Grandpa Olson pondered this for a moment, then said, "From what's on the computer and putting it together with the way your mother operates, she is not going to be satisfied with what is on the disk. Terri will want to have irrefutable proof, so I would say she's going to bring this guilty bastard back to Seattle. If she does, there is probably another computer involved somehow."

When he awoke the next morning, Gavin saw it was a nice day, so he called Becky and asked her to come over. Gavin told Becky he had something to show her when Gavin turned on the computer for Becky to see. His grandpa and grandma Olson came in too. They still were not able to believe it. After Becky saw what was on the computer, she said, "Wow, I have read every book in the Towner High School library. I have watched all sorts of movie mysteries on TV, and I watched a lot of shows about real life forensics. Nowhere have I ever seen anyone go to this length. Does your mom know about this yet?" Gavin said, "It will be her last Christmas present tonight, and I would like you to stay and see it." Becky said, "Thanks, Gavin, I wouldn't miss it for the world."

Meanwhile back in Minot, Terri was starting to go stir crazy. The TV let her know the storm was almost over. It said the snowplows were out, and Highway 2 would be clear by ten o'clock tomorrow morning. Terri went to bed and had a restless night's sleep. She kept thinking that she had not been able to keep her promise to clear Chris's name. Terri knew he would not be upset with her, but she was upset with herself. However, she was determined to keep a smile on her face.

Terri was up at seven the next morning determined to get home today. After getting dressed, she walked next door to the restaurant and ordered coffee and breakfast. Once she had finished eating, Terri kept drinking coffee until the waitress finally told her the roads were clear. As a snow plow had already cleared the snow off of the parking lot while she was in the restaurant. Terri packed up all the presents she purchased into the SUV and took off. All the presents were wrapped as Terri had plenty of time to do it while she was waiting for the snowstorm to be over. The roads were all clear, but were still icy. Terri still wasn't able to go more than forty-five miles per hour. But she wasn't about to wait until the highway department had sanded them.

As soon as she pulled into the farmyard, her mom and dad, Gavin, and Becky were all there with smiles on their faces. Terri thought something was fishy she just didn't have any idea what. One of things Terri had purchased while she was in Minot was several board games. So the family enjoyed themselves while playing one game after another and munching on homemade cookies and cracked nuts. Playing the games with her family and listening to the Christmas music in the background finally made Terri happy as she could be.

There was something Terri noticed when everyone thought she wasn't looking. She would catch her dad and mom, Gavin, and Becky giving each other sly looks. Terri knew there was something funny up with her family, and Becky for everyone looked like the cat who had swallowed the canary. When Terri would ask what was going on, they would just smile and say nothing.

Around eight in the evening, Terri's father said, "It's time for us to open our presents." Terri had such a wonderful time watching everybody opening their presents. Becky was very pleased with the iPod Gavin had given her. When it was all over and every last present had been opened Terri's parents told her, "Gavin has one last very special present for you." Gavin took Terri into her old room. Terri took one look and said, "What are you talking about? It is just my old computer, which has been out-of-date for years."

Gavin stated, "You just do not understand yet, Mom, watch this." With that, he turned on the computer, typed in the password, and the file opened. After reading the file, Terri just stopped and stared, not believing her eyes. Tears started welling up in her eyes, and tears were rolling down her cheeks.

"Over fifteen years has gone by, and it is been here all this time." Terri said, "This is the best Christmas present I have ever received." Then Terri gave a group hug to everybody.

Terri just had to know how this had all come about, so Gavin told her about finding the floppy disks. How he had tried hard to be able to find the password and then went to sleep. Then he told his mother about how his grandmother Sutton had appeared to him in a dream. Gavin said, "She actually gave me two passwords mom. The second one is for you, and it is F<:p91z*. Don't lose this password, Mom, I am sure you will need it before this is all over."

Terri said out loud, "We have you now, you sadistic bastard, and we know your alias is Conrad Roberts. I now know where you live, and you can bet your life I am coming to get you. When I am done with you, I will see you rot in a jail cell for the rest of your miserable life. I will somehow bring you back to Seattle. I will prove to the whole world Chris is an innocent victim and has been in prison for years, all because of you."

After talking to her parents and Gavin, Terri decided there was no sense for them to go back to Seattle until after the New Year. This made Gavin and Becky very happy. Grandpa Olson decided to take Terri's old snowmobile out of the garage, and got it running. Although Becky's snowmobile was a lot nicer, at least Gavin and Becky would be able to have fun together.

And fun the kids did have although Gavin was always there to help his grandfather with the chores every morning and every evening. Other than the chores, one didn't see very much of Gavin or Becky. On New Year's Eve, the whole family went to a New Year's Eve dance at the hall in Towner. Terri really enjoyed herself now she knew everything was going to turn out all right.

Terri danced with her father and her son. Other than those two dances, she sat on the sidelines and talked with old friends. None of her family told anyone about what they found. Terri did not want the press to accidentally get hold of it. When the time came, Terri would want all of the media there; and until then, no one would hear a word. She wanted it to be a total surprise.

Terri watched Gavin and Becky while they were dancing, reminding her so much of Chris and herself when they were their age. Terri commented on this to her mom and dad and they agreed. Grandma said, "If you notice, Becky resembles you in a lot of ways. I will say Becky and Gavin are both a couple of very good kids."

Chapter 58

The plane arrived back in Seattle just in time for Terri to drop Gavin off at Bellevue High School. It was a good thing both of them had slept all the way back. Afterward, Terri immediately headed to the Monroe Correctional Complex to see Chris. After she had hugged and kissed him, then sat down at the table. Terri told him, "Chris, I have some real important news for you, something you have been wanting to hear for a long time.

"But first, Chris, I am going to have to ask you to do something you won't want to do. I have been watching a television show, which tells all about parole board hearings. Chris, when you're parole board hearing comes up, you are going to have to tell them you are sorry for what you did." Chris immediately snorted and said, "What do you mean? Are you goofy, Terri? I will never admit to something I haven't done." Terri said, "Chris, darling, I know you didn't do it, and I will be able to prove it. But this way, you will be able to get out of prison faster. In all of the parole board hearings I have watched, the board have never released anyone who said they were innocent. The parole board only parole the ones who said they were sorry for what they have done.

"Chris, the good news is we have finally found something, which proves your innocence once and for all. But it's not enough. I am going to have LaShawn and Tatiana help me catch this bastard and bring him back here to Seattle. This might take a little longer than your parole board hearing, but I don't think by very much. I want you out so you will be able to face this asshole in front of a news conference. Also, Chris, in all of the time you have been in prison, I have never missed a forty-eight-hour visitation with you. I am sorry, but I will miss the next one. After this, I will always have you with me for the rest of our lives." Chris said, "Okay, sweetheart, I will trust you. Just be very careful, I don't want you getting hurt."

Terri told Chris, "I have proof right now, but I want more than this. I want the cops, the justice system, the news media, and the whole world to know what I know now." Chris immediately wanted to know more, for instance, who it was who had framed him. Terri told him, "You don't want to know. It would just make you very sick. All I will tell you is his alias is Conrad Roberts. Also, he has had a United States passport in the same name for years, more years than you have been here in prison. He was just waiting for the right person and the right opportunity to come along."

Terri mentioned, "We need to get a lawyer to help with the upcoming parole hearing. You know, Mr. Blankenship retired years ago." Chris replied, "Yes, I have been thinking about it too. When I was first in prison, I helped a young man get his GED. After he got out, he went to college and became a lawyer. Not just any lawyer, but one as sharp as they come. He also happens to have a lot of political pull. He comes to see me quite often here at Monroe. Brian probably would be glad to my lawyer, and I will contact him right away."

Terri embraced Chris and whispered in his ear, "The next time I see you, you will be a free man or very close to it." While driving back to Bellevue, Terri was contemplating everything she had to do. And in the midst of these thoughts, her cell phone rang. It was from the shop restoring Chris's Monte Carlo. Terri had forgotten all about the Monte Carlo. The restoration shop wanted her to come over. Seeing as how it was on the way, Terri stopped. She could not believe my eyes. The Monte Carlo was perfect, so she paid them and asked if they could hold it until Chris got out. Terri wanted him to be the first person to drive it.

After she got home, Terri sat down with the computer. She decided not to do a search on Conrad Roberts. He might accidentally find out someone was searching for him and leave. Knowing from the computer disk he had a business in Mauritius. Terri decided to find out everything she could about the place. She discovered it was an island nation off the southeast coast of Africa. It was approximately 550 miles east of Madagascar.

There were no inhabitants on the island when it was first discovered. Now there are over 1.2 million people living there. The population is a mixture of whites, Asians, and blacks. It is a world-class example of how diverse cultures can get along together. Also, Mauritius is the only known home of the dodo bird. There were thousands of these birds on the island when it was first discovered. But because they were very heavy and couldn't fly, they became extinct within eighty years after the first settlers had arrived.

Mauritius has a subtropical climate with hot wet summers and warm dry winters. The largest city and the capital is Port Lewis. There are many sugarcane plantations on the island. Seeing as how sugarcane is a large export of the island, it is inevitable rum will be produced there. The main airport is Sir Seewoosagur Ramgoolam international Airport.

After spending a whole afternoon looking at all of the statistics, Terri called Tatiana and LaShawn and asked if they could come over. After the couple arrived, she showed them the computer disk. The Wilsons were amazed. They could not believe anyone would be able to go to such an extent. Tatiana and LaShawn agreed this individual had to be brought to justice.

Terri explained to them all she knew and was able to find out about the island of Mauritius. She said, "I would like to bring the dirty heathen back to Seattle to face Chris and justice. When I bring him back, I want to rent a large hall. I want to make sure everyone who was involved in Chris's case to be there. I do know it's not their fault because all of the evidence was there. I just want them to know about it so someone else won't be able to pull off something like this in the future. I also want every media possible there to cover the story.

"Now I would like your help. You two have done everything possible to help me out in the past. I am hoping you will be able to help me in this last episode." LaShawn spoke up first. He said, "I know I can speak for Tatiana. We would have been insulted if you had not asked us for help. Terri, of course, we will help you." Tatiana said, "We are your friends, and this is what friends do for friends. Now we better get busy and start planning this trip."

Tatiana said, "The first thing we need to do is find a way for you to disguise yourself. Even then, you will not dare to get close to him. Even with a perfect disguise, your voice would immediately give you away. Depending on the situation, LaShawn or I will see if we can manage to have a drink with him. Then if we get a chance, we will slip something into his drink to knock him out."

LaShawn said, "I have got a idea. I have a whole bottle of Percodan. If it won't knock him out, nothing will. After he is unconscious or even semiconscious, we will take him back to his home. Once we get him there, maybe we can find out what he has been doing for the last fifteen-plus years. Maybe if we're lucky, we may be able to find out what's left of the money."

Terri spoke up, "But after we capture him, how are we going to be able to bring him back to Seattle?" Tatiana said, "I think I have figured that one out. If he has a United States passport, and I'm sure he does, he will have kept it validated. We will put him into a wheelchair and keep him comatose. We will tell the airlines he is very sick and wants to see his relatives in Seattle before he passes away."

LaShawn sat thoughtfully for a moment before speaking then said, "This could possibly work. I think we better play it by ear on that one. If worse comes to worse, I will get in touch with the corporation I work for with an explanation of course. I am confident the corporation will let me fly back and get the company jet. Regardless, we will have to figure out what we will be doing from one minute to the next. I wouldn't be surprised if our hearts aren't in our throats before we get back to Seattle."

Tatiana said, "The next thing we need to do is search for disguises for Terri. I think it would be best if we make her appear as if she is an old lady in her mid seventies." Tatiana and Terri went out and purchased several different styles of gray wigs. She also bought four outfits, which looked like they were for older women. Tatiana insisted Terri buys this stylish, silver-embedded cane. Tatiana laughingly told Terri, "If nothing else, you can hit him over the head with it." The girls stopped at a beauty salon where the saleslady was told Terri was going to a costume ball. The saleslady showed Terri how to apply makeup to make her look as if she were in her seventies.

Terri booked a flight to Mauritius for the sixteenth of January. Gavin would be having his meals at Tatiana's mother's house. He said he would be all right staying at home alone. Gavin is a good son and I totally trust him. Still, Terri couldn't resist telling him to stay out of trouble and don't have any parties. Gavin said, "Mom, you know me better than that. I wouldn't do anything stupid especially at a time like this." Then Gavin gave Terri a big hug, telling her, "Good luck and to be careful."

After everything was arranged, LaShawn, Tatiana and Terri were off. Terri already called the hotel in Mauritius and made room reservations. Terri made all of the reservations in LaShawn's name. She did not want her name coming up anywhere even by accident. Everyone decided when they got to Mauritius, it would be LaShawn who would make discreet inquiries. The threesome were all suffering from jet lag by the time they arrived. Terri got a rental car and immediately checked into their hotel. Once there, no one did much except sleep for an entire day. Once everyone was finally totally awake Tatiana ordered room service. Terri did not have a disguise on yet and did not want to take any chances; besides, they were all very hungry.

After finishing dinner, LaShawn left to see if he could find out any information. Tatiana and Terri stayed in the hotel suite. Tatiana wanted to watch the local news, so she turned on the television. However, everything on the local channels were in French. But she did find some English channels; however, they weren't local ones. Around 10:00 p.m., LaShawn came back, saying he had been to a local bar listening for any word of the person for whom they were looking. "After several hours without hearing anything, I mentioned I was a friend of Conrad Roberts. I told the men in the bar I would like to look him up if I knew where to look. This almost started a riot in the bar. It seemed like everyone there knew him and disliked him.

They said, 'Conrad is a very wealthy man, but he is cruel, heartless, and a womanizer.'

"The men in the bar told me, 'If you really want to find that scum of the earth, you need to go to the Verdant Repose Bar. Conrad Roberts likes to go there because it has sidewalk seating. There he will sit and watch women pass trying to find a way to lure some poor unsuspecting woman to his table. Invariably, he will offer to buy them a drink. When she accepts, Conrad will put a knockout drop in her drink when she's not looking.

"'When the lady begins to get groggy and has no idea of what she is doing, Conrad will put her in his limousine and take her to his mansion. There he will take advantage of her.' After telling me all of this, I started to hear a lot of muttering and murmuring around the bar. I quickly realized I had made a big mistake by saying I was a friend of Conrad Roberts. I was afraid the men in the bar were working up their nerve to attack me.

"When I saw the crowd was starting to get hostile, I told them I knew Conrad from years ago when he was just a working stiff. I told the crowd as far as I know he wasn't anything like this back then. So I bought everyone in the bar a drink, telling them, after hearing what he was like now, I didn't want anything to do with Conrad. I swore them to secrecy, asking them not to let Conrad know I was even here. After hearing this, the crowd calmed down and assured me they would not let anyone know I was in town."

Chapter 59

LaShawn, Tatiana, and Terri debated about what they should do next. Tatiana insisted she should go to the bar and sit outside at an unoccupied table. Then when Conrad came up and offered her a seat at his table, she would try to slip some Percodan into his drink. LaShawn, of course, wasn't too crazy about the idea. Terri suggested, "Let's just scope out the place first, then decide on what to do."

Terri said, "LaShawn, tomorrow why don't you go take a look at the Verdant Repose Bar. Check out everything about the place you can. Also see if there's a place across the street where I can remain hidden and still be able to identify him. Don't in any way let on it is Conrad Roberts who you are interested in. In the meantime, Tatiana and I will find an electronic shop. I will purchase small transmitters, which have ear buds for each of us. We should be able to find microphones so small we can hide one in Tatiana's bra. In this way, she can let us know right away if she is in trouble. Also, I can hide across the street and let you know for sure it is him. LaShawn, you will sit at the same table you did the day before. Because you have been there before, no one should pay any attention to you. This way, you'll be able to be right there when Conrad comes in, and when I let you know it's the right person, then Tatiana can walk right in behind him."

Tatiana remarked, "I think your idea will work. If Conrad asks me to sit down for a drink, I will. Then if he asks what I want to drink, I will ask him what he is having. Then I will ask Conrad to bring me the same thing. After our drinks are served, I will figure out a way to get him to go back up to the bar. When he leaves the table, I will switch drinks with him." Then Tatiana said, "LaShawn, after Conrad leaves the bar tomorrow, could you discretely follow him home. It would be a big help to us, so we will be able to know where to take him after he is comatose."

The next day after LaShawn left to go to the Verdant Repose, Terri put on a gray wig and one of the outfits purchased in Seattle. Tatiana helped her with the makeup and insisted Terri use her cane. As she walked by a mirror on the way out, Terri couldn't help laughing. Afterward, Tatiana had to touch up her makeup. The girls were able to find an electronic store having just what was needed. On the way back, Tatiana and Terri both put on a microphone and ear buds. Terri had Tatiana walk a block ahead of her. They were able to talk to each other, and the transmitters worked perfectly. (In reality, Terri wouldn't need them to talk to her.) However, Terri all felt safer if they all had them on just in case. In case something out of the ordinary happens, the three will be prepared. But Terri is sure Conrad feels very safe after being here for years.

After Terri caught up with Tatiana, they both marveled at how well the transmitters worked. Both of them went back to their hotel suites to wait for LaShawn. LaShawn showed up a little later and was very elated. He said, "When I was at the Verdant Repose bar, your guy came in. I mean, of course, providing he is the right person. If it was him, then today was very disappointing. Every time a good-looking lady would come by, Conrad would invite her to sit down and have a drink with him.

"Every one of the ladies turned him down. Evidently, the word is out about him. I am sure he was hoping to find some new talent, someone who had never heard of him. Conrad drove up to the bar in a Rolls-Royce. Hopefully, he doesn't have a chauffeur."

LaShawn followed Conrad home from a distance, watching him turn into his mansion. It is an awesome three-story building with the large stone fence totally surrounding it. There was a metal gate which opened for him. Evidently, he had a remote control. However, there is no guard shack or guards.

After a good night's sleep, Terri awoke, thinking, "Today is the day of all days." Terri got dressed putting on a different gray wig and an older lady's business suit. Terri applied her makeup and an oversized pair of sunglasses. When the three friends arrived at the Verdant Repose, Terri went to a restaurant across the street LaShawn had told her about. She ordered breakfast and asked if the waiter if there were any newspapers which were written in English. The waiter brought Terri one which she used mostly to cover her face.

LaShawn was already ready seated at the Verdant Repose at an outside table with a glass of cognac sitting in front of him. He was studying a newspaper in front of him. Half hour later, a Rolls-Royce rolled up, and a man got out. Terri quickly spoke into the microphone, saying, "It's him." LaShawn gave a slight nod to acknowledge he had heard. Conrad Roberts went to the outdoor seating area and found a table. Almost immediately, Tatiana walked past him.

As Tatiana strolled by, Conrad stood up and bowed, always the gentleman. He said, "Ma'am, I am all alone, would you be so kind as to give me the pleasure of your company?" Tatiana looked at him as if she were unsure. "Please," Conrad said, "your company would give me great pleasure." Tatiana said, "Well, if you insist" and sat down. He introduced himself to her as Conrad Roberts. Tatiana thought to herself, "Conrad Roberts my ass, you old reprobate."

Conrad asked Tatiana if he could bring her something to drink. She smiled and asked him, "What are you having?" He replied, "A Cuba libre," Tatiana told him, "That sounds absolutely divine. I haven't had one of those in ages, so please make mine the same." Conrad stood up and walked to the bar. Tatiana was able to see he was taking his time. When Conrad came back, he sat a drink in front of Tatiana. The other one he set on his side of the table. Just as he started to sit down, she said, "Oh, Mr. Conrad, I see they happen to have those little umbrellas stir sticks. I collect them, and I noticed these are quite unique. Would you be so kind as to get me one of these?" He bowed, saying, "Anything for the lady."

While Conrad had gone back to the bar, Tatiana switched their drinks, then just sat there like she was some dizzy dame like Conrad thought she was. After he came back to the table, Conrad handed her the umbrella stir stick. "Oh, thank you," Tatiana gushed. "It is so pretty. I collect them. I must have over a hundred of them at home." She was trying to make Conrad think she was scatterbrained.

Tatiana took a small sip as Conrad sat watching her. Conrad made some small talk, and Tatiana could see he was waiting for her to finish her drink. Conrad finally said, "We better finish our drinks before they get warm." With that, both drank their Cuba libres in one gulp.

Tatiana thinks for just a moment Conrad realized what had happened because he got a funny surprised look on his face, then pretty much went catatonic. Tatiana called in her microphone for LaShawn and Terri to come and help her. As they carried Conrad past the bar, the bartender gave them a wink and grinned at them. He gave them a thumbs-up and drew his fingers across his lips, indicating his lips were sealed. It looked as if Conrad Roberts was a hated man in Port Louis.

When LaShawn got Conrad to where his Rolls-Royce was parked, LaShawn plucked the keys out of his pocket. After unlocking the car, he placed Mr. Roberts on the backseat. LaShawn then promptly handcuffed him with plastic ties, then LaShawn took off. Tatiana and Terri followed in the rental car. When he got to Conrad's home, LaShawn pressed a remote control on the visor, and the gate opened at once, and we all went through. LaShawn closed the gate behind them.

When they came to the garage, LaShawn pressed another button, and the garage door opened. They immediately put both of the cars in and closed the door. LaShawn took Conrad Roberts out of the car and into the house. The house was absolutely palatial. As Terri and Tatiana were staring in amazement, a maid happened to walk in. Tatiana immediately grabbed her and set her down on the couch. Terri asked the maid if anyone else worked there. She said, "Only my husband. He is the gardener."

Terri told her, "If you and your husband will listen to us, we will not do anything bad to harm either of you. We are just here to take Mr. Roberts back to the United States. He was very a bad man when he lived there." The maid replied, "He is very bad man here too. When he can't find a woman at the bar, he come back here and rapes me. My husband and I are very scared to do anything. Mr. Conrad says he will kill us and have all of our families in Cambodia killed also."

Tatiana and Terri had the maid take them to find her husband while LaShawn stayed with Mr. Roberts. When the maid told her husband what they were doing, he immediately started crying. He grabbed Tatiana and Terri, hugging and kissing them, saying, "Thank you, thank you. You take devil away, very good, very good." The maid and her husband told us Mr. Roberts had been a very rich man when he came to Mauritius "He much richer now. He plays the European and Asian stock markets, very, very wealthy man. Maybe he have another place someplace else? Sometime he leaves then come back months later. We were very happy when he was gone."

Terri and Tatiana returned to where LaShawn was keeping a close watch over their bad boy. Conrad was just starting to come out of it. Terri took off her wig and sunglasses to let him have a look at her. She could see he was stunned. She jabbed Conrad with her cane, telling him, "Don't say a freaking word, dick weed. I would really enjoy killing you. You have made Chris and I lose over fifteen years of our lives, so keep your mouth shut."

LaShawn tied Conrad up more securely, then the maid went and got the knockout drops which Conrad used on women. Tatiana put some in water and made him drink it. The gardener and his wife took them to a room with no windows. It had a heavy door with the lock and a hasp, plus a deadbolt on the outside of it. They placed Mr. Roberts inside, first searching the room and taking everything in his possession.

Next, Terri and Tatiana searched the home, finding the office with a large safe and two smaller safes. LaShawn found an extensive wine cellar, and outside there was an Olympic-size swimming pool. There was also an outside barbecue grill complete with a fridge. LaShawn located some nice rib-eye steaks and started grilling them. The maid and her husband whipped up an excellent garden salad.

After everyone finished dinner, Terri went to find Conrad's office. There were two separate computer systems in the room. She got on the first one. When Terri turned the computer on, she found a file which needed a password. Terri thought, "Possibly this might be the password Gavin had given me." So she typed in F<:ip91z*. It just said wrong password; instead of trying to fight it, Terri turned the computer off.

Terri then turned to the other computer. When she turned it on, it had a different format. Again, it was asking for a password. Again she typed in F<:ip91z*. This time the file opened. It was a very extensive file covering everything owned under the name of Conrad Roberts. On it he had listed all of his bank accounts in different offshore banks. All of his stocks and shareholdings; in fact, everything he owned was on this file.

The best part of the whole deal was once you are in this file you would be able to transfer everything with the click of a button. Terri called LaShawn and Tatiana in to show them Conrad's files. Terri said, "I would like help recording everything I have transferred. I would like a written transcript of everything." LaShawn asked Tatiana to help Terri. "I want to feed the prisoner and keep an eye on Conrad."

The first thing Terri did was sell all the stocks and shareholdings, sending the money to his offshore bank accounts. When Terri was finished, she asked Tatiana what the total was. Tatiana told her, "It came to slightly over $558 million." The girls were totally flabbergasted at the amount. Terri told Tatiana, "We aren't finished yet. Here are the combinations to the safes." When Terri opened them, they yielded a total of $20 million in United States currency. What really surprised them was Terri found the paper titles to the mansion, the Rolls-Royce, and a Gulfstream G450 jet airplane. As unbelievable as it seems, everything was all signed. Terri went to have a talk with LaShawn. She asked him, "Tell me about the jet charter service you have been planning on starting? Have you taken any action on it as of now?"

LaShawn replied, "I am still a few years away, but I have incorporated a company. I get paid very well for what I do. I have saved over $8 million. However, I still need a couple more million for operating expenses. Then there's the matter of the airplane itself. I was planning on getting a used airplane just to start out with. I also have a friend who I can hire as a copilot, but as of now, it's about five years in the future."

Terri said, "LaShawn, give me the numbers for your bank account. Your jet charter service is now in full operation. Conrad Roberts is about to invest $12 million in your account. Plus, out of the goodness of his heart, he is also donating a Gulfstream G450 for services rendered." All LaShawn could do was stand there and look at Terri with his mouth open. When he finally spoke, he said, "You have got to be kidding me, Terri?" She said, "No, LaShawn it is all true. It is the very least I can do for you and Tatiana after all you have done for us."

LaShawn gave Terri a big hug, saying, "Well, that takes care of the problem of how to get Conrad back to Seattle." Then he asked, "Did you happen to find his passport?" Terri said, "Yes, it is in the name of Conrad Roberts, and it is current. Will you need a copilot for the airplane?" Terri asked. LaShawn said, "Yes, I will call my friend Ralph right away and tell him he has a new job. I'm sure it will take him at least two days to get here. In the meantime, I will go and take a look at the Gulfstream G450."

After LaShawn had left, Tatiana and Terri sat down with the gardener and his wife to have a talk with them. They found out their names were Kou and Suzy Chang. Terri told the Chang's she was putting the mansion and the Rolls-Royce in their names. Terri also gave them $8 million in cash. Kou and Suzy almost got dizzy jumping up and down and running around in circles and giving Terri and Tatiana hugs. They said, "Thank you, thank you, we have worked for bad man for too long."

There was one more thing Terri had to take care of. She transferred all the money from Conrad Roberts's numbered offshore accounts. This was all sent to numbered offshore accounts she had set up of over the years. Terri would eventually put some of it back where it belonged—the investors who had been swindled years earlier.

When LaShawn returned, he was grinning from ear to ear. He said, "When this is all over, Tatiana, if you want to, you will be able to quit your job. If you desire, you can be the new stewardess in our airline. You will not believe this airplane. It is the coolest and most plush plane I have ever seen in my life. While I was at the airport, I had them service and top it off with fuel. It will be ready to go as soon as Ralph gets here. Ralph, is on his way. When I spoke to him, I told him to get as much sleep on the trip here as he can because we will be taking off as soon as he arrives.

"Before Ralph arrives, there are a few things we need to do. We need to stock up the Gulfstream with food and drink. This plane has been used very little and is in excellent shape. We will need a wheelchair to take Mr. Roberts on and off plane. We will need to keep him comatose at those times. As far as anyone else is concerned, we are taking him back to see relatives in Seattle for one last time."

Tatiana asked me, "If I was going to bring Conrad's computers along with us, Terri told her, "Yes, because I don't know what is on the second computer. Maybe sometime in the future, I will have a forensic analyst to see if they can find out what is on there. It would be just out of curiosity because we already have everything we want."

Chapter 60

Meanwhile back at Monroe prison, Brian Edwards, Chris's new lawyer, came to the prison to talk to him. Brian was only thirty-five years old and had only been a lawyer for three years. Yet in those three years, he had proved himself to be a formidable lawyer. Brian gave an aura of importance just by the way he walked and talked. The expensive tailor-made suit he wore didn't hurt his appearance any. His handsome, square-jawed face and piercing blue eyes has shook up many a witness.

Brian shook Chris's hand firmly, saying, "I am not only your attorney, I am also your friend. I would not be here today if you had not talked some sense into me. First, you helped me to get my GED. You talked me into furthering my education. You also talked to my grandmother so she would help me go to college.

"Chris, I came to tell you your parole hearing is scheduled for this afternoon. I submitted letters to the parole board. The letters are from me, from your wife, from many former inmates whose lives you have helped turn around. There are also many letters from prison guards. They all wrote saying you have been a model prisoner during your incarceration. The guards state you have not caused one problem in all the years you've been incarcerated. In fact, the opposite is true you have helped to calm down many unruly convicts.

"In all the years you have been here, you have been the picture-perfect prisoner. You have helped instructors teach their classes. You have helped to calm down volatile situations. Everyone in the prison is pulling for you. In any prison, pretty much every inmate will try to tell you they are innocent. Even the most hardened criminals here think you were railroaded. No one not even the prison guards think you have committed any crime and certainly not murder.

"However, this happens to be a parole hearing. The people on the parole board don't know you like we do. They will have read everything about you. Why you are here at Monroe prison. How you have acted while you were incarcerated. The parole board members will have read all the letters submitted to them. But the main thing all of them being at the hearing is, watching you closely both your words and actions while questioning you."

At two in the afternoon, Chris was escorted into a large conference room. It had a long table and sitting on chairs on the far side of the table were the six parole board members. Chris was asked to have a seat on the other side of the table. A man of about forty-five with a crew cut and glasses asked, "Chris, if you are paroled, what would you do?" Chris answered, "I would join my wife and son. Hopefully, I would find a job and become a useful member of the community.

"In Monroe prison, I have met yet many young men who have strayed down the wrong path. I would like to dedicate some of my time to helping young people like this. I would show them there are better ways to live. This, added to the fact if they are going the wrong way in life, will put them behind prison bars."

Then a lady wearing a gray business suit, who had a heart-shaped face with a small scar by her lip, asked, "I see here at one time you stepped between a guard who had his back turned and a brutal convict with a knife in his hand. Why did you stop him?" Chris replied, "I did not want the guard to be hurt. Plus, I knew this convict would definitely stab someone in the back. But he wouldn't be able to do it if someone was facing him."

A man with a beard and mustache asked the next question. Judging from his appearance, Chris is sure he was a psychologist. "How come in all the time you have been at the Monroe Correctional Complex you never gotten angry or disobeyed guards?" Chris replied, "That is simple. It is not my nature. Anyway, what possible good would it have done?"

A lean sixtyish man with dark hair graying at the temples asked, "What happened to Felix Wells's body?" Chris answered truthfully, "I don't know. He was alive the last time I saw him. I feel terrible it happened. This haunts me to this day [which also happened to be the truth. Whatever had happened had cost me over fifteen years in prison]." Of course, Chris didn't tell the parole board this. He hoped the board thought this was an admission of his guilt, which of course it wasn't.

The rest of the questions Chris was asked were pretty much repetitious. He remained cool and calm and answered all of their questions to the best of his ability. After two more hours of questioning, the parole board told Chris he could leave. They told him the board would review the findings and would let him know the results in three days. He hopes he will get paroled. Chris needs to be home with Terri and Gavin.

After Chris returned, Brian told him, "Since I am your attorney, the parole board will let me know the results first. The second I hear anything definite, I will let you know. Chris, I want you to keep hoping for the best, but don't start thinking your parole is a sure thing. You can never be sure of how the parole board hearing works. The letdown would be terrible if you are positive you're going to get paroled, and it doesn't happen."

Ralph landed in Mauritius right on schedule. He was a heavyset short white man. Ralph was very charming and jovial. LaShawn informed him of everything which had happened leading up to this. After LaShawn told Ralph they had the person who had done this and were taking him back to face his comeuppance in Seattle, Ralph slapped his leg and chuckled out loud. He said, "It looks to me like Mr. Roberts has been waiting for his final destiny for a long time. I'm glad you have let me help him to fulfill his final wish."

LaShawn had stocked the airplane in anticipation of the long flight to Seattle. Terri rented a wheelchair accessible van and gave Mr. Roberts some knockout drops LaShawn loaded him into the van. Everyone said their good-byes to Kou and Suzy Chang and headed for the airport. The plane would be heading northwest through Africa fueling up as needed. LaShawn planned on landing in London for a brief stop. Finally, they would cross the Atlantic to Kennedy airport in New York. There they would have to go through customs. Last, we would fly across the United States landing in Seattle.

Ralph and LaShawn filed their flight plans and received the go-ahead for takeoff. Before Terri knew it, they were in the air. Terri understood why LaShawn was so impressed with the Gulfstream G450. It was total luxury with eight large leather chairs, which would recline so one would be able to sleep on them. It also had a small bedroom in the back. Also it had a small galley in front were Tatiana and Terri were able to prepare the meals.

The prisoner kept trying to bribe Terri. Conrad went so far as to sign everything he had in Mauritius over to Terri. She neglected to tell him, "she already had everything in her name." However, this would give her back up just in case it was needed. Terri kept the document, which everyone witnessed and signed. Ralph, being a notary public, attached his seal to it. Terri asked, "Conrad, what good do you think this did? We are still planning on turning you over to the authorities." Conrad arrogantly replied, "The justice system will never find me guilty. In fact, I was not stupid enough to put everything I own in one place. I happen to be smarter than the average bear, in a short time, I will have more money than I ever did."

Terri got very tired of listening to Conrad. It was like listening to water run out of a faucet. She shoved a sock into his mouth to shut him up. Later,

Terri told him, "I will remove the sock if you just shut up." Conrad nodded his head yes. Oh, blissful relief. After which he only spoke when he was spoken to.

When the plane was over the Atlantic Ocean, Terri placed a call to Brian Edwards, their attorney. Terri told him she had their man and was on the way back. Terri asked Brian if he could rent a large hall, then arrange a news conference. She told him, "I would like to have the judge, the prosecuting attorney, and the lead detective from Chris's trial to be there. I would also like reporters from all the media, newspapers, television, radio, etcetera, to be there."

Brian finally told Terri to stop talking. Then he simply stated he had just received a telephone call. "Chris is scheduled to be released in two days." Terri was so excited about the news she accidentally hung up the phone. Then she had to immediately call Brian back. Terri told Brian, "I have got to ask you something else. Could you have a wheelchair accessible van available? We will be landing at Boeing Field. I will call you later to let you know what time to expect us."

Terri was absolutely thrilled to hear Chris was getting paroled. Terri jumped up and hugged everybody, except Conrad Roberts of course. He knew enough to keep his trap shut. Tatiana and Terri prepared a nice dinner, putting Percodan in Conrad's. The plane was nearing Kennedy airport, so Terri needed Mr. Roberts to be comatose at that time. The captors enjoyed a nice meal, and shortly afterward, Conrad was out like a light.

After landing at Kennedy airport and were cleared by customs, the airplane was serviced and refueled. When the plane was back in air, Terri called Brian Edwards back, telling him the plane would be landing at Boeing Field at 5:15 p.m." Brian said that he would be there with a wheelchair accessible van." Brian asked where they would be taking Mr. Roberts. Terri told him, "Tatiana and LaShawn have a very secure room in their basement."

Brian stated, "We should take turns guarding him. You haven't waited this long only to have him disappear." Terri agreed. After hanging up, Terri told everyone what Brian said about pulling guard duty. Tatiana made a quick phone call. When she was finished, Tatiana told them she had talked to her four brothers. "Her brothers agreed to help them. When Conrad sees the size of them, he won't be very eager to escape. Everyone on the plane is tired from the long trip. This way, we will be able to get some much-needed rest."

Before the girls knew it, they were on the ground in Seattle; and true to his word, Brian Edwards was there waiting for us. LaShawn put Conrad into the wheelchair, which he placed into the van. Then everyone was off to Bellevue. LaShawn quickly put Conrad into the secure room in Tatiana and LaShawn's basement. Two of Tatiana's brothers were already there waiting for Them. The brothers told Terri, "Don't worry we will keep tight security. We will keep watch for eight hours. Then will change off with our other two brothers. We can keep this up for a very long period of time. Don't worry we know what we are doing, and there are other things you have to take care of."

Brian Edwards informed Terri, "Chris will be getting out of prison tomorrow. I will be going to Monroe prison with you and Gavin. At six o'clock tomorrow evening, I scheduled a press conference. I have the judge, the prosecuting attorney, and lead detectives coming. I also have a few other police officers who will be there. I have contacted every media outlet. I informed them to let all of their networks in on this because it is going to go national.

"I did not even let the media know what this is all about. I just informed them it was groundbreaking news which concerned them. The news reporters were all very inquisitive as to what was going on. I told them they would find out when the time comes. But the news reporters definitely would not want to find about this secondhand. Don't worry they will all be there. They are too curious not to come."

When Terri finally got home, she grabbed Gavin and whirled him around the room. Gavin asked Terri, "What's up, Mom?" Terri told him, "We have brought the guy who framed your dad back to Seattle. We could not have done it without you finding what was on the floppy disk. Not only that, but tomorrow morning, we are going to Monroe prison to pick up your dad and bring him home. Brian Edwards will be picking us up at seven in the morning. Then tomorrow evening, we will have a press conference. We will prove to the world your dad is innocent."

All of sudden, Gavin was just as excited as I was. He asked me if he would be able to see the prisoner." Terri told him, "Yes, you will see him sometime tomorrow. You already know who he is, but we can't tell your dad who he is or let him see him. Your dad might try to kill him." Gavin and Terri were really strung out. Terri made some popcorn and mother and son watched a silly movie to settle them down. Thankfully, both were tired when the movie ended, so both would be able to get some sleep. They were going to need it for tomorrow is going to be a long day.

Terri was up and ready to go by five o'clock next morning. She went to wake up Gavin, but he was ready to go too. Terri and Gavin watched the early morning news, then would pace the floor. Terri tried different topics of conversation, but nothing seemed to work. Both of them were just too keyed up. Time was not on their side. It just seemed to drag on and on. Finally at seven o'clock, there was a knock on the door.

When Terri opened the door, Brian Edwards stood there with a box of donuts and three cups of coffee in his hands. Brian said, "We better take the time to eat these now for it might be a long time before we get a chance to eat again. I know donuts are not the best thing for you, but at least it's something to fill the void."

Brian, Terri and Gavin arrived at the Monroe Correctional Complex at 8:30 a.m. Then had to sit and wait and wait. At twelve noon, Brian said, "This is enough of this crap." Brian started making a series of phone calls. He must have contacted the right people, for twenty minutes later Chris came out grinning from ear to ear. Terri, Chris and Gavin started crying and hugging each other. Terri told Chris how much she loved him. "From now on, you are going to have a hard time getting out of my sight."

Chris tousled Gavin's hair and gave him a hug, saying, "You're almost as tall as I am now. By the time you are done growing, you will be a couple of inches taller than me. What do you say this weekend we try catching a couple of baseballs. I would really enjoy that." Gavin returned Chris's hug, saying, "Dad, you know how wonderful it is to finally have my father home?"

On the way back to Bellevue, Chris asked Brian, "What did you do to get them to release me? The guards were playing games with me, taking their time just making me wait. Then all of a sudden, everything changed. The guards couldn't get me out of there fast enough." Brian laughed. "And did I ever mention to you the man who is now the vice president of the United States was once one of my professors at law school?"

For the first time ever, Terri thoroughly enjoyed her trip back from the Monroe Correctional Complex. They were almost back to Bellevue when Terri's cell phone rang. It was Tatiana. She wondered if all of them would stop by because she had made a huge dinner and wanted everyone to be there. Terri looked at Brian, Chris, and Gavin. They all nodded yes. Terri told Tatiana, "We will be there in twenty minutes."

Terri parked at their house, and even there she could barely find a place to park. All the parking spots between their home, Tatiana's home, and her mother's home were taken. Chris wanted to go in to look at their house. Terri winked at him and told him, "I will give you a personal tour later, especially the bedroom, but right now we have a lot of planning to do."

"What do you mean a lot of planning to do?" Chris asked. Brian and Terri looked at each other dumbfounded. They had been so excited about Chris get getting out of prison Brian forgot to tell him about the news conference. Brian took it upon himself to fill Chris in. He said, "After your son found out how you were framed and put in prison, your wife Terri with her friends LaShawn and Tatiana Williams decided they needed the ultimate proof. The three made a long and hellacious trip to Mauritius. There the three of them managed to capture the man responsible for your being in prison and brought him back to Seattle.

"We are having a big news conference at six o'clock tonight. This will prove once and for all to everyone in the world you are innocent. It will also prove an innocent man can be sent to prison for a crime he did not commit." Chris asked Brian, "Who and where is this guy? Can I see him? Do I know him?" "Yes, you know him," Brian answered, "and no, we won't tell you who it is, and no, you cannot see him until the six o'clock meeting tonight. We want you to be able to show genuine surprise."

Brian and the Sutton family walked over to LaShawn and Tatiana's home. After getting there, everyone had to hug Chris and tell them how glad they were he was out of prison. The house was packed. In addition to all of us, Tatiana's mother and four brothers were there. Lynn Anderson, Rodney Crowder, and of course, Ralph was also there.

Tatiana rang a bell and announced dinner was served. There was southern fried chicken, mounds of mashed potatoes, gravy, corn on the cob, and homemade biscuits. Everybody dug in. Chris really outdid himself. He said, "This sure beats prison cooking" as he helped himself to seconds. "Chris, you better be careful," Tatiana whispered, "or you won't have room for homemade apple pie."

Later, as the group sat around trying to figure out how they were going to the news conference. It was decided Brian, Chris, Terri, and Gavin would travel in one car. They would then all enter the conference room first. Then Tatiana, LaShawn, Ralph, Lynn Anderson, and Rodney Crowder would come in and sit in the seats in front of them. After everyone was seated, Tatiana's mother and her four brothers would enter the room bringing in the so-called Conrad Roberts with a hood over his head.

After sorting everything out, everyone just sort of mingled around. Terri saw Gavin talking to Tatiana's brothers they took him down to the basement evidently to see Mr. Roberts. Chris went into the kitchen to get another slice of apple pie. When he came back, Chris asked Tatiana how she had become such a wonderful cook. Tatiana pointed at her mother, saying, "There's the guilty one." Her mom just burst out laughing.

It was finally time to go to the meeting. When the first group got there, reporters kept asking them, "What's this earthshaking news?" Brian Edwards replied, "You will see for yourselves in a few minutes." He waited until the rest of our group arrived, except for Tatiana's mother and her four brothers who would come in later with the prisoner.

Brian Edwards stepped up to the podium. Immediately, a hush fell over the conference room. He started with, "The law in the United States is a wonderful thing. It serves a much-needed place in our society. It helps to keep thieves, rapists, and murderers off of the street. But once in a while, the law can be tricked into making a mistake."

Brian asked Chris to come up to the podium. He said, "This is Chris Sutton. Chris was paroled today after serving more than fifteen years in prison. Chris was in prison for a murder he did not commit. I'm going to irrevocably prove to you once and for all he did not commit this crime.

"You may have heard about this murder. The forensic evidence seemed to be irrefutable. Chris Sutton took an Alford plea for manslaughter to save himself from a sentence of life imprisonment. Or perhaps even the death sentence. It was not the fault of the leading homicide detective or even the prosecuting attorney or the presiding judge. The forensic evidence was there and was undeniable.

"This murder took away Felix Wells, an outstanding member of the community. Shortly after, Chris was placed in the Monroe Correctional Complex. All the assets of the Felix Wells Investment Firm just vanished. This amounted to over $200 million. Along with it, two of the firm's top executives disappeared.

"Terri Sutton, Chris's wife, was determined to prove to everyone her husband did not commit this horrendous crime. For fifteen years, she traveled the world seeking to find out who had framed her beloved husband, Chris. The husband Terri had known since they were babies. The husband Terri had started dating when both were still in high school. The husband Terri had married while they were in college. Chris and Terri thought they had the perfect life until some low-down scoundrel framed Chris for the murder of Felix Wells.

"This past Christmas, their son, Gavin, found a floppy disk at his grandparents' home in North Dakota. His mother had been an employee at the Felix Wells Investment Firm. While Terri was there, she saw a computer in a secretive room and downloaded it on floppy discs. Terri never got the chance to find what was on the floppy discs. Then a tragedy happened, and she forgot all about them. There they sat in her parents' home for over fifteen years.

"Somehow, Gavin Sutton managed to find the password and opened the file. He was able to find out the what, when, and where of the crime. Terri knew at this late date, she would not be able to get Chris out of prison early, but she could full well prove his innocence. With the help of some very loyal friends, Terri traveled halfway around the world. Terri and her friends succeeded in bringing back to Seattle the perpetrator of this crime." Speaking into a walkie-talkie, Brian whispered, "You can bring him in now."

Entering into the large conference room were Tatiana's four brothers with the prisoner who had a hood over his head. Their mother proudly brought up the rear. The four brothers placed him bound hand and feet on a chair beside the podium. Brian Edwards reached down and pulled the hood off, at the same time, saying, "Ladies and gentlemen, may I present Felix Wells to you." The crowd gave a collective gasp.

Chapter 61

Brian Edwards said, "I will now read to you what was on the floppy disk."

Years ago, when I was still in high school, I decided I was going to have it all. I went to cemeteries where I found the names of some boys who were born in the same year I was. The only thing difference was they had died in infancy. I knew it would help to have good false identities, so I took their names including Conrad Roberts to obtain birth certificates. With these, I obtained several Social Security numbers. From the Social Security numbers, I would eventually get driver's licenses and passports. I have always kept these current as well as those of my own name Felix Wells. I knew sometime in the future I would become Conrad Roberts.

I started investing in stock markets when I was still in high school. I became very successful, and by the time I was in college, they were calling me the boy wonder. I just seemed to have the Midas touch. What people didn't realize is I was doing just as well in other countries only under other names. As Conrad Roberts, I was doing just as well in the European and Asian markets.

As Conrad Roberts, I bought a beautiful villa in Mauritius. As Felix Wells, I started the Felix Wells Investment Firm. I decided I wanted to do away with Felix Wells. I was tired of him. I started thinking I had made all this money for investors, but they still wanted more. Most of the money is my own, and they don't deserve anything. I decided to end Felix Wells life and take every last cent from the firm and put it in Conrad Roberts's name. I finally decided on a great plan.

In a medical book, I found a person could lose two liters of blood before his organs started shutting down. This was of course if the person was in good shape physically. So I began searching for a physician who wasn't honest and needed money. I found a doctor who wanted to return to his home in Ecuador. I told him I needed to have the blood drawn for a medical experiment in the future, and I would pay him for it after it was to be done. Also after the blood was drawn, I would need an immediate transfusion. After he had agreed to do it for an exorbitant price, my next job was to find just the right scapegoat.

At my annual Christmas party, I was talking to Chris Sutton. I asked him if he ever went hunting. He told me no, but he had a .38-caliber Smith & Wesson pistol he used for target practice. Chris said he didn't even have any bullets for it anymore. I realized at the time I had found a perfect scapegoat. When Chris placed his empty glass on a coaster, I carefully picked it up by the coaster, knowing his fingerprints were on the glass.

I placed the glass gently into a plastic container and sealed it. This way the glass would not get dusty. With this I know for sure I had found my patsy. Now I would have to find a way to get into the Suttons apartment. I thought about it for a couple weeks, then an idea popped into my head. I ordered a brand-new Buick for Terri Sutton. When it came, I put it in the back corner of the parking garage. I went and asked Terri if I could borrow her car.

I drove the old piece of crap to the nearest locksmith and had every key on the key ring duplicated. I knew one of the keys would be the key to her apartment. I called a wrecking company to tow her old car off. Terri was tickled when she got her new car. Little did she know her troubles were just beginning.

During the time I was waiting for just the right moment, I put my plan into practice. I bought a pistol just like the one Chris had described. I bought an old house in the country far away from any neighbors. I found a place where I could get pig's blood. I took a small sponge and soaked it in pig's blood. I made two portable stands—one with a clamp to hold the sponge, the other one to steady the pistol.

I practiced shooting the sponge soaked with pig blood. I finally got both stands just at the right height and the right distance. I did very careful measurements. I wanted to have everything exact for when I did it for real. I checked to make sure the blood splatter on the wall and on my shirt was just right. After several test firings, I realized I only needed the stand with the clip for the sponge. Because I would be shooting so close to the sponge, there was no way I could miss.

When I was done with the testing, I had the house torn down. I gave the land to a neighbor. Now I just have to wait for when the time is right. I know Chris and Terri were planning a long vacation in June. Just before they leave, I will enter their apartment. I will wear rubber gloves. Once I am in the apartment, I will try to find a shirt of Chris's from the dirty laundry. Hopefully, he will also have a pair of old shoes. I will put the shoes and shirt in separate laundry bags. I will try to find Chris's comb and hopefully find some hair and put it in a baggie. Then I will locate Chris's pistol. Most people keep their guns by the nightstand.

When I have obtained my blood, which has been drawn from myself I will soak a small sponge with my blood. I will mount the sponge on the stand at the height of my heart. I will have already wrapped cellophane around my body to keep my DNA from getting Chris's shirt and shoes. After putting on Chris's shoes and shirt, I will place the pistol almost up to the sponge and shoot it.

This should leave high-velocity blood splatter on Chris's shirt. There will also be a bullet in the wall from Chris's pistol. The bullet will also leave high-velocity blood splatter on the wall. I will place the rest of the blood on the floor. After which, I will proceed to walk through the blood with Chris's shoes on. This will leave the tracks of the shoes in the blood. Plus, it will also leave my blood on the soles of Chris's shoes. I know forensics experts can trace shoe imprints to a specific shoe.

I will check the wall and the shirt with a magnifying glass to check for any tiny particles of sponge. If there are any, I will carefully remove them with a tweezer. I already purchased an identical Monte Carlo to the one Chris drives. I will park the Monte Carlo in my driveway without any license plates on it. When I am finished, I will toss the pistol in my neighbor's yard. After Chris and Terri leave for vacation, I will take shirt and shoes back to their apartment. On the afternoon before I do this, I will call Chris Sutton. I will disguise my voice and tell him about a good job in Everett. This will keep Chris from having an alibi for the time when this all happens.

All of a sudden, Felix Wells let out a scream. This caused Gavin to burst out laughing. It also set Chris off. Quick as a flash, he was up and had Felix Wells by the throat. The rest of our party jumped up and formed a living shield around Chris. Terri had warned all of them there was a possibility of this happening.

Chris instantly had a knife to Felix Wells' throat. He looked out at the audience and yelled, "You sent me to prison for over fifteen years for murdering this piece of shit. Now what are you going to do when I actually do kill this asshole?" Everyone in the room was going ballistic. The media were talking rapidly into their microphones. Television cameras were zoomed in on Chris and Felix. So many flashbulbs were going off it looked like it was the Fourth of July. Felix Wells was crying and begging for his life.

The judge and the prosecuting attorney were both trying to talk at once. Finally, the judge got everyone silenced then he spoke in his judicial manner. He said, "Chris, it is no fault of the justice system you were locked up at the Monroe Correctional Complex. It was completely the work of this evil, wretched person. But still the legal system usually works. Think, Chris, what will be harder on Mr. Wells, to be dead or to live life behind bars?"

Then suddenly, Chris dropped Felix Wells back into his chair. Turning, he grabbed Terri and started crying. Chris said, "I couldn't force myself to do it, Terri. I have never taken the life of any living creature. I wasn't able to do it this time either. The only way I could ever kill someone is if they were putting you or Gavin's life in danger."

The police then came and put handcuffs on Felix Wells and led him away in his wheelchair. The media were all trying to get a statement from them. Brian Edwards once again rapped on the podium. When attention was once more focused on him, Brian Edwards announced, "This is not all there is to the story. I am now going to turn you over to Terri Sutton."

When Terri stepped up to the podium, she said, "The first thing I am about to say is for my darling husband Chris. I tried from the very start to prove your innocence, and I never stopped trying. However, I was on the wrong path. Finally, when I thought all was lost and I was in the deepest despair, our son Gavin stepped up to the plate. He was one who found the floppy disk. He was the one who opened it. Gavin was the one who solved the puzzle.

"We still had to bring Mr. Wells back to Seattle to face justice. Our good friends LaShawn and Tatiana helped me to do this, as they have helped me every step along the way. Chris, I want you to know I saw you take the knife from Tatiana's kitchen. I did not try to stop you because I knew the Chris I love could not hurt a mouse. But I had to let you prove it to yourself and to the world.

"The next thing is for the good people who had invested their money in the Felix Wells Investment Firm. When Felix Wells absconded with $200 million, $100 million of this was his own money. The other $100 million were from investors. I have control of all Wells funds. He signed them over to me. I imagine his conscience was bothering him. Plus, the fact I had already transferred all of the money over to my own bank accounts.

"I will be paying $300 million of this money to the investors. This will be giving them their investment back threefold. We have all of their names on file. Lynn Anderson and Rodney Crowder will be helping me with this. I think this will be a good return on their investments. Chris and I will be keeping half of what's left of the money. The rest will go to the people who have helped us. LaShawn and Tatiana Williams will be getting the largest portion of the share. We also we will also be setting up an account for battered and abused women."

After Terri finished, they were deluged with questions. As Terri and Chris were about to leave the meeting who should show up but Tony Lindsay. Tony said, "The reason I disappeared was I had joined Interpol. I had felt so sorry for Chris and you I had joined Interpol to see if I would be able to help. Plus the fact it is a very good job. Whenever I got a chance, I would search for Russ and Marvin. But I was also on the wrong track. Three months ago, Russ and Marvin were almost caught by Interpol, but once again, they were able to elude capture."

On the way home, Terri asked Gavin a question, "I noticed every time Felix Wells squirmed in his chair, you smirked. When Felix screamed, you busted out laughing. What's the deal?" At first, Gavin was reluctant to tell his parents. Finally, he said, "Remember when we were back in North Dakota for Christmas? Well, after I found out what was on the floppy disk and you had decided to go after him, Grandpa Olson took me to the side telling me, 'Gavin, you have helped me on the farm for several years now. I know the way your mother works. Come hell or high water, she's going to bring that feller back. However, I know the law is not going to do diddly-squat. If you ever get a chance, Gavin, I would like you to use this on him. Then he handed me a brand-new elastrator complete with rubber bands.

"So today while everyone else was sitting around and just visiting after dinner, I went and talked to Tatiana's four brothers. I told them what I wanted to do, and they all said they would be mighty pleased to be able to help. So we went down to the basement. There they held him for me while I completed the job." Chris and Terri burst out laughing, and there were high-fives all around.

Epilogue

The day after the press conference, Terri took Chris to the driver's license department. There Chris had to take his driver's test, both the written and driving, for he hadn't had a license in fifteen years. When Chris was finished, his parents picked Gavin up after school. As Terri started to drive, Chris asked her, "What is going on now?" She told Chris, "I have not been able to get you any presents all the time you were in prison. So I saved up all of this money to get you one really big one." When they arrived at the place where the Monte Carlo was, Chris walked around the car several times admiring it. Chris told Terri and Gavin, "This is the fifth best present I have ever received."

Gavin asked, "Well, Dad, what was the best present that you ever got?" Gavin sounded a little disappointed until Chris hugged them both. He said, "The best present I received was marrying your mother. The second best present was when you were born the third best present was getting out of prison, so I can live my life with you and your mom. The fourth present was last night when you guys proved my innocence to the world. This fifth present is also very special. It shows me how much you and your mom love me. It is terrific, and I think it looks better than brand-new."

Terri and Chris called Dawn Hendrickson and asked her if she would like to start a shelter for battered and abused women. She said, "I would be very happy to have the chance." Together they purchased an eight-unit apartment complex. Chris and Terri help her when they are not busy traveling. Terri had been to so many exotic places, but she was not able to enjoy them. Now with Chris by her side, they have the time to enjoy the finer points of those places.

Gavin continued his education at Bellevue High School. Now the family go back to visit Terri's parents every Christmas, and Gavin still goes back to Towner every summer. He and Becky still plan to go to the University of

North Dakota. Gavin still plans on taking over his grandparents' farm. Terri is sure when he does, Becky will be there with him as his wife.

As for Felix Wells, because of the fact he had not killed anyone and also due to the fact his investors got back all of their money, no, thanks to him, Felix got by with only serving five years in prison. Chris and Terri think he kind of enjoyed prison, for when he was released he had a sex change. Felix had his name legally changed to Felicia Wells, then he disappeared.

It really doesn't bother them. Chris was proven innocent and Chris and Terri were just happy to be together again. Terri thinks Felix still has a big stash of money hidden somewhere else. He hinted to this fact on the plane trip back from Mauritius. Terri still has the second computer, which has a file she couldn't open. Perhaps someday she will have a computer forensic expert take a look at it. Terri doesn't know if she will ever get around to that. Of course, you never know some time Chris and Terri might need a little excitement in their lives.

Index

A

Alford plea, 109, 111, 278, 289
Anderson, Lynn, 74-76, 78-79, 87, 91, 110, 121-23, 129-30, 136-37, 169-70, 195-96, 204-5, 277, 284
anniversary, 68-70, 91, 175, 289
Argentina, 242-43, 249-50, 289
artwork, 101, 103, 107, 109, 113, 234, 289

B

Becky, 199-201, 203-5, 207, 210, 216, 218-22, 228, 251-52, 254-55, 257-59, 287-89
Bellevue, 48, 55-56, 62-63, 72, 86, 101, 114, 117, 120, 143, 198, 222, 256-57, 261, 276
Bellevue High School, 48, 189, 236, 252, 260, 287, 289
Bellevue Wolverines, 189, 252-53, 289
Berwick, 50-51, 289
Blankenship, Arlen, 100-101, 103, 105-6, 108-10, 116, 261, 289
blood, 101-2, 162, 234, 281-82, 289
bobbers, 33, 165, 289
Brasilia, 182-83, 189, 289
Brazil, 170, 172-73, 183, 188-89, 195, 202, 209, 212, 289
Buck, 197, 199, 203, 216-17, 220, 222, 251
Buenos Aires, 242-46, 249, 289
Butte, 46-47, 99, 289
butterflies, 134, 289

C

coffee beans, 133, 289
Colombia, 208-11, 214, 224, 229, 244, 289
Colombian prisons, 228, 231, 289
Connor, Michael, 97-98, 289
convicts, 116-17, 124, 137, 167, 186, 232, 234-35, 271-72, 289
Costa Rica, 122, 129-33, 135-36, 141, 289
crime, 104, 106, 110, 116-17, 138, 167, 177, 201, 204, 212, 224, 229-30, 233-34, 253, 277-78
crocodiles, 135, 289
Crowder, Rodney, 74, 78, 87, 110, 121-23, 136-37, 170, 195-96, 204-5, 208, 277, 284

D

Devlin, Hank, 131, 153-54, 170, 177, 231, 238, 243-44, 249-50

E

Earlene, 241-42
Edwards, Brian, 137-40, 171, 271, 273-80, 283
English, 135, 149, 152, 173, 176, 229, 239, 241, 246-47, 252
Evanston, Clark, 176-78, 180-84, 188, 192, 208, 224-25, 229-31
Evanston, June, 177-78, 180-84, 188, 192, 208, 230
Everett, 92, 102, 234, 283
evidence, 101-3, 109-10, 147, 161-63, 231, 234, 262

F

Falkland Islands, 242
farm, 9, 22, 25, 40-41, 43, 46, 48, 94, 97-98, 147-48, 165-66, 197-98, 205, 251, 254-55
farmers, 40, 43, 200, 211, 217
farmer's market, 90
favelas, 172, 179-80
Felix Wells Investment Firm, 72, 74, 85, 90, 110, 115, 118, 121, 137, 147, 189, 195, 278, 280, 284
Flash, 114-15, 143
floppy disks, 92, 255, 257, 259, 275, 278, 280, 283-84
Fred, 131-32

G

GED, 116, 118, 124, 137-39, 171, 185, 187, 261, 271

Global Airlines, 71, 77, 111, 123, 126, 129, 131, 147
graduation, 40, 88-89
Grand Cayman Island, 137, 141-42
guards, 117, 124, 126, 128, 185, 228, 232, 235, 249-50, 266, 272, 276
Gulfstream G450, 269-70, 273

H

Hell's Fire, 44-45
Hendrickson, Dawn, 194-95, 205, 207-8, 230, 287
horses, 44, 147, 197, 200, 203, 217-18, 222, 252

I

inmates, 117, 124, 126, 171, 185, 271
Interpol, 177, 181, 188, 208, 224-29, 284

J

Jackson, Tom, 149, 153-54, 170, 177, 231, 238, 243, 245-46, 248-49
Jacobson, Russ, 72-75, 78-79, 84-85, 87-89, 110-15, 120-23, 131-32, 149-55, 159-63, 181-83, 204-9, 212-14, 223-32, 237-38, 242-47
Jamaica, 153-57, 159-60, 164-65, 167, 169-70, 177
Joe, 131-32
Judy, 157-58

K

Kingston, 155-57, 159, 161

L

license plates, 102-3, 108, 282

lie detector test, 109
Lindsay, Tony, 75, 79, 83-85, 87, 90, 110, 121-23, 129, 136-37, 169-70, 195-96, 204-5, 284

M

Maoris, 241
McCluskey, Sean, 225-29
Medellin, 208, 211-15, 223-26, 231
Medellin SWAT team, 226-28
Minot, 22-23, 38, 148, 164, 210, 216, 254-55, 258
monkeys, 69, 134-35
Monroe Correctional Complex, 7-8, 111, 115-17, 124, 126, 136-38, 140, 146, 167, 185, 187, 231-34, 260-61, 271-72, 275-76
Mount Rainier, 52, 68, 89, 116, 173
Mueller, Marvin, 79, 110-15, 120-23, 126-29, 131-32, 149-55, 159-63, 177-79, 181-83, 188-89, 204-9, 212-14, 223-32, 237-38, 242-44
murder, 8, 100, 102, 116, 131, 189, 194, 201, 211-12, 271, 278
mutton punching, 44-45

N

New Zealand, 240-42
North Dakota, 9, 22, 32-34, 50-51, 88-91, 94-95, 98-99, 134, 146-48, 203-5, 210, 216-17, 237, 251, 254
nude beaches, 148, 151-52, 170

O

Ocean Shores, 61-63
offshore banks, 122, 137, 141, 155, 269
Olson, Gloria, 10-11, 15, 23, 33, 37
Olson, Sam, 10, 15, 33, 37

P

Philipsburg, 148-49
Poas Volcano, 135
police, 96, 98, 100-103, 105-6, 108-10, 112, 138, 153, 157-59, 161-62, 179-81, 206, 226-27, 240-41, 247-48
Princess Juliana International Airport, 148-49, 154
prison, 7-8, 106-7, 109-10, 116-18, 124, 126-28, 138-40, 171, 187-91, 228-29, 231, 233-35, 259-61, 271-72, 275-78
prison guards, 7-8, 187, 271
prison life, 118, 171, 190
prom, 35
prosecutor, 108-9, 138
prostitutes, 157, 193, 206, 215, 231-32

R

raccoons, 12
Ralph, 270, 273, 277
Reggie, 187
Richard, 147-48
Rio de Janeiro, 170, 172-75, 179, 188-89, 191, 232
Roberts, Conrad, 259, 261, 263-70, 273-74, 277, 280
Rogers, Ben, 117-18

S

Saint Martin, 147-50, 154-56, 159, 165, 167, 170, 232
San Jose, 130-33, 135
Sao Paulo, 183, 189, 243
Seattle, 46-47, 52, 88-90, 98-100, 142-43, 149-51, 164-66, 169, 203,

205, 250, 259-60, 262-63, 270, 273-76
Seychelles, 238-39
slums, 161, 172, 206, 211-12
Sugarloaf Mountain, 173
Sunshine, 203, 220-22, 251
Sutton, Clovis, 9-11, 13-15, 23, 33, 37, 43
Sutton, Gavin Christopher, 7-8, 126-31, 143, 145-48, 164-72, 188-90, 196-201, 203-5, 207-8, 216-22, 232-33, 235-37, 251-60, 275-78, 283-84
Sutton, George, 9-10, 13-16, 19, 33, 38

T

Towner, 9, 18, 23-24, 27, 37, 40-41, 43-44, 58-59, 89, 94, 164, 198-200, 220, 251, 254-56
Towner High School, 24, 35, 257
tracking bug, 177
turtle farm, 142
turtles, 135, 142

U

United States, 41, 52, 95, 123, 136-37, 146, 172, 189, 199, 214, 253, 261-62, 268-69, 273, 276-77
University of Washington, 34, 36-37, 47, 50, 68, 124

V

Verdant Repose, 266

W

website, 192, 194-95
Wellington, 240-41
Wells, Felix, 71-72, 75, 78-79, 81, 83-85, 87-90, 100-102, 106, 110, 113, 115-16, 278, 280, 283-84, 288
Williams, LaShawn, 150-51, 156-62, 164, 167-69, 172-73, 175-76, 178-83, 208-15, 223-25, 231, 237, 245-46, 262-63, 265-70, 273
Williams, Tatiana, 48-51, 55-60, 77, 104-8, 110-25, 127-35, 141-43, 146-70, 172-75, 177-80, 193-95, 208-11, 237-50, 262-63, 265-70
Wilson, Jack, 44-45
Wilson, Vern, 101-3, 116

Edwards Brothers Malloy
Oxnard, CA USA
May 13, 2014